PROLOGUE

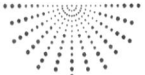

LONDON, EIGHT YEARS AGO

A swirling blur of laughter and light...the ballroom's dancing floor too crowded with bodies too hot and vibrant with energy both banked and exerted...smiles too care-free to give a toss about anything approaching respectability... hearts beating too fast and reckless with fizzy effervescence...

The atmosphere of Almack's season-opening spring ball was much *too* everything.

At least, that was how it felt to Lady Beatrix St. Vincent.

She'd been whirled across gleaming mahogany these ten dances in a row with ten different eligible gentlemen, and she felt not a twinge of ache in her feet or a care for the perspiration beading down her spine.

She only felt the triumph of the night.

Her triumph.

In the ladies' retiring room, she dipped her fingers in a bowl of fresh lavender water and pressed cooling fingertips to flushed cheeks. Just a quick respite to collect thoughts and emotions that were fluttering much too chaotically in her brain for her to catch hold of even one.

Actually, that wasn't true.

1

In the mirror, she gazed into her own gray eyes. Reflected back was the single, overwhelming emotion she'd gone nearly buoyant with...

Irrepressible joy.

Tonight was her come-out ball.

Yes, it was taking place at Almack's alongside seven other young ladies making their debuts, which was significantly less magnificent than what society would've expected of the daughter of a marquess. But the marquess in question was the Marquess of Lydon, a charming scoundrel from the moment he could cock his lopsided smile. As Beatrix's mother had perished within a couple of years of having given birth to her only child, society would suppose it a lack of interest on the marquess's part that had his daughter making her debut at Almack's.

By contrast, two years ago, her bosom friend, Lady Artemis Keating, had a lavish private ball thrown for her by her brother, the powerful and wealthy Duke of Rakesley. Though Beatrix hadn't been out, Artemis had insisted she attend, and it was the most glorious ball she could ever have imagined.

Beatrix was pragmatic.

A glorious come-out had never been in the cards for her.

No matter.

This come-out at Almack's would do, and really, it had to, for it was the best she could muster.

Indeed, she was the daughter of a marquess—which was only partially what had gained her entrance into this ballroom.

In actual fact, she'd achieved this night through her own planning and determination. She'd dreamt of a future that would be nothing like her previous twenty years of life and now, at last, it was within reach.

A good, solid husband with whom she would beget good, solid children.

Really, was a good, solid future too much to ask?

Devil
TO
PAY

Sofie Darling

OLIVER-HEBER BOOKS

The Race of the Century

The thrill! The pulse-pounding exhilaration!

Hark ye!

Attend, one and all! The most anticipated and electrifying Thoroughbred contest of this century -**Nay, of all time!**

Only and Exclusively this Season's Winners of The 2,000 Guineas, The 1,000 Guineas, The Oaks, The Derby, and The St. Leger shall vie for the prize of

£10,000

To Claim the Mantle of Greatest Champion

SATURDAY 21ST OF SEPTEMBER

IN THE YEAR OF OUR LORD 1822

EPSOM DOWNS

Society would credit her father with this achievement. It was what fathers did for their daughters, no?

Except Lydon's idea of a good, solid childhood had been to take his daughter to the horse races two or three times a week. Well, *take her to the horse races* implied her presence had been desired. More accurately, she'd been treated like an extra appendage one was obligated to drag everywhere one went.

At those race meetings, she'd amused Lydon and his wastrel friends. They'd taught her to exclaim, "Blimey!" and they slipped her a bit of betting money—sometimes a penny, other times a guinea. It depended on how fortune treated them the previous night. They'd all gotten a grand old jolly out of watching the little lady stroll up to the betting post and place her wagers.

But she'd made the most of it, hadn't she?

At first, she'd bet on the horses with the silliest names or the jockeys with the prettiest silks. Over time, however, she'd learned to wager based on odds and weather conditions and whispers about a horse's soundness. She'd become quite skilled at it. After all, what was a little, extra appendage to do but keep her ears ready and her eyes keen and soak in her surroundings and develop skills that might've done her no favors in a ballroom, but provided a compensation she wouldn't have attained otherwise—*money*.

Her own money.

Race after race, year after year, she squirreled away those winnings.

So, if she felt a trifle smug with triumph tonight, she'd earned the feeling. Those squirreled-away winnings had gained her a place at Miss Adelaide's School for the Refinement of Young Ladies, enough new dresses for a season, and a come-out ball.

This.

A chance at a good, solid future.

A *real* future.

As she exited the ladies' retiring room, she smiled a greeting toward a young lady she knew from Miss Adelaide's. In the smile reflected at her was the same giddy excitement she'd met in the mirror not thirty seconds ago. Before she reentered the ballroom, she tucked herself into a quiet nook and attempted to quiet her heart that begged leave to race again. She took one deep breath, then another, before she heard it—the low murmur of male voices on the other side of the silk screen.

It was a question—*"And Lady Artemis?"*—that had Beatrix pressing her ear to painted silk.

"She was the prize when she debuted," said another voice. "But that was two years ago."

"She's Rakesley's sister," said a third voice. "She's still the prize."

Beatrix could only agree. Artemis was the daughter of one wealthy, powerful duke and the doted-upon sister of another wealthy, powerful duke. The size of Artemis's dowry would, of course, make her the prize of every season until she eventually picked a husband.

Even if a small, unworthy part of Beatrix experienced a pang of envy, she didn't begrudge her friend her freedom. Just as Beatrix couldn't help the accident of birth that had led to her unlucky parentage, neither could Artemis help that which had granted her the best.

"She's a headstrong chit, though," said another gentleman—or perhaps the first. They all sounded alike.

"Why hasn't she married, anyway?"

Though she'd never voiced as much to her friend, Beatrix wondered the same. The season of Artemis's come-out, though, there had been a lord. The second son of an earl, in fact. Quite handsome, in further fact. He and Artemis had danced at every ball—then...nothing. Artemis never spoke of him again, and Beatrix sensed she couldn't ask.

"Word has it that Rakesley has given her access to her fortune."

"A mistake handing over that kind of blunt to a lady."

"How many new dresses does a lady need, anyway?"

The round of laughter that followed set Beatrix's teeth on edge.

In the conversation that ensued, the gentlemen began reciting the names of other young ladies—and their perceived chances in this season's marriage mart. Breath held, Beatrix waited for her name to be spoken.

And waited…

And waited.

At last, a voice said, "What of Lydon's daughter?"

A pause followed—one that drew out a few beats too long.

"Do you mean Lady Beatrix?" came a question that sounded… bewildered.

Her heart hammered against her ribs. She might not ever breathe again.

"What of her?" came another question.

Less question and more…*scoff.*

The thin laughter that followed wasn't the jolly sort, but rather the sort with a streak of cruelty running through. Her ears began ringing, even as they felt like they'd been packed with cotton. A slick of perspiration coated her palms.

Then came the question—the one that would come to shape the trajectory of her life from this point forward.

"Who amongst us would be saddled with the Marquess of Lydon for family?"

"If she had a curve or two on her bones, one might be tempted…"

"You danced with her, didn't you, Sadler?"

"It's her come-out," explained a voice, presumably Sadler. One could hear the shrug in his voice. "I felt bad for her."

"Besides," came another voice, "the patronesses have threatened to ban any gentlemen caught not dancing."

Beatrix's buoyant evening of triumph crashed to a sudden and ignoble end.

All her hopes and dreams, too.

Of their own accord, her feet began moving. Not toward the ballroom—this night had provided her with enough dancing to last her the rest of her days—but to the receiving hall, where she communicated a sore stomach to a footman. As she waited for her evening cape, she remembered to have a message sent to the ancient great-aunt-once-removed that she'd left dozing in a corner of the ballroom. The distant relation was serving as her sponsor for the night and chaperone for the season.

A few minutes later, Beatrix was outside, hands clasped tightly before her, fingernails digging crescents into her palms through silk gloves as she awaited the carriage she'd hired for the night. Then she was seated on leather squabs and rattling across wet London cobblestones, the steady *clip-clop* of horse's hooves echoing in their wake.

Somehow, she'd managed to accomplish all this with a dense, unresolved sob caught in her chest. Though utterly shattered, she held onto this caught sob, for it felt like the only thread holding her pieces together.

With its release, she would entirely fall apart.

She would not—*could not*—cry.

She'd endured enough shame for one night.

Yet the question came—and kept coming…

Hadn't she done everything right?

Except it wasn't the correct question.

Hadn't she done everything she could?

The answer was swift and brutal.

It wasn't enough.

She wasn't enough.

She never would be.

She hadn't fooled anyone—only herself.

That good, solid husband and those good, solid children and that good, solid future...

A mirage.

And in the way of all mirages, it had evaporated into nothingness the instant her grasp attempted to close around it. All that remained was endless desert stretching ahead of her for an eternity of miles and years.

Her intellect and wits were all she could depend upon in this world—*as ever.*

They'd served her this far—and simply would have to keep doing so.

CHAPTER ONE

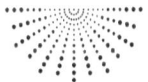

*D*ev stood amid the throng of society pleasure-seekers and experienced the satisfaction that never lasted beyond the inhalation and exhalation of a single breath.

Of course, they would come, a small voice reminded him.

This was Prinny's Stand, and today was the running of the Oaks, the fourth major horse race of the season.

Few would refuse that invitation.

It had been a good few years since King George IV was called Prinny—and it had been even longer since he'd graced the stand with his exalted presence. Centered in the middle of the horse-shoe-shaped course, the raised pavilion was the best vantage point from which to observe Epsom Downs, as it offered unimpeded views. Mostly, the stand went unused, save for when the king occasionally allowed a friend to use it.

Which wasn't how Dev had secured it for his viewing party of the Oaks horse race today.

The short of it was he'd offered an exorbitant sum of money to the king—which had been ignored.

Three days later, he'd offered twice the sum of the initial offering—which had also been ignored.

A day later, he'd offered twice that sum—which had been accepted.

Now, here he stood, hosting a viewing party in Prinny's Stand.

He'd left no luminary uninvited, from powerful duke to impoverished baron—and all the marquesses, earls, and viscounts in between. Many invitees had accepted, even a duke. A down-on-his-luck duke, it had to be admitted, who was singularly intent on stuffing as many canapes and pouring as much champagne down his gullet as one man could possibly stomach within the period of an hour, but a duke, nonetheless.

In truth, none of the highest tier of the highest tier of society had accepted.

Dev had to make do with the dimmer stars of the aristocratic firmament.

Not that he gave a toss, for the one person who did matter *had* accepted.

The Countess of Bridgewater.

Strictly speaking, it had been her husband, the earl, who had sent their acceptance.

But Imogen would be here.

That was all that mattered.

And she would ignore Dev.

He wasn't sure she'd once glanced his way these last two years.

Which told him all he needed to know.

She couldn't look at him directly—not if she was to continue with her farce of a marriage.

His mouth tipped into the half smile that had sent many a lady's heart into a flutter, Dev circulated through the room, exchanging greetings with lords and ladies who were still trying to understand this newcomer—some said *interloper*—into their vaunted ranks.

Lord Devil.

The name the *ton* had taken to calling him, both behind his back and to his face on the not-so-rare drunken occasion.

He didn't mind.

"Landsdown," said Dev on a greeting nod. "I hope you're finding the day to your satisfaction."

The Viscount Landsdown's smile suggested he couldn't believe his luck in having secured the attention of Lord Devil. "Oh, yes, yes, yes, indeed."

Landsdown wasn't an impoverished lord, precisely, but rather one living below the means he would prefer, most definitely. This might be a room filled to bursting with exalted lords and ladies, but its truer nature was a room full of sycophants. In their host—*Lord Devil*—they saw two entities. A man with the incorrect blood flowing through his veins...and a man who was a goldmine.

With this lot, for one to overlook the former, a man better be flush with the latter. Otherwise, he was of no use to them.

Dev was under no illusions about the realities.

"A quick little goer on the turf is your Little Wicked," said Landsdown. "Reckon she'll take it today?"

The charming smile Dev had inherited from his Irish mother went tight. *Little Wicked.* The Thoroughbred he'd won in a card game. The horse was supposed to have taken the Triple Crown. Yet here they were, three races into the season, with the fourth about to be run today, and she hadn't a win to her name—only second-place finishes.

Today, he needed the filly to fulfill her promise and *win*.

"Today is her day," said Dev, all abundant confidence.

Arrogance, the *ton* called it.

Lord Devil was a man who didn't know his place.

But Dev knew in his heart what it truly was.

Ruthlessness.

He *didn't* know his place.

But he did know this: He wasn't here to court their acceptance and join their rarified ranks.

He was here to vanquish them.

For the lords and ladies surrounding him and enjoying his hospitality, life had started on a ladder near its top rung, but with a single condition—they would occupy that single rung all their lives. Dev, on the other hand, had started approximately in the middle. Yet though the wrong blood flowed in his veins, life had gifted him an option that few others in this room comprehended —he could climb.

And climb, he had.

And climb he would continue to do.

He didn't crave the respect or love of this room.

He had a single desire.

And when she arrived, it would be on the arm of another man.

So, he would continue climbing, steadily, rung by rung—until she was on *his* arm.

Then, only when it was too late, they would know themselves for the conquered.

"Deverill," came a gruff voice at his back.

His mouth curved into his first genuine smile of the day as he turned and shook the hand of the solidly built man who stood several inches shorter. "Shaw," he said, undeniable relief pulsing through him.

From the cock of Shaw's eyebrow and the slight frown turning down the corners of his mouth, however, Dev understood his business partner wasn't best pleased to be mingling amongst *fancy folk*. A serious man to his core, Shaw didn't hold with the frivolity on display. He accepted the champagne coupe offered by a server and held the glass with an air of delicate uncertainty, as if it might shatter in his working man's hands at any moment.

Dev was unable to resist asking, "Enjoying the festivities?"

Shaw snorted. "The shipment of steam jackets arrived from Birmingham at dawn. Engine assembly can resume."

It took little for Dev to shift focus when it came to business. "Starting tomorrow?"

"Aye."

The steam jackets for their newly designed engines had arrived cracked a month ago, so they'd needed to be recast. In the lifetime of an engine's operation, the steam jacket handled an enormous amount of pressure. The tiniest flaw could result in the loss of life. Such an issue couldn't be tolerated or ignored.

Dev nodded with satisfaction. "Good."

Ten years ago, it was Shaw who had given Dev his start.

Dev had grown up modestly, the only son of a baron's estate manager and housekeeper. As a child, Dev's mind had been as quick and nimble as his fingers, and it was known for miles around that he could repair any broken-down old thing, even fashion mechanical improvements and inventions, too. Lord Whitsby saw a future gem in the younger Deverill and paid to have him schooled. Not a first-rate institution like Eton, but a school where he could become educated enough to take over the running of the estate someday.

That was the plan, at least.

The school, it turned out, suited Dev's interests perfectly, and he excelled. The mechanical arts came as naturally to him as breathing. Of particular interest was the steam engine. Greater and greater efficiency in its mechanics was required, which would lead to smaller, more portable engines and the use of less coal. Not a year later, Dev had fashioned a design he knew would accomplish those goals, but he'd lacked the funds and resources to put his designs into practice.

Until he met Mr. Seamus Shaw.

One evening, it had amused Lord Whitsby to invite Dev to a supper party. He'd inquired about Dev's studies and explained to the gathered friends and family that he was having Dev educated to be his future estate manager. Whitsby met the praise of his guests with smug satisfaction. When Dev began explaining his mechanical interests, Whitsby's demeanor turned into the condescending and dismissive with statements like, *Young Dev's little inventions litter the entire estate* and *There's no mining on my lands.*

After dinner, Mr. Shaw approached Dev and asked him to explain his steam engine invention in further detail, which Dev happily did. At the end of the conversation, Shaw offered to enter into a business partnership with Dev.

Dev had yet to reach his nineteenth year.

Within twelve months, he'd repaid Whitsby for his education, plus interest. The baron had groused about young men not knowing their place and friends poaching servants, but he'd accepted every last farthing.

Ten years on, Dev had never once regretted that turn in his life. With his experience running factories, Shaw had proven an excellent partner.

"Now, the ladies parading around this room. They think blunt grows on trees." Shaw tucked his thumbs into his waistcoat pockets and rocked back on his heels, a habit of his. "They don't understand a working man's mind."

Dev knew to the syllable what Shaw's next words would be.

"Not like my daughters."

Shaw's daughters... The man had three of them—and he would be most obliged if Dev would take one to wife. He wasn't fussy about which.

Which Dev had no intention of doing.

A flash of brown sun-streaked hair with a jaunty little bonnet perched atop caught the edge of his vision.

Imogen.

He knew it from the instinctive tightening of every muscle in his body.

Imogen had been at that fateful dinner party, of course. After all, Whitsby was her father. Though a few years younger than Dev, they'd grown up alongside each other.

Further, they'd had an understanding.

Or so he'd thought.

He felt the usual pull—to gravitate toward her and enter her orbit. That pull was as familiar as the sound of his own voice.

He resisted—which had also become familiar.

Imogen was another man's wife.

Not his.

Not yet, anyway.

A sudden frisson of excitement shimmered through the crowd. The horses had begun assembling at the starting line.

Before this season, Dev had never attended a race meeting in all his life. Then one night, he'd won a Thoroughbred off a dissolute, young earl named Clifton in a card game. Dev's first thought had been to sell the beast. Given the room's reaction to his acquisition of the famous Little Wicked, he'd known he could get a pretty penny for the filly. But he'd picked up a particular scent in the air—*opportunity*.

The owner of a Thoroughbred would have access to society of a higher tier than Dev had yet achieved, for he hadn't moved past associating with lords in gambling den card rooms. However, as the owner of Little Wicked, he would be mingling with the elite.

The *ton* would have to begin taking him seriously.

So, he'd hired the best trainers and grooms his money could buy—even succeeded in wooing the Duke of Richmond's favorite jockey into his stables.

And the gambit had worked.

Dev was immediately christened *Lord Devil*, as much for his black hair and piercing blue eyes as for his mountainous pile of blunt—and was invited to all manner of society soirées, musicales, and balls.

To be sure, he was a novelty for the *ton*, but he was being allowed into the room and that was the point.

More specifically, he was now allowed into rooms with Imogen.

Shaw in tow, he found a place at the central balcony from which to watch the race. He searched the line for Little Wicked's racing colors of purple and black and immediately found her. He didn't know the names of the competitors lining up beside her and, frankly, he didn't care. He only kept a tally of the salient facts. Little Wicked had placed second in the Derby yesterday—and every other race of the season. So, she was running the filly's race today in the hope that she would win and qualify for the Race of the Century in September, where she would run against the four other winning three-year-old Thoroughbreds of the season.

The other owners didn't agree with him running Little Wicked in every race, but the fact was the filly enjoyed it. Truly, she was a delightful horse—a thought that had never once occurred to him regarding any horse in all his life. But *delightful* applied to Little Wicked. Though she stood at sixteen hands and possessed all the power and muscle of every other Thoroughbred out there on the turf, she also held an intangible lightness of body and spirit.

The air went electric in the specific way it always did in the instant before the firing of the starting gun. Just when it felt as if the tension would surely break with the passage of a single more second, the pistol fired and the horses lurched into motion.

Two seconds later, the pistol fired again, signaling a false start.

The crowd groaned in unison, everyone understanding it was to be *that* sort of race. Dev could tolerate one false start, and even two, but by the fifth or sixth, his nerves were ready to jump out of his skin. He couldn't comprehend why the sport tolerated it. But then horse racing was a notoriously corrupt business, and false starts were part and parcel of the whole. A blackleg or a tout would pay off the starter to fire off a certain number of false starts. The idea was to rattle the jumpier of the horses, and since Thoroughbreds were a breed notorious for becoming unnerved easily, the ploy usually worked.

Except with Little Wicked.

A filly of even temperament, she serenely returned to her place at the starting line and did it all over again.

And again, it turned out after the next firing of the starting gun.

The third firing, however, was the charm, and the race was on as Little Wicked jumped to an early lead—and held it...through the first straight and turn...through the tricky turn at the infamous Tattenham Corner where she'd very nearly got tangled up with the Marquess of Ormonde's Filthy Habit in yesterday's Derby. But that wasn't a problem today, for no other horse was within ten yards of her.

Usually, these races were the longest three minutes of Dev's life. Today, those minutes flew past, for by the time Little Wicked crossed the finish line, she was half a furlong ahead of her nearest competitor.

"That a girl," cheered Shaw beside him.

Dev's fist clenched at his side, the only outward indicator of the depth of his satisfaction.

But a moment's satisfaction was all he felt—never more than a moment.

The next instant, the craving for *more* hit him.

Now, Little Wicked was through to the Race of the Century, where no one would be able to deny him his place amongst the elite.

Shaw slipped away with a farewell nod as congratulations poured in from all around. These lords and ladies might've been second- and even third-best aristocrats, but they understood who was keeping their coupes of champagne full to overflowing. Dev was the man of the moment.

From the periphery of his vision, a pair of figures drew close.

The same pair he'd kept track of from the moment they'd entered the stand.

Intentionally, he didn't turn their direction until they'd stepped within a few feet of him. Even then, he somehow kept his attention trained on Viscount Landsdown, who had reappeared at his side, though he didn't actually see the man or hear the words issuing from his mouth. At last, a masculine throat cleared.

Then Dev turned.

Before him stood the Earl and Countess of Bridgewater. Where Imogen exuded dewy spring vibrancy with her clear willow-green eyes and hair streaked with sunlight, the earl lent the atmosphere an air of decay. He'd reached the age where the life a man had lived the previous fifty or so years caught up with him. From the broken blood vessels blossoming across his nose and the dry pallor of skin that spoke silently of decades of dissolution, the earl exuded a rot that emanated from the core of him.

Bridgewater was in no way worthy of the model of perfection at his side.

Dev could hardly stand it.

"Well done, old chap," said the earl in his aloof Etonian accent that spoke of ancient privilege extending back centuries to William the Conqueror.

The rejoinder perched on Dev's lips, however, went unspoken. The earl had hardly broken stride as he moved through the crowd that was already dispersing now that the race was finished.

As for Imogen, she hadn't spared him a glance—as she hadn't since the decision was made that she would become Bridgewater's wife.

Hot fury streaked through Dev.

But it wasn't the sort of fury that lashed out.

It knew how to bide its time.

In fact, that was one of his particular strengths—to take his fury and channel it into a single-minded goal.

The feeling…the *craving*…for *more*…it ever hit him in moments like this.

Nothing would ever be enough until Imogen was his.

That was what he knew in the deepest part of his soul.

And he wouldn't stop until he'd made it so.

CHAPTER TWO

HYDE PARK, A FEW WEEKS LATER

*B*eatrix shifted on the hard, out-of-the-way park bench and swept a wary eye over the stack of letters in her lap.

She'd been ignoring them, though they were a large part of the reason she'd ventured to Hyde Park on a day that threatened imminent downpour. In truth, such an outcome wasn't an unusual prospect. London weather had defeated many a merry-maker—and writer, in her case.

Except the idea of returning home just yet filled her with a sense of gloom grayer than the sky above. The house was cold and dank. Too still and too quiet. They'd lost their last housemaid yesterday. The only servant who remained was Cumberbatch, Lydon's ancient valet, who Beatrix took care of more often than the other way around, as he was too lofty to care for any less noble personage than the marquess himself.

She moved her attention from the stack of letters that were too stubborn to disappear and returned it to the pencil in her hand and the journal below it. Her gaze roved across Hyde Park's lush green turf toward Rotten Row. Perhaps a few aristocratic goings-on would be worth recording. If anyone noticed her—

unlikely—they would think she sat here writing all manner of wretched poetry that tore at the soul.

A snort escaped her.

She could scarcely manage to put meat on the table twice a week.

She couldn't afford a soul.

But society didn't know that. They thought she held herself above them and considered herself an intellectual superior.

In fact, she wasn't writing about herself at all. She was writing about *them*—who was talking to whom...who was ignoring whom...who was cutting whom...what lady was laughing too hard at which lord's jokes...

In other words, the subject matter spilling from her pencil was such mundane folderol, it was about the farthest one could fall from the exalted heights of poetry. For what she was writing accomplished the most basic task of all. It provided food for her stomach—and sometimes there was even enough to spare to put wood in the hearth.

Writing for a newspaper—a turf rag, more specifically—earned her keep.

Under the guise of a pseudonym, of course.

Further, she'd discovered a few more shillings happened her way when she mixed in tidbits of society tattle. Really, the goings-on of Rotten Row could be considered turf gossip, if she remained focused on the lords and ladies who raced Thoroughbreds. After all, several of them were here today.

There was Gabriel Siren, the new Duke of Acaster, riding his mount with such obvious discomfiture Beatrix sympathetically shifted on her bench. While he didn't own any Thoroughbreds, he was a financial backer of the upcoming Race of the Century in September, so gossip about him would be relevant. He was riding toward Celia Calthorp, the Dowager Duchess of Acaster and the widow of his predecessor. If proof was ever needed that the *haut ton* was a small world, here it was. Besides, gossip about the duchess was relevant, too, as her filly Light Skirt had won the One Thousand Guineas, the second major race of the season, putting her through to the Race of the Century. That could be what she and the duke had to discuss. Though, going by the intent expression on the duke's face when he looked at the duchess, Beatrix sensed…*more*.

She traced a line between their names and scratched a question mark.

A thought for another time.

The Earl and Countess of Bridgewater trotted into view. As ever, Beatrix's mouth filled with a bad taste at the very sight of the earl. He was a good enough looking man in the middle of his fifties, who many ladies found attractive. Yet, for those gifts of title and looks, the man faced the world with an ever-so-subtle curl to his mouth that couldn't have been interpreted as anything other than a haughty sneer. Further, she didn't like the whispers about how he treated his horseflesh. *Drove them into the ground*, was the common agreement. The earl was not best pleased that his favored Thoroughbred hadn't placed in the top half of any race this season.

As for his countess, Beatrix had no opinion whatsoever on the woman. She was a beauty. Of course, she would be. Theirs would be a marriage made for dynastic purposes, which was nothing new under the sun. No young lady as lovely as the countess spent her youth dreaming of marrying a man twice her age. But if the slight curl to her ladyship's mouth was any indicator, she would be matching her husband for haughtiness within the decade.

Beatrix's eye that missed very little kept roaming. No sign of the Duke of Rakesley and his new duchess. Quite a little scandal that elopement had caused.

She gave her head a bemused shake. To think she'd shared a supper with them when she'd visited Somerton not two months ago without an inkling of what had certainly already been simmering beneath the surface. Not for the first time, the idea struck her that she might not be an entirely reliable society gossip.

Her gaze moved along and lit upon a newly familiar gentleman riding a gorgeous gray hunter.

Gentleman.

That was the word of interest to her.

For the man wasn't a gentleman, however much he pretended.

*Mr. Blake Deverill...*steam engine entrepreneur and upstart man about Town.

Or as society had dubbed him—*Lord Devil.*

Strictly from an objective position, he was composed of all the elements that made a man handsome—and a few that set him apart. Beneath the charcoal-gray superfine, his shoulders were broad, likely muscular, too. His hair, the black of a raven's wing, was thick and appealingly wavy. He had a strong jaw, sharp cheekbones, and a straight nose.

Those were the elements that rendered him handsome in the commonly held sense.

As for those that set him apart... The glacial aquamarine blue of his eyes beneath straight black eyebrows... Those eyes pierced and prodded. They held a demand for the world.

And his mouth... It was at complete odds with the rest of him with its full, pillowy lips.

A lovely mouth, Lord Devil had.

Though Beatrix had never been kissed in all her life, she imagined that mouth most kissable.

The truth was—an uncomfortable truth, to be sure—every one of her senses perked to life at the very sight of him.

Whose wouldn't? she thought a bit defensively.

The man possessed the sort of charismatic energy that made it next to impossible to remove one's eyes from him.

Yet another quality that set him apart.

Now, Lord Devil could sell a few gossip rags.

Her pencil stopped.

She might give the idea of writing about Blake Deverill further consideration. He was a man who had made his way in the world through his own intelligence and determination.

And ambition and ruthlessness.

It wouldn't do to make an enemy of him.

She had enough problems as it was.

With a mind toward solving a few of them, she tucked her writing journal into her satchel—which left the stack of letters patiently waiting on her lap.

Some opened...others decidedly unopened...

All dreaded.

She started with the opened ones. Better the devil you know —or something like that.

Bills.

To a one.

None earned by her, but that hardly mattered.

They affected her.

She plucked a different journal from her satchel and began moving her finger along the column of figures, hoping she'd transcribed a few incorrectly. That the five guineas here was, in fact, five shillings... Or perhaps this bill for seven quid was actually a credit...

She'd written every single figure correctly.

Down to the penny.

She eyed the unopened letters.

They weren't necessarily bills.

Except...they most definitely were—for they were addressed to the Marquess of Lydon. He didn't receive any other sort of mail, and she received no mail at all, except for her weekly letter from Artemis, who had run off to the wilds of Yorkshire, improbably, only to establish a horse sanctuary.

Actually, not improbably.

Artemis had lost her beloved Thoroughbred, Dido, during the season-opening race and had been utterly devastated. But in true

Artemis fashion, she'd found a way to channel the loss into something useful—she'd established a horse sanctuary on the estate she'd inherited from her grandmother. Though it might be better described an any-animal-that-happened-down-the-lane sanctuary. There was even a one-eyed sheepdog named Bathsheba, who Beatrix sensed was in the running for Artemis's best bosom friend.

With each letter, Beatrix could see her friend's customary brightness of spirit returning, and if that was what it took for Artemis to return to herself, then Beatrix had no choice but to be glad for her.

In the stack presently occupying her lap, however, there was no such letter to cut through the gloom.

She lifted the top missive and felt no qualm about breaking the seal. Someone had to—and heaven knew it wouldn't be Lydon. No, that onerous task was hers alone in their household of three, when one included Cumberbatch—which one must. Not only was he another mouth to feed, but the fact was she interacted with the old valet more often than she did with Lydon, who popped into the house once or twice a week and only then at odd times and intervals.

The opened letter confirmed what she'd already known—a bill. Twenty quid for a new pair of boots? She'd paid five shillings for the boots presently on her feet—seven years ago.

A sudden, wet plop landed on the bridge of her nose, startling her into the present.

A raindrop.

The rain the sky had been promising all morning had announced its arrival.

Further, it was keeping its other promise by fully opening at once and pouring sheets of water onto all heads with the bad luck and poor judgment to have been out of doors in the first place. Threats of rain tended to keep their promise in London.

The park transformed into a flurry of wet chaos as horses

bolted this way and that, ladies exclaiming in both delight and distress, lords fumbling about with the leather hoods of their curricles, all scurrying about in desperate search of shelter and scattering to the four winds.

Beatrix shoved journal, pencils, and bills into her satchel—though she'd been sorely tempted to let wind and rain carry the latter away. Bag in one hand, the other clamped onto her bonnet, she braced herself against the heavy sheets of rain blasting into her face, pointed herself in the general direction of home, and willed her feet into motion. She knew where she was going—*approximately*—so she didn't particularly need her eyes.

Then she heard and felt it—the thundering of hooves... approaching...*fast*. Of a sudden, a frenzied blur of motion appeared and was nearly upon her before she could blink. A shocked cry flew from her mouth as she instinctively hunched into a protective huddle and pivoted—twisting her ankle in the process and producing another cry, this one strident with swift, sharp pain. She collapsed to the ground, losing her grip on the satchel as reflex had her attempting to cushion her fall with an extended hand. The sudden pain in her wrist elicited yet another cry.

The rider jumped from his mount and lowered into a crouch above her, incensed blue eyes six inches from hers. "What are you thinking, woman?" he shouted into her face. "Running blind on a horse path during a rainstorm?"

For an instant, Beatrix felt no pain—only sheer incredulity at both question and questioner.

The audacity!

As for the man who asked it...

She blinked away the rain collected in her eyelashes, for surely they were casting illusions. But, no, those accusatory eyes... They weren't merely blue. They were the most glacially aquamarine-blue eyes one was ever likely to behold.

Lord Devil.

27

"What was *I* thinking?" she blasted. "That I wanted to get out of the rain?"

The words had hardly left her mouth before her ankle and wrist were barking their displeasure, and the ensuing gasp of pain resolved in a groan.

Without hesitation, his hands were upon her, one closing around an elbow and the other clamped around her shoulder. Indignation shot through her. "What, pray tell, do you think you're about? Isn't it enough that you've run me down with your horse? Now you're accosting me?"

Incredulous black eyebrows winged together. "Oh, blast it, woman, would you rather be carried away with Noah's flood? Or accept my help?"

Beatrix's heart beat out three heavy thuds as she considered her options.

Even as she knew she had only the one.

She exhaled a lengthy, resigned sigh.

And relented.

CHAPTER THREE

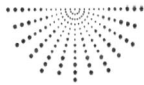

*O*f course, the sky opened onto Dev's head.

The universe did have a way of demonstrating its sense of humor.

Or it was precisely what he needed to cool the foul mood that had beset him.

The day had been ticking along nicely. He'd spent the morning sketching some new plans that had seeded in his brain. When that happened, there was nothing for it but to seat himself at his draftsman's table, pencil perched between thumb and forefinger. Sometimes, all it took was a few minutes; others, a few hours. On the odd occasion, a few days. For Dev, the world stopped until the idea had flesh on its bones.

Fortunately, today had been an hour spent at the draftsman's table, then another hour's worth of business correspondence. Then it was off to Hyde Park, where he would meet up with Gabriel Siren.

He corrected himself.

No longer Gabriel Siren, but Gabriel Calthorp, the newly minted Seventh Duke of Acaster.

Dev hadn't seen the man since his elevation to the second-highest tier of English society—just a single rung below the king. The duke had been a silent partner in his steam engine business with Shaw these last few years, and Dev wanted to get a feel for Acaster as he was now.

One thing Dev wouldn't tolerate was interference in his business. Everyone had their place in its success. Acaster invested pounds; Shaw oversaw operations; and Dev was the talent.

It was simply the truth.

Within thirty seconds of conversation, however, Acaster had put Dev's mind to rest. The man was the same as ever, even if he was now a duke.

It wasn't the duke who had incited Dev's present foul mood.

It was what had come after.

Namely, Imogen.

She and Bridgewater had approached him and Acaster on their mounts. Promptly, the earl had offered greetings to the new duke—greetings he wouldn't have offered weeks ago when the man had been a mere Mr. Gabriel Siren. Bridgewater ignored Dev—as if he hadn't hosted the man and his wife in Prinny's Stand at the Oaks three weeks ago.

The message was clear.

When Dev wasn't of use, he didn't exist.

In truth, Dev expected as much from Bridgewater. But Imogen…

They'd once been friends.

Once, they'd been even more.

He didn't believe the act they'd shared made her his.

But…hadn't it made them each other's?

And though no promise had been spoken, hadn't it been made with their bodies and writ upon their hearts?

Then Bridgewater and Imogen had moved on to extend greetings elsewhere.

The black mood that had descended upon Dev was swift and implacable.

He'd tossed Acaster a surly grunt of farewell and urged his hunter in the opposite direction.

It was then the heavens decided to open.

He didn't immediately rein in his horse or reduce his speed. The punishing ride felt too good—the pounding of hooves rattling and jarring him, freeing his mind of all but the raw elements of gusting wind and frigid rain that met his face like individual cannon blasts. It was exactly what he needed.

What came next wasn't.

Around a bend in the horse path, a figure appeared out of nowhere, dashing straight for him. He had only the split of a second to turn his mount before inflicting serious injury. Immediately, the figure—a woman—fell to the ground on a sharp cry of pain.

Instinct had Dev jumping from his horse, who hadn't yet come to a complete halt, and shouting, "What are you thinking, woman?"

The instant they flew from his mouth, he knew them for the wrong words—and unfair.

She could ask the same question of him—*fairly*.

From there, it only got worse.

When he made to assist her to her feet, she flinched back, as if he were attempting to assault her.

In Hyde Park.

In broad daylight.

At last, however, she gathered a modicum of sense and allowed him to assist her to her feet.

With the rain pelting every available surface, she was as soaked as he, and yet sopping wet, the woman weighed near to nothing. He'd encountered kittens composed of more solid substance.

And Dev had another observation to make about this

Woman—one that should've been apparent the instant she'd begun lashing him with her tongue.

She was a lady.

One he'd never encountered.

But then he wouldn't have.

This lady, came a quick third observation, was the sort who would fade into the background at a society gathering. The showier sort tended to catch his attention, in the general scheme.

The instant she was upright on her two feet, she shook off his hand and exclaimed, "You're a bloody menace, is what you are."

He owed her an apology—it was even possible she was correct about the menace part, too—and he was opening his mouth to say exactly that when her eyes went wide and—*yet another*—cry of distress issued from her mouth. He followed the direction of her gaze and found her satchel had sprung open. Neat white squares of paper fluttered haphazardly across the grass all around them.

"Blimey!" came another exclamation.

Blimey?

Wasn't this woman a lady?

But he had no time to contemplate the conundrum when she fell to her knees and began frantically gathering every square within reach—the seals identifying them as missives.

Dev's brow creased. She was only using one hand, rather awkwardly. "Are you injured?"

Without meeting his eyes, she gave her head a tight shake and continued about her business.

She must've tried to break her fall with the hand she was coddling. The wrist might be sprained or, worse, broken. Again, he began speaking words that were long overdue. "I must apolo—"

Her head whipped around. Gray eyes, fringed with thick, wet lashes, blazed up at him. "Are you just going to stand there?"

Right.

Like a newly released coil, he sprang into motion, gathering sopping wet missives and passing them over to her, which she accepted without a single thank you. She might've been a lady, but no one had taught her manners.

He straightened and glanced around, squinting against the lashing rain for evidence of more escaped missives, but found none. "I think that's all of them."

It was only after she'd clamped her satchel shut that Dev noticed one more item. Not a letter, but a journal. He'd just lifted it off the grass when another yelp sounded at his back. He swung around to find the woman struggling to her feet again.

"Would you please accept my help?"

The stubborn clench of her jaw and curt shake of the head was all the answer he received, leaving him no choice but to watch the lady struggle to her feet, increment by *slow...excruciating...interminable...*increment.

Once on her feet, triumph shone in her eyes, as if she'd passed some sort of test.

All Dev saw was a woman who was causing herself an unnecessary deal of pain and hassle out of sheer bloody-mindedness. He'd never had any use for the bloody-minded. They got in the way of their own interests, and he couldn't fathom that compulsion.

The rain continuing its unabated downpour, she took a sodden step.

And as Dev could've—*should've*—predicted, she yelped.

He reacted before he could think and grabbed her by the elbow before she could fall again and find a way to blame that on him, too. "It's your ankle, correct?"

She gave another tight nod. "You can let go of me now."

Gingerly, Dev did as told and stepped back carefully, as if she were a house of cards that would collapse at the faintest whisper of a breeze.

Then...*nothing.*

She didn't move.

He didn't move.

In this strange negotiation, they'd reached an impasse.

"Do you plan to stand there until—*when?—night?*" A vision of her hobbling through Hyde Park into the wee hours came to him. The woman was stubborn enough.

"Until my ankle feels sufficiently able to continue on." The wince that crossed her face belied her matter-of-fact tone.

Dev's brow dug a trench into his forehead. "Until your ankle *feels sufficiently able to continue on?* Do you plan to stand rooted to that patch of earth for the next few weeks, then?"

She tried for a dismissive laugh. "I can assure you—"

"You can assure me of nothing until a physician has taken a look."

She heaved a great, condescending sigh. He almost bought it. "Can you please leave now?"

"Not until I've done two things." She would see she wasn't the only stubborn participant in this conversation.

"Which are?" Genuine exasperation radiated off her.

"First, I offer you my sincere apology." He meant every word. "I was riding recklessly, and I'm solely at fault for this entire situation."

Without acknowledging his first point, she said, "And your second point?"

"You must make use of my horse."

A single eyebrow lifted in question. "Pardon?"

"It's obvious you won't make it home on your two feet, so I insist you make use of my horse's four."

"That, I can assure you, won't be necessary."

He'd expected as much—and had a counterpoint ready. "If you can take three steps without yelping or wobbling, I'll let you be on your way."

"What gives you the right to dictate ultimatums to me?" She tried planting a fist on her waist, but gasped and let it fall to her side. That would be the injured wrist.

He crossed his arms over his chest and cocked his head, his message clear.

He was waiting for her to speak sense.

She heaved another of her great sighs, but he sensed a slight relenting—and a further shoring up of determination. It would take more than a little opposition to make the fight go out of this lady.

Her jaw clenched, she took a slow, testing step.

No wobble.

No yelp.

She cut him a sharp glance that said *see?*

He spread his hands before him peaceably. "Two more steps, and you're rid of me forever."

He caught a glimpse of emotion as it passed behind her eyes— *uncertainty.*

Forever was only two steps away.

Dev tensed with anticipation. He needed to be ready if she did, indeed, wobble. She wouldn't fall again—not on his watch.

If she wobbled?

More like *when.*

She took a second step, her relief palpable when she didn't wobble or yelp. He admired her tenacity.

Her sense of relief, however, would prove her downfall, as she followed that successful second step with a hasty third. The yelp that scraped across her throat was sudden and instinctual, an honest reaction to pain.

But she didn't wobble, so Dev stayed his impulse to rush toward her.

Instead, he waited.

Eyes squeezed shut, she went still. As if the possibility existed that when she opened her eyes, he would be gone and this strange interlude would've never happened.

He cleared his throat.

Her eyes remained closed.

Still, he waited.

Then, her mouth moving as little as possible, out mumbled two stubborn words. He angled forward as if he hadn't heard them. "What was that?"

Her eyes slid open, opaque gray piercing through thick black lashes. Once one got past the sharpness of those eyes, it became apparent the woman had remarkable eyes...arresting eyes.

"*All...right,*" she said, each syllable distinctly enunciated, those remarkable, arresting eyes throwing daggers.

His mouth twitched, but he managed to keep a smile suppressed. The movement, however, was enough to catch her attention. Her gaze lingered a few ticks of time too long on his mouth, before sliding away.

As the torrent of rain had blessedly subsided into a light mist, he retrieved his hunter, who was sheltering beneath a sprawling oak and led him to the woman. Her knuckles shone white, so tightly was she clutching the satchel before her. For a silent moment, they stood facing each other, the understanding in her eyes matching his.

There was only one way for her to mount this horse.

With his help.

The five feet that separated them... Well, it might as well have been five miles.

For the first time in Dev's adult male life, he had no idea how to bridge the gap between himself and a woman who had consented to him putting his hands on her.

But this blasted woman couldn't bloody well walk.

Right.

He took a measured step forward, as if he were negotiating with a feral cat who would scratch his eyes out if she took a mind to it.

When she didn't respond with a step backward, he eased another step forward.

Now, they were within touching distance. The next move was hers. Though she didn't seem to understand it.

He cleared his throat, like a nerve-beset green youth. "You'll need to place your hands on my shoulders."

Gray eyes glared up at him. "I resent this entire situation."

"I'm aware."

Her shoulders lifted and fell on a deep breath.

At last, slender, gloved hands came to a tentative rest on his shoulders. Her head tipped back, so she could hold his gaze. No shrinking miss, this lady, even as the pheasant feather in her hat drooped and wet tendrils of hair clung to pale cheeks and hung lank about her shoulders.

Her eyes... They weren't merely remarkable and arresting.

They were beautiful.

She cleared her throat.

And irritated.

Those eyes most definitely glittered with irritation.

Right.

He supposed he needed to speak the next words... "And now I'm going to put my hands on your waist."

He didn't understand why, but he sensed she needed to be warned, even though she must've understood where he would have to put his hands.

She nodded, and for the split of a second, emotions other than irritation flashed behind her eyes.

Uncertainty...vulnerability.

Here he was, about to put his hands around the waist of a lady in the middle of Hyde Park.

An *unmarried* lady, that vulnerability spoke.

It was just him and her, here.

Her dark, straight eyebrows lifted with annoyance and most definitely impatience, and he snapped to.

And wrapped his hands around her waist.

CHAPTER FOUR

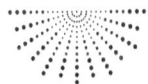

*B*eatrix hadn't experienced the feel of a man's hands on her person in...*years*.

Since the last time she'd danced with a man.

Since her come-out ball, to be exact.

These hands... They were strong hands, long-fingered and most definitely up to any task set beneath them.

And the shoulders beneath her palms were broad, the dense muscles pure banked energy.

And there was his scent...*woodsy and clean*, like pine and sea.

All such reasonable observations were swept away, however, when those strong, long-fingered hands tightened around her waist and lifted her as if she weighed naught more than a feather pillow.

Then her sodden bottom was squeaking across wet saddle leather, and her hands were lifting away from those broad, muscled shoulders and grabbing the pommel for support. Her palms felt...*tingly*. She swallowed and attempted to steady herself against the novel sensation. She was clearly stirred up from having almost been run down by a horse.

And who wouldn't be?

Indignation revived itself and pounded through her.

His head tipped back, and piercing aquamarine eyes met hers. She tried not to stare too deeply into those startling eyes. She'd heard tell of their transfixing nature and had dismissed such whisperings as hyperbolic tittle-tattle.

Now, she saw it hadn't been exaggeration in the least.

One could sink into the depths of that aquamarine gaze and never surface again.

She gave herself a firm mental shake.

Now who was succumbing to hyperbole?

She dragged her gaze away from him and set busily about securing herself.

"It isn't a sidesaddle," he said. "Will you be safe once the horse starts moving?"

She nodded without meeting his eyes. She understood how she would appear to this man—*haughty...cold...aristocratic... contemptuous.*

She would take all the armor she could muster.

He snorted and grabbed the horse's reins. "And I suppose you'll tell me where we're going?"

Beatrix opened her mouth, then as quickly closed it. He would know where she lived. A knife of panic cut through her—and as quickly dulled.

Lord Devil most definitely would *not* be entering her house.

"Little Stanhope Street."

He gave an assessing nod. "Fashionable address."

Only a fashionable address would do for the Marquess of Lydon.

She wouldn't be saying that to Mr. Deverill.

Through the thick blanket of London fog that had replaced the pouring rain, they began picking their way through the park until they reached Chesterfield Gate. Then they were on the slick cobblestones of Park Lane, followed by a turn on Hertford Street. They weren't the only people braving the weather, but they might as well have been, for Beatrix's attention was decidedly fixed on Mr. Deverill. Even when she was attempting to concentrate her energies elsewhere, ready to redirect him if he made a false turn, he ever remained within the edge of her vision.

He was impossible to look away from.

Concern for her appearance wanted to rear its head, but she refused to allow it.

Soon enough, she would see for herself the rumpled mess she was.

Mortification could wait until then.

When they turned onto Little Stanhope Street, she called out, "Number Ten," as if she were directing a servant.

Actually, she would never speak to a servant thusly.

Anyway, she could've just as easily have said, *"Locate the shabbiest townhouse on the row, and that's me."*

She would leave that bit unspoken.

Soon—*too soon*—he would see for himself.

How she hoped for the heavens to open up a second time. Rain heavy enough so one couldn't see one's hand in front of one's face, much less the great black strips of paint flaking off the trim and front door of Number Ten.

But she encountered no such luck as they slowed to a stop before her address.

Mr. Deverill began moving around to the side of the horse, and an idea born of absolute necessity came to her. If she could just hook her good foot into the stirrup...and grab hold of the pommel with her good hand...while twisting her body around... it would only be a short hop to the ground and she would have dismounted without his touching her.

Her first win today—or for the last several hundred, if one was counting.

The plan, however, wasn't as easily executed in reality as in her imagination, for she hadn't accounted for her satchel. It would have to remain clutched in one hand while she attempted the maneuver.

But she managed with only a few grunts until...*the twist*.

The twist that had her sprawled on her belly and clutching the opposite side of the saddle to prevent herself from crashing to the cobblestones.

Thusly, she remained—her breath tight in her lungs...her heart rattling against her ribcage...her bottom in the air.

Behind her came a snort.

Possibly—*very probably*—a suppressed laugh, too.

Mortification fired through her, swift and hot.

His throat cleared, and she waited for him to ask... "May I be of assistance to you, my lady?"

"As it happens—"

Oh, how she wanted to refuse him.

"Yes, my lady?" he asked, patiently—*too* patiently.

She couldn't refuse him.

And he knew it.

"*Yes*," she blurted without an ounce of grace.

"Your wish is my command, my lady."

He was laying it on a bit thick with the *my ladies*, wasn't he?

How she longed to tell him where he could stuff his *my ladies*.

But as she was entirely reliant on him at the moment, well, she couldn't.

Yet.

Large hands found her waist, their heat penetrating layers of soaked wool and muslin, firming their grip. All rational thought flew from her brain, as he carefully eased her down...down... down...in a humiliating, inelegant slither off the saddle.

Her feet hit yet-slick cobblestones, and despite the warmth of his hands, she felt frozen. Though she faced away from him, in the space between their two bodies she sensed...*something*.

Something she'd never experienced in this way with another person.

Awareness.

She gave herself a brisk shake, both mental and physical, and stepped out of his grasp. A great, sudden yelp instantly followed.

She'd forgotten her injured ankle.

He reached out to steady her, and her palm shot out between them. "You've done enough, Mr. Deverill."

Oh, the ice in her voice could form glaciers.

His head cocked in question. "*Mr. Deverill?*"

"Isn't that your name?"

"It is," he said slowly. "But how do you know it? Have we been introduced?"

She shook her head. "We haven't. If we had, you would've forgotten me within ten seconds of our parting." An edge of acid ran the length of the hollow laugh that issued forth. "All society knows Lord Devil."

His gaze narrowed. "Then you have me at a disadvantage."

"A rare occurrence, I dare say."

His mouth pursed and released.

Her eyes were left with no choice but to watch.

Simply, he had the loveliest mouth she'd seen on man or woman.

"And if I might be so bold as to ask your name?"

She drew herself up to her full, inconsiderable height and resisted the urge to adjust her bonnet, which had gone precariously askew. "I'm Lady Beatrix St. Vincent."

"A name replete with aristocratic forebears, I presume."

She felt her mouth do something odd.

It twitched.

Then, out of the murky gray sky, for there was no clear blue around, she was restraining a sudden tide of laughter that demanded release. Hysteria, it had to be. Or...

This situation was...

Funny?

She summoned every shred of willpower yet in her possession and suppressed it.

She didn't want to share a laugh with this man.

Instead, she asked, "You're not expecting an invitation for tea,
are you?"

Enough scorn infused her voice to turn the ocean into dry
salt.

Something dark and inscrutable passed behind his eyes, and
they went flinty as stone. "Of course, *my lady*."

Another *my lady*.

Blimey.

Dignity hanging about her in fraying tatters, she tore her gaze
away from the magnetic Mr. Deverill and turned, taking the steps
carefully, one by one.

Once she'd made it to the top—without yelping once—she
heard at her back, "A physician will be at your door within the
hour."

She glanced over her shoulder, a refusal ready on her mouth.

"*Answer it*," he said, then turned on his heel and strode down
the street.

Once the front door clicked shut behind her, Beatrix pressed
her back against solid oak and exhaled the breath she'd been
holding these last thirty minutes.

"Blimey."

What in the blazes just happened?

She'd nearly been trampled by a horse...a horse ridden by
none other than...*Lord Devil.*

And...he'd put his hands on her.

Twice.

A groan of no single emotion, but a blustery whirlwind of
them escaped her.

Of a sudden, a scent hit her nose.

Was that the smell of...*scorch?*

"Cumberbatch?" she called out, alarm bells ringing through

her. Taking an instinctive step, she yelped from the ensuing streak of pain.

Down the corridor, a head with precisely twelve gray hairs on it popped into view. "That'll be evening tea." His voice lacked any sign of apology—as usual. "Did you bring the castor oil for my bunions?"

Blimey.

With all the hullaballoo with Mr. Deverill, the castor oil had completely slipped her mind.

Her hand was already wrapped around the door handle as she called over her shoulder, "I'll be back in half an hour."

A decided limp to her step—with Lord Devil gone, she could call it what it was—she hobbled down the front steps and made her slow way down Little Stanhope Street. Cumberbatch would be pettish throughout evening tea if she didn't bring the castor oil for his bunions—and massage it into them. A chore that would turn the stomach of many a lady, to be sure. But Cumberbatch was well into his dotage and his fingers had long gone knotty with arthritis and, most importantly, he had no one else.

Neither did she, really.

Most mornings over the kitchen table and most evenings across the dining room table, it was the grumpy presence of Cumberbatch who sat opposite her.

Both of them had long been discarded by Lydon.

All facts she'd reconciled herself to.

Anyway, company was company, and the truth was she didn't think Cumberbatch viewed her as his ideal companion any more than she viewed him as hers.

They were stuck together.

Mr. Deverill's eyes stole into her mind, hard as granite.

He hadn't liked her dismissal of him.

Too bad.

She wouldn't be inviting the man into her home for tea—now or…*ever.*

A man like Lord Devil would see her living circumstances for what they truly were.

No.

She couldn't bear that.

And there was his unnerving effect upon her.

She couldn't endure that for any length of time, either.

Not that it was a concern.

She'd been out of his presence for longer than ten seconds.

Which meant he would've already forgotten all about her.

Which meant, of course, she could forget all about him.

CHAPTER FIVE

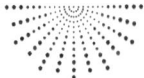

ST. JAMES'S SQUARE, A FORTNIGHT LATER

L ady Beatrix St. Vincent.

Dev's gaze narrowed.

Here, writ plain in black and white in the betting book that had appeared in the Duke of Acaster's card room, was the name of the lady he'd mostly put out of his mind this last fortnight.

He'd only intended to glance at the book casually, as one did either for a laugh or to join the action.

But that name was enough to stop his eyes cold in their tracks.

Lady Beatrix St. Vincent.

A prickle of guilt needled through him.

He *had* come close to running the woman to ground with his horse.

Thankfully, the physician had assured him there had been no bones broken and no real harm done. The lady would recover unscathed.

And that had been the end of Dev's association with Lady Beatrix St. Vincent.

But here was her name in the gentlemen's betting book at a ball.

Which usually wasn't a positive development for the lady in question, as gentlemen's betting books skewed *ungentlemanly* when it came to the fairer sex.

The bet regarding Lady Beatrix, however, appeared tame enough.

£50 shall be awarded to the gentleman able to persuade Lady Beatrix St. Vincent to dance with him.

Fifty pounds? Dev's brow dug into his forehead. *To dance with a lady?*

He'd met the lady in question.

He'd even put his hands on her.

Out of necessity, of course.

The point was the bet gave the impression she was a gorgon. Though Dev could attest to the fact that she was stubborn as a mule, she wasn't a beast worthy of mythology.

Yet…she was no malleable bit of fluff either.

It was those eyes of hers—*remarkable…arresting…beautiful.*

Eyes that held a magnetism.

An idea teased him.

He could try his hand at winning this bet.

He might not even mind it—as a personal challenge.

As quickly as he made to act upon this surely unwise idea, a hand cut across him and penciled a line through the entry. Dev questioned the young gentleman at his side. "Did someone already win?"

"Injured ankle," came the mostly indifferent response that explained everything.

Again pricked that needle of guilt.

Injured ankle.

He was the cause of that injury.

Another memory pushed forward and swept that feeling aside like an icy wind.

"You're not expecting an invitation for tea, are you?"

The scorn in her voice still turned the blood to bile in his veins.

As if the idea of sharing tea with riffraff like him was too incredible to entertain.

Lest he forget his place in the hierarchy.

Right.

"I was going to win that fifty pounds," came one voice.

"Oh, you think so?" rejoined another.

"I'm sure you're just her type," scoffed a third.

Dev turned to find himself surrounded by a herd of young bucks.

"Lady Beatrix has a type?" continued the first with eyebrows lifted for comic effect.

"It would take Attila the Hun, old chap."

This got a round of laughter.

Likely, Dev should've walked away and left the lordlings to their nonsense. Yet...

He teetered on the edge of knowing something more about Lady Beatrix St. Vincent, and he found he wanted that information.

Very much.

"Does Lady Beatrix not enjoy dancing?" he asked.

A simple enough question.

"Oh, that's putting it mildly."

"How so?"

"Lady Beatrix is on the shelf."

"A spinster?" Dev couldn't say he was surprised. She possessed the air of a woman yet untamed by a man.

That sounded wrong, even in his own mind.

She possessed the air of a woman yet untamed by love—or even lust, for that matter.

"Decidedly so."

"Had her come-out years ago—"

"Weren't you still in leading strings, Portney?"

A roar of laughter burst forth.

"And nothing came of her debut season."

"Probably just did it out of obligation."

"She might not be the sort who's interested in marriage," offered Dev.

Why was he defending her? While he didn't pretend to know what sort of woman Lady Beatrix was, he did know she was the sort who knew her own mind.

"Oh, she's definitely that sort." Portney's eyebrows crashed together with confusion. "The sort who's *not* that sort."

"And that's what the dancing bet was about?" asked Dev in an attempt to steer the conversation toward the information he sought.

"It's a standing bet at every ball."

"Has been for years."

"To see who can convince Lady Beatrix to dance a single dance."

"And has she ever been convinced?" Dev found he wanted to know.

"Not once."

"And there's the father."

Dev was getting more information than he'd bargained for, yet he couldn't not ask… "Who is her father?"

"Lydon."

Dev searched his mind. He knew of only one Lydon… "The marquess?"

"The very one."

"The Marquess of Lydon is Lady Beatrix St. Vincent's father?"

"Indeed."

From what Dev had observed of father and daughter, two

more different people couldn't exist. How was that supremely self-possessed woman the daughter of the dissolute Marquess of Lydon? Every time Dev saw him, the old wastrel was thirty or so cups into his drink and a hundred or so pounds in debt to a dealer.

That was Lady Beatrix's *father*?

"She's always been a bit high in the instep for us mere mortals."

Now, *that* fit within Dev's experience of the lady to a T.

A few nods all around, and talk, predictably, turned toward more felicitous conversation—horseflesh.

Dev let it proceed without him, for his mind hadn't stopped chewing on the previous one.

So, that was Lady Beatrix St. Vincent, all laid out for him. A few surprises, yes, but his overall impression of her remained largely unchanged.

Except he knew one thing more about the lady than did anyone else in this room.

Just as they were observing her and storing up opinions, she was doing the same with them.

And Dev had the proof sitting in his suite at Mivart's.

Her journal.

The one he'd picked up in Hyde Park and neglected to return to her.

He'd spent an entire meal entertained by its contents, for within its pages wasn't the meaningless drivel about her day or fussy prose about her feelings. Rather, the pages were meticulously segmented—date and location at the top with a vertical row of names to the left and details to the right. What certain lords and ladies were wearing; with whom they spoke; who they ignored. No salient detail was left unnoted.

Further, the entries varied with the venue. If it was a horse race, then it was wins and losses, too. If it was a ball, it was who danced with whom and who was the biggest flirt. And if it was

Rotten Row, choices of horseflesh and conveyance were noted alongside names.

Names like Lord Devil.

Those few details had Dev's eyes running over them for three straight minutes.

Face—handsome; hair—black; eyes—blue; lips—full, pillowy, kissable(?)

His lips… They were a salient detail? And their kissability, too?

In truth, he'd been told as much by no few women, but he wouldn't have counted Lady Beatrix St. Vincent amongst their ranks.

Well.

Then he'd slipped the journal into a drawer and put it from his mind.

Yet, tonight, he couldn't help wondering what observations Lady Beatrix was storing up about the ball—and if he and his possibly kissable lips made an appearance.

As he began making his way toward the ballroom, he nodded greetings toward lords and ladies along the route. He didn't smile or gush effusively. Though he was *only* a wealthy, self-made man in the eyes of these people, he wasn't a bootlicker.

They would come to him on his terms.

A delicate balance, that, when one was attempting to insinuate oneself into their world. And tonight, he saw he'd—*mostly*—done it. Of course, as he and Acaster were business partners, the duke would have invited him to this ball.

That wasn't the achievement.

It wasn't simply that he was mingling amongst the cream of the *ton*.

He was being pulled into conversation by lords and treated as if he were one of them.

As one who'd come from the outside, it was in the near imperceptibilities that Dev was able to see. No plucky lordlings asking who his family was when they knew the answer full well. No condescending waggles of eyebrows when he spoke in his less-than-aristocratic accent that held a hint of Irish from his mother.

Though Dev wouldn't make the mistake of believing they didn't think him a slightly lower organism than themselves, they'd anointed him Lord Devil, and in giving him a title had made him—*almost*—one of them.

Close enough, anyway.

For now.

The gaiety of the ballroom was in full swing as happy strings sang beneath bows and buoyant feet danced in unified rhythm and the chandeliers above blessed all proceedings below with sparkling, prismatic light. Dev lifted a coupe of champagne off a passing tray and took a sip. As ever, his eyes were on the move, assessing the gathered. It was only after he'd done two full sweeps of the crowded ballroom that he realized he was looking for *her.*

Lady Beatrix St. Vincent.

No sign of her, though he wondered if he would recognize her. The only time he'd ever met the woman she'd been bedraggled, mud-streaked, and soaked to the bones, resembling more wet cat than daughter of marquess.

Her eyes, however...

He would know them anywhere.

Except it was a different pair of eyes that caught his gaze on its third sweep of the room.

Clear, willow-green eyes.

Eyes that hadn't met his in two years.

Imogen.

Her head tipped to one side, and her mouth lifted subtly to the other. Her fresh, pristine beauty—the brightness of her eyes... the roses of her cheeks...the perfect bow of her lips—put every other lady to shame.

Then she placed her hand into that of the gentleman standing before her and was whisked into the whirl of the waltz.

The contact had lasted but the split of a second, yet it felt… *intentional*.

A feeling winged through him, but not the one he would've expected.

He would've thought to feel joy or a sense of triumph, but what he was left with felt strangely hollow.

After two years, that was all? asked a small voice.

He dismissed the voice.

Of course, that wasn't all.

After two years—*at last*—it was the beginning.

Yet, surprisingly, before that instant of contact, he hadn't thought of Imogen once tonight.

His mind had been occupied by a different lady altogether.

He conducted a fourth sweep of the ballroom and, again, yielded nothing.

"Could you tell me something?" came a sultry feminine voice at his side.

He glanced around to find a lady regarding him with a saucy smile on her rouged mouth to match the one dancing in her eyes. She possessed the twinkly look of a woman who had dared herself to do something and was surprised to find herself doing it. Yet, at the same time, she didn't have the look of a lady who had never done such a thing.

"It would be my honor to impart any information to a lady of your consummate beauty," he said with a slight bow.

He was laying it on with a trowel, but if one couldn't lay it on thick at a ball where the champagne was flowing and spirits were running high and hot, then where could one? Besides, he'd told no lie. The lady was a beauty with her hazel-green eyes and lush figure.

"Why is it they call you Lord Devil?"

A corner of his mouth lifted. He knew it for his wicked smile. "I believe the title to be ironic."

"Oh?" She poked out her bottom lip in a pout.

"Oh, yes." His voice had gone low and conspiratorial. "I'm *such* an innocent."

Appreciation shone in her eyes as they slowly roved up and down his person. "Let us hope not."

A laugh startled from him. When he'd decided to muscle his way into the *ton*, nothing in his previous life had prepared him for the forwardness of its married ladies and widows. Not that he'd actually been an innocent. But these ladies could be...*direct*.

The lady held out her hand, each silk-gloved finger bearing a different jewel. "I'm Lady Standish."

He lowered into another bow. "It's my pleasure to make your acquaintance, Lady Standish."

She took a step, their body positioning now implying a relationship more intimate than mere recent acquaintances. "You may call me Susan. No one has addressed me with such familiarity since my husband, the late earl, went to meet his Maker a year ago." Her smile turned knowing. "And, oh, how I do miss the familiarities."

So, a widow.

A *willing* widow.

"Perhaps you could show me..."

The rest of her words fell on deaf ears as Dev's gaze performed another scan of the ballroom and locked onto the figure he'd been seeking.

Lady Beatrix St. Vincent.

It was a miracle he'd spotted her at all, as she'd tucked herself away into a nearly hidden corner.

No longer was she sopping wet. Rather, her presumably dry sable hair was pulled back into a matronly chignon, accentuating her arresting gray eyes. Her dress was simple white muslin with no adornment, the waist a little higher than the current style dictated as waistlines were dropping. It hung loosely on her, revealing the sharp line of her collarbone, giving her a waifish appearance. He supposed one such as her didn't overly concern herself with mundanities like sustenance.

Lady Beatrix St. Vincent was one of *those* aristocrats. Descended from old family that didn't need to care about fashion or any such *nonsense*. The sort with nothing to prove to anyone. The sort who wore her shabby nobility like a badge of honor.

Yet he recalled a fact about her person—the feel of her waist in his hands.

A waist so small his fingers could almost meet around it.

Too small, somehow.

"Now," said Lady Standish, the lowered octave of her voice pulling Dev back into the moment. The look in the lady's eye said she wasn't going anywhere until she had what she wanted.

Him.

"Come with me," she said. "I have a secret I wish to impart to you."

"A secret?" he asked, only too happy to play along. The lady was a welcome distraction from…other ladies. "But we've only just met."

Some ladies enjoyed working for it a bit. The tease given only heightening the pleasure received.

"And after I've had thirty minutes of your time," she said, seduction in her eyes, "we'll have a secret shared."

It was certainly no secret what she was saying beneath her words.

And…*why not?*

Why not pursue a little dalliance?

After all, he as yet remained a free man, unclaimed by any woman of his acquaintance.

CHAPTER SIX

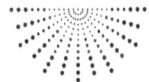

*E*very ballroom had one.

The perfect stretch of wall from where one could stand and observe, unobserved.

The Duke of Acaster's ballroom was no exception.

From here, Beatrix could memorize all the details, both large and small, that she would note in the journal she kept expressly for the purpose.

The journal.

It had been a casualty of *that* afternoon in Hyde Park—*lost.*

She'd returned to the very spot where she'd practically been trampled by Mr. Blake Deverill's horse. It hadn't been there—and left no sign of ever having been.

The panic she'd been holding carefully at bay had immediately assailed her. What if someone had found it? She would be exposed and shunned from society.

The next instant, her good sense had come to her rescue. Her name wasn't written inside, and she couldn't be identified by her handwriting. The fact was no one could point a finger in her direction as the author—or authoress, as the case was.

Besides, what had she written that was particularly scandalous? Names…dates…locations…adjectives…a few adverbs.

Well, some of those adjectives and adverbs could've been construed as somewhat…*pointed*. Further, she supposed one might wonder about all those names, dates, and locations in relation to those *pointed* adjectives and adverbs.

But, again, her name was written nowhere within its covers.

Which might've been a tell in and of itself.

If she'd mattered one jot in society.

So, panic subsided, she'd gotten on with it and purchased a new journal, spending precious coin she nearly didn't have.

Now, from her perfect nook, she noted that Lord Oxnard had danced twice with Miss Barclay, while Lady Oxnard, a known hand at Macao, was otherwise occupied in the card room.

Beatrix's immediate impulse was to find Artemis and share a snicker.

Except she couldn't.

Artemis was in Yorkshire, and she had to accept the possibility that Artemis might not return to London at all. While she didn't need or desire a wide circle of friends, it was nice having the one with whom she could share a gossipy giggle at a ball. A letter once a week wasn't the same.

Maybe she could make a new friend. Except…she wasn't sure how precisely one went about it. She'd only been lucky enough to happen upon her friendship with Artemis.

Really, though, how did one make friends?

She could venture from her protective stretch of wall, she supposed, and stand at the periphery of the dancing floor with the other spinsters and wallflowers. From there, she could strike up a conversation with one or two of those spinsters and wallflowers and—*possibly*—have a new friend.

At least, that was how the sequence of maneuvers followed in her mind.

Except...

She was likely a good five years older than the oldest spinster who yet harbored the hope of being picked, and she was a good ten years older than the wallflowers.

She would have nothing in common with any of them.

There was the further fact that she didn't dance, so it would be awkward to stand there with a silly, hopeful smile on her face, as if she were waiting for a gentleman to pick her.

Her reason for not dancing wasn't that she didn't enjoy dancing.

She did—immensely, in fact.

The freedom of being swept into the flow of music and whirled around and around and around, giddy delight buoyant in one's chest, was the closest humans came to flying.

Or, at least, that was how she remembered it from eight years ago.

She didn't dance for two reasons.

First, she had a reputation to uphold. These last eight years, she'd adopted a manner of, well, indifference to gentlemen and frivolities like dancing—and it had succeeded. No one suspected a single, solitary truth about her life. Society assumed she held herself above such things and, mostly, let her be.

Her second reason for not dancing was loosely related to the first. These last few seasons a merry-go-round of unmarried gentlemen had been making sport of her refusal. At every ball, several would seek her out, discovering her private nook, and asked her to dance. She refused each and every one. Yet they seemed either too caught up in their own interests or, plainly, too stupid to realize she understood what was happening.

With absolute certainty, she knew a betting book was involved.

It was the only explanation for the, frankly, insulting behavior.

Tonight, however, she'd only been asked once and thus had only to refuse once, able to cite her injured ankle. Really, it might be worth feigning a permanent limp, for the strict truth was her wrist and ankle were mostly healed, which was, of course, down to the physician sent by Mr. Deverill.

In the end, when her knocker had sounded, she'd done as he'd commanded and opened her front door, both appendages thoroughly throbbing by then due to her additional excursion to Shepherd's Market to procure Cumberbatch's castor oil.

Before she could even greet the man, the physician had briskly informed her there was no point in refusing his services as he'd already been compensated. From there, he'd efficiently determined nothing was broken and wrapped her limbs, all the while teaching her how to do it herself. He'd even asked if she had castor oil, as it was known to settle the inflammatory tendencies of injured muscles. She'd assured him that, as it happened, she did have castor oil on hand.

Just now, a silver tray bearing a dozen coupes of bubbly champagne floated within arm's reach, and on impulse, she lifted one. Though she didn't usually imbibe libations at society events —after all, her livelihood depended on her mind being sharp— she decided tonight could be an exception.

By the time the coupe was half empty, her ankle was barking its displeasure less stridently and she ventured from her protective stretch of wall. Who knew champagne possessed healing properties?

Quite a few monks in France, likely.

Her attention bounced around the ballroom in time to the lively quartet of stringed instruments, allowing her to take in the atmosphere without making a single observation.

Was this how enjoyment felt?

It might even be tempting the corners of her mouth into a ceilingward position.

Then her gaze snagged on a figure on the opposite end of the dancing floor—a broad set of shoulders, to be exact—and all beginnings of a smile fell decidedly in the past.

Mr. Deverill...

Here.

Of course, he was here.

Where wasn't he these days?

And what a sight he presented, dressed in evening blacks cut to perfection across his form. Her gaze lifted and didn't stop lifting until it reached...his mouth.

Oh, his mouth.

A mouth that belonged on a woman.

That the possessor was a man—*this* man—well, it held a decided allure that she didn't understand.

Of course, these qualities were the easily observable that anyone could see.

If she were to record him in her journal tonight, what could she write that society didn't already know?

The rasp running alongside the deep timbre of his voice that held a soft note of Irish lilt... His scent of fresh pine and open sea that made one want to keep inhaling him... The spark within his eyes that spoke of intelligence and drive and something else, too—*ruthlessness.*

Society only thought it had dubbed him Lord Devil for his physical appearance, but it was that which sparked within those aquamarine depths that conjured the devil.

What more could she say that society didn't yet know?

The strength of those muscles beneath superfine... The feel of his masculine, long-fingered hands... That when they held one in their grasp, one felt entirely secure.

One could like that feeling.

If one didn't put it from her mind.

She was staring at his hands.

Her gaze shifted…

And found itself staring at his mouth—*again*.

She was just about to turn her attention to the opposite end of the room when she saw a lady approach him.

Lady Standish—an attractive widow of one year who had the reputation of pursuing her passions with, *erm*, great vigor.

Of course.

Of course, Lady Standish would try her luck with Lord Devil.

That little tidbit would most definitely be going into the journal tonight.

She averted her gaze. She didn't need to watch to know how events would unfold.

Her attention landed on an interesting figure—*the Duchess of Acaster*, the widow of the sixth duke and a renowned beauty.

Only a few months ago, she'd met the woman over a dinner held by Artemis's brother, the Duke of Rakesley. At the time, it had been widely assumed Rake would ask the duchess to marry him. Instead, he'd run off with his jockey and married her.

Leaving the duchess in the metaphorical lurch.

For Beatrix harbored a suspicion about the woman.

Bluntly, that she was penniless.

Beatrix knew the signs—the remade dresses…the fact that the duchess had never once hosted a party of her own neither before nor after she'd become a widow.

Tonight, however, the duchess was both playing hostess to this ball and wearing a vibrant fuchsia silk gown in the first stare of fashion.

Beatrix's mind was quick to fit the puzzle pieces together: The dress would've been a gift from the recently elevated Seventh Duke of Acaster as a way of showing his gratitude to her for helping him throw this come-out ball for his sisters, the Ladies Saskia and Viveca, and for introducing them around society.

Unbidden, another puzzle piece slotted into place.

As tonight's hostess, the duchess would've been the one to

oversee the guest list. She would've approved the invitation to Mr. Blake Deverill.

In the interest of gaining a feel for the man through eyes other than her own—for the gossip pages, of course, not to assuage her own curiosity—Beatrix found herself closing the distance between herself and the duchess.

The duchess's brow lifted in mild surprise to find Beatrix standing at her side. As it wasn't her way, Beatrix didn't waste precious time with small talk. "What do you know of *that* man?"

Since curious ears could be listening, she didn't name the man. She did, however, jut her chin in his direction. Though a good thirty men stood in that direction, there could be but one man—*truly*.

The duchess's eyes lit with understanding, even as she gave a little shrug that men surely found entrancing. Renowned beauties tended to render men entranced. Beatrix wouldn't know this from her own experience of the opposite sex, but she'd witnessed it aplenty in her years of observing balls from the periphery.

"Nothing, really," said the duchess.

Somehow, that answer confirmed something for Beatrix. "And yet he's here."

"I believe the duke has business dealings with him." The duchess conveyed utter indifference to the matter of Blake Deverill.

But Beatrix was getting at something bigger... "Don't you find it odd that a man none of us knew existed a year ago is suddenly everywhere?"

The duchess canted her head as if considering both the man and Beatrix's words. At last, she said, "He doesn't seem the sort of man who would be denied entry into any place he wanted to be."

An insightful observation, to be sure. But, still, it didn't satisfy an as-yet undefined feeling inside Beatrix. "Which only further begs the question," she pressed. "Why is he so hellbent on being in *these* rooms?"

In truth, she was posing the question to herself.

"Ah, I've found you, at last!" came an overloud exclamation from the ever-affable Earl of Wrexford, a man with the personality of an excitable spaniel.

The *you* in question was the duchess, who smiled her beautiful smile when it was clear—to Beatrix's eyes, at least—she wanted to wince.

Beatrix took the opportunity to slip away, even though a few lines concerning a budding courtship between the Duchess of Acaster and the Earl of Wrexford could bring her a nice chunk of coin. She had other matters to pursue.

Across the room, Lady Standish turned dramatically and directed a saucy glance over her shoulder toward Mr. Deverill.

The lady's meaning was clear.

He was to follow.

Would he, though?

Beatrix had her answer in a trio of seconds.

He followed.

Beatrix's feet would've been wise to remain planted where they were.

Or better yet, return to her protective stretch of wall.

What she shouldn't do was give chase.

And very, very wrongly, she did.

Her pursuit was neither swift nor nimble, but rather dogged —as she did all things in life, it seemed.

She entered a dimly lit corridor with all manner of paired-up couples—none the couple she sought. A door leading outside stood at the end, and she pushed it open only wide enough to cock an ear for the sound of voices.

On the verge of retreat, she heard it—the low murmuration of quiet conversation between a man and a woman.

Without conscious thought, her body followed her ear, and she was silently easing along the stone wall, toward those voices.

Deverill and Lady Standish stood below the terrace, which left Beatrix lucky. She could crouch in the corner and listen.

The first words she'd caught with any sort of clarity were those from a giggly Lady Standish. "Or even here, if you like."

Beatrix's brow crinkled. What could that mean?

A raspy groan escaped Deverill. "If you keep that up, I might just have to."

Oh.

Heat crawled through Beatrix, and suddenly her dress felt too confining. Really, she could hardly draw breath.

"That's the idea." Lady Standish's voice had gone a few octaves lower.

"Meet me in Mivart's in one hour."

"That long?" No mistaking the pout in the woman's voice.

"I'm worth the wait."

He would say that.

"And your room number?" asked Lady Standish, undeterred by his arrogance—possibly further intrigued by it.

"The entire top floor is mine. Tell the concierge you're my new amanuensis."

An incredulous scoff carried on the air. "Do I look like a servant?"

A masculine chuckle followed. "He'll know what it means."

Beatrix only just didn't snort.

Even she knew what it meant.

It meant Lady Standish was one lady of many.

Not that the lady in question would care.

After all, Lord Devil was one in many.

"But it's gone midnight." The lady's protest was weak.

"I work *all* hours, my lady," rumbled from his chest. "And I *always* deliver on time."

Beatrix knew what that meant, too. The blush burned the tips of her ears.

Before she could think through her actions, her feet were moving.

Within three minutes, she was out of Acaster's mansion and crossing St. James's Square.

One hour.

She had one hour—well, fifty-seven minutes—to see for herself how the devil lived.

CHAPTER SEVEN

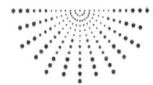

*L*ike a king.

That was how Lord Devil lived.

The instant the footman had opened the door to Mr. Deverill's suite, it was the aroma that hit Beatrix first.

Fresh pine...crisp sea...clean.

The man wasn't even here, yet here he was, conjured.

How did he smell so good?

Money.

That was how.

Deverill smelled like money. Not of the ill-gotten variety, but the sort gained by skill, intelligence, and determination. Whatever else the man might've been, one couldn't deny those qualities about him.

After it became apparent to the footman that Beatrix would not be slipping him a bit of coin, he shut the door with a mild sniff, leaving her alone in Lord Devil's lair.

She snorted.

Lord Devil's lair.

A bit dramatic, that.

But her first observation held. All rich, warm woods and

refined hues of cream and rose invited one to sit and relax. This suite of rooms with its delicious scent, stylish Rococo Chippendale furniture, original oil paintings—was that a Gainsborough? —eight-foot windows, and high coffered ceilings was fit for a king or a very wealthy duke.

She cast a longing eye over an overstuffed chaise longue situated beside a high window. That would be a perfect reading spot during the day. Filling out the drawing room were a sofa, two armchairs, a few console tables strewn about, and a painted silk screen done in the Chinoiserie style so popular this last century.

An object on the low table before the sofa caught her eye.

A small, flat box.

Unable to resist, curiosity had her crossing the room and picking it up. The box was light, which meant whatever was inside was likely very expensive.

Carefully, she slid the top off and gasped at the contents within.

Chocolates.

Three rows of three, each little sweet different from the one seated beside it—this one with a delicate leaf of gold on top, that one with a tiny purple violet, yet another with a single perfect coffee bean.

Beatrix's mouth watered, and temptation beckoned. It would only be the one. Deverill wouldn't miss it…

But he would notice.

For none had yet been eaten.

A shame, that.

With a sigh of resignation, she replaced the cover and returned the chocolates to the exact spot of table where she'd found them—before her mind could twist the logic around and she convinced herself it would be all right to take a single, wee chocolate.

She crossed to the dining area—she needed some necessary distance between herself and the chocolates—where she found a gleaming mahogany table that seated six. In the center sat a silver bowl filled with apples and pears, which would've been procured from a greenhouse, for the fruit was yet a few months out of season.

On impulse, she grabbed an apple and took a bite before she could think better of it.

She moaned.

Crisp and sweet with a delightful edge of tartness, not a hint of mealiness, it was the most delicious apple she'd ever tasted.

She took another bite, this one better than the first.

A word came to her.

Forbidden.

So, this was how Eve felt.

Perhaps it was the forbidden quality of the apple that enhanced its deliciousness.

Crunching into her third bite, she entered his bedroom. She wasn't certain what she'd been expecting, but it wasn't *this*. If pressed, she would've envisioned something resembling a bordello—all crimson velvets and gilded mirrors—even one on the ceiling. Not that she'd ever witnessed such a thing firsthand. But she didn't lack for imagination.

Yet strangely, this room that saw Deverill at his most vulnerable felt utterly devoid of him.

Except for his scent.

That lingered, as ever.

She savored another bite of apple and wandered into the bathing room. Stark white marble and obsidian black. She didn't stop, her feet carrying her into the dressing room. All clothing neatly hung or folded away. Nothing appeared to be out of place.

Deverill kept his life tidy.

Which rang true to her.

In the bathing room, her forefinger dragged along the lip of the tub and caught a large drop of water. This water would've come from his bath. Water that had touched his naked body. It felt like an unexpected sort of intimacy to be rubbing it between her fingers.

Her eyebrows crinkled, and she exhaled a sharp breath.

Her presence here was wrong.

And her reaction to being here... Frankly, it was getting a little strange.

She shouldn't be eating his fruits and ambling through his rooms and touching the little that remained of his bath water.

Her curiosity, insatiable as it might be, didn't give her the right.

She beheld the apple core in her right hand.

Blimey.

She'd eaten almost the entire, delicious thing.

Which she should regret.

But couldn't quite.

She needed to leave—and was intent on doing precisely that when it caught her attention.

Over by the window, a draftsman's table, large sheets of detailed mechanical drawings littering its surface. All done by Deverill's hand, she knew instinctively. What she was beholding was his work. The very work that had made him an obscenely wealthy man. Though she knew nothing of invention or the mechanical arts, she did know talent when she saw it.

Again, the question that had driven her here tonight returned.

Why would such a man give a toss about being accepted into the *haut ton*?

He seemed too intelligent for society nonsense.

She needed to let this go. She understood that. Deverill's business was none of hers.

And in this very moment, technically, she was committing a crime.

She needed to leave—*now.*

She'd only returned to the drawing room and was making a straight line for the door when the handle jiggled.

Within the space between one second and the next, her mind performed a quick calculation.

That door was on the brink of swinging open and admitting Deverill into his lair.

Blimey.

It wasn't conscious thought that had her feet scrambling across the room, making for the silk screen in a near dive, but instinct. She curled into a tight crouch and attempted to control her breath and calm her racing heart. As for her perspiring palms, there was no help for them.

It hadn't even been half an hour. But she reckoned it was the man's prerogative to come and go as he pleased in his own hotel suite.

The door clicked shut, and a metallic *clank* sailed through the air. That would've been the room key discarded into a bowl.

Heavy footsteps—*male* footsteps—strode deeper into the room.

Breath held to the point of bursting her lungs, Beatrix shifted so she could peer through the long crack between screen panels.

Deverill.

As he hadn't immediately begun searching the rooms for her, she could only thank her lucky stars that the concierge hadn't informed him of the lady awaiting him in his suite.

The solid length and width of his back was to her as liquid hit crystal. He was pouring himself a whiskey.

She could use one of those herself.

To celebrate her escape from this room.

If that ever occurred.

He set the crystal tumbler on the dining table, and she harbored the hope that he would go to his bedroom. Instead, he removed his gloves, revealing an ostentatious ruby ring on his left pinky. She hadn't ever seen him without gloves, so she wouldn't have known about this ring. It wouldn't be inscribed with a signet, because he wasn't a lord. The rich quality of gold and size of the ruby, however, proclaimed his right to be anywhere he pleased. Then he shrugged off his evening coat and draped it over the back of a chair.

If only he would leave the room…

He reached up and tugged at his cravat, loosening, then discarding it. His shirt fell open into a narrow V, revealing a dark smattering of chest hair.

She tried to swallow, but her mouth had gone too dry.

He took one shirtsleeve and began rolling, fold by fold, revealing a forearm sinewy with muscle and a dark dusting of hair.

A bead of sweat rolled down the side of her face. She'd gone hot—*too hot*. Such heat couldn't be beneficial to one's health.

When he began rolling up the other sleeve, she considered the possibility she might combust on the spot.

A light *tap-tap-tap* sounded at the door.

He opened the door with a playful flourish, and Lady Standish dramatically swept inside.

Certain dread crawled through Beatrix. Now that Lady Standish was here, Deverill was sure to be removing more than gloves, coat, and cravat.

Blimey.

She needed to be gone.

Actually, what she needed was not to have been here in the first place.

Good sense arrived at too late.

"Welcome to my humble abode," he said to Lady Standish without an ounce of humility.

The lady took in the room around her, the critical glint of assessment in her eye clear. "I suppose it's serviceable enough."

Beatrix nearly snorted.

Here she'd been thinking Lord Devil lived like a king.

"I wasn't sure the concierge would let me in," she continued on a huff.

"Oh?"

"He gave me a bit of blather about Mr. Deverill having a busy work night. The man *winked* at me. The cheek!" she exclaimed. "I have half a mind to take it up with his superior."

Beatrix almost felt badly, considering she was, presumably, the additional party contributing to the *busy* work night.

"Well, now that you're here..." No mistaking the wickedness inflecting Deverill's voice. "Are you ready to fulfill your amanuensis duties?"

Beatrix could groan—but didn't.

Lady Standish closed the few feet between them. "*I* give the orders."

The lady's back was to Beatrix, which left her with an unimpeded view of the amused, indulgent curl of Deverill's mouth that spoke of familiarity with the game Lady Standish was playing. She touched light fingertips to Deverill's chest and began trailing down until they reached the buttons of his waistcoat.

Beatrix couldn't breathe.

Lady Standish began undressing Deverill—and Beatrix couldn't not watch, her face pressed so close to the crack between the screen panels her eyelashes brushed it with every blink. Waistcoat discarded, the lady tugged his shirt free of his trousers with a giggle. Then the garment was up and over his head and joining the waistcoat on the floor.

At the sight of his bare chest and the stacked rows of muscles on his stomach, Lady Standish gasped.

Behind the hand that had flown to her mouth, so did Beatrix.

One would need a good five minutes to count all the muscles rippling across stomach, chest, and arms, so defined and...*male*.

She'd never beheld anything so male in all her life.

What would it feel like to touch such a powerfully built man?

Unbidden, the memory of the water from his bath returned.

That drop of water knew.

Lady Standish's hands kept moving...*down*.

Feathering along the waistband of his trousers...and further *down...*

Grazing across the *very* obvious bulge beneath superfine.

"Oh my," she giggled, "is that a devil in your trousers demanding to greet me?"

"It does have demands," he said on a deep rumble.

"I believe investigation will be necessary." One could hear the shiver in her voice as her hand tightened on the bulge—which somehow had grown *bigger*.

Deverill sucked in a breath.

Another gasp flew from Beatrix—but her hand smothered it too late.

Deverill went stone still, and his gaze shifted.

Toward the screen.

Beatrix froze.

Likely, he was staring at the lovely painted landscape on the silk screen. Serene lake scenes might be a favorite of his.

She didn't know him—not truly, anyway.

His gaze narrowed...

On hers.

Or had it?

She couldn't be sure, but just in case it had, she didn't move, breathe, and or even blink.

For her part, Lady Standish didn't seem to have noticed anything different about Deverill beyond his use for the night. He grabbed her hand and brought it to his mouth, applying a kiss to the back, like a gentleman—as if that very hand hadn't just been caressing the rather substantial bulge in his trousers.

"I've just remembered I have an early meeting tomorrow morning," he said, apology in every word.

"Early meeting?" asked Lady Standish, as if the concept were entirely foreign to her.

In all fairness, it likely was.

"And I must prepare beforehand."

"*Prepare beforehand?*" scoffed the lady. Another foreign concept aired.

He lifted his hands in the universal gesture of helplessness. "The vulgar ways of business, I'm afraid."

"You would..." The lady huffed. "You would rather..." The lady puffed. "Than..." In her fit of pique, complete sentences eluded her. "With *me?*"

He gave another lift of helpless hands, which proved too much for Lady Standish, who whirled in a great flurry of skirts and angrily jerked the door open, only to slam it shut behind her.

The room went silent.

Until this moment, Beatrix hadn't known silence could, in fact, be *this* silent.

Deverill lifted his tumbler of whiskey off the dining table and took a long pull.

She squeezed her eyes shut and waited.

Muted footsteps crossed the room.

She squeezed harder, and still, she waited.

Any second now rough hands would wrap around her arms and haul her to her feet, then toss her from this room like so much rubbish.

Except... What her ears caught was undefined movement on the opposite side of the room.

One eye carefully slitted open—then blinked in disbelief.

There, directly across from her, he sat with his legs sprawled, one arm stretched along the curved spine of the sofa, tumbler in hand.

Somehow, his utter maleness was... *enhanced.*

His gaze shifted...

And met hers through the crack in the screen.

She gasped—*again.*

Idly, he said, "You can come out now."

Somehow, around the solid lump in her throat, out came the truth. "I'd rather not."

CHAPTER EIGHT

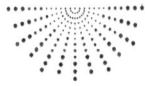

*T*hat voice.

Recognition hung just beyond the edge of Dev's memory.

"You'll have to come out eventually." He was only pointing out the obvious.

The obvious was met with silence.

And stillness.

The woman wasn't coming out.

They were at an impasse.

He supposed it was within his rights to stride across the room, tear the screen away, and forcibly remove the woman, but in truth, this was the most interesting thing to have happened to him in weeks. It was even almost fun.

Still, she left him with no choice but to say, "You have exactly ten seconds before I send for the law."

"No!" came a shout as the woman sprang to her feet and scrambled out from behind the screen, nearly tipping it over in the process.

And here was hazy memory come to solid life.

Lady Beatrix St. Vincent, as he lived and breathed.

Here, in his hotel suite.

Life could deliver some unexpected twists and turns, and that was a fact.

Cheeks flushed, eyes bright, her breath coming in sharp, shallow sips, she stared out at him. From the little he understood of her, he knew this much. She wasn't the sort of woman who was lost for words.

Yet here she stood before him, exactly that.

He settled deeper into sofa cushions and crossed an ankle over the opposite thigh. A flash of irritation passed behind her eyes, and her jaw clenched and released.

His air of indolence annoyed her.

Good.

He wanted to poke at her…

Prod her…

Push her…

And test where her limits lay.

"You think I won't have you arrested because you're a lady?" He had to ask.

She didn't flinch. "I don't know what you're capable of, Mr. Deverill." She'd found her voice, but behind all that bravado, he detected a telltale wobble. "You did try to run me down with your horse."

Her spark had certainly returned. "Are your ankle and wrist recovered?"

He hoped so. He didn't like the echo of guilt he felt when he recalled her injuries.

"Quite."

As if she would have said anything else.

He returned to the main subject. "I believe the law would find the case against you compelling, to say the least."

Her eyes flashed gray steel.

"You're guilty of both trespassing in my rooms and of spoiling what was promising to be a very pleasurable interlude with Lady

Standish."

She crossed her arms over her chest. A defensive stance. "I got carried away was all."

"*Carried away?*"

The woman had nerve. He would give her that.

"It happens."

In that instant, Dev saw something. Something a man like him was especially attuned to.

Opportunity.

And he understood something else.

Now wasn't the time to push it. Going at this skirmish head-on with an adversary like Lady Beatrix wouldn't get him anywhere—especially when it wasn't yet clear where *where* was.

A pivot was necessary—for the moment.

"How did you know this was my suite?"

A natural enough question, given the circumstances.

She shifted from one foot to the other, indicating a distinct and new discomfort. "Isn't it known you have rooms here?"

"Likely." He would give her that. "But how did you get *inside* my rooms?"

Her lips remained firmly pressed together.

"This suite occupies the top floor," he continued. "And the door wasn't forced. Unless you possess untold talents of the magical variety, you didn't scale the walls or fly."

A slow, silent second ticked past, then another, as his words hung in the air like a lead weight. Just when he thought she wouldn't respond, she heaved a resigned sigh. "I overheard you."

"*Overheard* me?"

She gave a brusque nod.

"You'll have to do better than that."

"With Lady Standish." The admission sounded as if it had been extracted with a pair of pliers.

He was beginning to understand… "At Acaster's ball?"

Another curt nod.

Of course… "So, you knew to tell the concierge you're my amanuensis."

Mutiny shone in Lady Beatrix's eyes, as if to say she'd given him all she would.

"That would explain the concierge's *impertinence*. The man must've thought we were having an impressively wild night."

She averted her eyes. Was that the hint of a blush staining her cheeks?

"So, you're not only a trespasser, but an eavesdropper, too."

A strangled sound that might've been a protest escaped her, but that was all the defense she could muster.

He'd only spoken the truth.

And speaking of the truth… "Which reminds me."

He uncrossed his ankle and shifted forward to slide a drawer open from the low table before him. "I have something of yours."

The object he'd retrieved gave a satisfying little slap on the tabletop, punctuating the moment.

Her journal.

A strangled cry tore from her throat, and she took a reactive step forward before she remembered herself and the situation she'd become embroiled within.

"This is *yours*, no?"

Here he was, pushing her again. Yet she made no move to take it. He could only imagine the amount of self-control that took.

He lifted the journal and began paging through. "The prose is a bit sparse, but even so, it makes for interesting reading, given all the names belonging to members of the *haut ton*."

Perhaps he was pushing it too far, for she'd somehow gone both pale and flushed. He wondered if she might even rather be arrested on the spot than endure this treatment.

"Some of the notes…" he continued thumbing through. "Well, less than flattering some of them. Shall I read a few favorites aloud?"

She heaved a deep, resigned sigh. She knew there was no

stopping him, so better to get it over with. He could admire the pragmatism.

He cleared his throat. *"Lord Wrexford—human spaniel, only lacking wagging tail; competing with A for attentions of D of A?"* Dev glanced up. "I suppose you won't be decoding names for me?"

Lady Beatrix threw darts at him with her eyes.

Oh, this was fun.

"Lady Neale—rumor true; hair experiment gone wrong; green strands poking out from beneath wig." Dev closed the book and let it rest on his lap. "I reckon the lady wouldn't care to have *that* bandied about."

Lady Beatrix lifted her chin. "I suppose there's a point to all this?" she asked in the cool, clipped, aristocratic voice she'd been gifted at birth.

The tone that deigned to address the lower organism before her.

Of a sudden, Dev was having less fun. Another memory slid into place... Her addressing him thusly on her doorstep, scoffing at the very idea of inviting him in for tea.

"The point of all this?" he returned, his voice gone cold.

"Really," she continued, "what's in that journal is none of your concern."

She was attempting to turn it around and put him on the back foot. Well... "Try again."

Her hands clasped before her, her knuckles gone white with tension. She understood she wasn't leaving this room without a confession. "I write."

"Clearly."

"For a few turf rags."

"Hair experiments gone wrong don't fall within the purview of turf rags. *Try again.*"

She attempted an indifferent shrug. "I pepper in a few society morsels from time to time."

Here, Dev's sharp eye proved useful, for he saw straight

through her words to what she was really saying. "The daughter of a marquess is a grubby, gossipmongering newshound."

She opened her mouth—then snapped it shut. She managed on a croak, "It's a lark."

Which was a lie.

This woman didn't *lark* about.

He shifted forward and extended the journal across the table. It took her only the split of a second to realize he was returning it to her before she snatched it away and held it behind her in tightly clasped hands. Her stance in combination with her white muslin gown conjured a vision of innocence.

Which she wasn't.

Actually, he had no doubt she was an innocent in the carnal sense, but she'd intruded into his rooms, which placed her in an undefinable in-between space.

Before him in her innocent pose stood a different sort of lady, and…

He was intrigued.

He reached for the box on the table and slid off the lid. *Chocolates.* In truth, he hadn't much of a taste for sweets, but the hotel liked to provide him with small offerings every so often, which he took home to Primrose Hill every week. Mama liked the caramels best.

"Is that all, then?" asked Lady Beatrix.

He glanced up, ready to inform her it would be *all* when he said it was *all*, but he caught something in her eyes and the words arrested in his mouth. If he wasn't very mistaken, that was the specific gleam of…*hunger.*

On impulse, he took a chocolate between forefinger and thumb. "Forgive my sweet tooth." He bit down on a chocolate and even groaned for effect. "Do you care for chocolate?"

"A bit."

Dev extended the box. "Have one."

Temptation beckoned.

She angled slightly forward, poised on the verge of accepting...

Then she blinked, and her shoulders squared. "It's not proper for me to be in your rooms."

He snorted. The woman had some audacity. "For a variety of reasons, in fact. The first being that you weren't invited."

Again, he scented opportunity in the air.

Now.

This was the moment to push it.

"What would you do *not* to be arrested?" he asked, mildly, as if he were inquiring about the weather.

A response took her only a moment. "Just about anything."

"Just about?"

"Within reason."

"Well, that's not *anything*, is it?"

She swallowed against a surely dry throat. "Anything."

And here it was—opportunity splayed open before him.

His for the plucking.

He wasn't finished with Lady Beatrix St. Vincent.

Really, he'd only gotten started.

"What should I ask for?"

If she'd been a cat, the hair along her spine would've bristled to a stand. "A gentleman would let me leave with a mild admonishment."

"Would he, now?" Dev nodded, slowly, consideringly. "'Tis a truth universally acknowledged that gentlemen have no imaginations." He shrugged. "And I'm no gentleman. Nice effort on your part, though. You do have spirit—for a lady."

He could see her mind racing behind her eyes. Any moment now, she was going to flee this room and never look back.

And he wasn't finished with her yet.

"Here's what will happen." His became the voice of reason. "You will leave now, and I will call on you tomorrow once I've decided what to do with you."

Arresting gray eyes narrowed with wariness. "Where?"

"At your humble abode, of course."

"At my…*house?*"

Her mortification at the idea of having him in her home was more than clear—which only made him more determined. "At your townhouse on Little Stanhope Street."

Lady Beatrix wasn't about to give up that easily. "Why not a coffee house? Or the park?"

"*Your house,*" he repeated. "I'll be there at ten o'clock."

"In the morning?" she squeaked. "I thought you had a meeting tomorrow morning."

He suppressed a laugh. "My meeting will be finished by then," he said. "Ten o'clock *sharp*. I'm always on time. Now," he continued, "you may go."

She didn't need to be told twice as she all but flew from the room, the door a loud, decisive slam behind her.

Dev finished off the remainder of his whiskey before making his way to his draftsman's table. He hadn't been lying tonight. He did have an early meeting, which, of course, in typical circumstances wouldn't have precluded what he and Lady Standish had been about to get up to—before Lady Beatrix St. Vincent had put a stop to it.

As he thumbed through the plans he would put to Shaw in the morning, a feeling strummed through him. An excitability when on the verge of an advancement. While Shaw wasn't involved in the invention process, he was a keenly intelligent man who would ask the right questions and test the soundness of the idea. Further, with Shaw's experience of manufacturing, he would be able to create a timetable for when the product could be feasibly produced.

As with all technology, it was a race, for his competitors were having the same or similar ideas. So, it was all down to not only whose ideas were best, but whose ideas could be implemented and brought to market fastest—and, really, it was the latter that mattered most.

It wasn't until Dev was lying in bed an hour later that his thoughts returned to Lady Beatrix—and the rather interesting question mark she presented in his life.

Why had she trespassed in his rooms?

What was he going to do with her?

What opportunity did she present?

She was a lady—the daughter of a marquess, in fact. No doors in society were closed to her.

So, how could he benefit from that?

Really, it came down to his end goal.

Imogen.

And could Lady Beatrix be useful in, at last, having her?

CHAPTER NINE

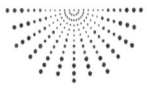

NEXT DAY

*H*er booted heels a swift *click-clack* down the corridor, Beatrix caught a quick glimpse of the pendulum clock on her way to the kitchen.

Nine fifty-five.

Five minutes until Lord Devil arrived.

Lord Devil...

Indeed.

Lord Devil, *here*, in her house.

After a sleepless night of tossing and turning and mostly staring at the crack in the ceiling that bisected the entire width of her bedroom, she'd risen with the dawn and looked at the house with fresh eyes. Truly, the place had fallen into a state of ruin.

She'd immediately set to work and hadn't stopped since. Floors swept... Surfaces dusted and tidied... That sort of thing.

The plan her mind had worked out was a simple one. When Deverill arrived, she would usher him from the front door to the nearest drawing room. Strictly speaking, that was the widest swath of the house he needed to experience.

He shouldn't step through any floorboards, if he kept to that path.

Beatrix kept to paths, too.

Except she didn't always keep to paths, did she?

Last night, she'd strayed off the path in rather spectacular fashion.

And today, she was to pay for it.

Blimey.

Still, one thing had gone right for her today.

Lydon never made it home last night.

Which was no great surprise. He might spend three of thirty nights in the house.

She offered up a silent, but fervent prayer that he would not shamble in during her tea with Deverill. It would be too much.

Too much.

Ironically, two words that were coming to define her life—a life characterized by its inability to have enough.

It would've been funny—if only it were.

She entered the kitchen and noted Cumberbatch's napping presence in a corner. Too late, she'd realized she should've scoured London for a maid willing to work for a morning.

As it presently stood—and would proceed, unless a sudden catastrophic event struck London—Cumberbatch would serve tea.

Palms damp with perspiration, she reached for the kettle that had just reached the boil and poured water into the only unchipped teapot in the house. That it didn't match the only pair of unchipped teacups—which didn't even match each other—was something she would simply have to live with.

Perhaps Deverill wouldn't notice.

She snorted.

The man lived like a king.

He would notice.

A loud harrumph came from Cumberbatch's corner.

Her snort must've startled him awake.

She estimated she had fewer than two minutes before the clock struck ten.

"Be sure to serve at a quarter past the hour." The instruction served as a settling of her own nerves rather than a reminder for Cumberbatch. There was nothing wrong with his memory.

"Aye, aye." He waved her off in the long-suffering manner he'd adopted these last few years. "A valet serving tea. What's this grand old world coming to, eh?"

Beatrix let the familiar lament wash over her as she gave the tray another once-over. The tea was brewing up to an almost dark brown—if she squinted hard enough. There was cream, even if it was watered down. No sugar. Bad for the teeth, anyway. Perched atop a pair of small unmatched plates were the prizes of the morning—two precious scones. She'd set out first thing and procured them expressly for this tea. She couldn't resist a deep inhalation. It had been several months since anything that smelled so delicious had inhabited the four walls of this kitchen.

Sadly, the tray lacked butter, but nestled within a small bowl was a wee dollop of strawberry jam she'd paid an extra tuppence for. London prices were extraordinary these days.

Still, she was strangely proud of this hard-won tea tray. She would be able to serve Deverill a proper, if paltry, tea.

Right.

Dong, came the low thrum of the pendulum clock. The first chime of ten. Improbably, the clock yet remained in the house. Items of value tended to vanish during the night in the House of Lydon.

Ten o'clock.

Her heart a racehorse in her chest, she gave Cumberbatch a parting nod and, somehow, willed her feet to move toward the front of the house, every other step marking the next chime. The tenth chime sounded, and she stopped, the silence deafening as she anticipated the rap of the door knocker her bones knew was coming. One second loped past…then another…

But not a third.

Breaking the stillness so suddenly as to give her a start, three solid raps of the knocker echoed through her and down the corridor. She swallowed against a dry throat and waited three more seconds. The slowest three seconds of her life, though her racing heart didn't know it.

It wouldn't do to appear eager.

At last, with fingers that wobbled, she slid the bolt. Her hand curled around the door handle, she hesitated. Once she opened this door, there would be no turning back.

Except she'd passed that point the instant she opened the door to Deverill's hotel suite last night.

She'd entered his rooms—and his life.

She saw that now—too late.

Now, she would face the consequences.

She pulled the door open and beheld the man on her doorstep who stood with a decided male power to his stance and a small parcel in his hand.

A confounding thought came to her. She'd encountered this man in any number of ways—sopping wet...clad in impeccable evening attire...undone in a state of near undress. But never like *this*—in the full glory of a sunlit morning looking every inch a gentleman with his clothes of the finest quality and latest style, tailored to perfection on a form that, despite all his finery, held an undiminished masculinity.

Lord Devil wouldn't be ignored. He was too imposing and too handsome and the glint in his eyes said he knew it.

He removed his hat and offered her a shallow bow. It couldn't come across as anything other than ironic.

"Mr. Deverill."

An awkward beat of time ticked past as they stood silent, facing one another not unlike adversaries, before she had the presence of mind to move aside and allow him entry.

"I didn't know ladies opened their own doors," he said as he stepped past her.

She followed her plan and led him along the prescribed path into the drawing room, understanding his sharp blue eyes were taking in every inch—the threadbare carpets...the quarter inch of dust coating the chandeliers she'd been unable to reach... She could hardly stand it—simultaneously wanting to jump out of her skin with nerves and melt into the floor with humiliation.

Her feet led her straight to the settee where she took a seat, expecting Deverill to lower onto the settee opposite.

Except he wasn't the sort of person to follow the expectations of others.

He remained standing.

And not only standing, but on the move, ambling from one corner of the room to the other—from the cracked marble hearth...to the bare patch of wall with a faint rectangle imprinted where a painting of some value had once hung...to the glass case of miniature animal figurines that were of no value at all or they would've long found their way to Lydon's favorite pawnbroker.

All this—and more—Deverill observed.

Hands clasped tightly on her lap, Beatrix wasn't sure she could bear another second of it.

"Your lot doesn't believe in buying anything new, do you?"

Your lot...

Aristocrats.

Was that what he thought?

Well, who was she to disabuse him of the notion... "We take pride in our heritage."

What a load of rot.

Still, he might buy it for a penny.

The aquamarine depths of his eyes flickered with amusement. "Is that what you call it? *Heritage?*"

A thin ribbon of relief fluttered through her. It appeared the

91

universe would leave her with a shred of pride—even if it was purchased with a lie.

At last, he lowered his imposing form onto the opposite settee. She wasn't sure she imagined a cloud of dust puffing up around him as he settled back, the ancient piece of furniture creaking ominously. He set the small parcel beside him atop frayed damask.

Which left them no option but to stare at each other across a low table whose walnut inlay curled up at the edges. Direct and unflinching, Deverill's eyes were an otherworldly hue. But that wasn't what was interesting about them.

His eyes weren't cold. When he smiled, as he did now, they smiled along with his mouth.

Genuine.

Whatever else his immortal soul might be, it held not a bit of falsity.

She wasn't sure if that was good or bad.

"Now," he said. "You can start by telling me precisely why you were trespassing in my rooms last night."

So much for small talk.

Instinctively, she squared her shoulders and was opening her mouth to reply when his head cocked to the side, as if he'd caught an irregular sound.

Then she heard it, too.

Just beyond the door…faint…

Shuffle…clank…shuffle…clank…

Beatrix's stomach plummeted to her feet.

Blimey.

That would be Cumberbatch making his—*interminable*—way down the corridor, carrying the tea tray.

Deverill's brow creased, but he didn't express a word out loud —*blessedly.*

After what felt like thirty years, but could've been no more than thirty seconds, Cumberbatch appeared in the doorway, tray held precariously before him, his mien dour and noble in the manner of a servant proud of his house. He and Beatrix might know the lie, but the outside world wouldn't. At this moment, she felt immeasurable gratitude for the old grumbler.

Porcelain clanking ominously, he tottered into the room.

Deverill was regarding the proceedings as he regarded every-thing—*directly...unflinchingly...*

Unsparingly.

Beatrix cast her gaze toward her hands clutched in her lap. It was the safest option.

With every *clink* and *clank*, she winced.

Deverill would've noticed that, too.

Who knew disaster could unfold so...*very...excruciatingly... slowly...*

Deverill shifted forward and muttered, low so his voice wouldn't carry, "Does he need assistance?"

The icy glare Cumberbatch shot Deverill froze the response in Beatrix's mouth. "Of course, I don't need assistance," he intoned. "'Tis you who will need assistance, young man, if you dare to assist me."

Deverill gave a nod that communicated both apology and suitable humility. Cumberbatch, however, was in no mood to accept either. "Do you know what they called my right fist when I was coming up in the rookeries?"

Beatrix knew the answer, but decided it best to let Cumber-batch inform Deverill himself.

"*Destroyer of Worlds*," said the valet with a firmness that communicated his right fist could still wreak proper destruction, if called upon. "Now, I left that life behind when the Marquess of Lydon fancied having a boxer for a valet, but Destroyer of Worlds could be prevailed upon to come out of retirement."

By now—*bless the heavens*—Cumberbatch had reached the table. So very slowly...so very deliberately...he bent forward with the tray held at a stiff right angle. It was all Beatrix could do not to wrest the tray from his hands and set it down herself. But if she took such action, Cumberbatch would be in a sulk for the rest of the week.

So, she sat, with her jaw clenched and her hands clasped tight, and kept half an eye on Deverill, his eyebrows reaching new heights of alarm as teapot, teacups, scones, and scrumptious strawberry jam threatened to slide off the tray and tumble onto the table in a messy heap.

Messy heap.

Well, there was a phrase that summed up her life these days, now wasn't it?

However, by some mercy of the universe, no such happening occurred. At the very last moment, Cumberbatch released the tray and, miraculously, it landed flat. To be sure, there was a great clatter of porcelain that set Beatrix's ears ringing and tea had spilled into the strawberry jam, but all wasn't lost, which she would count as a win.

Wins were so very few and far between.

She mustered every last ounce of dignity yet in her possession and said, "Thank you, Cumberbatch."

Already turning, he grunted and began very, very slowly shuffling out of the room.

Once she decided the valet was safely out of earshot, she said, "Cumberbatch's hearing is excellent."

"Oh, I think we've established that."

She found herself biting back a smile as she reached for the teapot and commenced with the ritual of serving tea—pouring them each a cup, then placing a scone to either side of the table, the strawberry jam accessible between. Deverill took his teacup and saucer and settled back, watching her as he sipped tea that wasn't much stronger than water.

Beatrix reached for the scone that she, at last, had permission to eat. Deliberately, she tore off a crisped edge with the intention of consuming the crumbly pastry with the elegant indifference of a lady. But one bite led to another delicious bite and, of a sudden, the scone was gone—save the final bite, which had become lodged in her throat. She reached for her teacup and swallowed a rather large, very decidedly unladylike gulp.

When she glanced up, it was to find Deverill watching her with a subtle cant of the head. In an instant, a flood of realizations crashed through her. She'd eaten her scone neither elegantly nor like a lady. In fact, the possibility—nay, *probability*—existed that she'd devoured it in fewer than five bites. Further, in her haste, she'd disappointingly forgotten the strawberry jam.

And Deverill had quietly watched.

As if she were an animal at the zoo.

Well, she might not have behaved all that dissimilarly from one.

The heat of mortification thrummed through her.

He shifted forward and, with the hand not holding teacup and saucer, pushed his scone across the table—toward her.

She should've experienced a doubling of humiliation.

And she almost did.

Almost.

But the scone yet held a hint of warmth from the oven and it would be a sin to allow the strawberry jam to go untasted...

She lifted the pastry from the plate and willed her fingers to go slow—first, splitting open the scone...then spreading a thick swathe of jam across the crumbly surface, making sure to save some for Cumberbatch. Strawberries were a particular favorite of his.

So it was that Beatrix ate Deverill's scone, too.

And perhaps with a little more ladylike finesse than she'd consumed the first.

Afterward, she couldn't say.

It had been a fever dream of deliciousness.

She reached for her tea and took a delicate sip.

All the while, Deverill hadn't moved a muscle. "All finished?"

"I like scones."

"Now, will you answer the question?" he asked. "Why were you in my hotel suite last night?"

As she'd been about to do earlier, she offered him the truth. "I wanted to see how you lived." She couldn't not add, "For my grubby gossipmongering, of course."

A dry exhalation sounded through his nose as he settled back into his creaky settee and took a sip of tea, never once taking his eyes off her.

The man was contemplating her.

And she wasn't certain how she felt being the object of his contemplation.

Whatever he was seeing, it was too much.

Something she hadn't volunteered.

And she didn't like that.

But she saw something, as well.

It was too late for him not to see it.

It had been so from the moment she'd invaded his private rooms and set all this in motion.

Consequences.

There were consequences when one crossed such a man.

And a devil to pay.

CHAPTER TEN

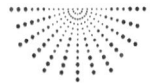

*D*ev crossed an ankle over a thigh and let the facts of the woman before him assemble themselves.

He'd walked into her townhouse today armed with firm certainties.

Lady Beatrix St. Vincent was the pampered daughter of a marquess, accustomed to getting her way. A lady who lived in the same luxury as other peers of the realm. A lady of the old guard, who was too good for new things. A lady who didn't invite the riffraff in for tea.

But he saw now he hadn't been armed with facts at all.

He'd been carrying assumptions.

Now, they were crumbling beneath the weight of the realities.

Her out-of-date gown at the ball... The day dress she wore now, in fact... The flaking paint on the front door... The worn-down, cracked, creaky, threadbare, moldering *everything* of the interior... The way she'd eyed his chocolate last night and ate not one, but two scones just now—like a wolf.

These were the facts regarding Lady Beatrix St. Vincent.

When she hadn't invited him in the other day, it wasn't snobbery.

It was…

Shame.

And that shame, once it joined with the facts, left one with but a single, unexpected conclusion.

He shoved forward, set his teacup down, planted his forearms on his knees, and clasped his hands before him. Instinctively, she shifted backward, as if he were invading her space.

Good.

As he had last night, he scented opportunity.

"You're…*poor.*"

The statement left no room for equivocation.

She visibly bristled, the gray of her eyes gone to steel. "I'm the daughter of a marquess."

He didn't relent. "Poor as Job, in fact."

"I'm a lady."

He nodded. "And you're living in near penury." He wasn't letting her off the hook, but he needed a different angle. "I've looked into your writing *lark.*"

She tried for an indifferent shrug. "An occasional pastime."

Dev narrowed in… "Five or so published articles a week is more than occasional."

She allowed the clench and release of her jaw to provide her answer.

"This writing *lark* of yours puts food on your table."

Her eyes shone with mutiny.

"And the society gossip you pepper into your articles—"

"Horse racing and society go hand in hand," she cut in.

"That gossip puts a little more food on your table."

Her gaze cut toward the window, as if she could see through the grime.

Dev went on, undeterred. "I came here to ask you—"

Her gaze flashed to meet his. "You mean to *bully* me."

What she might've lacked in material wealth, she made up for with an abundance of courage.

"I came here," Dev continued, equably, "to *convince* you to write nice things about me here and there."

"Because of last night?"

"If you choose to see it that way."

"I don't see how a few write-ups in the turf rags will lift the esteem of society."

The lady was quick, he would give her that. "You're not wrong."

Her head tilted in question. "What is this all about, Mr. Deverill? Why would you want to unearth anything about me? I'm nothing to you."

"Oh, you're someone, Lady Beatrix," he said, dry. "You're the someone who broke into my hotel suite last night." He realized he was turning his pinky ring and stopped. "Besides, I make it a point to know everything there is to know about anyone that I'm going into business with."

A little, disbelieving laugh escaped her. "You and I aren't going into business together, Mr. Deverill."

Oh, she wasn't going to like the next part of this conversation. But opportunities and angles were coming to him, and there was one in particular that held the glimmer of promise... "Now that I've properly met you in your home and seen your circumstances firsthand, I think we might have a use for each other."

"Now that you know I'm penniless," she said, blunt—antagonistic, even.

Dev lifted empty hands, helpless to the facts. "You've seen how I live, and now I've seen how you live."

He let the tit-for-tat settle into the air—and waited. In any negotiation, this moment inevitably arrived—the impasse. Ironically, one had to arrive at the impasse before progress could be made. What it came down to was who had the most patience and the most nerve. One needed both to come out on top.

"Will you never stop speaking in riddles, Mr. Deverill?" At last, her patience had run out.

"It's simple, really," he said. "You marry me."

Oh, he had nerve to spare.

Lady Beatrix blinked. Her mouth fell open for the space of three incredulous seconds before she snapped it shut. It opened again. "*Marry* you?"

"Well, agree to marry me."

"You jest."

"I'm not known for jesting, in the general sense."

A scoff born of sheer incredulity scraped across her throat. "I won't agree to marry you."

Dev sensed now was the moment to ease up a hair, even as he continued to press forward. Another opportunity like Lady Beatrix St. Vincent wouldn't fall into his lap again so easily. "*I* know that, and *you* know that, but society doesn't have to."

"So…you're proposing…an *engagement?*"

"In the eyes of society, yes."

"Why would I agree to such a thing?"

If she wasn't careful, she would form permanent grooves in her forehead.

Finally, they'd arrived at the crucial moment. "Because you need money." He glanced around their decaying surroundings to illustrate the point. "And I can give it to you."

He could practically see the race and whir of her mind as his proposition penetrated deeper with each passing second.

"You would pay me to *pretend* to be your fiancée?" A beat. "Why?"

"Don't you wish to have…*more?*"

Complicated emotion flashed behind her eyes. "I'm getting by."

"But you can do more than get by."

"You still haven't answered my question. *Why?*"

Dev felt like that *why* encompassed what was being explicitly asked—and more, too. For now, he would address the explicit.

"As you've mentioned, you're the daughter of a marquess. A *lady*. No doors are closed to you."

She nodded. She understood this.

"But..." she began.

Tension crept through Dev. She was about to ask about that other *why*.

"Why is it so vital to you that those doors are open?" Her head tipped to the other side, as if in doing so she could view an angle she'd missed. "By every measure, you've achieved complete success."

Temptation pulled at Dev.

The truth.

To tell this woman the truth.

To tell her that every success was a mere a milestone on the road to gaining what he truly wanted.

What he'd always wanted...

Imogen.

The temptation passed.

The woman before him wouldn't understand that sort of passion for another person—the sort that penetrated through skin and bone and into the very cells of one's being until those very cells were composed of nothing else.

So, he said, "My business interests will benefit, of course. Not to mention a solidifying of my position in society, which, of course, will serve to benefit my future progeny."

She sat back and watched him speak—and didn't believe a word issuing from his mouth. "Oh, yes," she said. "One must consider one's *future progeny*."

Dev snorted. He couldn't help himself. She was calling out his half-truths, and he didn't mind all that much.

It made no difference.

By the end of this little *tête-à-tête*, he would have what he wanted—her agreement.

"If we were to pursue this idea of yours," she said, "do you have a plan for announcing our engagement to society?"

"I do." It had come to him only three seconds ago.

"Which is?"

"We'll cause a little sensation."

"*A sensation?*"

"Nothing you won't be able to walk away from with a relatively intact reputation."

Lady Beatrix uttered a dry laugh. "I have about six months before my place on the spinster shelf is official. A little sensation would give me a bit of panache, I dare say. But…"

"*But?*"

"But…how much?"

"*How much?*"

"How much money are you willing to pay me to create a *little sensation* with you?"

A fair question, but he wanted to push her and he knew exactly how… "You know, I could turn you in to the law."

His words, however, didn't have the intended effect. She didn't appear rattled. In fact, she looked cooler in this moment than she had since he'd entered her house. "Is that so?"

"It is."

She smiled and she shook her head, slowly. "That end has been missed."

"You think?"

"I'm no longer in your hotel suite," she said, the very voice of reason. "The burden of proof that the daughter of a marquess has trespassed in your rooms would lie squarely on your shoulders."

"The chewed-up apple core in my rubbish bin could bear witness."

Her mouth twitched with a smile it was unwilling to release. "The apple had no business being that delicious."

A sudden guffaw startled from Dev. *Audacity*. The woman possessed both audacity and a sense of humor.

A thought occurred to him—one he hadn't yet allowed himself to believe.

This partnership could work.

"Five thousand pounds," he said.

Lady Beatrix's gasp could've been heard all the way to the Western Isles. *"Five thousand pounds?"*

"Not a penny more."

She stared at him, aghast. "I would've done it for several thousand pennies *less*."

"I want you to fully invest in the role."

Her brow creased, as if she were only now seeing him for the first time. "You're swimming in gold, aren't you?"

"Something like that."

But it wasn't greed for what she could squeeze out of him shining in her eyes. It was interest—and curiosity. "And this is all for your *future progeny*?"

Her skepticism was unmistakable.

But she didn't have to believe him.

"I'm a man who gets what he wants."

"I can see that, Mr. Deverill."

What Dev saw was a question perched on the tip of her tongue—the one that would naturally follow.

And what is it that you actually want, Mr. Deverill?

He had no intention of answering that question—now or ever —so he pivoted. "Of course, you'll immediately require a new wardrobe."

Her eyebrows winged together. He'd caught her on the back foot. "I'm wearing my best day dress now."

"It won't do." Though the change in subject had been strategic, Lady Beatrix's wardrobe did, indeed, need to be addressed. "It's wool, brown, buttoned up to your chin, and about ten years out of date."

"I don't care about that."

"It's not the sort of dress that tempts a man into creating a sensation."

He got a snort by way of reply.

"I am Lord Devil."

"And?"

"*And* I would only court a stylish woman."

"I'm not spending a penny of my money on new clothes. That's not part of our agreement."

"I can't have the woman I'm courting looking like a pauper."

"I'm the daughter of a marquess. No one thinks me a pauper."

Even as he lifted it, Dev knew the raised eyebrow was a fair bit of cheek.

"And you'll need a new servant or two."

"I'm not replacing Cumberbatch."

"An *additional* servant or two," he amended.

The woman shimmered with pique and exasperation and looked thoroughly unconvinced. "Why on earth would I spend my money on servants and dresses?"

"Why wouldn't you?"

"I'm scraping along just fine."

"*Scraping along?*"

Her gaze shifted toward her favorite patch of filth-crusted window. She didn't dignify his question with a response.

Sudden insight struck him. *Scraping along* had been Lady Beatrix's life for so long she didn't know another mode of existence. Here was a woman adapted to making do with what she had.

And Dev saw something more.

He may have been the son of a humble estate manager and a housekeeper and she the daughter of a marquess, but his life had always had so much more than hers.

"To be clear," he said, "you have no intention of purchasing new dresses for our engagement?"

"Our *pretend* engagement," she corrected him. "And the answer is of course not."

Sometimes in a negotiation one must retreat and reassess. They'd reached that point—which didn't mean Dev would concede the point, not at all.

"I almost forgot," he said, reaching for the parcel at his side. He pushed it across the table. "A gift."

Her eyebrows crinkled with confusion. "*A gift?*"

"For you."

For some reason, he felt like that last bit needed to be said. This woman wasn't accustomed to receiving gifts.

Tentatively, as if a jape were possibly being played on her, she took the parcel and set it on her lap.

"Aren't you going to open it?"

"Maybe."

"Open it."

Hesitant fingers hovered, then forefinger and thumb pulled the string and the four sides of the box fell open. She gasped with a squeak closely resembling delight at the variety of chocolate confections staring up at her. She tore her eyes away to meet his.

"Aren't you going to try one?"

He found he liked this role.

Lord Devil—*tempter.*

He couldn't help wondering what other temptations he could throw this woman's way.

She picked up a chocolate and considered it. Very clearly, she wanted to eat it. A single bite was all it would take.

But she didn't.

She took a nibble and savored it. Then another nibble, and savored it, too, as she consumed the chocolate bite by dainty bite in a manner Dev wasn't sure he'd ever appreciated a single thing in his life.

"One thing more," he said.

"Yes?" she asked, distracted. She was eyeing her next chocolate.

First, Dev noticed something. "You have a smudge of chocolate...*here.*" He tapped the corner of his mouth.

Her tongue darted out and began working on the area.

As he watched the tip of her pink tongue, a surprising happening occurred. His mouth went dry.

He tore his gaze away and cleared his throat and returned to the subject of *one thing more...* "You and I are not adversaries."

Her tongue stopped, and her eyes narrowed warily, as if searching for his angle. "We're not?"

He shook his head. "I don't see any reason we should be."

She reached for her second chocolate and took a contemplative bite. Her eyes drifted shut for an instant of bliss. But he could see she was turning his words over in her nimble mind. At last, she nodded. "I think you're right."

"In fact," Dev continued, emboldened, "we should be friends."

Her brow crinkled. *"Friends?"*

"Our arrangement won't work if we don't like each other. So..."

He extended his hand across the table. She regarded it as if she'd never beheld a man's hand before and made no move to take it. Then—*at last...tentatively*—she reached out. His hand felt like a clumsy bear paw against the slender elegance of hers. He'd thought her hand would've been cold. But, no, Lady Beatrix's hand was warm and composed of firmer substance than it appeared.

Much like the rest of her, he suspected.

He liked the feel of her hand.

His gaze lifted, and he found himself not only holding her hand, but staring into her eyes—those remarkable, arresting, beautiful gray eyes of hers that he now saw held a hint of violet.

Her brow lifted expectantly, and he realized he'd been holding her hand a few ticks of time too long.

He released it and cleared his throat, his sense of purpose

returning. "In three days, the Duchess of Haver is hosting a musicale."

Lady Beatrix nodded. "I received an invitation along with everyone else who is summering in Town. You're invited, too?"

"Surprised?"

"The thing is," she began, and Dev knew he was in for another of her little insights. "If you're being invited to the musicales of duchesses, I don't understand why you need me."

"Oh, you're very necessary to my purposes, Lady Beatrix."

"And it's at the musicale that we will create our little sensation?"

"Yes."

She stood, signaling the end of tea. "Then I believe our arrangement is ready to proceed." She hesitated. *"Friend."*

A smile curved Dev's mouth as he came to his feet. Lady Beatrix had a sense of humor. He couldn't help wondering how many people knew that about her? Fewer than a handful, he suspected. He was seeing a side of her she didn't easily reveal.

And he knew it to be as fragile as a robin's egg.

Perhaps they would end up becoming actual friends.

"Lead the way, *friend.*" He followed her to the front door. Once outside, he donned his hat and said, "I'll see you three days hence."

She hesitated the split of a second, a flash of uncertainty passing behind her eyes. Then she nodded and closed the door.

In that split of a second, she'd reconsidered.

Then reconsidered again—and let their arrangement stand.

As his feet hit the cobblestones of Little Stanhope Street, Dev understood something. He was one step closer to his goal. No doors would be closed to him with Lady Beatrix St. Vincent as his future bride. The *ton* would have no choice but to take notice.

And so, too, would Imogen.

Oh, Imogen would notice.

The next three days would be crucial, for there he felt on

shaky ground. Lady Beatrix could easily reverse course. He must find a way to bind her to their arrangement.

As quickly as the problem presented itself, so did the solution.

Of course.

It had been before his eyes the entire time.

It wouldn't be through threats of exposure or verbal acrobatics or bullying that he would bind her to him.

How did one attract a Bea?

With honey.

Or chocolate, as the case happened to be.

CHAPTER ELEVEN

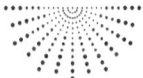

THREE DAYS LATER

*B*eatrix had been approached for conversation by no fewer than five ladies this evening.

While she might converse with that many ladies over the course of a night out in society, she didn't within the first quarter hour of arrival.

As with gentlemen asking her to dance at balls for the last few years, she would've suspected a betting book wager of some sort —except she knew why she was being approached.

It was her mode of dress.

At the height of fashion, to put it simply.

Though she and Deverill were to create a *little sensation* together this evening—during the intermission, to be exact—she was causing a little sensation all on her own.

"You must give me the direction of your modiste."

"I'm afraid I can provide you her name, but not her address," replied Beatrix. "She came to me."

An intrigued lift of eyebrows conveyed no small bit of surprise—for the fifth time tonight.

And for the fifth time tonight—or five hundredth, more like—

the feeling that she'd been caught up in a whirlwind fluttered and tumbled through her.

These last three days... How quickly her life had transformed.

The very afternoon after she'd entered into her arrangement with Deverill, a housekeeper, a maid, and a cook had arrived on her doorstep, along with a pantry's worth of food.

It sounded like the beginning of a joke.

But apparently, it was no joke.

It was her life.

For his part, Cumberbatch observed all with a canny lift of an eyebrow and his mouth pressed into a flat line.

Blessedly, he hadn't asked a single question.

Of course, he hadn't needed to.

They both knew the answer.

Deverill.

Next arrived the modiste, Madame Dubois, who required nothing of Beatrix other than she strip down to chemise and stockings and allow her measurements to be taken. The woman had *ooo*ed and *ahh*ed over Beatrix's porcelain skin and dark sable hair. *"And that black fringe of lashes... Oh, ma chérie,"* she'd exclaimed. *"Vibrant colors for you."*

"*Erm,*" replied Beatrix. It seemed the only thing she was capable of saying.

The woman hadn't noticed, as she industriously set about her work of measuring and jotting notes. *"You will stand out, rest assured."*

Stand out?

Beatrix had never stood out once in her life. At least, not for the right reasons.

The following morning, the new garments began arriving— everything from practical boots to satin slippers; from kidskin to silk gloves; gossamer stockings to sturdy stays. Then there were the dresses in a rainbow of bold colors. Riding habits...morning dresses...day dresses...evening gowns...ball gowns.

She'd been unsure she could wear such dresses, for they were bolder in other ways, too. The necklines lower…the fabric thinner… A lady held not a single secret while wearing such dresses. Yet she couldn't deny they were in the first stare of fashion. No one would look askance at her, beyond idle curiosity about Lady Beatrix St. Vincent's sudden new sense of style.

As for further evidence that her life had utterly altered… This morning, the maid had served her hot chocolate in bed.

That hot chocolate was the most delicious thing she'd ever tasted.

Divine was the only word that fit.

The new cook was French.

Overnight, Beatrix's life had changed.

That fateful night in Deverill's hotel suite, she'd discovered he lived like a king. But what she couldn't have known was that, after one shook hands with him, one lived like a princess.

Part of her longed to give in to the magic of it.

But a central problem lay with magic.

It only lasted so long.

Eventually, the spell broke—and one was flung back into stark reality.

No.

She wouldn't—*couldn't*—accept the magic as reality.

The return to earth would be too devastating.

"The style of dress quite suits you, Lady Beatrix."

Lady Neale held a mean, little glint in her eye that had Beatrix bracing for the backside of the compliment.

"You don't look a year over seven and twenty."

Beatrix swallowed back a sudden chirrup of laughter.

She'd just been insulted directly to her face, all but called a spinster outright. Except the barb glanced away. Society's arrows had long stopped finding their mark.

Though sorely tempted, she refrained from returning Lady Neale's veiled insult. She wouldn't make the observation that one had to squint very hard to see the faint sheen of green that yet lingered in her hair.

So, she nodded and began ambling through the room in the hope that movement would discourage questions about her modiste.

How very conspicuous she felt.

The feeling crawled across her skin and prickled the fine hairs to a stand. She didn't care for the sensation.

Deverill, however, did.

She understood that.

He knew he drew eyes and didn't shy away from them.

Which was how she knew he hadn't yet arrived.

Though a vibrant affair, the mingling hour before the music began wasn't yet enlivened with the specific energy Deverill produced in any room he entered.

Again, she found her mind running through his stated reasons for the arrangement they would set in motion tonight—business interests…position in society…*future progeny*.

All very good reasons.

All very solid reasons.

All very believable reasons for a man on the rise.

Yet there was something those reasons weren't—the deeper reason.

His true reason.

There was more to the pretend engagement they were about to embark upon than he was telling her.

But what she'd decided was—and this was the important part —she didn't care.

£5,000.

It was the windfall she needed.

Sure, it wasn't enough to make her an heiress, but it was enough to start her life over.

Start over?

The end of her twenties was in sight. It wasn't a stretch to say her life had never gotten started in the first place.

This arrangement with Deverill... While it felt like a whirlwind had taken over her life, it also felt like momentum—*forward* momentum.

Her life had never had that sense of progressing from one stage to another. Oh, after years of saving her meager horse race winnings, she'd once thought it had—but that had been an illusion. The truth was, eight years ago, she'd fallen into a bog and had lacked the means to pull herself out of it. All she'd been doing in the intervening time was keeping her head just above the muck.

But this arrangement with Deverill... It held the allure of possibility coming within reach.

For the first time in a very long time, a forgotten feeling blossomed within her—*hope*.

She could have a life.

It wouldn't be what she'd envisioned at twenty, but that was all right. She was realistic about her prospects. A widower, perhaps... A third or fourth son, even... With a dowry of £5,000, she could be wed. A possibility she hadn't allowed herself to consider in years.

But now...she could dream again.

"Is Lydon about perchance?" came a question at her back.

She turned to face her interlocutor, Lady Berenger, and nearly groaned. The mention of her father tended to elicit that response. "I do not believe he is," she replied neutrally.

A condescending smile curved the lady's lips. "Ah, well, he wouldn't, would he?"

Beatrix didn't want to ask—truly, she didn't—but she must. Though to do so was to fall into Lady Berenger's trap. "And why is that?"

The lady gave a bright, tinkling laugh. "The card room is closed tonight," she said. "And even if it were open..."

Beatrix braced herself. As bad as this conversation was, it was about to get worse.

Lady Berenger leaned in conspiratorially. "The play would be too rich for his coffers, I dare say."

Beatrix couldn't control the clench of her hands at her sides. "Indeed, you do dare say."

The lady's eyes narrowed with gratification. She'd hit her mark. "No need to get uppish, Lady Beatrix. A new dress notwithstanding, everyone in society knows the House of Lydon is in shambles."

Swift anger soared through Beatrix, whipping her blood into recklessness. "Is that Lord Spivey I see near the terrace doors?"

Lady Berenger shrugged a creamy shoulder. "Why should I know?" However, the blush creeping up her décolletage told a different story—one of keen awareness.

"Oh, I thought you would since he and your husband are bosom friends and known to be generous with one another. By all accounts, they share absolutely everything." Now, it was Beatrix leaning in conspiratorially. "I've even heard it whispered they share—"

She left the *you* unspoken.

But Lady Berenger heard it. The blood drained from her face, and she blinked before hastily excusing herself.

Beatrix shouldn't have done it, she knew that. She didn't think herself a petty or uncharitable person, but when one stood on the fringes, one gathered insights about others and heard little whisperings, too.

She experienced a niggle of doubt regarding the arrangement she'd made with Deverill.

Simply, she wasn't sure his plan would succeed.

She wasn't exactly the most popular or known lady in the *ton*, even if she was the daughter of a marquess.

She was the daughter of a *debt-ridden, debauched* marquess.

An important distinction.

Still, as he said he would, he'd paid out half of the agreed-upon £5,000, so she would be giving his plan her all.

£2,500… That was the amount presently hidden away beneath the floorboards under her bed.

Oh, yes, she would be giving his plan her very best effort.

Then he would pay her the other half.

Money… For the first time in her life, she had a substantial amount of it. Money had always seemed more like a shapeless concept than a tangible thing. But now, against her skin, the slide of new silk and fine muslin—*luxurious…decadent…possibly sinful…*

She liked it.

Further, though she was nearing confirmed spinsterhood, she felt…*lovely.*

Her place within society had been set these last eight years, but this new stylish dress suggested her place might need to be reevaluated.

Which only helped her purpose along.

This lovely dress—and the conferred loveliness of her in it—suggested to society that she might be a catch.

Of a sudden, she felt *it*—an alteration in the air. A dip in the volume of the crowd, followed by an immediate buzzing spike, even louder than the volume that preceded it.

The intriguing Lord Devil had arrived.

Oh, the figure he cut in society.

A veritable collector of superlatives was Lord Devil.

He wasn't the tallest man in the room—but rather the most imposing.

So, too, was he the best dressed and most handsome.

And the most magnetic.

It was those eyes of his.

Eyes that held a wicked glint—and wicked secrets. He might even share them with you—but only if you were very lucky.

Oh, where had that last thought come from?

Her own wicked places, she supposed. For she held wicked places within herself, she'd recently accepted.

Or perhaps it was Lord Devil himself who stirred those places to life.

That, more than anything, was his effect on a room.

And upon an individual within it.

"We should be friends."

She didn't have many friends.

Really, just the one—Artemis.

And a man for a friend?

That man?

But...why not *that* man?

Out of everyone populating this room, he was a person she could respect.

And he was helping her achieve what she wanted in life—a good, solid future.

Why not be his friend?

Who would suspect?

The spinster Lady Beatrix St. Vincent entered into an arrangement with Lord Devil?

Such a notion existed so far beyond the realm of possibility as to be delusion.

Yet this delusory notion wasn't only possible, it was an appealing one, too. She'd become so accustomed to feeling alone —even viewing the world as a hostile place, at times—that this notion of friendship with someone who knew a few private truths about her held appeal.

Even as it should have inspired a healthy dollop of caution.

When she'd reached out to seal their arrangement and his fingers had closed around hers, she'd almost snatched it back. The warmth of his hand...the strength...the way it pulsed with life...

Deverill's was the sort of vibrancy that was impossible to contain or control.

She would do well to remember as much.

The ringing of a small brass bell cut through the spiky buzz of the crowd. The music was set to begin henceforth, if everyone would take their seats.

Beatrix's heart struck up a little dance against her ribs as she made her way down the central aisle. Typically at these affairs, she sat in the back—the better to observe all. But Deverill had instructed in his note that she take her place in the front row.

So, here she sat in her new finery, sweat-slick palms clasped tightly in her lap, gaze fixed straight ahead—the observed.

Tonight, *she*—Lady Beatrix St. Vincent, who had been dismissed as a spinster by all society—would create a *little sensation* with the man they called Lord Devil.

Once everyone had taken their seats—a small gathering of a hundred or so—the soprano recently arrived from Italy took her place beside the pianoforte. Gentle notes began flowing from the instrument, and she opened her mouth and produced the most heavenly sound Beatrix ever heard. Until this moment, she hadn't been aware the human voice could be so transfixingly lovely.

Yet, even as her soul longed to be swept up and transported to Italy, she had an assignation tonight.

This lovely dress on her back…

It hadn't yet been earned.

So, with subtle taps of her fingers, she kept time with the music and a tally of the seconds and minutes. Once ten minutes had ticked past, she inhaled a deep, bracing breath and stood—and attempted to tamp down mortification. All eyes were certainly on her and not the soprano, who was surely throwing eye daggers Beatrix's way for intruding upon the brilliance of her performance.

Well, there was no help for it, as this was a key part of Deverill's plan. The gathered would notice when Lady Beatrix excused herself.

So it was that she let the momentum of destiny carry her down the aisle.

The momentum of destiny?

Wasn't she one for dramatics tonight?

The answer to that question was a resounding *yes*.

In fact, she'd only gotten started.

CHAPTER TWELVE

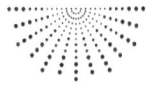

*F*rom the corner of his eye, Dev watched Lady Beatrix.

Any moment now, she would stand and draw every eye toward her.

She wouldn't like the *drawing every eye* part of this business.

But that was rather the point.

Just when he began to doubt her nerve would hold, she shot to her feet like a spring and all but dashed down the center aisle.

She was going through with it.

He slid his pocket watch from his waistcoat and held it discreetly palmed in his hand. He would give it three minutes before he followed.

As the soprano's voice lifted into another impossible register and swirled through the air, he experienced the twin thrills of anticipation and momentum—that feeling when a plan was proceeding precisely as it should.

Lady Beatrix was playing her role.

He was playing his.

And unbeknownst to her, Imogen was playing hers.

She was in attendance, as he'd known she would be.

And tonight, for the first time since she'd impossibly married Bridgewater and become a countess, Dev had ignored her—or pretended to. He hadn't attempted eye contact or proximity.

Not even when he felt the heat of her gaze upon him.

He sensed a question therein—and that was good.

He would have her wondering about this change in him. Imogen had always been so sure of herself. It served him tonight if she were a little less so of him. Otherwise, how could he convince her that he was besotted with Lady Beatrix St. Vincent?

The minute hand of his pocket watch struck twelve. The three minutes were up.

He'd taken a seat in the second row, so he would have to inconvenience every lady and gentleman he passed on his way to the center aisle. Annoyed shifts of knees to the left and right... A few ladylike huffs of annoyance...

He'd made a spectacle of himself.

They would remember.

Earlier, he'd walked from the ballroom to the conservatory, so he knew the path to take. Lady Beatrix, of course, wouldn't have needed to exercise such precaution. She would know this mansion, as she knew fifty others like it populating the West End of London. This was her world, lest he forget.

And that was the interesting thing—when he was around her, he tended to.

She wasn't like other aristocrats.

And it wasn't because she was poor, as he'd so eloquently informed her.

There was no artifice to her.

When he'd suggested they be friends, admittedly, it had been strategy. The next several weeks of being in one another's company would proceed better if they weren't adversaries.

But also...

He'd said it because he thought it could be true.

He and Lady Beatrix could be friends.

At the conservatory door, he stopped and surveyed the magnificent space with its soaring glass ceiling now dark with night and palm trees that nearly reached the highest point in the center. Lush with exotic greenery from every corner of the world, this room proclaimed aristocratic wealth and privilege more distinctly than any other room in the mansion. Gilt and silk furnishings and crystal chandeliers could be easily bought, but one came into possession of these exotic trees, shrubberies, flowers, and orchids—not to mention the Grecian marble statuary scattered throughout—with contacts from around the world and no expense to spare. One didn't purchase such finds with credit.

His gaze caught on a still figure bent over an especially vibrant orchid.

Lady Beatrix.

She was dressed at the height of fashion in her new finery tonight—a silk dress in a sapphire hue with white satin gloves reaching just below her elbows. Her lady's maid had arranged her hair in a coiffure that accentuated both the volume and luster of her sable locks and the graceful column of her neck.

His gaze found itself following the delicate line of her clavicle.

A man's tongue wouldn't be able to resist that line—to test its feel...to know its taste.

Dev stopped himself right there.

Lady Beatrix wasn't his to test and taste.

And she wasn't his doll to dress up.

He'd only procured the clothes—and the housekeeper and the maid and the French cook and the pantry full of food—so she could play the role of his fiancée believably.

That was all.

He cleared his throat.

She froze, mid-sniff. Her head angled, and surprised, remarkable...*arresting*...eyes met his, holding them as she straightened.

Her eyes.

The sapphire hue of her dress brought the subtle violet within the gray forward, further deepened by the thick, dark fringe of eyelashes—*beautiful*.

But Lady Beatrix's eyes were more than remarkable, arresting, and beautiful.

Unflinching and possessed of a rare openness, one had to be stout of heart to brave looking into those eyes. One wouldn't be able to hide from that inquisitive gaze—at least, not for long.

"The conservatory for our *little sensation* is a bit cliché, no?" she asked. Except she wasn't asking—she was telling.

A blade of steel ran through the understated beauty before him.

Dev found a smile twitching about his mouth. "Then what better place?"

A laugh sounded through her nose. "You owe the soprano at least five dozen roses for upstaging her performance."

He didn't hesitate. "I'll send her ten dozen."

Lady Beatrix shook her head on another dry laugh and began wandering along the periphery of the cavernous space...always keeping opposite him and...*watchful*. "Do you know where we shall, *erm*, position ourselves?"

Discomfort and nerves shimmered off her, belying the pragmatism of her words.

He glanced around. "We need to be visible from the corridor beyond the doors."

She wrinkled her nose. "A bit obvious."

"Tonight isn't about subtlety."

She continued her amble, pausing before a large palm in examination. "What about here?"

Dev shook his head. "It isn't sufficiently visible from the doors."

She walked purposely toward a bright spray of fuchsia on the other side of the room. "Would this suffice?"

"It has rather aggressive thorns. I can see them from here."

He understood what she was doing. She was avoiding the obvious place where they should stage their *little sensation*—the marble Greek statue planted dead opposite the double doors. *Too obvious*, he supposed.

He propped an arm on its base. "I believe this is the perfect spot."

Lady Beatrix appeared unconvinced. "Define perfect."

"A clear view from the door."

A resigned sigh issued from parted lips. "I suppose. However, I'm not sure anyone will notice us in the slightest with *that*"—she motioned in the general direction of the statue's perky, unclad breasts—"for our backdrop."

Dev's mouth curved into a smirk. "They'll think we've been overcome by lust."

She squeezed her eyes shut for an instant. Then they popped open, and she said, *"Right.* Shall we get on with it?"

Dev's smile broadened with triumph, then froze.

One problem yet remained.

Namely, the ten or so feet of distance between them—and how to bridge it.

The nervous skittishness of Lady Beatrix's eyes said she'd arrived at the same problem.

"This doesn't have to be awkward." He said it in an offhand manner meant to put her at ease.

She crossed her arms over her chest. "Who's being awkward?"

Best he left that question unchallenged.

He took a step forward and sensed she'd willed herself not to take a responding step backward.

As starts went, he could think of worse.

* * *

THE TIME HAD ARRIVED.

For Beatrix to play her role—of besotted lover to the man known as Lord Devil.

Head cocked, attentive, he was waiting.

For her to make the next move.

"Shall I…" She had no idea where to go with the question. "Just tell me where to stand."

"Where you are is perfect, only…"

"*Only?*"

"Only I shall need to move closer to you."

Within his eyes and between the syllables of his words, he was requesting permission.

She nodded.

He moved closer.

"I believe some parts of us will have to touch."

She swallowed. "Of course."

"Would a hand be asking too much?"

It was a joke.

Even the sort of joke spoken between friends.

Yet she couldn't quite conjure a smile.

Wordlessly, she extended her hand, and he took it.

A frisson of anticipation purled up her spine and crawled through her veins. Her lungs forgot how to draw breath.

"May I remove your glove?"

Her brow crinkled. "Is that necessary?"

"We're lovers."

Beatrix suppressed a gasp.

Lovers.

Except…forming an umbrella above that word and all her interactions with the man before her hung another word.

Pretend.

All this was a game of pretend.

She nodded.

He took white silk between forefinger and thumb and tugged —one finger, then another, until the glove slipped loose and free.

He had strong, capable hands—hands accustomed to work. She'd felt them upon her that day in Hyde Park. But not like *this* —his skin bare and warm against hers.

Truly, she'd experienced his hands upon her in more intimate places.

Except did the touching of two hands lack intimacy?

One experienced the world through one's hands.

So, to touch the hand of another person…

To know they felt yours, too…

What could be more intimate?

Further, she understood in a way not born of experience, but rather instinct, why women wanted *this* man's hands upon them.

In the distance, her mind registered applause. The first half of the musicale had concluded. Guests would start stretching their legs and mingling and wandering through the manse, possibly— *probably*—toward the conservatory.

Her heart hammered in her chest, and she grew suddenly too hot. Deverill stepped closer. Space remained between them, but with her hand in his and the positioning of their bodies combined with the seclusion of the setting, no doubt would linger in the mind of the casual observer as to the goings-on between Mr. Blake Deverill and Lady Beatrix St. Vincent.

A small group of ladies strolled past the open conservatory doors, and Beatrix braced herself for what was to come in the next second. The ladies glanced their way…

And kept moving without sparing even a second glance.

Surprise, along with a hefty dollop of indignation, swept through Beatrix. Was it so far beyond the realm of possibility that she would indulge in a bit of impropriety?

"I believe we need to be more obvious," said Deverill.

"And I suppose you have ideas for how to go about that." The statement left her mouth dry as dust.

No mistaking that glint of wickedness in his eyes, curling one side of his mouth. "Myriad," he said. "But one will do."

She swallowed. His gaze, which caught everything, followed the movement.

"I'll place my hand on your waist." His voice held a dark, raspy edge. "With your permission, of course."

Beatrix supposed that fell within the boundary of a *little sensation*. Still… "Not too low on my waist. On the ribs."

His brow lifted in question.

"I don't want to be ruined," she said, tightly.

"Aren't I compensating you enough for your services?"

No denying the implication within that *services*. She could choose to be insulted—or to stand her ground. "I might want to marry someday."

His head cocked. "Oh?"

Her back was beginning to ache beneath the rigid squareness of her shoulders. "I would like for my options to remain open."

A strange conversation to be having when one hand was holding one of hers and his other hand was settled on her waist and *her* other hand was resting on his shoulder, the heat of his body meeting hers through superfine, his delicious scent mixing with the floral aroma of exotic flowers in bloom.

The close, humid atmosphere of a conservatory was most… *intoxicating*.

She picked up a sound—muted footsteps…the low murmuration of voices punctuated by the odd trill of sudden laughter…

Another group of ladies was approaching.

"Ready?" he murmured.

She nodded a barely perceptible *yes*, even as a panicked *no, no, no* tore through her.

The group reached the open iron-and-glass doors, and Beatrix thought she might've caught a few second glances from the corner of her eye. Yet there was no indication that a *little sensation* had been achieved. She wasn't even sure they'd inspired the lift of a mildly scandalized eyebrow.

Deverill's brow furrowed with perplexity.

Though it pained her, Beatrix had to say something. Though it meant she would have to return the money—and the dresses... and the servants...and possibly the food...and most definitely the French cook who prepared the most divine hot chocolate in the whole world... "I fear," she said, "you may have been wrong in your choice of partner for a *little sensation.*"

Deverill's eyes narrowed into aquamarine slits. "How do you mean?"

"Well," she began, "I'm Lady Beatrix St. Vincent, all but confirmed spinster. And you—" She leaned back and swept her gaze up and down his person. "Are *you.*"

"Meaning?"

"*Meaning* the casual observer likely thinks you're picking a stray palm frond from my hair." She took a sip of air to brace herself for what she must say next... "Bluntly, no one would expect a dalliance between us. Society would think everything else first."

Oh, the mortification that burned through her. The heat of a thousand suns couldn't touch it.

But it had to be faced.

Yet Deverill didn't release her or demand the return of his £2,500 or the dress off her back. He simply said, "I see."

He possessed the look of a man who had made up his mind about something.

More lively conversation drifted into the conservatory from the corridor. Another group was approaching.

"What are you thinking?" she asked, wary.

And she knew what other look he possessed.

The look of a man who hadn't given up.

In fact, he might've only gotten started.

He angled his head in assessment, which illustrated the strong line of his jaw.

She only noticed because she was so close to him—within his embrace, in fact.

"Do you trust me?"

CHAPTER THIRTEEN

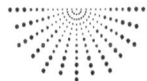

"*D*o *you trust me?*"

The question, and the intensity with which it was asked, did nothing to calm Beatrix's nerves.

"I'm reserving judgment."

The hand at her ribs slipped lower on her waist and firmed.

Every muscle in her body tensed, even as a strange, contrary part of herself began to thaw. He lifted her hand and placed it on the back of his neck, the fine black hairs tickling her palm. "This is the only way," he muttered.

Her mind went completely and determinedly blank.

The *only way?*

She could see no *only way.*

All she could do was hold very, very still—and watch his beautiful mouth speak words that eluded comprehension.

"Double the money."

She blinked.

"Place your other hand on my neck, too," he directed.

She obeyed.

Apparently, she was only capable of behaving as he instructed.

The crowd grew louder...*closer*...and a sense of urgency gathered momentum.

It was only in the next split of a second that she understood.

Double the money...

Ten thousand pounds.

She blinked with sudden comprehension. "Kisses weren't part of our arrangement," she somehow spoke.

His brow creased. "Pardon?"

"You heard me," she whispered in a rushed hiss.

"I cannot kiss you without your permission." The way he spoke the words gave the impression this was a problem he'd never encountered. "I'm not that sort of man."

The shift in power nearly stole Beatrix's breath away. He might've paid her a small fortune to enter into their arrangement, but for this—*a kiss*—he needed her permission.

She could say *no*.

Which, contrary person that she was, only made her want to say...

"Yes."

And she lifted onto the tips of her blue satin slippers and pressed her willing mouth to his shocked one.

For a man possessed of such hard, unassailable edges, his mouth was unimaginably soft. Except *unimaginably* wasn't the correct word. For she realized now, somewhere in a hidden corner of her mind, she *had* imagined the soft feel of his mouth.

Pillowy...but firm.

Every individual part of her seemed to develop a mind of its own the longer the kiss went on. The tightening of her arms around his neck... The sway of her body into his... A little cause and effect there. But, *my*, what a hard, unyielding body she'd swayed into. And her tongue...

Her tongue, of its own instinctive accord, darted out and swiped across his bottom, beautiful lip.

A single, swift swipe was all it was, yet...

A low growl sounded in the back of his throat.

That growl penetrated skin and bone and resonated through her, producing sensations… Sensations that *begged…implored… demanded…* This pretend kiss… It felt like it wanted to turn into something else…

Something *more*.

Of a sudden, in the not-too-far-off distance, a chorus of shocked gasps and exclamations sailed through the air of the conservatory.

A heartbeat later, Beatrix tore her mouth from Deverill's and took an inelegant, scrambling step backward, light fingertips pressed against kiss-crushed lips. For the complicated split of a second, she and Deverill held each other's gaze. And in that moment, she saw reflected at her a note of surprise that mirrored her own. Her gaze slipped lower and took in his beautifully swollen mouth and for a wild moment considered kissing it again.

And she might've been bold enough to do so but for the gathering of a crowd at the periphery of her vision. Just as she couldn't quite believe what had happened, neither could they.

Lady Beatrix St. Vincent…*kissing*…Lord Devil.

They wouldn't have believed it if they hadn't seen it with their own eyes.

And even then, it was a struggle.

Without taking his gaze off her, Deverill reached into an interior coat pocket and produced an object.

A *shiny* object.

As if she were observing from a place above and beyond herself, Beatrix watched him fall to one knee and extend the shiny object toward her.

More gasps followed.

The shiny object was a ring—a deep red cabochon ruby set in a band of gold.

His beautiful mouth was moving, but she could hardly hear him through the cotton in her ears.

The words, "My sweet Bea," snapped her to.

Not only her given name, but a shortening of it.

A pet name.

"Will you do me the great honor of becoming my wife?"

Rapt, anticipatory silence descended on their audience.

"Say *yes*," he muttered beneath his breath. "And drum up a tear of happiness while you're at it."

But Beatrix was trapped outside herself and unable to will her mouth to move.

"A nod will do."

And, somehow, she managed to nod what passed for a *yes*.

More gasps and murmurings followed, as the silence broke and the small crowd rushed forward to offer their slightly confused congratulations to the happy and unexpected couple.

And that was their *little sensation* enacted.

Though, as Beatrix accepted and mutely endured the confounded congratulations and lifted eyebrows, she couldn't be sure of something.

That the kiss had been purely for the stage.

It was that swipe of her tongue across his bottom lip...

She still tasted him—sweet and smoky, like whiskey.

She was the only person in this room who knew the taste of Lord Devil.

The unique sensation of being watched skittered across her skin and had her scanning the crowd to locate the source—a lady.

The Countess of Bridgewater.

But the countess's gaze didn't linger. It had already shifted toward...

Deverill.

She wasn't merely or idly observing him as one might do in the circumstances, but rather staring.

As for Deverill, he was meeting the countess's gaze—*unflinchingly.*

Deverill and the Countess of Bridgewater...

Those two knew each other...

Well.

Intimately?

Again, a certainty crept through Beatrix. Deverill wasn't being transparent about his motivations for this pretend engagement. It wasn't about business interests or social connections or future progeny.

It was about—possibly...*probably*—the Countess of Bridgewater.

Beatrix was being used in a game different from the one he'd claimed.

Which was...

All right.

For she, too, had her own motives in play—and a future to secure.

As quickly as it had descended, the moment lifted and there was no more room in her whirring mind for thought as she was swept along in a tide of congratulations and questions she couldn't answer. *Would it be a spring wedding?... Or an autumn wedding?... Or a special license wedding?* She understood what the last question meant—was she in need of a hasty wedding that couldn't wait nine months?

Fortunately, Deverill kept his head about him as he stated that his beloved betrothed—laying it on a bit thick, there—was understandably overwhelmed by events and the two of them would be leaving the musicale posthaste.

Beatrix took their early exit for a bit of nimble strategy on Deverill's part—leave society with a juicy morsel of gossip and let them turn it into a seven-course meal overnight. News of their *little sensation* would be everywhere by dawn.

Once they were settled inside his coach-and-four, him seated across the footwell, they remained silent for the short drive to Little Stanhope Street. Beatrix directed her gaze out the window and watched the shadows of Mayfair roll past. As they approached her townhouse, he gave three hard raps on the carriage ceiling, and it slowed to a smooth stop.

Without the clatter of horse hooves and all the noises associated with a carriage in motion, the silence stretched long. She needed to say something. But where to start?

"The ring..." She held her hand up to the moonlight streaming through the window. Deep crimson absorbed the light and glowed. "It's the correct size."

"You have a slender hand." He shrugged. "I took note when I shook it."

"It's very similar to the one you wear."

"I thought it would be a nice touch."

"To further the myth of us." She wasn't proud of the tartness of her voice.

He didn't seem to notice. "I almost went with a sapphire, but a ruby suits you."

"Why is that?"

"You have a bit of fire about you, don't you, Lady Beatrix?"

A smile wanted out, and perhaps a small one escaped, but she realized she did have something to say... "It's too much."

"It's not."

"Like everything else." Now that she'd finally gotten started, she couldn't stop. "The new wardrobe...the house staff...the hot chocolate in bed...the ten thousand pounds."

The *magic*, she didn't say.

"But you're my fiancée."

"I'm *not* your fiancée, and that's rather my point."

"In the eyes of the world, you are."

"So?"

It wasn't the reality.

He needed to understand that.

Actually...

It was her who needed to understand it—and keep it in mind at all times.

The magic he presented was too seductive.

But he appeared unmoved as he continued. "In the eyes of the world, you are my future wife."

"*And?*"

"And as such, you must maintain a certain standard of living."

"This is about *you*, then."

"It's about appearances, and how important they are in your world."

"*Appearances.*" The word nettled beneath her skin and found purchase. "*Appearances.*" She laughed.

Blimey.

From his seat opposite, he watched her, silently.

The logic of appearances was something she understood.

The maintaining of them wasn't magic.

It was, in fact, the furthest thing from it.

"*Appearances,*" she repeated. "It's simply the same stuff and nonsense that has dictated my life from birth."

With that, she pushed open the carriage door and hopped down to the cobblestones before Deverill could get it into his male brain that she was in need of assistance. Before she shut the door, she had one last thing to say. "I can live with that."

The parting image she held of him was of his eyebrows gathered into an expression of utter and complete confoundment.

Good.

That man who had it all needed to be confounded every so often.

When this pretend engagement ended, so would the *magic*.

And she understood that was all right.

Better than all right.

For when this pretend engagement ended, her real life would, finally, begin.

The good, solid life she'd been denied for so long would be hers to pursue.

At last.

CHAPTER FOURTEEN

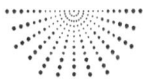

HAMPSTEAD, TWO DAYS LATER

*D*ev hadn't planned on spending his afternoon at the horse races.

It was the middle of the week, and a man had work.

But a man also had a pretend fiancée to keep track of.

So, on his way up to Camden this morning, he'd directed his coachman to Little Stanhope Street to see how the new servants were faring and, most importantly, if he still even had a pretend fiancée after...

The kiss.

That kiss had kept him awake these last two nights.

For a very simple reason.

The kiss between him and Lady Beatrix...

It had been her first.

And the part contributing to his restless nights was clear.

The kiss had its origin in pretense.

Which didn't sit easily inside him.

No one's first kiss should be for others.

It should be real.

Yet...there had been a sliver of a moment when he'd felt the glide of a soft, tentative tongue and an inclination toward surrender.

Within her…possibly, within himself.

It was within surrender that a kiss became real.

Right.

When he'd arrived at Little Stanhope Street, however, he'd found her gone.

"It's Wednesday, of course," her ancient servant Cumberbatch had informed him.

"Of course." Dev nodded slowly—and uncomprehendingly. "If you could just refresh my memory…"

"She'll be at the race meeting in Hampstead."

Of course.

Cumberbatch squared his sizeable, long-limbed form in the doorway. "You're not out to make Lady Beatrix your side bit of trifle, are you?"

Dev noted the clench of Destroyer of Worlds at the old valet's side. Arthritic or not, that fist was ready to defend Lady Beatrix's honor.

After assuring Cumberbatch of the purity of his intentions, Dev had set off for Hampstead by way of Camden first. He and Shaw had established their factory there, as it was on the Grand Junction Canal. England's canal system gave them water transport access to Birmingham to the north and the Thames to the south, making it an excellent logistical location for the receiving of supplies and the export of the finished product.

After having walked the factory floor, covered a few items of finance, and shared a new idea with Shaw, Dev set out again. But he hadn't proceeded to Primrose Park, the grand estate he'd purchased for a multitude of reasons—its proximity to Camden, its vast grounds, and fine stables for keeping Little Wicked and everything and everyone that accompanied the keeping of a Thoroughbred—which included, but wasn't limited to: trainer, grooms, stable lads, and even other horses.

No, he'd directed his coachman to Hampstead. It was only a couple of miles farther north, and Dev was curious.

In his investigation into London's turf rags, no writer by the name of Beatrix St. Vincent had turned up.

However, one Lady Godiva Gallop did.

After he'd finished laughing—and still yet, the name produced a chuckle—he'd read her every article. She was a good writer, thorough and knowledgeable on all matters related to horse and turf.

Today, he intended to see her in action.

Hampstead was a small racecourse—if it could be even called a racecourse, for no railing ran along the track. Only a few posts marked furlongs from point to point in a large field that was filled with a different class of race-goer than would be found at Epsom Downs or Newmarket.

It certainly wasn't the sort of racing course where one was likely to find a lady.

Unless that lady was Lady Beatrix St. Vincent.

Or Lady Godiva Gallop, as it were.

Not that she needed this work any longer. With the £2,500 she'd already received and the £7,500 she would pocket once the terms of their arrangement had been met—terms Dev was aware he hadn't made entirely clear to either her or himself—she could live any sort of life she wanted.

Which would require her spending some of that money.

Which she had no intention of doing.

I don't want to be ruined... I might want to marry someday.

Lady Beatrix was saving her pennies, shillings, crowns, and pounds for a chance at marriage.

In the moment, he'd been surprised by the admission, but upon reflection, it made sense.

Didn't everyone have ambitions and dreams that they carried in their heart, but didn't wear on their sleeve?

Yet...the idea that he was providing a dowry for her to marry another man when all society was under the impression she was to marry *him* produced a strange, unsettled feeling—one he had no interest in exploring.

At Hampstead, the day wasn't a beautiful one—the clouds that hovered above could go one way or the other—but an afternoon's races provided no small amount of entertainment for the all-manner-of-folk constituting the crowd. There were the horses, jockeys, trainers, grooms, and lads weaving through, either having finished a race or making their way toward the starting line. Then there were all the others who found themselves at a Hampstead race meeting on a Wednesday afternoon—the race-goers themselves and the gamesters who profited off them, the blacklegs and touts shouting odds around the betting post drawing the largest crowd.

Though Dev owned a Thoroughbred, he had no experience of a race meeting of this loose variety. It was after a particularly raucous group of soldiers strode past, laughing and jeering and already deep in their cups, that he spotted her—*Lady Beatrix*, standing in the shadow of a lean-to, pencil in one hand, journal in the other, scrawling notes, half an eye on the racecourse as horses warmed up for the next race.

Already a small woman, she possessed an uncanny ability to shrink not only her body, but somehow her entire personage into near invisibility. If one wasn't expressly looking for her, one wouldn't see her.

Another detail struck him. She wasn't wearing a single stitch of her recently acquired wardrobe, but rather was dressed in attire years out of fashion.

He supposed it was all part of her desire to remain inconspicuous, but it annoyed him—mightily.

He took a step to communicate precisely that, but wasn't quick enough, for another man approached her from the opposite direction. Tall and rangy, dressed impeccably but flamboyantly with a bold chartreuse paisley waistcoat, and an ostentatious diamond stud winking in his left ear, Dev would've put the man near five and twenty.

Dev didn't like the look of him.

With that cocksure tilt of the mouth and the bold glint in his eye, the man was a blackleg.

What business could such a man have with Lady Beatrix St. Vincent?

Before he could question his right to do so, Dev was in motion with swift, determined strides. Lady Beatrix caught the movement, and her eyebrows crashed together in both shock and consternation. He suspected he was scowling and attempted to relax the muscles of his face.

The blackleg crossed his arms over his chest and widened his stance as he watched Dev approach, the rogue displaying an appropriate amount of wariness and an unspoken amount of readiness. Here was a man accustomed to unpredictable situations and ready to meet any eventuality.

When he reached Lady Beatrix's side, Dev didn't hesitate to slip his hand around hers and lift it to his mouth. "I hope you weren't waiting very long, my sweet."

She blinked. "I, *erm*," she managed. "No."

Dev wasn't sure why he'd done it.

Claimed her, that was.

Except, actually, he did.

As of two nights ago, the world thought her his, and if that were actually true, he wouldn't stand for some East End ruffian harassing her.

In fact, it wasn't strictly true—and he still wasn't standing for it.

Hardened to a point, his gaze cut toward the blackleg. "And you are?"

It hadn't escaped his attention that he yet held Lady Beatrix's hand—and found his fingers twining through hers.

SOFIE DARLING

"Blaze Jagger," she answered for the blackleg, as she subtly reclaimed her hand.

Jagger's brow lifted with surprise. "You know who I am, Lady Beatrix?"

"Everyone associated with horse racing knows who you are, Mr. Jagger."

"I'm flattered."

"I'm not sure you should be."

That pulled a hearty laugh from the rogue—which Lady Beatrix didn't join.

"And your business with my fiancée?" Dev asked—*demanded*.

He might've been taking this claiming too far.

Jagger appeared unbothered. "As I was standing at my stretch of betting post and gazing upon the world around me—as a man does on the oddish occasion—a question smacked me solid on the head." He didn't wait for them to inquire. "Why doesn't Lady Beatrix St. Vincent ever place bets on the ponies with me?"

She gave an unbothered, one-shouldered shrug. "I don't bet on the ponies with anyone."

Jagger let the words sink in, then nodded his acceptance of them, before reaching into an interior pocket and pulling out a pair of calling cards. He handed them each one.

Dev gave the contents a quick scan and felt his brow reaching for the sky. "*The Archangel?* That's Gabriel Siren's—" He corrected himself. "The Duke of Acaster runs The Archangel."

"And don't forget his sister, Lady Tessa," said Jagger.

Dev waited. He wouldn't be baited.

"Now, a duke's a busy man," continued Jagger. "And he'll like his hands clean. So, he and his sister cut me in to run the place."

The logic held. A duke wouldn't be managing the floor of a gaming hell on a nightly basis. Dev slid a glance toward Lady Beatrix. Her mind was plainly awhirl and storing this information for not-so-future use, perhaps as Lady Godiva Gallop.

Jagger continued to address her. "You could drop by if you

142

fancy a roll of the Hazard dice or spin of the Roulette wheel sometime." A beat. "Or even a nice, little chat."

She didn't hesitate. "I fancy neither Hazard nor Roulette, and I don't have nice, little chats."

A beat of time ticked past where Jagger contemplated Lady Beatrix.

"And there you have it," said Dev. Enough was enough. "Good day, Mr. Jagger."

The moment teetered on the head of a pin as Jagger appeared on the verge of saying something more. Instead, he tipped his hat in farewell and pivoted on his heel. In a matter of seconds, he'd disappeared into the dense crowd.

Dev shifted his gaze and found inquisitive gray eyes fixed upon him. "Why are you here?"

Not one to beat about the bush, Lady Beatrix.

"I was in the area." A version of the truth.

Her head canted. "Oh?"

"My factory is located in Camden."

"Camden is south of Hampstead," she pointed out.

"Well, not *in* the area." He reached for a point that would appease her stubborn adherence to logic. "Can we agree it's in the vicinity of the area?"

One skeptical eyebrow dropped; the other remained lifted.

Progress, he supposed.

"Can't a man enjoy a day at the races with his fiancée?"

"I suppose he could."

She wasn't buying it, and Dev couldn't say he blamed her. A change of subject would be the better part of wisdom... "Should I run Little Wicked at the smaller courses like Hampstead?"

Suddenly, she was regarding him like he was the biggest dolt in London. "Most definitely not. A horse of her standing should only run in the major races of the season. Will you be running her at Doncaster for the St. Leger?"

"Will my answer be published in the *Turf Times* by one Lady Godiva Gallop?"

Her mouth twitched, but no smile broke through. "She makes no promises."

"What do you think?" He truly wanted to know. "Should I run her?"

She considered the question. "It's clear the filly loves to run. But, no, I don't think you should."

"Because it's a longer course?" he asked. "I've heard the conditions can get rough."

She shook her head. "Little Wicked is already in the Race of the Century. You would be exposing her to unnecessary risk. The problem is she's too fast."

"*Too fast?*" That was a new one on Dev.

"She will have caught the attention of the blacklegs, and you're not in league with them as far as I know."

"I'm not."

"Unless they're backing her, she's at risk. In truth, you've been reckless with her already by racing her on back-to-back days. Do you have a man to keep watch over her?"

"As his occupation?"

"Horse racing is a dirty sport, and you don't want to learn that lesson at the cost of Little Wicked."

Dev knew the voice of experience when he heard it. "I'll see to it."

"She's an intrepid filly," said Lady Beatrix. "Hold her back until the Race of the Century in September."

Dev usually had to take time to consider advice, but he found he trusted Lady Beatrix.

One beat of silence expanded into another, longer one.

They seemed to have run out of things to say.

Except they hadn't.

Dev knew what needed to be said—or rather, acknowledged.

"Do we need to talk about the other night?"

CHAPTER FIFTEEN

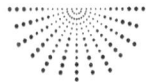

*L*ady Beatrix's gaze skittered away and a light blush pinked her cheeks. "What's there to talk about?" she asked, all frustrating innocence. "The night was a success."

"The kiss," said Dev, blunt.

Her gaze swung to meet his. "Is the money still doubled?"

"Yes."

"Then, no."

More silence expanded into the air between them—the only patch of quiet in all Hampstead, considering how dense and raucous the crowd had become.

Still, he had yet one more thing to say to this woman. "Your new clothes…"

Her gaze narrowed.

"You're not wearing them."

"This isn't really the sort of crowd who can appreciate a lady dressed in the first stare of fashion." The dry note in her voice said she didn't care too much about it herself.

Still… "But your ring."

Her expression went from mildly mocking to wholly incredulous. "I couldn't wear that here."

"Why not?"

"Are you trying to get me robbed or murdered for my flash clothes and jewels?"

"You're the daughter of a marquess," he said, slowly, as if it needed explaining to her. "You're entitled to wear every jewel beneath the sun whenever and wherever you like. You could bring a manservant to protect you."

Her brow lifted with open skepticism. "Are you suggesting I bring Cumberbatch with me everywhere and let Destroyer of Worlds dispatch with the ruffians?"

Dev wasn't giving up. "I'll hire someone."

Her eyes rolled skyward. "All so I can wear a ring?" She exhaled a long-suffering sigh. "Oh, Mr. Deverill."

A feeling stirred to life inside Dev. He rather liked the way his name sounded from her mouth. The woman was exasperated, but the note in her voice suggested she accepted him for who he was.

In the way of a friend.

"Call me Dev."

Mischief sparked within her eyes. "Not Your Excellency Lord Devil?"

He snorted. "That blasted nickname. They've turned me into a fetish for ladies. Dev will do." He asked the next question as a matter of course. "May I call you Bea?"

That pulled a smile from her. "Because of my sting?"

"Because Lady Beatrix is a mouthful, and we're betrothed." The last point should've been reason enough, but there was yet another... "And I like it."

The final point was the entire truth.

The mischief faded from gray depths. "Why don't we start with Beatrix?"

He nodded. It would have to do—*for now*.

"The ponies are lining up for the next race," she said, changing the subject. "Shall we move closer for a better view?"

"Ponies?" he asked while they walked. "Actual ponies?"

"Oh, yes," she said. "You've only attended the major races, where only Thoroughbreds are run."

Actually, that reminded him of a question he'd always been too embarrassed to ask. "What makes a Thoroughbred, anyway?"

Surprise flickered within her eyes before she replied, "Thoroughbreds were produced when Arabian stallions were mated to native English mares. The shape of head is like that of an Arabian, finely sculptured. But the sturdy English stock makes them bigger than their Arabian grandsires. They stand at sixteen hands and more. Quick and elegant, you'll have noticed, and built for stamina."

"Ah."

"On small courses like Hampstead," she continued, "there is no oversight by the Jockey Club and therefore fewer rules. So, on any day, all types of races can be run. Thoroughbreds one day, ponies the next. Cocktails are gaining popularity."

"Cocktails?"

"Half-bred horses," she explained. "But those races are usually ruined when someone smuggles a Thoroughbred in."

"Didn't you just say Thoroughbreds are half bred?"

"Oh, not for decades. They're an official breed now." She cast her gaze toward the racecourse itself. "I don't think the smaller courses like Hampstead will survive much longer."

"It's a convivial enough atmosphere, and it's packed with race-goers." Both facts were obvious, even to the casual observer.

"This is common land, which is the problem," she explained. "The local gentry have started insisting on compensation for its use. Further, since the Jockey Club doesn't oversee common-land races, they're even more corrupt than the average corrupt horse race."

Dev couldn't deny it. He was impressed. Beatrix knew this

world as well as she knew the back of her hand. Out of necessity, one could say. After all, her deep well of knowledge served her articles, which had put food on her table—for years, he suspected. But that didn't account for the full extent of it... "You love it out here, don't you?"

She tore her gaze from the track where the ponies were lining up for the blast of the starting gun. "I always have."

The truth, her eyes told him, but a complicated one.

Her cheeks went bright with passion. "Racing has everything. Open spaces, beautiful animals, dastardly scoundrels, noble competitors, money changing hands too fast for honest accounting, greed, duplicity, and soaring triumph in the end. On any given afternoon, on any given racecourse, the hooves of Thoroughbreds, ponies, and any other four-legged animal on offer pound out a dozen Greek plays—some tragedies, others comedies. The drama of the sport is literally bred into it." She shrugged. "Also, I need the money."

Dev couldn't let that pass unchallenged. "You *did* need the money. Now, you have—"

The word that wanted to follow felt wrong to speak.

Me.

It felt like a promise—and he and Lady Beatrix St. Vincent had no promises between them.

They had an arrangement and a payment schedule.

That was all.

Her mind seemed to have heard the same *me* and performed the same calculation—with the same intention to leave it unacknowledged and unspoken. Her gaze shifted and settled on the line of horses. She pulled the small journal and pencil from her reticule and wet the pencil tip with her tongue.

Pencil poised above paper, she was ready for the race to begin.

"Well, well, well," came a voice behind them.

It was an aristocratic voice—and one soaked in whiskey, at that.

Yet the voice held an edge.

Beside Dev, Beatrix froze, and her eyes squeezed shut as if denying the reality of that voice at her back.

But it proved to be composed of quite solid substance when it boomed, "If it ain't the happy couple."

She released the breath she'd been holding and turned, her shoulders square with tension. Dev pivoted alongside her to find a ruddy-faced, barrel-bellied aristocrat shambling toward them.

In an instant, Dev knew the man.

The Marquess of Lydon...

Beatrix's father.

The two shared the same gray eyes and the same fine, straight nose—but that was where similarity ended.

"Lydon," she said once he'd come closer than shouting distance.

A laugh rumbled from the depths of the marquess's belly. "Hear what the chit calls her own father?"

Before Dev could come up with a diplomatic response—how did one answer such a question, anyway?—Beatrix cut in. "By your name?"

"And the mouth on her?" Lydon continued addressing Dev. "You're certain you don't want a sweeter bride?"

In that instant, Dev understood something. In his haste to have what he wanted, he hadn't gone through the proper channels. He hadn't asked Lydon for his daughter's hand.

"Your lordship," he said, very properly, ignoring the unlady-like snort that sounded at his side. "Will you grant me the honor of taking your daughter's hand in marriage?"

He didn't need to glance at Beatrix's face to know it had gone pale with horror.

"The chit doesn't have a dowry." Lydon barked what passed for a laugh. "I rather misplaced it a while back."

Clearly, he got a grand old kick from what passed for wit with him.

Beatrix flinched.

Dev opened his mouth to spout some romantic rot about living for love, not a triviality like money. But it was the canny glint in Lydon's eye that had the words dying in his mouth.

"What's she worth to you?" asked the old scoundrel.

Money.

That was what Lydon saw when he looked at Dev.

So, it would be a negotiation.

"The question is, my lord," began Dev, his voice gone to stone, "what's she worth to *you?*"

Lydon gave a shrug. "A little here, a little there."

That answer had Dev's hackles rising. "A hundred quid?" He measured the sum as a decent starting point for a negotiation with a marquess.

"Per week?" Lydon nodded contemplatively. "That should about do me."

A strangled noise sounded in Beatrix's throat. Dev paid it no heed as he held Lydon's gaze, wondering if he should demand a shake on it. This pretend future father-in-law would be an expensive one.

Sudden insight struck him.

Beatrix had been dealing with this all her life.

Lydon directed a too-serious bow toward Beatrix. "Daughter." He turned to Dev. "Welcome to the family."

And with that, he was off, sauntering into the distance, a whistling tune trailing in his wake.

Welcome to the family.

An unexpected feeling expanded within Dev. Those parting words—and one in particular—imbued the exchange with a strange solidity.

Family.

Of a sudden, this pretend engagement to Beatrix felt less like a game of pretend and more...*real.*

Her gaze remained affixed to the distant point in the crowd

where the marquess had disappeared from sight. "When I was a child," she began, "Lydon didn't allow me to call him Papa or even Father. *Lydon*, he'd insisted." Her eyes rolled toward the sky. "He's impossible."

Family.

Dev was about to say as much when he felt it—a raindrop on his nose.

Beatrix must've experienced a similar sensation for she held out her hand and tipped her head back, directing her attention toward clouds that had grown considerably blacker in the last five minutes. "We have about thirty seconds before—"

But she was unable to complete the sentence before the clouds opened and unleashed their heavy burden directly on top of their heads. Without hesitation, he grabbed her hand. "Come with me," he shouted, feet already on the move toward his waiting carriage.

She offered no resistance as they dashed across the racecourse grounds, race-goers and horses alike running around in a mad scramble as they attempted to secure shelter from the sudden onslaught. A few more minutes of this deluge, and one would need a rowboat to paddle home.

Soon, they reached Dev's carriage and clambered gracelessly inside. With the rain belting an unrelenting tattoo on the roof, they each collapsed onto opposite benches. Soaked to the skin, hair clinging to her face in sodden strings, Beatrix was a mess.

"Have you caught a chill?" he asked, already shrugging off his overcoat.

"I'm all right," she dismissed, curtly. The shiver that visibly ran up and down her body told the lie.

"Your lips are turning purple." It needed to be said.

"I just need to get home."

"London will be a tangle of traffic. It'll take three hours to get to Mayfair in this weather."

"Best we get rolling, then."

She was a headstrong one.

When her teeth started chattering, Dev made a decision. "We're not returning to London."

"We're not?" she asked through clenched jaw.

"Primrose Park is a few miles from here."

"*Primrose Park?*"

"My estate."

Her mouth curved into what would've been a smile—*of sorts*—if it didn't look so painful. "Is there no problem you can't solve?"

"I haven't encountered one yet." In fact... He thrust his great-coat across the footwell. "*Here.*"

"I can't take your coat."

"You can." A stubborn second ticked past. "And you will."

She made no move to accept the garment. Instead, the blasted woman crossed her arms over her chest.

If she wanted to play it that way... "Or I take the seat beside you, and you use my body for warmth."

She simmered with pique before grudgingly accepting the coat. She slipped one arm, then the other, into the sleeves and brought the collar to her chin, wearing it backwards so it resembled more blanket than garment. Large, wet-lashed gray eyes stared out at him. She muttered something, but through the cacophony of rain on the carriage roof, he couldn't make out her words.

"What was that?"

She exhaled a deep, long-suffering sigh. "Thank you." What might've been a smile curled a corner of her mouth. "*Friend.*"

Dev knew the smile that curved his own mouth was a smug one and that it would irritate her no end, but there was no help for it. His sense of gratification was too strong. He gave the ceiling three firm raps to differentiate the sound from the rain. "Primrose Park," he called outside to the coachman who was hunkered into his duck-cloth overcoat that was imperviable to all varieties of English weather.

The carriage lurched into motion, and Dev settled back into plush leather, his only view the woman before him, who was fixedly staring out the window.

He resisted the urge to right her hat, which sat on her head at an askew angle.

It might prove too large a test for their fledgling friendship.

So, he, too, directed his gaze out the window and let the carriage drive him home.

The evening would be an interesting one.

CHAPTER SIXTEEN

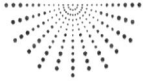

PRIMROSE PARK

*A*ll done in sky blue and cream, every available inch of wood gilded to within an inch of its life, the bedroom was nothing less than what Beatrix would've expected—spectacularly opulent.

And new.

She'd expected that, as well.

Too new—its silks too shiny, its colors too vibrant to be seen as anything resembling tasteful in the eyes of society.

Gauche.

Old titles and older money didn't appreciate vivacity in its displays of wealth. Since the French aristocrats had gotten their heads lopped off for such obvious flaunting, English aristocrats had learned their lesson from their cousins on the other side of the Channel and kept their privilege relatively muted these days. They rather liked having their heads attached to their necks.

Yet this bedroom belonged to Mr. Blake Deverill... *Lord Devil* —a man who wasn't a lord in any real sense, yet he existed in a world without limits.

What must it feel like? To experience life thusly?

She would never know, of course, but she found it refreshing to dip her toe into these unexpected waters of his.

She lifted the dress that was laid out on the bed. Brown... slightly worn...able to be buttoned by its wearer...incongruous with its surroundings...

It was the dress of a servant—and meant for her.

The dress was dry and clean; she didn't mind.

Outside, the weather continued its offensive, lashing the windows and tossing solid oak canopies as if they were willow trees.

She would be staying the night.

Extraordinary.

She would be staying the night in Lord Devil's house.

Beyond extraordinary.

It stretched the limits of belief.

The only silver lining she could think of was that she wouldn't be ruined, as society didn't know of her presence here.

She'd just finished buttoning the dress, scented subtly of lavender, when a light *tap-tap-tap* sounded on the door. She opened it to find a servant waiting to lead her to the dining room. As she navigated one long, freshly painted corridor after another, she saw that the rest of Primrose Park was as newly refurbished as the bedroom.

Blimey, how much money did Deverill have, anyway?

The dining room, of course, dazzled, with its plush Aubusson carpets, rich mahogany wainscoting and long central table to match. White marble fireplaces mirrored one another to either end of the rectangular room, and a solid wall of windows surely overlooked an exquisitely manicured garden during daylight hours. But this was night, and the storm continued to rage outside, so the sparkling panes would have to wait until morning to reveal their delights.

Her gaze immediately found Deverill, one arm comfortably propped onto the fireplace mantle as he held a whiskey tumbler and conversed easily with two older servants—a tall, upright man who bore the air of an estate manager and a woman of middling height who could be none other than Primrose Park's housekeeper with her tidy appearance and quick, darting eye that kept abreast of all happenings within a fifty-foot radius of her. She'd noted Beatrix's presence before Beatrix had noted hers.

An odd thought occurred to her.

Here was Primrose Park, a decidedly aristocratic country estate, being run in a uniquely democratic, even bourgeois manner.

Deverill's gaze found Beatrix's. His ease held, as she felt herself tense. She couldn't yet relax around him—even if they were *friends*.

She only just didn't snort.

"Lady Beatrix," he said, pushing off the mantle, "I see you managed to get dry."

As all eyes landed on her, she managed not to squirm. She never did like being the center of a room's attention. "Only just."

That got a smile from the other man and a cant of the head from the housekeeper. "A hot meal will set you to rights," said the woman, efficient feet already on the move. Her voice held more than a hint of the Irish.

Deverill stepped to the dining table and pulled out a chair. "My lady," he said, indicating she take the seat.

As she stepped around him to take the proffered seat, she couldn't resist a quick inhalation—just a sip of air. The air smelled so delicious around that man.

"Are your footmen out for the night?" she asked as she lowered onto saffron velvet.

It was a distancing question, but also one of genuine curiosity. An estate like Primrose Park should have a footman attending the master's dinner. Several, in fact.

But Primrose Park, clearly, wasn't like other estates.

"We haven't yet gotten the knack of footmen," said Deverill, taking his own seat at the head of the table, to Beatrix's left.

Her eyebrows lifted. *We?* Was the man now referring to himself in the royal *we?*

Before she could inquire, the housekeeper returned and set a large dish in the center of the table. A shepherd's pie, if Beatrix had to hazard a guess. A stray thought wondered if the formal dining room of Primrose Park had ever served a dish of shepherd's pie before Mr. Blake Deverill had become its owner? The scrumptious scent of savory meat and veg hit her nose, and her mouth watered and she decided she didn't care.

The housekeeper stood aside while two maids brought in a few more dishes and finished setting the table. Then the estate manager pulled out a chair for the housekeeper, and they settled into their places across the table from Beatrix.

Eyebrows crinkled together, she flashed a question toward Deverill. The blasted man was regarding her with clear amusement. "Lady Beatrix," he said, "may I introduce my parents, Mr. and Mrs. Deverill, to you?"

Beatrix felt her mouth wanting to gape open. She didn't allow it. Instead, she summoned every good manner that had been instilled within her—at finishing school, *not* at home—and said, "I'm so pleased to make your acquaintance."

That got a smile from each of the Deverills, and Beatrix felt a measure of relief. "No need to stand on formality with us, my dear," said Mr. Deverill.

"Blake," said Mrs. Deverill, reproachfully. It only occurred to Beatrix that, of course, his mother would call him by his given name. "You've gone and played a jape on poor Lady Beatrix?"

A sheepish smile acknowledged his mother's admonishment. "I might've been having a bit of fun," he said in the manner of a son who had charmed his mother from the moment of his birth.

It actually explained much about the man.

"No, I thought..." In her attempt to mitigate the situation, she might make it worse by finishing that sentence. Beatrix closed her mouth.

"You thought my parents were Primrose Park's estate manager and housekeeper?"

"I..."

At last, she was saved from digging herself deeper into the hole of her own making when Deverill said, "Well, you would've been right."

Again, Beatrix felt her eyebrows lift. Honestly, she'd never felt so aristocratic in her life.

"Now, Blake," said Mrs. Deverill without heat.

Deverill shrugged in a gesture of resignation. "I can't stop them."

"A lordly life of leisure isn't for the likes of us," said Mr. Deverill.

"How can you know if you don't try it?" asked his son, but there was no mistaking the wink in his voice. The argument had the worn-in timbre of one that would remain ever unresolved.

"A man must make himself," said Mr. Deverill. "Otherwise, what's the point of him?"

Mrs. Deverill nodded approvingly at her husband and reached for the shepherd's pie. She began spooning portions onto everyone's plates. "My son's favorite meal."

Beatrix cut a quick glance toward Deverill, who caught it and gave a little shrug. A smile pulled at her mouth.

When she took her first bite of the pie, her eyes drifted shut and she might've moaned. "I think," she began, "your shepherd's pie might now be my favorite meal, too, Mrs. Deverill."

It had been the truth *and* the right words to say. Now, everyone could relax and tuck in with ease. *Lady* Beatrix might be an aristocrat, but she wasn't a hoity-toity one.

As the meal progressed, she was able to sit quietly as talk proceeded around her. It was the conversation of a family who not only knew the details of one another's lives, but also shared in them. She rarely enjoyed a meal like this. Simple, delicious food...the company of people who adored one another.

And she liked one thing more.

Deverill hadn't introduced her to his parents as his fiancée. Their ruse for the *ton* didn't extend here—into the realm of his true family.

He had lines he didn't cross.

Which spoke well of him.

It was a question from Mrs. Deverill, however, that pricked her ear—and curiosity.

"And that Imogen?"

Composed of but three words, the question held a sharp blade running through its abbreviated length.

"Now, now, dearest heart," said Mr. Deverill, quelling.

"*Imogen?*" Beatrix found herself asking—as if she had the right.

She never could resist a pursuit when her curiosity was stirred.

Deverill gave his head a curt shake, the glint in his eye warning her off.

His mother, however, would heed no such warning. "She would be the Imogen who was the daughter of Baron Whitsby. The Imogen who Blake grew up alongside." She sniffed. "The Imogen who ended up a *countess*."

"Mama," said Deverill, "Lady Beatrix is the daughter of a marquess."

Mrs. Deverill fixed Beatrix with a look of sympathy. "None of us can help the accident of our birth, can we, love?"

Beatrix gathered she might've just been insulted and further gathered she didn't mind very much. In fact, a laugh bubbled up and spilled over. She didn't laugh very often and was a bit out of practice, which was the only explanation she could find for how long it went on.

Mr. Deverill gave a bemused shake of the head, while Mrs.

Deverill gave an approving nod. Their son settled back and watched, his expression unreadable.

At long last, Beatrix swiped a tear from her cheek. "Are we speaking of the Countess of Bridgewater?"

"Know her, do you?" asked Mrs. Deverill. It was clear she wouldn't count such an acquaintance in Beatrix's favor.

"All nobs know each other," said Mr. Deverill. "There's only so many of them."

Before Beatrix could assure them how very correct an observation that was, Deverill pushed back from the table and shot to his feet. "Would you like to meet Little Wicked, Lady Beatrix?"

"Oh, Blake," said Mrs. Deverill, "let the lady finish her meal." She met Beatrix's eye. "Would you care for a second portion, love?"

Beatrix thought it better to place her fork down. The stormy expression in Deverill's eyes said he wasn't truly asking. "I've quite taken my fill, Mrs. Deverill. I've never encountered a tastier shepherd's pie, I can assure you."

Then she was following Deverill through the house, one corridor after another, and through the kitchens, which filled with sudden quiet at the unexpected presence of the master of the house. In the boot room, before they stepped outside, she was handed an aged greatcoat to ward off the rain. The violence of the weather had abated to a steady downpour, so it was a quick dash across the grounds to the stables, which were a hive of activity, even at this evening hour, as lads and grooms scrambled about, attempting to soothe high-spirited horses still spooked from the storm.

In her time, Beatrix had seen all manner of stables, from the shabby and inexpertly run to the tip-top fitted out with only the best. Deverill's stable fell into the latter category with its spacious stalls, high, airy ceiling, and general air of cleanliness. He might have known nothing about horses or the world of racing, but he was a conscientious owner, one who did right by his stable. He'd hired the best to maintain it. Beatrix could only admire the resolve.

When they reached the last and roomiest box at the end of the central aisle, Deverill broke his silence. "Here's our best girl."

A chestnut beauty at sixteen hands high, Little Wicked was being groomed with steady smooth strokes by a lad humming a soothing tune, though the filly had no look of wildness in her eyes. If anything, she was basking in the attention.

"I've only seen her on the racecourse. Never this close," said Beatrix, her voice low, so as not to disturb the quieting atmosphere. "She's a beauty."

"Isn't she?"

"And you take good care of her."

Deverill snorted. "Coddle and spoil her, more like."

"Thoroughbreds are bred to be spoiled."

He dug into a pocket and came up with a lump of sugar. The filly stretched her neck and gentle lips took it off his extended palm as he stroked the velvet of her nose with his other hand.

"Is Little Wicked a one-off for you?" The question had been at the back of Beatrix's mind for some time. "Or are you out to establish a bloodline of racers?"

"I haven't decided yet." He appeared content to leave it at that.

She had another observation to make. "The field is almost set for the Race of the Century."

"Aye."

"The competition will be fierce." She was aware her voice had taken on the tone she used for extracting information for her articles.

Deverill cast her a knowing glance. He'd detected the tone. "Aye."

She figured she might as well continue as she'd started. "There's the Duke of Rakesley's Hannibal. His stable won't have eased up on training."

"Oh, I know all about the methods of Rakesley's stables."

She sensed a truth hidden just beyond sight. "How is that? Stables are secretive and guard their methods closely."

"If you must know—"

"I must."

"—When I won Little Wicked in that card game off Clifton, I knew nothing about horse racing. I thought the game rule number one was that everyone cheated."

Slow dread churned through Beatrix. "What did you do?"

"I hired a spy." He gave an unconcerned shrug.

If he thought she would let such a provocation pass, he didn't yet know anything about her. "You installed a spy in the Duke of Rakesley's stables?" She couldn't keep the incredulity from her voice.

"Aye," he said, nodding. "The practice is shockingly common." Another shrug. "I'm certainly housing a few spies in my own stables as we speak."

"That's beside the point." Her next question was most inappropriate, but so, too, were her entire dealings with this man. "Did you learn anything of value?"

"Nothing the grooms and trainers I'd hired didn't already know."

"And the spy?" she asked.

"You don't know how to let a matter drop, do you?"

Beatrix proceeded as if he hadn't spoken. "Is the spy still in Rakesley's stables?"

A dry laugh sounded through Deverill's nose. "In a manner of speaking."

She lifted her eyebrows and let them ask the next question for her.

"The duke up and married her."

It only took the split of a second for the implication of those words to sink into the air and find purchase in Beatrix's mind. "Are you saying the new Duchess of Rakesley was a—"

Deverill held up a single finger, staying the rest of the question in her mouth. "*That* does not find its way into one of your articles."

Fair play, she supposed. Deverill had no way of knowing that since Rakesley was the brother of her best friend, no gossip about him would ever flow from her pen. "Then you'll know," she said, "that Hannibal will be tough to beat."

Deverill nodded. "As will the Duchess of Acaster's Light Skirt and the Marquess of Ormonde's Filthy Habit. In fact, Little Wicked has yet to beat any of them."

"Then there's whoever wins the St. Leger in September."

"Aye." His attention returned to Little Wicked. "I know little about horses and racing, but there is something special about this filly, isn't there?"

Beatrix's eye assessed Little Wicked from muzzle to haunch. "She has a magic to her."

He nodded appreciatively. "*They* will have to beat *her* in the Race of the Century—not the other way round."

A question had been nagging at Beatrix for days—since before they'd entered into their arrangement, in fact. If there ever was a time to ask, it was now. "Why?"

Intense aquamarine eyes shifted and met hers. "*Why* what?"

"Why did you keep Little Wicked and become part of this world?"

Unreadable emotion flicked behind his eyes before he lifted them toward the ceiling. "The rains have passed."

And Beatrix heard it was true.

The rain had, at last, worn itself out, and the stable had gone silent.

"We'll be able to leave in the morning." He gave Little Wicked's muzzle a parting stroke and strode down the central aisle. "It's getting late," he tossed over his shoulder.

That was one way to avoid answering a question.

She knew the satisfaction of having struck a chord, even as she experienced the frustration of having been dismissed.

Her feet scrambled to catch him and only just did so as he was passing through the wide gate into the stable yard. However, she'd misjudged the solidity of the ground beneath her feet.

Or, rather, the slickness.

One moment, she'd drawn abreast with Deverill, a demand that he explain himself poised on her lips, and the next, the world went suddenly sideways as her foot skidded across a slick cobblestone and gravity had her tumbling arse over head.

Or it would've done.

A pair of quick, masculine hands shot out and grabbed her—and pulled her upright...

Into his broad chest that had all the give of a brick wall.

The tip of her nose could attest to the fact.

Her heart threatening to hammer free of her ribs, she went still and assessed herself. All seemed as it should be.

Well.

As it should be was also *not* the case.

For a pair of strong arms yet held her, leaving her no choice but to feel the length of his body along the length of hers...the warmth of him...the strength of him... She tipped her head back to inform him she could, indeed, stand on her own two feet, unassisted. But her gaze only made it as far as his mouth and the words became stuck in her throat.

His lips.

She'd dreamed of his lips.

It was shamefully true.

The beauty of them...the *feel* of them.

Of their own will, her feet were lifting onto the tips of her toes. Then her mouth found a will of its own, too, and was pressing to his...

Soft, yes...

Firm, too...

Delectable...

Kissable.

Lips that invited one to keep kissing them.

His hands tightened around her upper arms, and gently, he set her away from him, breaking the kiss as quickly as it had begun.

Aquamarine eyes glittered with bemusement. "What was that about?"

"Confirmation." She supposed that was the best word for it.

His eyebrows creased together. "*Confirmation?*"

"That your mouth is as kissable as I remembered."

A dry, flummoxed laugh escaped him. "An empirical exercise, then?"

When he put it like that… "Precisely."

CHAPTER SEVENTEEN

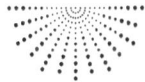

*I*t was possible Lady Beatrix was trying to be the death of him.

"So, this kiss..." Dev attempted to grab hold of the thought that had been hounding his heels since their kiss in the conservatory. "This kiss was an exercise?"

She blinked, drawing his attention to the dark fringe surrounding her gray eyes. They were more beautiful in this moment than he'd remembered.

"Pardon?" she asked.

Oh, how to articulate to her something he hadn't fully articulated to himself.

"The first kiss had been a show for others, and this one a confirmation for yourself?"

"Yes."

And it struck him like a thunderbolt... "That's not how kisses are supposed to be."

There.

That was his nagging thought articulated.

"Not a first kiss," he continued. "And certainly not a second kiss."

And Dev understood.

He had a kissing situation to rectify.

His hand slid around her waist, to the small of her back and snugged her against him. With his other hand, he cupped the back of her head. The breath had caught in her chest. He knew because if it hadn't, it would be whispering across his mouth. "A kiss shouldn't be a cold exercise," he muttered nearly against her lips. "A kiss should be hot and messy and desperate."

How small she was in his arms. Delicate, even.

"A kiss," he said, "should be like *this*."

And he lowered his mouth onto hers.

Slow and deep, this kiss was for her.

And perhaps for him, too.

For with this kiss, there was confirmation he sought, too.

Of an ineffable something that sparked between them.

Objectively, Lady Beatrix St. Vincent was pretty. There was nothing special about her scent or the color of her hair or the mode of her dress, which when left up to her was decidedly indifferent. Yes, her eyes were beautiful, but even so, beauty abounded in the world. Beauty was a superficiality that, in truth, had never held much interest for him.

But now, as he held her against his body and tangled his fingers through rain-damp hair and ran his tongue across her lower lip and pulled a feminine sigh from her parted mouth, he understood at a fundamental level there was something special in *this*.

In the spark between their bodies.

In the spark between their minds.

It was the latter spark he found most alluring.

That had him pulling her tighter to him and easing her until her back met the stable wall, tangling his tongue with hers, bending his knees so to press his cock suggestively against her, leaving no doubt about what effect a kiss—a *proper* kiss—should incite.

Her body's instinctive response only stoked the flame, as her hips gave a reactive swivel and her fingers wove through his hair. Breathless with newly discovered urgency, here was a woman entirely given over to a kiss—*his* kiss.

To make a woman so reliant on her intellect lose all control... Gratification soared through him, even as an elemental determination stirred.

The determination to see her completely undone.

This determination was wholly carnal, and he understood how close he was to taking it even farther—to completion.

No.

The voice in his mind was firm and final.

He couldn't take her against a stable wall.

No.

Before he could argue away what he knew was right, he placed his hands on her shoulders and broke away. A cry of frustration escaped her, as she slumped against the wall for support. Eyes bright, cheeks flushed, lips swollen, she stared out at him in obvious shock.

All he wanted—*body...mind...soul*—was to lean forward and kiss her again.

For confirmation.

No small amount of irony there.

She lowered her gaze, as if to gather her thoughts, and gasped.

And Dev became aware—of his raging cockstand.

Any attempt to cover it or shift his stance would only foreground the fact of it further, possibly render it a conversational topic.

Simply, there was no diminishing it.

She swallowed, and her gaze remained fixed.

When her gaze didn't lift of its own accord, he cleared his throat. Wide, gray eyes startled up and met his. So many emotions battled within those eyes—*guilt...curiosity...knowledge...*

Desire.

She might've been an innocent, but she understood the meaning of a man's raging cockstand.

"The, *erm*," she began on a croak. She cleared her throat. "The Countess of Bridgewater."

Dev hadn't been sure what her first words would be after what had transpired between them these last five minutes—one never knew with Lady Beatrix—but it hadn't been those.

"What about her?" he asked, wary.

"She's your reason." The sentence stood on its own for a beat of time before she expanded upon it. "For the acquisition of Little Wicked. For entering the world of horse racing. For our pretend engagement."

Dev held his silence.

She rightly took it as confirmation—*annoyingly*. "She's why you're out to prove yourself to the *ton*, no?"

Now, *there*, she'd missed the mark. "I have nothing to prove to those people."

She smiled, chastened, but undaunted. "You're correct. You don't. Take it from one who was born into their ranks, you're better than the lot of them." A slight pause before she amended, "With a few exceptions."

He crossed his arms over his chest and waited. She had yet more to say.

"But that doesn't change the fact that all this is about her. You're trying to prove something to the countess."

The certainty with which she spoke facts she couldn't, in fact, be sure of irked Dev. "*Imogen*," he said, the correction a reflex—a telling one.

Beatrix shook her head, firm and clear-eyed. "The countess will never be Imogen to me."

He could see there would be no getting out of this conversation without a spilling of the truth. "Imogen and I have known one another since childhood, but it wasn't until our teen years that friendship turned into something else."

"Infatuation."

"If you want to call it that." *Obsession* might've been more fitting. "I went away to school, and she—"

"Got married."

"Not that quickly. After school, I went into business with Mr. Shaw, and we started our steam engine business. We'd even made a success of it before she married."

Realization dawned across Beatrix's face. "You only lacked one thing." He didn't care for the hard, sharp glint that had entered her eye.

"And what was that?" he asked, even as he could predict the answer.

"You weren't an earl."

"What a very cynical lady you are." He wasn't above deflection. Still, she needed correcting. "It was Imogen's father who wanted an earl in the family."

Beatrix shook her head. "Women cannot be forced into marriage."

Dev was growing decidedly irritated with this woman. "You know nothing of the matter." Each syllable dripped ice.

"Oh, I know a few things," she said, undeterred by his sudden coldness. "Over the last several years, you've grown rich as Croesus. So, you thought what better use for all that hard-won blunt than to insinuate yourself into the *ton*—into your Imogen's world —and win your beloved back the way you've won everything." A beat of time calculated for drama ticked past. "With your money." A triumphant, little smile curled about her mouth. "Am I close?"

Though Dev's back teeth wanted to grind together, he didn't deny it. The blasted woman had hit the target close to dead center.

Close, but not quite.

"What you've described is the first step."

Beatrix's brow lifted, then realization lit within her eyes. "You mean divorce."

He nodded. The woman was quick, he would give her that.

She shook her head. "It would be next to impossible for her to secure a divorce from Bridgewater. They don't have children, but even so, the laws are notoriously strict."

"Imogen won't be applying for a divorce."

Beatrix's eyebrows winged together. "Pardon?"

Dev didn't owe her this explanation, yet he felt compelled to offer it. "Bridgewater needs money."

The words hung in the air while Beatrix's mind raced through them. Her brow released, revelation writ clear. "And *you* have money." As he'd known she would, she'd worked it out. "You're planning to offer Bridgewater money to divorce the countess."

"A fortune, in fact," he clarified. "I've made several; I won't miss one."

Beatrix's brow lifted with plain skepticism. "You truly believe Lady Bridgewater will cause the biggest scandal the *ton* has seen this century by agreeing to divorce the earl she worked so hard to secure?"

The question was blunt—and genuine.

"Imogen"—the Imogen Dev knew in his heart of hearts— "doesn't give a toss about any of that," he growled. "Her father worked for that title. It means nothing to someone like her."

"So, you've made yourself so successful and so impossible to ignore that she will leave Bridgewater to take up with you?"

Did she have to make it sound so...*tawdry*? So lacking in romantic feeling?

She crossed her arms over her chest, and the cant of her head shifted to the other side. She wasn't finished. All Dev could do was brace himself for the impact.

"And you would want someone like that?"

The breath stopped in his lungs. The blood might've stopped flowing in his veins. "Someone like what?" He'd never wanted anything else.

"Someone of such little substance that she would be swayed by money and...*things*. Someone who can be bought."

How was it that someone as intelligent as Beatrix couldn't see this? "I'm not proposing to *buy* Imogen. I'll present her with the option of a better life."

"What if she likes the life she has?"

Dev snorted. "Satisfaction with a life spent with the Earl of Bridgewater? Let's be serious."

Though disbelief shone in her eyes, Beatrix, at last, gave a nod. It wasn't curt, but firm...*decided*. She'd made up her mind about something.

Dev now knew her well enough to detect the signs.

"I know what you must do."

The statement was delivered with such certainty that he had to ask, "You do?"

She nodded, slowly, contemplatively. "Here's the thing about aristocrats. We love a country house party, and it so happens late summer is upon us, which is the season for house parties. *And* it also so happens that you own the perfect country estate for hosting a—"

"*House party*," Dev finished for her.

Though clear doubt sounded in his voice, Beatrix was becoming visibly more convinced of her rightness by the second. "It's actually perfect. You'll have every opportunity to flaunt your enormous wealth, and the *ton* will have every opportunity to be the recipients of it, which is a favorite pastime. You simply cannot lose."

"And inviting a parcel of aristocrats to Primrose Park will help me win Imogen?"

"The Earl and Countess of Bridgewater will be at the top of the guest list."

"They might not accept the invitation."

"As the owner of a moderately successful racing stable

himself, the earl won't be able to resist a look at your stables, and the countess won't be able to resist getting a look at..."

She let a meaningful lift of her eyebrows finish the sentence.

"*Me?*"

"Presumably."

A laugh startled from Dev—it couldn't help itself—and though Beatrix's plan was bold and unexpected, he thought it might be a good one.

"We must act swiftly," she continued, "as invitations need to be sent out within the next couple of days." She nodded in time to an internal dialogue. "Before the end of the month."

"That soon?"

"I see no need to wait."

Ah... "All the sooner to collect the second portion of your payment."

Even in the moonlight he detected the blush pinking her cheeks.

His own mind began making deductions. "I'll need to hire someone accustomed to managing such parties."

"You will, but I shall supervise."

"Oh?"

A smile tipped one side of her mouth. "I'd hate to think all the blunt I spent on finishing school was wasted."

"Blunt *you* spent on finishing school?"

"No one else was about to."

"How were you able to do that?"

"When I was a child, it amused Lydon and his cronies to give me betting money at the races."

"And you won?"

She shrugged a modest shoulder. "More than some."

Dev tried not to let his surprise show. Lady Beatrix was an altogether different sort of lady.

"And I saved it all."

"For finishing school?"

"A portion of it."

She hadn't quite answered his question. If she yet remained in possession of a farthing, she certainly hadn't spent it, considering the near penury of her living circumstances.

The lingering question must've shown on his face, for she continued. "The remaining nine hundred pounds was to have been spent on one shining season on the marriage mart."

No mistaking the irony there.

Her one shining season hadn't gone to plan.

"You didn't marry."

"No one wanted to shackle themselves to the Marquess of Lydon, not even through his daughter."

"Surely, that wouldn't have mattered." Dev's hands found themselves wanting to clench into Destroyers of Worlds.

"At the first ball of the season, the gentlemen ranked all the young ladies who had come out."

It was the flatness of her voice that gave her away—that gave away the residual hurt.

Through dread, Dev asked, "What were you ranked?"

"Oh, they didn't bother ranking me."

It was worse than he thought.

But with that answer, she confirmed her *why* for him—why she'd entered into their arrangement. "With the money from me, you're providing yourself with a dowry."

She didn't deny it. "A chance at a good, solid future with a good, solid husband."

Dev nodded, even as he privately thought *good* and *solid* sounded like a dead boring way to slog through one's days. But he supposed her life until now had provided a certain motivation toward uniformity.

Lady Beatrix St. Vincent wasn't only clear-headed, intelligent, and pragmatic.

She was *strong*.

A bemused laugh issued from her mouth that was yet a little kiss-swollen. "Well, that's the air clear between us, isn't it."

Dev chuckled along with her. "Like old friends."

Her eyebrows formed a quizzical line. "I've never had a friend like *you*, Lord Devil."

That pulled another chuckle from him.

"Can I ask you something?"

"Anything." He found he was in the mood to mean it.

"*Anything?*"

He spread his hands wide. "I'm an open book to an old friend such as yourself."

She gave a wry shake of the head, even as her curiosity remained undeterred. "If you're so in love with the countess, then why do you, *hmm—*"

She was searching for a word, and Dev couldn't wait with any but held breath.

"Why do you *kiss* other women?"

She wanted to say more, that was clear, but she'd said enough with the aloud *kiss*—and implied yet more beneath her words.

Dev cocked his head. "Do you imagine me some sort of— *what?*—noble celibate?"

She blinked.

"Sir Lancelot, I'm not, I can assure you, Beatrix. I think you're fully aware of that by now."

Her mouth parted slightly and looked as if it wanted to gape open. She snapped it shut. Then opened it again. "Do you want to hear what I think?"

If he was being honest… "Maybe…" Or… "Possibly not…" But actually… "Yes."

The fact was he wanted to hear what she thought—*irritatingly*.

"How you think of the countess…"

"*Imogen.*"

"What she represents to you is…" She looked as if she'd

decided to leave the sentence unfinished. Then she said, "A fantasy."

Dev might have to rethink the parameters of this friendship. "How I *feel* about Imogen is real."

Beatrix considered him for the space of three uncomfortable heartbeats, then gave a noncommittal shrug—and let the matter drop.

"It's getting late." It couldn't have been later than half eight. "I'll walk you to your rooms."

"I can see myself there." She turned on her heel. Apparently, she was as eager to be rid of him, as she tossed over her shoulder, "I bid you good night."

And he was content to let her have her way.

After a quick consult with his head groom to ensure all was ticking along smoothly in the stable, Dev made a slow journey toward the house, the night sky now bright and crisp with starshine, two women on his mind.

The one who had always been there—and the one he'd invited in.

A strange paradox had opened within him, and unlike the sky above, his mind was less clear than it had ever been.

It had to do with the kiss.

Not the first or the second, but the third.

The kiss that had naught to do with calculation or confirmation.

A kiss born of the stuff of the best kisses—pure, naked wanting.

A kiss with the power to crack open a dichotomy in a man's mind.

And like the sky above, he suspected a storm would have to sweep through before all became clear again.

CHAPTER EIGHTEEN

LONDON, A FEW DAYS LATER

*B*eatrix nodded approvingly at the tea presentation, and the maid gave a small curtsy and departed.

She released the breath she hadn't been aware of holding.

Every day was like this.

Every morning, her eyes opened on a new day, expecting this life she'd somehow fallen into to have been a dream.

Then the chambermaid arrived to open the curtains and deliver the hot chocolate she'd become positively addicted to and Beatrix realized she would be living inside the dream one day more.

Now, it was evening, and her nighttime tea had been delivered, along with a separate tray that overflowed with correspondence.

It had been a long while since she hadn't served herself tea.

How different her life was since Blake Deverill had entered it —a house full of servants…said house rendered spotless due to said servants…a pantry full of food…a French cook to prepare said food…a wardrobe stuffed with new dresses…and a tray full of correspondence.

And not just any correspondence.

Invitations.

Her status as the daughter of a marquess had always ensured she was invited everywhere—to balls...to soirées...to musicales... and such.

But the invitations now filling her correspondence tray were of a different variety. They were invitations for morning strolls and afternoon teas. The sort of invitations extended from one lady to another so they might further their acquaintance.

And it was down to a single lie: Lady Beatrix St. Vincent was the fiancée of Mr. Blake Deverill.

These ladies wanted to meet with her to get to the bottom of a single, fundamental question.

How had the unremarkable, spinster-adjacent daughter of the wastrel Marquess of Lydon secured the most exciting man to enter the *ton* since Lord Byron took himself off to the Continent?

How had such a woman captured the affections of such a man?

Members of the *ton* were beside themselves attempting to uncover that particular truth.

Oh, doubtless the gossip was bursting with theories abundant. But that was all they were—*guesses*. There were no facts.

Only she and Deverill knew the truth.

And she planned to keep it that way.

To distract herself from thoughts of that man, she poured herself a cup of tea, and while it cooled, she reached for a raspberry biscuit. A sweet ever held the power to consume her entirely—for a blissful moment, at least.

But it was no use.

As had become usual, one thought of Deverill led to another, then on to an inevitable destination.

The kiss.

That was yet another way her life had changed since he'd entered it.

She'd been kissed.

Thrice, in fact.

The first kiss had kindled her curiosity.

The second had confirmed the pleasure of the first.

But the third kiss…

Blimey.

A kiss should be like this.

The third kiss had revealed the previous two kisses to be mere shadows of a kiss.

She hadn't known a kiss could unsettle the very foundations below a person's feet.

But really, that was only the beginning of what she hadn't known a kiss could do.

A kiss should be hot and messy and desperate.

And that was precisely what the third kiss had been—*hot... messy...desperate.*

Fingers that yet held a residual tremble reached for the top letter in the correspondence tray.

Anything to distract herself from that kiss.

It preyed too much on the mind.

As she thumbed through missive after missive, it was exactly as she'd thought. Invitations, with a few bills for Lydon sprinkled in—*of course*. It was a good thing her father was a peer of the realm, for if he hadn't been, he'd likely be serving a decades-long sentence in the Marshalsea for debt.

The next missive produced a smile as she lifted rich cream parchment to her nose. *Honeysuckle.* Just as she'd instructed.

She snapped the crimson wax seal on the invitation and took in the gold-embossed contents she'd dictated, word for word:

To the most esteemed Lady Beatrix St. Vincent:
The pleasure of your company is most cordially desired
at the
Primrose Park estate
of

Mr. Blake Deverill
Entertainments will commence on
28 July
and conclude on
1 August

Beatrix's eye caught on a word, and her brow lightly crinkled. *Desired.*

It had been a word, in fact, that had been much on her mind these last few days, and there it was, staring up at her, brazenly.

Requested would have been the more proper word.

Now that impropriety had begun to govern her behavior, it was slipping into her lexicon, too.

Yet, even the fussiest peer would have difficulty turning down this invitation—even with its whiff of the improper.

For Beatrix, however, it held a whiff of something else, too—*hope.*

The future she'd so craved was almost hers.

At this house party, Deverill would win the countess. And if he couldn't win her at his beautiful, luxurious estate where his every advantage would not only be displayed, but forced into one's face, then there never had been any hope for him, anyway.

And Beatrix would have her final payment for pretend-fiancée-services rendered.

Her *dowry.*

Soon.

So soon she could almost taste her future.

Her gaze reluctantly slid over to the other stack of letters—the debts. On a resigned sigh, she reached for the top one and cracked its seal. She wouldn't miss receiving these in her good, solid future.

She scanned the contents, knowing what to expect, and blinked.

Somehow, this debt letter wasn't what she'd expected at all.

Her eyes moved across it again.

And again.

And...*again*.

If she was putting the sequence of words together correctly—and by now, she should have been—Lydon's debts were no longer *debts* in the plural sense.

Rather, they were now *a debt*.

A debt owned by a sole entity.

Blaze Jagger.

The vision of a rangy, handsome figure filled her mind's eye. The young, arrogant, cocksure blackleg who had introduced himself to her at the Hampstead races.

That man now held all Lydon's debt and the note on the very Mayfair townhouse she'd occupied all her life.

Her attention caught on a string of numbers, and the bottom fell out of her stomach.

£19,881.

Such a precise number.

Enough to send Lydon into bankruptcy and have everything unentailed seized and sold.

Everything, that was, that Lydon hadn't already sold himself.

The roof over her head was as good as gone. She should start packing her bags for the crumbling family pile in Bedfordshire.

Except...

She did have money, didn't she?

Or, at least, she would very soon.

A sob formed in her throat and sat there, a hard, unresolved knot.

Likely, it would sit unresolved for the rest of her days.

She must pay Lydon's debt.

If she wanted to keep both the roof over her head and her good name, she had no choice.

And like that, her dowry and her good, solid future disappeared before her eyes.

To think, for an instant, she'd allowed herself to envision one.

Blaze Jagger.

The name cut through her like a curse.

With sudden determination, and ignoring the tears of fury and frustration and no small amount of hurt, she shot to her feet and dashed into the receiving hall. A frenzied search of her reticule found the item she sought.

A calling card.

Mr. Blaze Jagger
Tom of All Trades Extraordinaire
The Archangel

Resolve steeled within her.

Blaze Jagger, Tom of All Trades Extraordinaire, wanted her to pop in to The Archangel for a nice, little chat?

Oh, they would have a chat, indeed.

But it wouldn't be nice.

* * *

THE ARCHANGEL

Dev gave the Hazard dice an indifferent toss and stifled a yawn.

It was just as well he threw out on the first roll.

He was dead bored.

Typically, he enjoyed a rattle of the Hazard dice or a game of Macao as much as the next man. But it was habit that had him here tonight, as he made a point of frequenting The Archangel once a week. To show that he belonged to one of London's most exclusive gaming hells. That he belonged everywhere any lord of the *ton* belonged.

Really though, the night's work had already been accomplished in that capacity.

In fact, he was feeling fairly gratified at the moment. The Earl of Bridgewater had just deigned to inform him personally that he and the countess would attend the house party at Primrose Park. Further, the earl had made it abundantly clear that he intended to tour the stables and meet Little Wicked.

Beatrix had been correct on that point.

The woman was correct on many points, in fact.

Dev loved a good plan, particularly when matters behaved as they should and proceeded as expected.

And he had Beatrix to thank.

A clever woman was Lady Beatrix St. Vincent.

A clever woman who wanted to waste herself on a good, solid future.

He gave his head a bemused shake.

There was no accounting for wants and desires.

And just as he didn't understand hers, she didn't understand his.

Fair play.

He gathered his markers and began making his way toward the exit when a figure flashed at the edge of his vision. It would've been unremarkable, except…

It was a feminine figure—in an all-male establishment.

Which incited a boisterous buzz that washed through the club with the suddenness of a tsunami wave.

Recognition stirred as he pivoted—and there came confirmation.

Lady Beatrix St. Vincent…

Here.

At The Archangel.

Striding through the club like a Fury.

And she wasn't simply any woman causing a scene.

In the eyes of all in this room, this Fury was his fiancée.

Right.

Of their own accord, his feet were already in motion, alarm firing through him.

He reached the study in time to hear her call out—and for the benefit of no fewer than ten sets of ears, "Jagger, you and I have business."

Jagger had been conferring with the club's doorman, his back to her, but slowly, he turned, a single eyebrow lifted, his entire being glittering with arrogance. "Do we now, Lady Beatrix?" The smile curving his mouth was not unlike a tiger's as it held a mouse squirming beneath its paw. "And what business is that, pray tell?"

Dev doubted the ten sets of ears populating the room had ever listened so hard in all their lives.

Before Beatrix could respond with the answer ready on her lips, Dev was across the room and threading his hand through the crook of her arm. Startled gray eyes rounded on him. The next instant, they were shooting daggers.

He cared not.

The woman had already caused more than a minor sensation.

He had a scandal to avert.

"Let's take this conversation upstairs, shall we?" He kept his tone breezy and absent of heat. They could've been discussing the weather.

The arrogant glint in Jagger's eye didn't falter. "I'm content with the good lady having her say here."

"As am I," agreed Beatrix.

As were all The Archangel's patrons.

"*Private*," said Dev in a low voice that would brook no smart talk.

Jagger sucked his teeth before giving a shrug of a shoulder. "If you'll follow me."

He led them through the club—*paraded*, more like—and up the stairs to the second-floor office. Dev made sure the door was closed firmly behind them.

He knew that particular set to Beatrix's jaw. The woman was in deep dudgeon.

The few intervening minutes had neither cooled nor soothed her.

Jagger cocked a hip onto the large oak desk and crossed his arms over his chest—and waited with a smirk perched on his mouth.

"Lydon's debt," she bit out.

Dev didn't understand what she meant by it, but no curiosity shone in Jagger's eyes. "What about it?"

"You've bought every last note."

Jagger sniffed. "Oh, I'm sure there are more out there. He does get about."

Beatrix remained in no mood to engage in a bit of levity. She waited—and glowered.

"Must admit, though, to a bit of surprise that he came running to you about it."

Utter disbelief shone in her eyes. "You think Lydon opens his mail?"

Jagger spread his hands wide. "You got me there. I reckon he wouldn't."

"*Why?*" she demanded. "Why have you bought Lydon's debt?"

"An investment, if you will."

She shook her head. "No."

"*No?*"

"No one possessed of half a brain would invest in Lydon"

Jagger cocked his head. "Should I take that as a compliment?"

"Take it as you like, but I know one thing." The words hung in the air for an extra beat of time. "You're out to ruin him."

"I'm just holding on to the debts." An intensity entered Jagger's eyes that belied his easy manner. "For now."

Beatrix's sharp inhalation rent the air. She'd heard the truth as clearly as Dev had—and something more within the single space between those two simple words.

For now.

Not indefinitely.

When she opened her mouth to speak, her voice was low and rasped with emotion barely suppressed. "You can take possession of the Mayfair townhouse any time you like."

The smile that curved Jagger's mouth sent a ripple of foreboding through Dev.

"Now, now," said the rogue, his voice rich with condescension. "What sort of brother would turf his own sister out on her arse?"

CHAPTER NINETEEN

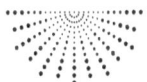

*T*he loudest silence Dev ever experienced expanded through the air until he thought it would surely burst from the tension.

The hot flush of high emotion drained from Beatrix's face. "I'm no one's…"

The next word—*sister*—died on her tongue as she stared into Jagger's eyes—

his opaque gray eyes…fringed with thick black lashes…

Certainty crept through Dev—the same certainty that would be creeping through Beatrix.

The infamous blackleg, Blaze Jagger, was Lydon's by-blow—her brother from the other side of the blanket.

"Soon," she said, her voice a reedy scratch across her throat. "Soon, I'll have funds."

Dev's brow dug trenches into his forehead. "Now, wait a minute."

Neither sibling heeded him.

"*Funds?*" Jagger looked plainly skeptical.

She swallowed. "I'll be able to pay off a sizable portion of the debt."

"*Beatrix.*" Dev attempted to imbue his voice with an authority he didn't hold. "You'll do no such thing."

He might as well have been issuing commands to the four walls, for all the consideration she gave him.

Jagger's attention remained wholly focused on her. "Now, dear sister Lady Beatrix, what are you thinking to do to secure that amount of blunt?" For the first time since they'd convened in the office, his gaze cut toward Dev. "Maybe marry some chap?"

"That's none of your concern," she said, her chin lifting. Dev was relieved to witness a return of her spirit. "I'll have it by the end of the month. Promise me you'll continue to hold the note until then."

"And what would the promise of a bastard like me mean to a lady like you?" asked Jagger. No small amount of bitterness laced the question.

Beatrix held her brother's gaze. "If you give your word, I'll believe you."

With those words, earnestly spoken, Jagger's pretense, arrogance, and condescension fell away as he stared intently into his sister's eyes. He would see the truth in there. Tightly, he nodded.

Dev knew a moment for farewell when he met it. "Jagger," he said, firmly. He glanced down. "Beatrix?"

A beat of time ticked past as brother and sister continued to regard one another. Then she nodded and allowed Dev to lead her out of the office and The Archangel. It was a silent ride through London as she stared out the carriage window. Her mind would've been awhirl with all that had transpired tonight.

Dev's certainly was.

Blaze Jagger…the bastard son of the Marquess of Lydon.

The holder of Lydon's debt.

None of which were problems of Beatrix's making.

All of which affected every corner of her life down to the very roof over her head.

It was only when the carriage was rolling to a stop that he realized he'd allowed the coachman to bring them to Mivart's.

Perhaps it was for the best.

Beatrix needed to give air to what was whizzing through her mind. Otherwise, she might burst from it.

Inside his suite of rooms, he strode to the liquor cart and poured two generous brandies, placing one in Beatrix's hand before guiding her to the sofa.

She hadn't yet spoken.

And it was making him nervous.

He sat on one end of the sofa, and she on the other.

She stared into the viscous amber depths of the brandy.

He cleared his throat.

She continued to stare into the brandy.

Slightly frustrated, he unbuttoned his evening jacket.

Her gaze flicked up and followed the movements.

Progress, he supposed.

In the name of progress, and of making himself comfortable, he unbuttoned his waistcoat and shrugged it off along with the jacket.

Her eyes tracked every movement from beneath black lashes.

His fingers wrapped around his cravat and tugged it loose.

Her gaze lifted, at last, and met his. "What are you doing?"

"Well…"

"Are you trying to distract me?"

Was he? "I don't think so." *Or was he?* "But I can continue if you think it will succeed."

His attempt at levity struck on deaf ears.

Actually, it was worse.

Her eyes went glassy with unshed tears.

"Beatrix," he said. But he didn't have any other words for her.

"I was so close." The tears fell in twin streams down her cheeks in the same instant a sob broke from her throat. "All my dreams," she cried, pounding a fist on her knee. "Gone…*again.*"

Dev never felt so ineffectual in his life. He couldn't simply sit here and watch Beatrix weep over her dashed dreams.

Those good, solid dreams of hers.

Even if those dreams weren't worthy of her, they were *her* dreams and he couldn't bear to see her shedding tears over their loss.

"Drink your brandy," he said, firmly—more firmly than he had a right to.

"I don't…want…*brandy*," she wailed.

An object on the table caught his attention. *Of course.* He had the box of chocolates open two seconds later. "Have a truffle."

Her bottom lip trembled as her gaze lifted. Sadness, anger, frustration, and annoyance shone out at him. But the tears didn't stop. "I don't want chocolate."

Again, his gaze cast about, and he grabbed the nearest moveable object—a blanket of the softest East Asian cashmere. "Are you cold?"

She huffed in bemusement. "Have you never comforted someone in distress?"

Actually… "I don't think I have."

"Well, you're not great at it." The words came on a wet hiccough.

"Tell me what I'm supposed to do."

"You're supposed to ask the other person what's happened."

"But I know what's happened. I was there."

She heaved a trembly sigh. "I suppose you were." She shook her head, utter disbelief in the movement. "What a family I have."

Dev judged it best to hold his tongue.

"But I was *so close* this time."

"None of it has to affect you." It had to be said.

"*That*," she said, "is not true. If I ignore it, say, and buy a modest house in a less fashionable part of London with my money from you, I'll have to sit by while my scandalous half-brother ruins my father for the entertainment of all London. In which case, I won't be left with a good name, and what self-respecting, decent man would have me then?"

Dev wished she wouldn't speak of herself thusly—as if she were chattel. It diminished all she was.

"Or," she continued, "I buy some time."

"With the money from our arrangement?"

She gave a tight nod. "Of course, it won't be enough."

"Beatrix—" She needed to hear this. "It will never be enough. Lydon won't change his ways."

She threw frustrated hands into the air. "What choice do I have?" She appeared to be working herself into another bout of tears. "I'll be penniless, but I'll have my name. Nothing new in that." Misery edged her voice. "Destined for spinsterhood either way."

Dev was tired of this. "Has it never occurred to you that a man would want you as...*you?*"

Her brow gathered as if he'd begun speaking German. "One hasn't yet."

"Your eyes," Dev found himself saying. "They are remarkable."

She blinked. "My eyes are...*remarkable?*"

"Arresting."

"*Arresting?*"

"Beautiful."

She touched light fingertips to her mouth.

He couldn't tell if her reaction indicated distress or utter befuddlement, so he continued for some reason absolutely due to a fleeting madness. "And your figure is lissome."

"*Lissome?*"

"Comely."

"*Comely?*"

"Desirable."

It was as if all the air had vacated the room.

Dev wasn't pleased with himself. These qualities of Beatrix's... They were the superficial.

"Your spirit…" Oh, he was entering some uncharted territory here… "Your spirit is fierce and bold." And yet he kept speaking… "And your intelligence is without equal." And on, he went… "And when you give over to an endeavor, it's with focus and passion."

"*Passion?*"

Dev nodded—and swallowed.

He might be in trouble.

Her pupils flared.

Her breath had become quick and shallow.

He was noticing the flare of her pupils and the quickness of her breath.

He was definitely in trouble.

Her gaze remained steady on him. "Are you telling me all this as my friend?"

No, Dev didn't—*couldn't*—say.

So, he nodded.

The safer option.

"Here's the thing." Her voice had become throaty and slightly breathless, and she'd shifted position on the sofa—closing the distance between them by half, in fact.

Dev remained very, very still.

"Yes?" he uttered. He couldn't understand why his heart thundered in his chest like a stampede of racehorses.

"I don't think I want to be your friend."

It was incredibly dramatic how it felt as if his stomach had dropped entirely out of his body. "You don't?"

She halved the distance between them again.

Again, he remained stone still.

"I don't think I *can* be only your friend."

Before his heart could perform more dramatics in his chest, his ear caught upon a word.

Only.

That *only* implied…*more.*

"What would you like to be?"

Now who had gone breathless?

"I don't want to define it."

There was much she was saying below the surface of those words, and he would give it air... "Would you like to be my something more?"

It was only they two in the wide world now.

"Yes."

CHAPTER TWENTY

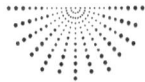

*W*ould you like to be my something more?

As if a simple *yes* could encompass the dire necessity pulsing through Beatrix.

As if she'd ever wanted anything more in her life.

"You've shown me what more a kiss can be. Now," she said, driven by an instinct that held demands, "I want you to show me where more *leads*."

"Beatrix…" The low rumble of Dev's voice quaked through her and settled deep within, made her knees squeeze together with ache. "This isn't a good idea."

She understood that.

Truly, she did.

But here was the thing.

She didn't care.

Tonight, all her hopes and dreams for a good, solid future with a good, solid husband had come to a crashing end.

So, tonight, she would have this man.

He didn't have to be good or solid or her future.

All he had to be tonight was her *something more*.

Again, she halved the distance between them. Now they were

separated by inches. So close she caught his scent of pine and fresh, salty sea and inhaled a sip of air that contained him and held it in her lungs, letting it penetrate her from deep within.

She hardly knew herself, driven as she was by this instinct. Emboldened by the way he watched her—both wary and desirous—by the way he held so still, as if he didn't trust himself to move.

As if doing so would incite an utter and complete ravishment.

This was power.

She would say it was power unlike any she'd ever felt, but she'd never experienced power in any sense.

But here she was, a mere woman, with the power to seduce the most attractive man she'd ever laid eyes on.

And she was going to use it.

She reached out and caressed his cheek, dark stubble scratchy against her palm, following the strong line of his jaw. Unable to resist, her thumb slid along his full bottom lip. Oh, how she ached to replace her thumb with her tongue.

"You have a reputation, Lord Devil." She hardly knew her voice.

"Aye." Nothing he wouldn't already know.

Oh, the bolt of desire his confidence arrowed through her.

With one hand she grabbed her skirts, as with the other she reached for his shoulder, and with a flurry of motion she moved inelegantly to straddle him.

Yet, still, his hands remained at his sides—even as she now sat astride him.

The thought occurred to her that women might attack him thusly on a nightly basis.

His head tipped back; he watched her as if from a great distance.

In fact, they were very close.

So close she could…

She gave her hips a bold swivel.

There.

She felt it.

Through the muslin of her chemise and the superfine of his trousers, his manhood—*hard...thick.*

It seemed the sort of implement that would be equal to any task.

A shiver crawled through her.

"Beatrix..."

Oh, how she liked the sound of her name pouring from his mouth on a plea.

"Now, Lord Devil, it's time you earn your reputation."

Within his fiery aquamarine eyes that pierced and prodded, she saw resistance give way to surrender, then harden into something that struck through her on an elemental chord—from man to woman.

Intention.

His intention to have her.

She lowered her mouth to his—*at last*—and his hands—*finally* —moved...from calves, following the seam of her stockings up to the garters above her knees...trailing along her thighs...across her bottom...up to her hips...grabbing hold as he pressed her hard against him, her sex grinding along his rigid length.

She gasped as novel sensation cascaded through her—all of it pleasurable.

"Oh, do that again," she murmured against his lips.

She felt him smile against her mouth.

And he did.

From the center of her sex, lightning spiderwebbed through her veins, nerve endings lit alive.

Heady and daring, this was the feeling of freedom. With this man, she could do whatever she liked, such was the communication between their bodies that didn't need words to be spoken.

And what she would like now was to see *him*...to feel *him* against her bare skin.

His mouth pressed against the crook of her neck, almost undoing her intention, but down his body her hands proceeded, awed fingertips brushing across the falls of his trousers...the turgid length of his aroused shaft.

The size of him.

Once, she'd seen a depiction of Michelangelo's *David* in a book on Italian art. In many ways, Beatrix could see how Deverill's form mirrored that of the hero's—muscles precisely delineated into near god-like lines and curves.

Except in this one area—his manhood.

The statue of David had in no way prepared her for what lay beneath the falls of Deverill's trousers.

Overcome with curiosity and determination, she settled slightly back and unfastened one button at a time, her heart seeming to double its rate with each button freed.

The cloth fell away, and she inhaled a gasp.

Bold.

His was a manhood with no need to apologize for itself.

Oh, the wickedness that sparked within his eyes. "Like what you see?"

How his wickedness delighted her.

"I'm not sure yet." She could be wicked, too. "Further investigation will be necessary."

A dry chuckle rumbled through him.

Driven by the necessity of the moment, her hand wrapped around him, finger by curious finger. So very, impossibly hard... and *hot*, yet...the skin soft like velvet. Instinctively, she moved her hand up its length, and a groan poured from his parted lips as eyes half-lidded with desire watched her explore him.

Though she straddled his legs, her thighs wanted to squeeze together with a fresh wave of arousal as he watched her pleasure him with her hand.

Emboldened, she squeezed tighter and moved with building confidence.

The raw desire in his eyes… She inspired that.

He slid lower on sofa cushions, his legs sprawled beneath her as he let her have her way with him—and watched.

Blimey.

Now she understood stolen moments between lovers, the willingness to risk all for…*this*.

On a groan, he reached out and covered her hand with his. "That will be enough for now."

Her brow creased. "I thought you were enjoying my, *erm*, ministrations."

"Let us enjoy some other *ministrations* before I enjoy myself too much."

Ah. He was afraid he would spill. She might've been new to this, but she understood the basic mechanics of the act.

In a swift fluidity of motion, he drew her tight into his body and stood. Instinctively, she wrapped her arms around his neck and pressed her mouth to his throat, the hard, alive throb of his pulse against her lips, as he carried her into his bedroom. The large, four-poster bed had the covers turned down, as it awaited the presence of its master.

Alive.

That was the word that best described the sensations whirring through her.

Her body had never felt more alive…*enlivened*.

When they reached the bed, he released the arm beneath her legs and set her on her feet. Her head tipped back. The look in his eyes—*determined…intent*—had her hands moving…reaching for the hem of his untucked shirt, pushing it up his torso and over his head, tousling his thick black hair. His hands responded in kind, fingers nimbly unbuttoning her dress, sliding it off her shoulders and letting it fall to the floor.

They each took a second to gaze upon the other revealed. Oh, his chest was as she remembered—broad…lightly fuzzed with fine black hair…muscles dense and well-defined.

SOFIE DARLING

But it was his eyes that called most to her, as they gazed upon her clad in naught but chemise and stockings. She'd lost her slippers somewhere in sofa cushions.

He wanted her.

Perhaps as badly as she wanted him.

Perhaps desperately.

A wicked smile tipped one corner of his mouth. "Shall I return the favor for you?"

"What..." The question faded as quickly as begun. She knew what favor. And... "Oh, yes."

Firm, masculine fingers wrapped around her waist and eased her back against the bed. As her bottom perched on the cushy edge, he moved forward, pressing her back, lying her down, the length of his body poised above, their faces inches apart. Into his eyes she gazed, and he into hers, their breath shallow and quick, mingling. He dipped his head and took her mouth with his in a slow, languorous kiss. The sort of kiss that slipped deep into a soul.

He angled his body slightly to the side of hers, supported by his forearm. His other hand slid across her skin, teasing a trail of goose bumps as it went—cupping her breast, giving the nipple a light pinch...across her stomach...into the curls of her mons pubis...

And still he kissed her, their tongues tangling, as a light fingertip grazed along her slit, pulling a moan from her as her hips tilted and pleaded for more.

Then she felt it—the slide of his finger...him entering her, slowly pushing inside.

Her sex had been waiting all its life for this moment.

For...*Blake Deverill.*

How full she felt as he penetrated her, her body discovering a rhythm with the motion. With each thrust of his finger, lightning shot through her veins. Her sex felt...*oh*...pleasured.

Brimming with so much pleasure.

Yet, still, it wasn't enough.

Something inside her had awakened and wanted—*demanded*—more, as she felt herself beginning to strain and take all of him. It seemed her quim wasn't opposed to begging.

And getting ideas, too.

If this was how his fingers felt, then how much *more* would his manhood feel?

The question produced a frisson of trepidation, but also... *need*.

She needed to know.

She tore her mouth from his. "Dev."

He angled slightly back. "You're sure?" He knew what she'd left unsaid.

"I am."

His gaze searched hers for another three seconds—the longest three seconds of her life.

He could say *no*.

And that would be the end of it.

Instead, he nodded.

Triumph soared through her. This man... He wasn't a perfect man, but he ever took her at her word. He trusted her to know herself.

Even if he, like she, knew that on the morrow another belief would come—that tonight had been the height of foolishness.

His finger eased from her, and her thighs squeezed together, aching at the absence of him. He slid off the bed and made short work of the rest of his clothing. Then he was reaching across her and slipping her chemise over her head. "What a beauty you are, Beatrix."

She nearly snorted—*nearly*.

It was the utter seriousness in his eyes that held it back.

Whether she believed his words mattered not. He believed them, and something in her blossomed.

Again, he eased his body onto hers, her legs opening to

accommodate him. The air between them grew intimate and close. As he took his length in hand, she tilted her hips to receive him.

No one had taught her this.

No one needed to.

Feminine instinct was her guide.

Then she felt it—the press of him against her. His mouth met her ear, and her name was easing from him as he pushed with slow, deliberate force. The breath caught in her lungs as he filled her, inch by inch. She'd seen with her eyes how very big he was. But seeing and feeling were two very different sensations. For a wild instant, she wondered how all of him could fit. Then he pressed yet another inch deeper, and she was adjusting to the feel of him all over again.

"Are you all right?" His voice was a rasped growl that sent shivers through her.

She nodded—and hoped she did so convincingly.

As uncomfortable as the surface of this act was, a deeper part of her absolutely needed him to keep going. *Slowly...slowly...*he penetrated her and she had to wonder if the length of him would ever end.

"We don't have to do more than this," he said into the space between their mouths, his voice ragged. "We can go back to what we were doing before."

She shook her head, adamant. "There's no going back, do you understand me?" She meant it quite literally, but it couldn't help feeling like a metaphor, too. Anyway, she wasn't asking. "Prove yourself to me, Lord Devil."

The light of challenge in his eyes, he reached beneath her and cupped her bottom, steadying her as he pushed *impossibly* deeper. It wasn't only the feel of him that required adjustment, but also this need...this feel of...*completion*.

Until this moment, she'd considered herself an entity complete unto herself.

But *this—him inside her...filling her*—offered a different possibility.

That she'd been incomplete.

Until she'd joined her body with his.

Until...*now.*

What strange, wondrous workings of the mind this act wrought.

He began to move, and the feeling of him consumed her, as all her senses heightened to take every bit of him inside. His male scent...his moans...the taste of him as her tongue followed a bead of sweat along his throat... But the sensation most acute was that of *feel*—her quim's slick acceptance of his hard length...the thickness of him stretching her...

Yet through that superficial pain pushed a deeper pleasure. This act...it felt, *oh*, good.

"Sweet Bea," he rasped. "You are perfection."

Sweet Bea.

She wouldn't have thought herself the sort of woman who would respond to a little endearment.

But it turned out she was.

Deeper, he impaled her—and deeper, she took him. His movements became more focused, somehow his manhood harder, as he drove into her. "Bea, are you..." he muttered. "Are you close?"

"*Close?*" The question a breathless gasp. "Close to what?"

"*Blast.*" Every muscle in his body went rigid with tension as he slowed his motion. "I need to—"

She wasn't about to allow him to finish that sentence. "*Stop?*" She gave her head a firm shake. "You're not stopping."

"But you haven't—"

Her legs wrapped around him. She wasn't certain what she was setting out to accomplish, except he wasn't going anywhere.

Long, demanding fingers tightened on her bottom as he became a different man altogether. Withdrawn into himself, into his pleasure, as he thrust with singular intention. An undefinable feeling began to pull through Beatrix, sparking a peculiar drive inside her. Of a sudden, she couldn't get enough of this man.

Then he was pulling away from her and, with an animal groan, spilling his seed onto the counterpane.

The abruptness of their separation opened a feeling inside her —a void.

How empty she felt.

She hadn't known she'd been living her entire life empty of him.

Sweaty, enervated, he collapsed beside her. Within those piercing eyes of his shone a peculiar emotion. "Please accept my apologies."

Guilt, that was what ran behind his eyes.

And something else, too—*shame*.

"You have nothing to apologize for," she said, very clear on this point. "I wanted this."

He gave a short, mirthless laugh and rolled onto his back, resting the back of his hand over his eyes.

"Now," she said, turning onto her side, facing away from him. "I'll have a short rest before I go home."

Behind her, she heard him exhale a long sigh.

Why was he behaving thusly?

Their coupling had been one of mutual want, and now she knew what all the fuss was about.

She couldn't regret it.

Her eyes drifted shut.

Yet…

She had to admit the act wasn't as transformative as plays, poetry, and novels had led her to believe—that a part of her that felt oddly unknowable had teased just out of reach and ultimately denied her a secret.

Perhaps, someday, it would reveal itself to her.

CHAPTER TWENTY-ONE

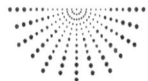

*D*ev lay on his back, watching night shadows dance across the ceiling, damnably awake.

Beside him, Beatrix snored softly.

He should have seen to her pleasure first.

He wasn't some green youth.

He was Lord Devil, for heaven's sake.

She had been the virgin.

And he'd left her unsatisfied.

The very idea gnawed at him.

Which it would surely do for the rest of his days.

And there she lay, sleeping peacefully because she didn't know any better.

She didn't know she should be hurling his reputation back into his face.

He groaned—*again.*

For the hundredth time tonight.

He shifted onto his side and let his gaze rest upon her nude form, porcelain skin illuminated by the soft light of the moon streaming through a high window.

He'd taken her for naught more than skin and bones during their first encounter.

She was thin, but lissome was the more accurate descriptor. There was no one perfect version of the female form—he'd dedicated much of his early twenties to discovering that for himself—but this woman was perfect unto herself.

As frustrated as he was about how tonight had proceeded—another groan escaped him—he couldn't regret it.

Refusing her had never been an option.

But he wouldn't hide behind that flimsy excuse.

The fact was he'd wanted her.

From their very first encounter, he'd been drawn to her, but now, he saw it for what it was.

Desire.

Desire to speak with her.

Desire to be in her presence.

Desire to touch some part of her.

Desire to please her…to spoil her.

Desire to kiss her—*properly.*

Desire…

To be *something more* with her.

So, he'd seen desire through to its natural resolution.

And botched it.

He flung the sheet away and swung his legs off the bed. He couldn't lie still another second with this frustration steaming inside him.

At the washbasin, he dipped a cloth into cooling water scented with some herb or another and wiped his face.

He could sit at his draftsman's table and work. A pencil put to paper always settled and focused his mind on straightforward problems and the clear solutions that followed.

However, as he squeezed the excess water from the cloth—he could use a quick wash while he was at it—he felt them.

Eyes upon him.

He glanced over his shoulder and found Beatrix curled onto her side, watching him, no mistaking the appreciation in her eyes.

"That was…" But she didn't seem to have the words to finish the sentence.

He didn't think he could bear to hear them, anyway. She might say something like *wondrous*, and he wasn't in the mood for well-intentional lies.

It hadn't been wondrous.

At least, not for her.

Truly, she didn't sound as outraged as she should.

"Yeah," was all he could say as he returned to the bed, cloth in hand, an idea forming. Before he could reconsider, he asked, "May I?" He was holding up the square of linen, his intention clear.

A complicated beat of time passed. Then she nodded, and relief washed through Dev.

A chance at redemption scented the air, and he wouldn't bungle it this time.

He lowered onto the bed beside her, and she rolled onto her back. Her eyes never left him.

"It will be cool on your skin," he said before smoothing the cloth along her arm, waking a trail of goose bumps. Her nipples tightened into hard buds, and it was all he could do not to lean down and take one into his mouth.

His cock came to life.

This cloth, meager as it was, was all that stood between his skin touching hers.

This cloth carried a heavy weight on its flimsy shoulders as, in truth, it was all that kept the moment from tipping over into a complete abandonment of reason.

The sigh issuing from her parted lips wasn't helping matters.

Somehow, he moved lower, to her stomach, paying a

moment's attention to her navel and producing a breathy, feminine giggle that nearly undid him.

Nothing new in that.

Everything in relation to this woman seemed to undo him.

As the cloth reached the juncture of her thighs—*her sex*—she bit her bottom lip and squeezed her knees together and exhaled a soft sigh.

She had the heavy-lidded look of a woman aching with arousal.

Aching with arousal...

How he related to the feeling.

He brushed the washcloth along the curls of her cunny and applied light pressure in the name of cleaning her, but he knew what he was doing. Within those curls lay a firm, little nub that existed solely for her pleasure.

Gently, he pushed her thigh. Her knees parted slightly. She was granting him access—and permission.

He tossed the washcloth aside, nothing between him and her as his forefinger slipped into those curls. Not every woman could achieve release from a man's cock.

Perhaps this was the way for her.

Hot...swollen with desire... Her sex was ready for him.

But not yet.

First, she would have her pleasure.

Her slickness invited him to apply a bit more pressure as he grazed the nub with intention. It was as if an electric current suddenly seized her body. One arm flung itself over her head and clenched the pillow above, and the other grabbed the bedsheet, as her back arched on a long moan.

Her nub slick and wet, he continued grazing his finger across it. Climax wouldn't take long. She was absolutely primed for release.

Her nipples, so taut and pretty, begged for his attention, and he could no longer resist their call as he dipped his head and took one into his mouth and sucked. A cry scraped across her throat—one of pleasure and need and frustration and utter want.

He stroked her firmer...*faster*... Though she didn't know it, climax was nearing.

Then her breath caught in her throat, and her body held in exquisite stasis, deliciously open with need. All that mattered in the world to her in this moment was what came next...

A duo of breathless seconds followed before she broke beneath a deeper thrust of his fingers, crying out, as her sex pulsed its release against him. He couldn't take his eyes off her as she tipped into utter abandonment of the self.

Though his cock demanded he take her now, he remained exactly as he was, his fingers feathering lightly across porcelain skin misted with perspiration and let gratification replace the frustration that had been gnawing at him. Her eyes slitted open. "That was..."

"*Wondrous?*"

He was ready to hear it now, if she were so inclined.

A smile fluttered about her mouth. "I think the feeling would just about fit inside that word."

A smile tipped about his mouth as he pushed to a seat and settled back against the headboard. He could almost ignore the raging cockstand that hadn't abated one bit.

She flipped onto her stomach and gazed up at him, her cheeks flushed and eyes yet bright from climax. The view of her pert bottom down the length of her back wasn't helping his unresolved cockstand situation.

Her gaze slid down him and widened ever so slightly.

She'd taken notice.

She reached for the still-damp washcloth. "Your turn." With slow deliberation, her gaze traveled up and down the length of him. "You're a full glory, Dev."

She hadn't called him Lord Devil or Deverill, but rather Dev. He liked it.

Was this the first time?

"But you know that, don't you?"

Dev's *yes* remained unspoken, but there were certainties a man held about himself. He knew women saw him thusly.

She laughed. Not mocking or dry, but thoroughly, genuinely delighted.

That he could delight her in some way was an aphrodisiac in itself.

Never mind what she'd started doing with her hand...moving the washcloth along his thigh...inches from his cock.

Oh, lord.

And up it inched, as she eased closer, too, her smile of delight fallen away, replaced by one of wickedness.

He was fit to burst.

"I suppose you've been told the obvious," she said.

"The obvious?"

"How very large you are."

"How would a sweet virgin such as yourself know such a naughty thing?"

"My virginity has been consigned to the past tense," she said, matter-of-fact.

The past tense in relation to her virginity was something he wouldn't think about right now. "My question remains unanswered. How would you know?"

"I've seen a rendering of Michelangelo's *David*, and you are noticeably larger than him. Proportionally speaking, of course."

An ironic chuckle escaped Dev. "One can only be grateful for small blessings."

A saucy glint in her eye, she tossed the cloth aside—it had been of little use, anyway—and feathered her fingertips up the length of him. He sucked in a sharp breath. "If you keep doing that..."

"What?" No mistaking the daring glittering off her. "You'll ravish me?"

The temptation to do precisely that crooked its finger at him and beckoned. "You're new to this," he said. "Can you—"

"Oh, I most certainly can."

A moment's hesitation, then his mind was made up. He reached out and wrapped his hand around her upper arm. She offered no resistance as he tugged.

"Shall I show you what *more* lovemaking can be?"

They shouldn't have done it a first time.

But now they *needed* to do it a second time.

Her leg crossed over his thighs and she came to a straddle over him, hovering above, her long, sable hair forming a curtain around them, seduction in her eyes as she said, "You're the expert, Dev."

Though he'd had her not an hour ago, the anticipation of having her again was nearly enough to kill him. To have her pert bottom in his hands...her soft mouth on his...her sweet cunny wrapped around his cock... Her hands on his shoulders, she shifted onto her knees so he could take himself in hand, the crown of his cock grazing her deliciously wet slit.

With held breath, she slid down his shaft, taking him in, inch by inch, her mouth against his neck, impaling herself on him.

She felt *so...damn...good.*

He held tight onto her hips, keeping the rhythm steady and measured as they began to move together. He wanted to savor every second...every stroke.

Even as he felt the familiar tightening that preceded release.

No.

Slow...measured...

Sweat trickled down the hollow of his spine, down the center of her chest, as he sensed a release of tension within her—her body's instinctual recognition that there would be no pain in this coupling, only pleasure.

Given that permission, he loosened his hold a degree and sank himself deeper into her.

She was ready.

She gasped. "Aren't you full of surprises?"

Together, they established a rhythm of give and take as she moved on him, seeking and discovering the pleasures to be had from one another's bodies.

Except this was something more than two bodies given over to lust and stealing pleasure and delight from one another.

Oh, there was pleasure and delight, but there was also intensity and intimacy of the sort that reached down into a soul.

A tup with this woman was more than a tup.

It was...

Something more.

The movements of her hips became more centered, focused... the sighs and moans and cries pouring from her mouth sharper. Urgency had begun pulling at her. There was yet more her body wanted from his.

And he would give it to her.

Here was a Beatrix he hadn't yet known. *Wild...untamed...free.* No shadow or reserve about her as she rode him and took what she needed. Her head tossed back, she cried out, release taking her of a sudden, her sweet quim pulsing around him.

Then he, too, could take no more of this exquisite torture and followed her over the edge, only lifting her off his shaft as he began to spill, taking himself in hand, his gaze upon her as he stroked himself to completion on a guttural shout.

As he collapsed back against the headboard, he reached for her, pulling her into his side, her head nestled into the crook of his shoulder as they hung above the bounds of the physical for a span of time that couldn't be accounted for.

He stroked her hair, and her fingertips lightly traced across his chest. "It was better the second time," she said in that direct way of hers.

He experienced the great satisfaction of redemption. "It tends to get better and better as you learn what your body likes and the likes of your—"

"*Lover?*"

He nodded.

This was no way to be talking. A future of them discovering the hidden pleasures of one another's bodies wasn't part of their arrangement. This night had been born of a specific madness that would dissipate with the morning light.

"Sleep," he said—though he knew he wouldn't.

His mind raced into the small hours of morning.

They'd become *something more*.

Something ill-defined.

Which didn't sit well within him.

He didn't like the ill-defined. He liked clearly delineated parameters. A man knew where he stood within such boundaries.

But *this*, the new territory he'd entered with Beatrix, it was uncharted. It turned the earth beneath his feet—earth that had been solid as granite his entire life—into shifting sand.

Something more.

He was left with a single certainty now—one that offered no reassurance.

That simple, ill-defined *something more* was far more powerful than it appeared on the surface.

It might even hold the power to turn his life entirely on its head.

CHAPTER TWENTY-TWO

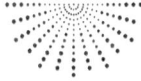

PRIMROSE PARK, TWO WEEKS LATER

*B*elow a crisp blue summer sky, Beatrix sat with her legs tucked beneath her and held a pleasant smile on her face—a smile that she suspected was more bland than serene —and attempted to appear as if she were attending to the other ladies' thorough discussion of London's best and worst milliners.

The guests had begun arriving at Primrose Park this morning, bursting with excitement for the house party all society was buzzing about, and already the entertainments were underway with an afternoon picnic on a gently sloping hillside. The acres and acres of Primrose Park's grounds had been meticulously planned with an idyllic, painting-perfect view at every turn— verdant rolling hills...elegant willow trees draped over the pond, providing a perfect frame for the stately manor house in the distance. Even the sky dared not be uncooperative today.

"And your hair, Lady Beatrix," said Lady Farthington. "You're doing something different with it these days."

A dozen sets of feminine eyes narrowed on Beatrix. "Am I?" The conversation had tipped from hats to what lay beneath.

"Most definitely." Her steely eyes narrowed. "Something *French*."

Nods of agreement all around.

Until now, Beatrix hadn't the faintest notion that a hairstyle could be a political statement.

"It's perfect for you," said Mrs. Shaw. "My girls were just commenting on the loveliness of your hair. Weren't you, my dears?"

The Shaw daughters dutifully and agreeably nodded.

Now, it was a blush warming Beatrix's cheeks. As the wife of Dev's business partner, Mrs. Shaw was outranked by every lady present, save her three marriageable daughters who sat demurely arrayed at her side. Upon their introduction this morning, Beatrix had suspected she would like the woman, but now she knew she did.

Lady Farthington began nodding. "I shall instruct my lady's maid to have a word with your girl."

"Of course," said Beatrix. She'd rarely encountered a gathering of women where hair didn't arise as a topic.

Blessedly, the conversation carried on without her as her gaze lifted to the sky and her mind drifted along with the cotton puffs of white clouds lazily idling above.

A majority of the guests had already arrived. The highest-ranking peer who had accepted the invitation was the Duke of Richmond. Though Beatrix was convinced it was only so he could see Primrose Park's stables and meet Little Wicked, who had gained no small amount of fame in her three years of life.

A few earls had accepted, too. The Earl of Wrexford, a man known for his unflappable amiability, and the Earl of Stoke, with whom Beatrix wasn't acquainted, but whose reputation preceded him. A licentious earl, if the rumors were correct. Likely on his way to ruin. In other words, an earl who wouldn't refuse an invitation to an opulent country house party.

Another earl had accepted, too—the Earl of Bridgewater.

Although, he and the countess hadn't yet arrived.

But they would.

Of that, Beatrix was certain.

All she had to do was call to mind the way the countess's stare had been fixed upon Dev on the night of their sensational, little engagement.

The countess would be here.

Dev.

The countess would also know him by Dev.

Beatrix was certain of that, too.

Now that her mind had cracked open the door she'd held firmly shut these last two weeks since she'd last laid eyes on the man—him lying in bed…only a sheet covering the lower half of his body—memory took permission to relive their first kiss.

And the second.

And most definitely the third.

But mostly that night.

A night that lived with a bit too much familiarity in her mind —and in her body.

She'd held very few expectations regarding the act of coitus. The whisperings amongst ladies had deemed it an act to be endured. But if she'd had any preconceived ideas, their first coupling would have satisfied them. *Nay.* It had far surpassed mere endurance, for she'd wanted Mr. Blake Deverill with every cell of her being.

Yet, it hadn't been transformative.

After, she'd still felt very much herself.

Then…they'd done it again.

And, oh, how she'd been transformed.

How the second time haunted her every waking—and sleeping—moment.

Which was why she'd avoided him these last two weeks.

Today, upon her arrival and the ensuing madness of ensuring all was running smoothly for the party—guests' myriad needs met, wants accommodated, and desires indulged; the supply of champagne bottomless—she'd somehow managed to speak to Dev only in public view.

She didn't trust herself with him in private.

She didn't trust herself not to beg him for a third time.

And a fourth…

Oh, there would never be enough times.

That was the truth.

Avoidance was simpler.

And necessary.

After all, this entire elaborate ruse had a single goal—for him to woo another.

Lest she forget.

In the distance, a pair of gentlemanly figures appeared. For a panicked second, she was sure one of them was Dev.

Neither was.

The one man was tall, but older and carried a hearty paunch about his middle. The other man was tall, too, but rangy…a confident swagger to his step…a flash of sparkle in his left ear.

Her heart kicked into a gallop, and she sat up ramrod straight. *No, no, no.* If she wasn't mistaken—and she wasn't—the pair of figures were none other than…

"Lady Beatrix, is that Lydon?" asked Lady Farthington.

Mouth dry as dust, all Beatrix could do was nod.

A few delighted titters floated on the air. "Now the party shall be a lively one," chimed another lady.

Lady Farthington squinted into the distance. "And who is that young man with him?"

Beatrix swallowed. She must answer. "That is Mr. Blaze Jagger."

No few gasps inhaled. "The infamous blackleg?"

"He now runs The Archangel," answered Beatrix.

To a one, the ladies fixed the entirety of their titillated gazes upon Jagger. The fact was her brother—no matter that he was from the other side of the blanket, that was how she'd come to think of him—was too appealing for his own good. The large diamond flashing in his ear only enhanced his dangerous magnetism. And the mischief in his smile…

Well, he would be seated well away from Mr. and Mrs. Shaw's impressionable, marriageable heiress daughters.

She would have a little chat with this come-lately brother of hers.

Of course, Dev had insisted on inviting Lydon. He was Beatrix's father; it was only proper. That Lydon was also a marquess, well, that was a bonus.

By the time Lydon and Jagger joined the picnic, there was no denying the frisson of excitement that had enlivened the ladies in a way discussions of milliners and fashionable hairstyles simply couldn't.

These were men—untamed, possibly dangerous men.

Untamable?

Few women were above wanting to know—or even finding out for themselves.

She would most definitely have a chat with Jagger.

A jolly smile in place—he was well versed in those—Lydon clapped his hands and rubbed them together briskly. "What's this harem of English roses I've happened upon?" He wasn't above mixing his cultural references.

The ladies, predictably, tittered. Lydon held a sort of charm, Beatrix supposed. That, and he was a marquess. Ladies naturally tittered and cooed over the charms—paltry though they might be —of a marquess.

Beatrix only realized she'd snorted after she'd done it.

Lydon's attention shifted. "Ah, there's my lovely daughter."

Until this moment, she had been merely annoyed.

Now, it was as if the Devil himself was fiddling on her last nerve.

"Lydon," she said, tightly, certain her face was making a mess of itself in its attempt to remain composed.

If he thought she was about to address him as *Father* for the benefit of appearances, he was destined to be sorely disappointed.

He sniffed and carefully lowered himself onto the pallet of blankets and pillows the servants had hastily arranged for him.

Seeing him there, lying about like a sultan on holiday and accepting a coupe of champagne from a footman, was altogether too much for Beatrix's continued well-being. She shot to her feet. "I, *erm*, I'm off for a walk."

Lifted eyebrows directed themselves her way, and Jagger shot her a wink.

Cheeky man.

She didn't bother glancing at Lydon as, without another word, she set out. Not for the manor house, but rather in the opposite direction—toward a dark and as-yet mysterious copse of woods.

They suited her mood.

She'd only made it thirty yards or so when she felt it—a hand on her upper arm. She threw an irritated glance over her shoulder.

Lydon.

Pique transformed into puzzlement as she swung around to an abrupt stop. Before she could open her mouth, he said, "I haven't had an opportunity to properly congratulate you on your impending nuptials, just the two of us."

"Haven't had an opportunity?" she asked, incredulous. "You haven't been home in weeks."

He shrugged, a marquess utterly indifferent to bourgeois standards of time. "A man has business to attend in the general course of life."

Her brow creased with a sudden suspicion. "You haven't left Cumberbatch in London, have you?"

The stubborn man had refused to come with her to Primrose Park. "I'm valet to a marquess, not your nursemaid." Then he'd extended an object toward her. "Now, you strap this little beauty to your thigh, and you'll be all right."

It was a knife.

A knife that presently lay undisturbed in her valise.

Cumberbatch meant well.

It was almost touching.

"The old bugger insisted on coming." Lydon shook his head, bemused. "Getting rather vocal in his opinions in his dotage. Might need a new valet soon."

Beatrix's fists clenched at her sides. "Don't you dare even think of it," she said through gritted teeth.

Cumberbatch was too aged to find another place.

He was theirs, for life.

Though they weren't within earshot of the party, they were within view, so Beatrix decided it best that she stay put and let Lydon have his say, rather than put on a spectacle of her running away and him chasing after her. "You have something to say to me?"

A serious glint entered Lydon's eye. "You'll want to get on those nuptials in quick order." He glanced around the grounds of Primrose Park meaningfully. "You've caught yourself a right keeper."

Beatrix felt not only the skyward lift of her eyebrows, but also the effect of having herself struck dumb.

"I doubted you had it in you." Doubts that yet lingered in his eyes, in fact. "No idea as to the *why*s and *how*s of this impending union, but you've done it. I'll say this for you—you've always been a clever one." And on he went… "Now, you get those vows spoken and that marriage register signed."

Beatrix's cheeks burned. The tips of her ears, too. The bald-faced audacity!

But as much as she wanted done with this conversation, she did have a matter to air… "You brought Blaze Jagger."

A statement of the obvious; the question implicit.

Why had he brought the fox into the henhouse?

Lydon remained unbothered. "Figured it was all the same to Deverill if I brought a new friend."

"*Friend?*"

Lydon kept surpassing himself in degrees of audacity. Jagger was many things—*adversary...family*—but not *friend*.

Lydon searched her eyes for any knowledge they might reveal. "Jagger might say some unpleasant things to you. Don't believe a word of it."

"And what might he say?" She didn't let Lydon answer. "That he's the holder of all your debt?"

Lydon gave a lordly sniff of dismissal.

"Or," she continued, "might he say he's my brother?"

That got Lydon's attention. "Load of rot. I shared a bit of fun with his ma on the rare occasion, and I'm guilty of—*what?*—*crimes?*"

Beatrix supposed that was as close to a confession as she was ever likely to get. "Why did you bring him here?"

"He expressed an interest in attending, and, well..." He shrugged, as if the remainder of the sentence didn't need to be spoken.

Beatrix was in no mood to humor her father. "And you're in no position to refuse him."

She would've thought such words would elicit a sniff or even a glower. Instead, he smiled—*brightly*. "If it isn't the man himself," he said, as if the sun to his moon approached.

And Beatrix knew before a sure, masculine hand lightly closed around her arm and a low, rumbly voice sounded in her ear. "Going somewhere, my love?"

Deverill.

She froze.

My love.

Of course, the endearment was for the benefit of others. After all, they were on display.

She turned sharply, and her mouth found itself disconcertingly close to his. Her gaze lifted and met his within that intimate space.

Until this very moment, everything about their arrangement had felt mostly theoretical.

Now, here it was being put into practice.

Was she up to the task?

Doubt pulsed through her.

In the wild instant that followed his *my love*, she'd believed it.

Or had wanted to believe it.

And she wasn't sure which was worse.

CHAPTER TWENTY-THREE

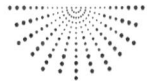

*B*eatrix didn't want to respond.
　　　　She wanted to run.

Dev understood that.

Well, too bad.

She'd made an arrangement with him.

He could release her from it, of course.

A gentleman might.

But he was no gentleman.

"Ah, the beauteous nature of young love." Thumbs tucked into waistcoat pockets, Lydon rocked on his heels, smug smile in place. "I'll leave you lot to it."

The old wastrel likely didn't think Dev caught the wink directed at his daughter.

She groaned.

"They're all watching," said Dev through his smile.

"So?"

The woman had no instinct for artifice.

"So, we're completely besotted with one another, remember?"

Something opaque and unknowable passed behind her eyes. Her brow creased with a little crinkle.

"Now," he said, turning them toward the picnic which had doubled in size with the return of the men, "let's show them how mad we are for each other." They took a few steps. "And smile, woman."

He risked a glance to find her face assembled into what could pass for a besotted smile—in the dark...perhaps.

With the return of the men, the gathering had broken into smaller groupings. Typical of Richmond, the duke was holding court and expostulating on all matters of the turf in the direction of a few earls and similarly assorted lords. Lydon had found a group of ladies suitably in awe of his every word. Meanwhile, Blaze Jagger maintained the skeptical lift of an eyebrow as a lord was earnestly imparting a matter of serious importance to him— likely how he would be repaying an outstanding debt very soon.

Jagger had been unexpected, though Dev should've seen it coming. The man was audacious and ambitious. He'd seen a way in, and he'd seized it. Dev would've been the biggest hypocrite in the world if he didn't understand and, further, sympathize.

Although, an eye would have to be kept on the man. Too many ladies, both married and unmarried, were casting intrigued glances in his direction.

But, really, Dev's main concern was for the woman at his side.

The woman who had only contacted him these last two weeks through letters.

He'd let her avoid him, but he wasn't so sure it was for her benefit.

Likely, it had been for his own.

"Deverill," came a call and corresponding wave. Shaw, beckoning him and Beatrix over to join him and his family.

"Do you mind if we sit with the Shaws?"

He didn't know why he was asking. This was his show.

"I like Mrs. Shaw," said Beatrix. "She seems a woman of good sense."

She was speaking to him again.

Progress.

As they settled onto the blanket, Mrs. Shaw asked, "Have you yet tasted a scone? They are truly scrumptious. I must have the recipe."

A chorus of feminine snickers sounded from the adjacent blanket. Mrs. Shaw had made it obvious she baked her own scones.

"Scones, you say?" asked Dev. "Second only to chocolate, they are Bea's favorite food."

Questioning gray eyes flashed up to meet his.

Bea.

He'd called her Bea in society.

Was that annoyance he saw?

A feeling of satisfaction twisted through him.

Some part of him wanted to prick and annoy her, for he realized something in this moment.

He was annoyed with *her.*

"In fact—" He lifted a scone and spread a dollop of clotted cream across its lumpy surface, followed by a swipe of sticky strawberry jam. He lifted the scone and met her eyes, which had gone wide. His intention was clear.

Her mouth remained stubbornly closed, her eyes mutinous.

"Come now, my love, we're amongst friends," he cooed. "Why deny yourself?"

And he realized with no small amount of bewilderment that he wanted this—to feed her.

He'd never fed a woman in his life.

A tense beat of time ticked past.

At last, she relented—and opened her mouth.

He felt the pull of a wicked smile as he slid it inside. She bit down. Unable not to, he watched her chew and swallow.

Then he noticed… "You have a smudge of jam just…" Without thinking, he reached out and pressed his thumb to the corner of her mouth. *"Here."*

And that would've been the end of it.

Except her tongue had the same idea.

So, in the instant he swiped, she did, too—and licked him.

Her tongue slick and soft against his thumb.

There was nothing soft about the lightning bolt of desire that streaked through him straight to his cock.

The moment stretched the limits of a single second as their gazes held, knowledge within, knowledge of each other...

"Oh, you must tell us the story of how you met," exclaimed Mrs. Shaw. "I'm certain it's incredibly romantic."

Beatrix dropped her gaze and turned her head subtly enough so his thumb no longer had an excuse to touch her. "It's not a terribly fascinating story," she said, quelling. She glanced toward the sky. "The clouds are beginning to look a little fearsome. Maybe we should go—"

"As usual, my sweet Bea is being too modest." He saw what she was trying to do and wasn't about to let her. "We met in Hyde Park."

Mrs. Shaw shifted forward, already rapt. "Oh?"

"In a rainstorm."

Mrs. Shaw looked ready to swoon.

"She'd turned her ankle." He decided it best to leave out the part where he'd nearly run her down with his horse, thereby causing said turned ankle.

"Oh, dear."

"In fact, this ankle here..." Guided by impulse, he reached down to where Beatrix's legs were folded to the side of her body and traced his forefinger along her boot and up to her slender ankle.

In a more formal setting, it would've been shocking. but Dev thought with the right charming smile curving his mouth he could just get away with it.

With that swipe of the tongue across the pad of his thumb,

she'd sparked a match to flame inside him and he was powerless against adding kindling to the fire.

He needed to touch her.

"Then what happened?"

"Well, as you may have noticed, my sweet Bea has a stubborn streak the length and width of the Atlantic Ocean—"

"Don't forget the depth, my darling," said Beatrix with a sugary smile.

"But I was able to convince her to ride my mount."

"Upon your first meeting?" This was from the eldest of the Shaw daughters, who clearly hadn't the faintest notion about double entendres. All three sisters looked as if they were bearing witness to a romance with the scope and drama of Antony and Cleopatra.

The tips of Beatrix's ears grew fiercely red as she shifted and discreetly tucked her legs beneath her, away from further explorations of his fingers.

It had been forward of him.

But he couldn't regret it.

"And was it love at first sight?" asked the youngest Shaw daughter.

The question was simple—a natural progression of the conversation. It should've been expected.

Instead, it rocked him back on his heels.

He opened his mouth, knowing the answer expected of him. All he had to do was speak that single word—*yes.*

Beatrix's eyes lifted and found his.

Dev closed his mouth.

He couldn't.

For it felt strangely transgressive to speak that *yes* to these people.

It felt...*complicated.*

Much like a first kiss was supposed to be, it was meant for the intimate space between two people.

In a sudden flurry of skirts, Beatrix pushed off the ground and shot to her feet. "I think I'll take that walk now."

And she was off, marching up the short rise of the hill as if she owned it.

Dev sprang to his feet. "Isn't she delightful?"

And he was off, too, in pursuit.

A few seconds later, he was by her side and threading his arm through hers.

For the sake of appearances, of course.

When they entered the woods and disappeared into its daytime shadows, however, she pulled away and he let her.

He let the silence between them expand, too.

Except a copse of woods was never silent, if one listened. The muted crunch of their footsteps. The soft susurration of a light summer breeze whispering through the trees. Crickets and birds singing their ancient songs. Toads croaking their chorus. A dog or a fox barking in the distance.

On, they wandered, her leading the aimless way that Dev was content to follow.

Content.

He wasn't content.

He was, in fact, *dis*content.

She behaved as if they'd never been friends or...*something more.*

Enough was enough.

"Do you plan on ever speaking to me again?"

"We've spoken," she tossed over her shoulder without breaking stride. "We're speaking now."

"You're being childish."

She let her forward-marching feet be her answer.

Discontent tipped over into bloody irritation. "Do we need to talk about it?"

He detected a hiccough in her step, even as she asked, "Talk about what?"

"The night," he said. "Or shall I explain in minute detail which night?"

She whirled around, eyes brimming with fear and fire in equal parts. "Don't you dare."

He had her—and it felt good to provoke her into genuine emotion beyond studied indifference. "Then I suggest you start talking about something else."

Gray eyes sparked with annoyance. At last, she said, "How did you acquire Primrose Park?" She began striding through the woods again, him at her back. "The same way you acquired Little Wicked? In a card game?"

Again, irritation snapped through him. "I'm not an actual scoundrel, you know," he fired back. "Everything I've acquired has been done so honestly." Well... "More or less."

She shot him a sheepish glance over her shoulder. "That was rather low of me. I apologize."

He nodded his acceptance, even if he didn't quite believe her. "Primrose Park was unentailed, and the lord who owned it deeply in debt."

"A common enough story."

"Indeed."

"You're good at it, you know."

"Good at what?" He was good at many things—a few of them she'd experienced intimately.

"At playing the aristocrat."

He snorted.

"Better than most aristocrats."

"All it takes is a mountain of money and a willingness to spend it on expensive things, like racehorses and country estates."

A laugh drifted over her shoulder. "That reminds me. I suppose I must thank you."

"Beatrix," he said. "May I walk beside you?"

Her hesitation was borne out by the dozen or so yards that passed beneath their feet. "If you must."

A few strides later, he was by her side. "Now, you may thank me."

Her mouth twitched, but she managed to hold a smile in check. "I must thank you for sending your parents on holiday."

"Oh? I was under the impression you liked them."

"I do," she said. "Very much, in fact, but I don't relish the idea of playing pretend as your fiancée beneath their observant eyes."

Playing pretend.

He didn't know why the phrase rubbed him the wrong way, except it did.

A thought for another time, perhaps.

Or perhaps not.

"Are they enjoying the Lake District?"

"According to the letter I received yesterday, yes."

"Good."

They walked on for a while in silence before she stopped and looked around. "Do you know where we are?"

"In the woods."

She heaved a great, dramatic sigh. "Where are we in relation to the manor house?"

"I haven't the faintest idea."

She lifted a bewildered eyebrow. "But these are *your* woods. How can you not know your estate lands?"

He lifted empty hands. "Alas."

"We're lost?"

"Define lost."

Her eyebrows dug trenches into her forehead.

"Beatrix," he said in a tone that could calm a spooked horse, "did you never go off adventuring in the woods as a child?"

"No."

For an instant, Dev was flummoxed. How could that be?

Then he remembered.

She'd spent many of her childhood days and years at race-courses with Lydon and his band of jolly rotters.

"Well," he said, "I can assure you we shan't be lost for long. England only has so much land. We would hit the sea from any direction, eventually. You can take the word of the son of an estate manager."

Her eyes searched his for another instant, then she nodded and started walking again. "You had a wonderful childhood, didn't you?"

He'd never given it much thought, but... "Yes."

Ahead, a clearing came into view—a second, smaller pond. The forest surrounding it lent a feeling of privacy. One could indulge in summer swimming here. It would've even felt wild, but for the Greek-columned folly on the other side with its grand, domed roof.

"You might be the owner of the most beautiful estate in all England, Lord Devil."

Before he could reply, a thunderclap sounded directly over-head, eliciting a startled cry from Beatrix before the sky opened —*one...two...three...*heavy raindrops followed by a sudden torrent. Lost as they were, a mad dash to the manor house wasn't an option. By unspoken agreement, they sprinted straight for the folly, arriving soaked through to skin.

Well, Beatrix was soaked to the skin.

He had his greatcoat for protection.

She stared out at him, sodden, stringy tendrils of hair clinging to her cheeks, lashes heavy with raindrops. The wet-cat metaphor came to mind. "Are there two people in England more likely to get caught out in a rainstorm?"

Dev laughed. He couldn't help it.

Beatrix didn't join.

She was serious.

His brow gathered. "Are you actually angry with the weather?"

"I'm not going to take it anymore," she exclaimed and strode out from beneath the protection of the folly—and straight into the rain.

All Dev could do was watch, bewildered, even as he admired her spirit. If anyone could take on the elements, it was Beatrix.

She made it about twenty yards.

Then she stopped. Her shoulders heaved up and down with, presumably, a great frustrated sigh, before she whirled around and dashed back to the folly.

She was now irredeemably soaked. Hair, a clumpy, tangled mess...boots emitting a soupy *squish-squosh* with every step...the fine muslin of her dress utterly ruined.

And utterly transparent.

Below her spencer, ivory fabric had found every inch of wet skin and clung on as if for dear life. Outlining...framing...displaying...every valley and hill... Her mons pubis a dark shadow beneath gossamer muslin.

Oh, she was a mess.

An utter, ravishable mess.

"You're staring."

His gaze lifted, and he didn't deny it.

Instead, he shed his greatcoat and held it out, bridging the few feet between them. "Here."

"I don't need your—"

"Spare us the ten minutes of back and forth and take the blasted coat, woman."

She looked as if she might fight on, then she snatched the coat from him and shrugged it on—*grudgingly*.

It wasn't only she who needed protection.

But he from himself—and his baser urges.

Urges which were presently rioting through his body and making their case.

Again, he experienced that contradictory spark of irritation.

She'd only taken his coat when presented with no other choice.

As if she couldn't bear any part of him touching her, even if it was only the residual warmth from his body.

As if she were playing another game of pretend below their other game of pretend.

This game of pretend, however, was solely between the two of them.

It sounded complicated, but really, it was simple.

She was pretending their night together had never happened.

That he'd never touched her.

That she'd never touched him.

That they'd never taken pleasure from one another.

Huddled into his greatcoat, she lowered onto the bench to wait out the storm.

But really, he suspected, it was to keep an eye on him.

As if he couldn't be trusted.

Or…

As if she couldn't trust herself.

That irritated him, too.

He propped a shoulder against a column and crossed his arms over his chest. "Now, who's staring?"

She ignored the question. "You'll catch a chill now that I have your coat."

"A real conundrum."

He didn't care about the blasted coat or potential chills.

The deeper source of his irritation with this woman struck him.

He was a man with something to prove.

He wanted to prove to her how he'd made her feel.

And how it could feel even better the second time.

Nay, the third.

He wanted to prove it so thoroughly, she couldn't ever deny it again.

He wanted her to blush simply from setting eyes on him.

He wanted...*surrender*.

He recognized another desire, too.

A too-familiar desire.

The desire to vanquish.

He ever carried it within him, this desire.

"We could share the coat." She made the offer offhand, as if it didn't matter all that much to her one way or the other.

But her eyes told a different story.

"Would you like me to share the coat with you?"

"I would be warmer."

He pushed off the pillar. "Once we start sharing the coat, there's no going back."

"I need you to share this coat with me, Dev. It's all I can think about."

It wasn't irritation or the need to prove her wrong or himself right that had him closing the distance between them, but rather a sort of will.

The will to possess her—and for her to know herself possessed.

It likely wasn't his best idea, but this desire wouldn't be denied.

And something in him wouldn't let her deny it in herself.

"What are we doing?" she asked.

"Nothing...*yet*."

CHAPTER TWENTY-FOUR

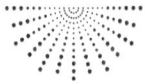

*S*ometimes the sharing of a coat was simply the sharing of a coat.

Any number of situations could necessitate it—*cold...wet*.

Both were in evidence.

Except the look of necessity flickering within Dev's half-lidded eyes had naught to do with exterior elements.

But only with what sparked between them.

It was spoken in that tiny three-letter word.

Yet.

As he closed the distance, Beatrix allowed her gaze to rove across him in a way she hadn't allowed herself...*yet*.

How gorgeous he was.

The rare man who incorporated ideals of both beauty and masculinity.

The rain had turned her into a sopping, wet mess.

But it had turned him into a god—black hair damp and tousled with a loose curl to it...clinging white shirt revealing the dense muscles of his arms.

And there was the swagger in his step—and in his smile, too.

How alive the air was around him.

How alive she was when he was near.

He moved with slow deliberation, as if not to startle her into bolting.

She was going nowhere.

He stopped just beyond her knees, and she had to tip her head back to hold his gaze.

Intention.

That was what glittered there, and it arrowed a bolt of desire straight through her.

It wasn't she who parted her knees but rather desire and need.

He reached down and pushed the clingy muslin up her legs. Then he kneeled between, so they were face to face, his body brushing against her inner thighs, that skin so sensitive and so alive to the large, male feel of him. She opened the coat and twined her arms around his neck so they both shared in the warmth. The world outside this intimate cocoon ceased to matter.

All that mattered was the ragged in and out of their mingled breath...the hard drum of their hearts...the heat that flowed between them...

He reached up and brushed his knuckles across her cheek, and her eyes drifted shut for an instant so her entire earthly experience was the feel of his bare skin against hers.

Then he angled forward and pressed his mouth to hers.

Before now, time had slowed its forward march, but with his soft, beautiful mouth moving against hers, urgency seared through her with desire unsated. Time sped up and, of a sudden, there wasn't enough of it.

At least, not for them.

It had been two weeks—and she felt it desperately.

Her arms tightened around his neck, bringing her body tight against his, her nipples pressed into his chest. He groaned into her mouth, as her legs hooked around his waist, bringing the rigid length of his manhood hard against her sex, pulling a gasp from her and a ragged groan from him.

More…she needed more.

Impatience guided her hand between their bodies and had trembling fingers grazing across his shaft.

"Bea," he groaned—*pleaded*—against her mouth.

All that stood between her and what she wanted was a thin layer of superfine.

A barrier easily resolved by determined fingers.

Only the flick of a few buttons and she would have it—him inside her.

She'd already moved to the second button when his hand closed around hers. On a frustrated cry, she broke from his mouth. "What are you thinking of?"

"*You*, of course."

She couldn't countenance the smile curling the corner of his mouth.

"Today," he continued with a patience that just might stir her to wrath, "we're going about matters in the correct order."

She attempted to remove her hand from his. He only tightened his grip. Oh, she was definitely becoming stirred to wrath. "What are you on about?"

"You…first."

"*Me…first?*" The man was making no sense.

Enigmatically, he nodded and shifted backward. Oh, the wickedness in his smile as his hands closed around her thighs and applied gentle pressure.

Uncertainty pulsed through her for a few, quick heartbeats of time, but quickly gave way to a stronger feeling—curiosity. Whatever it was he had planned, she wanted to know.

He angled down and pressed his mouth to the sensitive skin of her inner thigh. It felt…naughty…and delicious…and it tickled.

A giggle sprang from her.

He kissed her again—*higher*. Then yet higher, as he trailed slow, warm kisses up the interior of her thigh. When she thought he couldn't go any higher, she felt *it*—the slick, velvet brush of his tongue along her slit.

Every cell in her body sparkled into effervescence, and she gasped. His eyes remained steady upon her, a question within those aquamarine depths. "Some women don't like this."

Beatrix knew in an instant—she wasn't one of them.

Yet she said, "Then I think that leaves us with but one option."

How very unlike itself her voice sounded.

"Which is?"

"For you to do it again so I can decide what sort of woman I am."

It was a game and, *oh*, how she wanted to play.

He shifted forward on a low chuckle and again slid his tongue along her. Pleasure rippled through her as her head tipped back and he offered her a pleasure unlike any other with his tongue.

It felt so decadent and good...*too good*, possibly...transgressive, likely.

Except...if the body possessed the mechanism to experience this sort of pleasure, where lay the transgression in experiencing it?

And, *oh*, what an experience it was as his tongue—his *so* talented tongue—caressed her...flicked her... Every nerve in her body lit alive with this feeling as if they all ended in the patch of skin where his tongue met her quim.

One hand reached down and tangled in his hair as her hips inelegantly shoved forward, demanding more as a feeling built within her.

A feeling he'd taught her.

Need tore through her, breaking her down into elements, then cells of utter, inexhaustible ache, taunting...teasing...just out of reach, refusing to be sated.

He eased off the pressure against her, just an increment. In doing so, he was denying her what she wanted and giving her what she needed, because, *oh*, the feeling that taunted and teased now had her in its grip as her body went still and reached for... *oh...*

A cry tore from her throat as her body broke with release, her quim pulsing against his mouth until the pleasure became too much and she had to ease back from the intensity of feeling.

Her eyes slitted open, and she met his gaze across her body.

"I think we can safely say what sort of woman you are."

The words were spoken lightly, and she couldn't help smiling, but she found she couldn't quite agree. Before this man had entered her life, she'd thought herself a very different woman from the one she was proving to be.

It was as if she'd lost hold of the elements that identified her to herself.

She didn't know this woman.

A being composed entirely of want.

A wanton.

That was who she was—with him.

She hooked her hand around his neck and tugged. When her mouth met his, she tasted herself on his tongue. Somehow, she'd lost none of her earlier urgency. If anything, her need had only amplified in feeling.

She might not know who she was in this moment, but she knew what she wanted.

Him...inside her...now.

With a few efficient movements of his fingers his falls were unbuttoned and his manhood freed, its shaft so long and hard and so very ready. He reached under her and grabbed her bottom, pulling her to the edge of the bench so now his length slid along her sex. Oh, the hot, thick feel of him as he pushed into her one slow inch at a time, and she stretched around him to accommodate his demanding girth.

His hands tight around her bottom, he began to move in and

out of her, plunging deeper with each stroke. "Sweet Bea, you feel so good."

Sweet Bea.

She liked the pet name.

That was the truth.

Within this intimate act, there was no room for deception—especially not of the self.

They moved as one, and the coat fell away, unheeded. There was no question of the heat they were creating.

She'd been correct, it seemed.

The only way to prevent this outcome was to stay completely away from this man.

There was no safety in proximity.

They'd gone too far once—and now there was no going back.

Or, came a wicked suggestion.

Perhaps this was exactly what they needed.

Perhaps this time would provide satiety.

Perhaps now they could move on from this mad hunger.

For it was a madness.

Desperation seized her as she moved on him, taking him so deep inside, pain and pleasure inextricable. An act so of the body, even as she reached beyond herself into another realm.

This was what bodies were made for.

More than that, *this* was what *her* body was made for—to couple with him.

Deeper, he impaled her, and deeper, she took him. "Bea," he muttered against her neck, stubble scraping against that sensitive skin, sending pleasure skittering through her as he drove with a relentless intensity. "You feel too good. I can't last much longer."

Along with every other pleasure this man was wreaking upon her, here was yet another pleasure and the most heady of them all —his desire for her, so desperate and pleading.

On his next stroke, her sex found its release, and she cried out, pulsing around him, as she clung tighter to him. On, he drove into her, his shaft impossibly hard, following the path of his own pleasure, her body but a vessel for its giving. On a shout, release took him, and he tumbled into the oblivion where she waited for him, their bodies sweaty, panting, enervated, as he slowed his movement to an eventual stop, even as they remained joined, their breaths and heartbeats as one.

This hadn't been a gentle coupling of romance and soft beds.

This had been an act of desperation and need. A vulgar act... A *fucking*, to put it in the proper language.

Yet...it had also felt...*right*.

Until this moment, she hadn't known this truth...

There was the mind.

Then there was the body.

She'd been absolutely certain the former ruled the latter.

But that belief had never been tested.

Until now.

Now, she saw it as a neat trick of societal and self deception.

The truth was the body was content to let the mind think it ruled until...

Until a too-handsome man with a too-pretty mouth happened into one's life and laid waste to all the lies one had been telling oneself.

Here—on this bench—*now*—him still inside her—*this* was the truth.

And, for the rest of her life, she could never unknow it.

* * *

FACE NESTLED into the crook of her neck, Dev inhaled.

She smelled of crisp rain and woodsy forest and lemon soap and *Beatrix*.

So small and delicate in his arms, yet so substantial.

For there was she and he apart.

Then there was them together.

And somehow the substance of them together held a weight more substantive than it should have.

It defied the laws of the universe.

She angled back and met his gaze. "We should probably…"

She didn't need to finish the sentence.

He shifted and, slowly, slid from her, even as every cell in his body demanded he stay where he was.

Then time sped its progress and they were no longer touching and she set about the business of making herself presentable—or at least, somewhere in that vicinity.

She was a right delectable mess, and their tupping hadn't improved matters. Though now, seeing her even more mussed and delectable with her flushed skin and bright eyes, it was all he could do not to lunge forward and kiss her again.

She liked his mouth and being kissed by it.

But he stayed where he was and buttoned his falls, allowing her a moment's privacy while she saw to her clothes.

"It's stopped raining," he said, rising to his feet.

His ear picked up a flurry of movement at his back, and she appeared at his side. "We can try finding our way again, I suppose."

She held his coat out to him. He took it, only to place it on her shoulders. "You'll catch a chill, Bea," he said, firmly, to ward off her inevitable protest.

She gave a roll of her eyes and started walking, leaving the protection of the folly. As dusk approached, the forest lay awash in glorious golden light. Side by side, they walked without touching. His fingers itched to twine through hers. Their loss of contact had been too abrupt.

"That probably wasn't the best idea." He felt it needed to be acknowledged, if for no other reason than to make the next few days of close proximity bearable.

"It wasn't an idea at all," she said, her gaze fixed ahead. "Ideas come from the mind, and *that* originated from an altogether different place."

"Shouldn't we discuss it?"

"Do you want to discuss it?"

"Not especially."

"Me either."

Her answer had a contrary effect inside him. He hadn't wanted to talk about it, because he feared that in doing so they would strip it of its magic.

But *her* not wanting to talk about it had a different feel…

In fact, he was now convinced they most definitely *should* talk about it.

"Do you see that?" She was pointing ahead.

He followed the direction of her finger. A moment later, he saw it—a thinning of the woods.

And he understood.

They weren't going to talk about it.

Disappointment sheared through him, and the now-familiar irritation caused by this woman returned. But he didn't have time to voice his mounting frustration as they emerged from the woods and onto the drive leading to the manor house. She set out at a swift clip, but he kept pace at her side. Was she attempting to be rid of him?

Well, she wouldn't find it easy.

The manor house, with its three stories of wide, uniform windows, stared out at them as they approached. They were on display again, for who knew whose eyes were watching their every movement at this very moment?

Still, he didn't insist they lock arms.

As they crunched across the gravel of the forecourt's circle drive, a coach-and-four rolled past and came to a stop before the wide, stone staircase that led up to the front doors, which were now swinging open in anticipation of the newly arrived guests.

Beatrix shot him a tetchy glance. She understood just as he

did they would have to play the welcoming hosts and greet these guests.

Objectively and collectively, they were an utter, bedraggled mess—hair still damp and tossed about, clothing rumpled, and generally mussed by the elements and…each other.

Blessedly, Beatrix was still wearing his greatcoat, so she wouldn't be starting any scandals with the damp transparency of her muslin dress.

With nimble alacrity, the uniformed tiger hopped down from the carriage's back bench and opened the door with a great flourish. From its depths emerged the Earl of Bridgewater, looking his usual thunderous self. Dev's teeth reflexively clenched at the sight of the man.

"Deverill," he said, his gaze catching on Dev and Beatrix at once. "You're looking rather…" The lift of a single eyebrow finished the observation for him.

"Yes, well, rainstorms and picnics are rather like oil and vinegar. They don't mix."

Bridgewater sniffed. "Indeed."

Behind him emerged Imogen.

As ever, she looked the picture of exquisite perfection, from the artful arrangement of sun-streaked curls around her heart-shaped face to the delicate pink glisten of bow-shaped lips. She was the sort of woman who could make a man's lungs forget how to breathe. A rainstorm wouldn't dare touch a single hair on her head.

A perfect goddess.

Movement to his left caught Dev's attention.

Beatrix.

Discomfort shimmering about her, she held the look of a woman who would rather sink into the wet earth than stand here in idle chit-chat. "I must—" she began.

"Oh, Mr. Deverill," Imogen cut in, her voice dripping with delight.

A voice that usually held the power to make him drop everything.

Except in this instant, he had a different concern—*Beatrix*.

"Primrose Park is absolutely stunning," continued Imogen, oblivious to any concern but her own. A quality he usually found charming. "Isn't it, Bridgy?"

Bridgy grunted.

"But…" Imogen cast her gaze over Dev in assessment, as if she were only now really seeing him. "I've seen you look better."

"We, *erm*, got lost."

"And there was the rain," supplied Beatrix, which only drew the attention of Bridgewater and Imogen.

Dev saw he had a host's duty to perform. "My lord, my lady, may I introduce Lady Beatrix St. Vincent to you?" he asked and hastily added, "My fiancée."

My fiancée.

For the pulse of a single second, a feeling pinged through him.

Rightness.

For that flicker of time, that concept in relation to him and Beatrix felt…*right*.

Which, of course, was all wrong.

Bridgewater offered an indifferent bow in Beatrix's direction, and Imogen's head subtly canted as she took Beatrix in.

Drawing upon generations of noble forebears, Beatrix lifted her chin and squared her shoulders. Dev could only admire the effort. "I'm pleased to make your acquaintance." She turned toward Dev. "Now, I shall see myself to my rooms for a much-needed bath and tea."

The sharp glint in her eye told Dev she would brook no opposition.

Then she dashed up the front steps as nimbly and with as much dignity as a half-soaked woman wrapped in a man's great-coat that dragged on the ground behind her could summon.

Dev wished she'd stayed.

Or invited him up to her bedroom to take part in the bath with her.

He gave himself a mental shake.

"Now," said Bridgewater, "let's see those stables of yours, Deverill."

"Don't mind me," said Imogen.

"You can manage yourself," dismissed Bridgewater.

"I always do, don't I?" No mistaking the note of acid in the little laugh that followed in Imogen's wake as she swept around them and into the house.

As Dev led Bridgewater toward the stables, the reality of the situation began to set in.

Imogen had arrived.

The anticipation of triumph should've been firing through his blood.

Vanquishment and surrender were within arm's reach, he felt it in his bones. All he had to do was grab hold.

Yet, somehow, his appetite for it felt...diminished.

A novel experience, to be sure, for he never relented once he had a victory in sight.

But novel experiences, it seemed, were becoming rather the usual since Lady Beatrix St. Vincent had entered his orbit.

And these novel experiences with Beatrix... They brightened his world, didn't they?

In a flash, he understood the source of his prevarication.

To seize victory on the one hand meant to suffer loss on the other.

Simply, and likely selfishly, he wasn't ready for either outcome.

CHAPTER TWENTY-FIVE

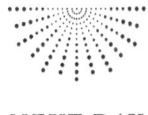

NEXT DAY

*A*s Beatrix traversed the corridors of Primrose Park toward the breakfast room with a bland smile affixed to her face, she felt rather proud of herself.

Somehow, she'd found the wherewithal to leave her bedroom.

Now, if only she could erase yesterday from existence.

Didn't the universe have limits on how many things could go wrong at once?

Surely, she'd pushed those boundaries as far as they could go.

But it seemed not.

Lydon arriving with Jagger... The rainstorm... The *something more* in the woods with Dev...

Meeting the Countess of Bridgewater looking, frankly, like an outright ravished mess.

Actually, the rainstorm might've been a blessing, for the mess caused by the rain hid in plain sight the havoc wrought by the *something more.*

And yesterday had been only the first day of the house party.

Blimey.

What fresh calamities did today hold?

Her feet came to a sudden halt. She could plead headache and take her morning meal in her bedroom, a time-honored practice of delicate ladies since King Arthur's court. After all, the Countess of Bridgewater had, indeed, arrived. Dev didn't need Beatrix around to woo the woman. In fact, it would be better if she wasn't.

In further shameful fact—and undoubtedly closer to the entire fact—she didn't think she could bear to watch said wooing.

Her feet had made up their mind to return to her room when she heard it—a rather robust bark coming from the direction of the breakfast room. Was that a dog?

On its heels came another sound—a familiar feminine laugh that had Beatrix's heart lifting in her chest. A few seconds later, she found Artemis dangling a slice of ham above a sheepdog who appeared to be missing both an eye and a leg. But the one remaining eye was fixed onto that slice of ham as if for dear life.

"Good girl." Artemis released the morsel, and the dog snatched it from the air.

"Artemis, you came," said Beatrix, rushing forward, unable to contain her delight—and relief. Until this moment, she hadn't realized how much she needed a true friend here with her.

A bright smile on her face, Artemis stood and enveloped Beatrix in a tight embrace. A hug from Artemis always contained a bit of ferocity. "Arrived at three this morning. The journey from Yorkshire cannot be overstated in its length and rigor."

"And I see you brought a friend." Beatrix smiled down at the dog, whose tail was wagging as if in hopeful anticipation of another piece of ham from her new friend.

"Meet Bathsheba," said Artemis. "I hope you don't mind her. She cannot bear to be away from me, so she comes with me everywhere. And to be clear, I shan't restrict her access to me by putting her outside. It would be cruel."

"Of course, she's welcome." Beatrix had no intention of separating them, but the way Artemis said it… She was such a privileged, doted-upon sister of a duke and took it as an absolute given that she would have her way. Somehow, her friend made it charming. "I can't imagine Dev—Mr. Deverill would mind."

Artemis took a step back without releasing Beatrix's hands and gave her a thorough up-and-down. "You're looking well."

"As are you."

Artemis had never been possessed of the ideal cream-and-roses English complexion, but rather of silky black hair, deep brown eyes, and lovely olive skin. In the months since Dido's untimely tragic death and Artemis's retreat to Yorkshire, the fresh northern air and days spent beneath the summer sun had lent her a golden glow. Her friend's brightness had returned.

Yet she was slightly altered, too.

One might call it maturity.

But Beatrix understood.

One didn't suffer loss without taking some damage.

"It appears Yorkshire is treating you well."

"Oh, yes." Artemis released Beatrix's hands and reached for her cup of tea. "I've become quite the wild thing in the north."

"It suits you."

"Doesn't it just?"

"And your horse sanctuary?"

Artemis snorted. "It's attracting every animal within a ten-mile radius." She didn't appear to mind.

"I've heard a rumor about a horse up there," said Beatrix, only now remembering. "A mythical lost Thoroughbred."

"Mm-hmm."

Back in the last century, a Yorkshire breeder happened to have a brother who was a merchant in Aleppo. This brother lucked upon a four-year-old Arabian stallion through one means or another—horse trading was a shadowy business—and sent the horse on to England, where he covered any Yorkshire mare brought to his stall. This stallion came to be known as the Darley Arabian, from whom a long line of winning Thoroughbreds descended, including the greatest of them all, Eclipse. However, it was in the breeding with the other multitude of mares that the rumored *lost* Thoroughbreds of Yorkshire descended.

Beatrix sensed Artemis was withholding information, so she did what she always did—she pressed. "This colt might be racing in the St. Leger? He had a silly name. What was it?"

"Radish."

"That's the one."

"Well," began Artemis with the determined lift to her chin that Beatrix knew well. "We'll see."

Just as Beatrix knew when to push, she knew when to retreat. "And Rake?" She poured herself a cup of tea. "Are he and his new duchess settling into the bosom of wedded bliss?"

"Oh, Gemma is wonderful," said Artemis with a genuine smile. "Whatever Rake did to deserve her, he needs to keep doing."

A pair of ladies entered the room, nodded their amiable morning greetings, and seated themselves near the far window.

Artemis's deep brown eyes narrowed on Beatrix. "But I don't wish to discuss any of that."

"No?"

"Grab a croissant." Artemis came to her feet. "We're taking a walk."

"For the dog?" Bathsheba appeared perfectly content.

Artemis shook her head. "For *you*."

A bemused laugh escaped Beatrix. "I don't need to be walked, Artemis."

"Oh, you do."

Nerves fluttered through Beatrix. She didn't want to discuss herself. She wasn't sure she could lie to Artemis.

And lies would most definitely be necessary.

Next thing, however, Beatrix was outside, Bathsheba bounding ahead as fast as a three-legged dog could bound, her stride matching that of Artemis—almost. Artemis was a good five inches taller than Beatrix and possessed of much longer legs.

The grounds of Primrose Park were lovely in the morning—sunlight imbuing the air with a soft golden glow, setting the dew on the grass asparkle. The estate was like a jewel box of perfection.

Beatrix spared the sky a suspicious glance. She didn't trust it after its behavior yesterday. The clouds appeared innocent with their puffy white indolence, but she knew better. They were wont to wreak havoc at a moment's notice. "Let's not venture too far from the house."

Artemis answered with a dubious lift of her eyebrows.

"Dev and I were caught out in a rainstorm yesterday," Beatrix explained.

Artemis remained unmoved in her skepticism.

"And soaked to the skin."

A vulpine smile curled about Artemis's mouth. "*Dev?*"

Beatrix's stomach dropped.

"Would this be the same *Dev* who is your fiancé? The same *Dev* who is known in society as Lord Devil?"

"Same and...same."

Artemis would, of course, want the details—the how and the why and the everything in between.

"Imagine my shock when an invitation to a house party celebrating the engagement of my dearest friend to one Mr. Blake Deverill arrived in the post." Past bewilderment yet echoed through the words. "I wasn't aware the two of you were acquainted. So, a whirlwind romance?"

"Something like that." Beatrix was being circumspect—and Artemis would seize upon it.

"Tell me all about *Dev*."

"Well," Beatrix began, her mouth gone suddenly dry, "he's handsome."

"Indeed."

"And very successful."

Artemis nodded, consideringly, and looked in no way satisfied by Beatrix's answers. When she opened her mouth surely to pursue the matter of Mr. Blake Deverill further, a cacophonous splashing sound tore through the air.

Beatrix, at last, noticed her surroundings.

Their ramble into the woods had led them to the little pond.

A delighted laugh escaped Artemis as she took in the sight of Bathsheba enjoying a swim. "Oh, what a lovely folly. Let's explore, shall we?"

"No!" shouted Beatrix.

Artemis shot her a bemused glance.

"There's a…" Beatrix searched her mind for something—*anything*—that would prevent them from entering the folly. She wouldn't be able to bear it, given…*yesterday*. "There's a… wild beehive."

Really, she should sound more affrighted than relieved.

Disinclined to argue the point, Artemis shrugged and whistled to Bathsheba, indicating they would keep walking.

Even as she strolled with her friend, Beatrix waited.

The interrogation was far from over.

It wasn't a minute before Artemis returned to the subject. "Now, tell me about *Dev*." When Beatrix opened her mouth to reply, her friend held up a staying hand. "And not what anyone can see with their own eyes and hear from any old gossip hound." Her gaze bored into the side of Beatrix's face. "Who is he, really? And why are you engaged to the man?"

The truth lifted its head and presented itself as an option.

After all, Artemis was her dearest friend.

No.

If she spoke one truth, it might lead to another, deeper truth… then another yet deeper.

"He's not really a devil, of course."

A surface truth.

A safe truth.

Artemis held her tongue and waited for more.

"He's very…" Oh, Dev was *very* a lot of things… "Sweet."

A truth a little less safe—one that teetered on the edge of dangerous. The sort of truth that could be a falling domino, if she wasn't careful.

Artemis's brow gathered. "Blake Deverill is *sweet?*"

"He is, actually." For some reason, she continued. "And thoughtful. Loyal, too."

Artemis snorted. "He would make an excellent dog."

Beatrix laughed. She couldn't help it, even as the thread of tension pulled tauter within her.

"But you haven't mentioned one thing," continued Artemis.

"What is that?"

"Love."

Oh.

Beatrix cleared her throat. A stalling tactic. She was utterly unprepared for this turn of conversation, though she shouldn't have been. "I feel…"

What did she feel?

A jumble with too much feeling.

That was the truth of it.

"I feel affection for him."

"*Affection?*" scoffed Artemis. "You're upsetting the entire balance of your life for *affection?*"

Beatrix nodded.

She didn't like this lie precisely because it didn't feel all that much like a lie.

What it felt like was the least safe truth she'd yet spoken.

Artemis stopped and turned, pinning Beatrix in place with the force of her gaze. "Beatrix, you can tell me."

"Tell you what?"

If a question could be a lie, this one was.

"Tell me what that man has over your head. Beatrix, I have means. I know the last several years haven't been the easiest for you, and really I should've said something before now, but I can help you."

Beatrix's cheeks burst into flame. She wasn't sure if she wanted to hug Artemis or give her a good telling off. She managed to say, "What Deverill and I have isn't blackmail."

"Then what is it?"

Beatrix tore her gaze from her friend and began marching. The instant she emerged from the woods, a sharp, feminine shout brought her to an immediate standstill. She met Artemis's gaze over her shoulder. "Did you hear that?"

Artemis held a hand to her forehead, her gaze scanning the open grounds. "*There,*" she said, pointing toward a flat stretch of land on the other side of the large pond. "A group is out shooting at straw targets."

A fleet arrow whizzed through the air, followed by a solid *thunk*, punctuating the fact.

"I suppose we should join them." A distinct lack of enthusiasm accompanied Beatrix's words.

"Indeed," said Artemis, distinctly enthusiastic. "You can introduce me to *Dev.*"

Beatrix didn't groan—only just.

As they neared the party, she took note of those present. Lord Bridgewater seated with his morning newspaper open before him, alternating his attention between paper and proceedings— sardonically, no doubt. Lord Wrexford's shock of copper hair announced his presence as he stood near Mr. Shaw and the eldest Miss Shaw, who was undoubtedly blushing furiously at the attentions of an eligible gentleman—an earl, no less. And off to the side, bows at the ready for another round of shooting, stood Lady Bridgewater and Dev.

There, the proof indisputable, was Dev's wooing of the countess commenced.

It was all Beatrix could do to keep placing one foot in front of the other in forward fashion and not pick up her skirts, whirl around, and leg it back to the woods.

Now that they'd moved closer, she saw Dev's bow had lowered.

And he was staring directly at her.

Her heart beat out a heavy thump in her chest. Through the sudden influx of blood rushing in her ears, she heard Artemis say, "I don't know what is going on between you and that man, and I suppose you'll tell me when you're ready, but I will say this: You've certainly chosen a handsome one to bestow your *affection* upon."

In that instant, a certainty came to Beatrix.

She would never tell Artemis—or anyone else, for that matter.

What existed between her and Dev—be it affection or *something more* or something else—it was only for them.

On the heels of that unsettling certainty came a wish.

That she had followed instinct earlier and gone back to bed.

And now, for her sins, she would have to watch Dev woo another woman.

How was she going to come through the next several minutes unscathed, much less the next three days?

CHAPTER TWENTY-SIX

*D*ev understood his role today—and the two opportunities it presented.

First, as host, he had the opportunity to give society what it wanted—opulence, the fulfillment of whims, and the general pleasure-seeking they so enjoyed. Since they did little else, he supposed frivolity was what they lived for.

This morning, pleasure came in the form of archery.

"It's too bad Richmond couldn't stay," opined the Earl of Bridgewater from behind his open *Times*.

Yesterday, once the Duke of Richmond had completed his thorough inspection of Little Wicked and the stables, he'd been gone by the evening meal.

"I have a filly I think would suit his stables," continued Bridgewater, offhand.

As he'd been a fringe member of the *haut ton* for nearly a year, Dev had gained the ability to parse between the lines of Bridge-water's *offhand* statement.

The earl needed money.

Which Dev knew, of course, as the fact was a central element of his plan to win Imogen.

Yet what aristocrat didn't need money?

Dev still didn't understand how that worked. Nobs took it as their right to have the finest of everything in life, yet they did nothing to earn the blunt to attain it.

The economics simply didn't work.

Except those very same economics worked for a man like Dev —and others like him on the rise. Those economics had yielded him Little Wicked, Primrose Park, and...

Beatrix.

What a strange thought.

But it was true when viewed from a certain angle.

If Lydon had managed his finances better, his daughter wouldn't have entered into an arrangement with a man like Dev.

Well, a man had to take his luck where he found it.

The absence of Richmond notwithstanding, the house party seemed to be a success with close to forty members of the highest echelon of society attending. Beatrix had been correct. If he invited them, they would attend and happily partake of his hospitality.

Most were still abed and would be so until the middling hours of the afternoon—the *haut ton* loved its late nights—but others were interested in partaking of activities and archery had been the one this lot had agreed upon.

His eye caught on a small cluster of figures. There stood Shaw, supervising his eldest daughter's shooting lesson, which was being taught by the Earl of Wrexford. Even from here, Dev could see both earl and young lady were blushing furiously. He was no matchmaker, but there was no mistaking how the wind blew there—a young earl and a young heiress.

Those economics added up.

"Mr. Deverill?" he heard at his back.

He knew the voice to the marrow of his bones—*Imogen.*

He turned and found her looking as exquisite as ever, her

plain brown wool shooting costume somehow only enhancing her lush beauty.

Being a countess did suit her.

"Would you care for a friendly round of archery?"

And here was the second of Dev's two opportunities as host presenting itself.

Time with Imogen.

His entire reason for hosting a country house party in the first place—lest he forget.

"Of course," he said. Her husband didn't take notice as he settled deeper into his newspaper.

The glint of competition shone in Imogen's eyes and smile. She was an expert in the sport of archery. Far superior to Dev, in fact.

He moved toward the target-shooting area where pairs of haystacks were set up beside each other. Fifty yards opposite stood corresponding pairs of haystacks. As they competed, they would shoot from one end to the other in rotation.

Dev couldn't understand why his feet felt heavy. He was getting what he wanted—time with Imogen. Yet his eyes kept darting toward the house every time a new figure emerged. But it was always a servant moving to this or that task set by the guests.

It was never Beatrix.

Where had she got off to this morning, anyway?

Shouldn't she be here, making Imogen jealous?

Really, she might be in breach of their arrangement.

But mostly, he was genuinely curious what she was doing this very moment.

She'd disappeared into the house yesterday evening—and he hadn't seen her since.

They still needed to talk.

Except…perhaps they didn't.

Now, he had this golden opportunity to spend time with Imogen.

It was possible the rest was up to him, and he didn't need Beatrix anymore.

The idea didn't sit comfortably inside him.

In fact, every cell of his body rejected it.

"Dev?" Imogen was smiling, but a question flicked in her eyes.

He'd been staring at the house again.

He accepted a bow from a waiting footman and joined her at the nearest pair of haystacks.

"Remember how we would spend entire afternoons seeing who could hit the most bullseyes?"

"I remember you always winning," he said. "That was a long time ago."

He didn't know why he said that last part—except it was the truth.

It *was* a long time ago.

More than ten years...*fifteen*?

Long enough for him to have been an entirely different person.

Imogen positioned herself at the line and fitted nock to string. Her body perpendicular to the target some fifty yards distant, she gracefully bent the bow, only an instant's hesitation to confirm her aim, then released her fingers. The arrow buried itself confidently in the center of the target, as if it had been an inevitability.

Dev couldn't begrudge Imogen the smugness of the smirk she turned on him. "Match that," she said.

She truly loved winning. She was at her most beautiful when she won.

It had been why, ten or fifteen years ago, he hadn't minded losing to her—the opportunity to view her beauty in full blossom.

Today, however, he felt mostly indifferent.

He followed suit and...didn't match *that*. He'd barely even notched the outermost white ring. "I'm a bit out of practice," he offered apologetically.

Imogen enjoyed winning, yes, but mostly she enjoyed a close competition that was, of course, followed by her win.

With the next arrow, she struck the heart again.

Dev missed the haystack altogether.

"Dev!" she exclaimed in frustration. "Are you even trying?"

He wasn't.

He cared not a whit who won.

He was just about to tell her exactly that when two figures appeared on the periphery of his vision. Two ladies, strolling into view from the direction of the pond. Was that a dog with them?

He didn't know the dog or one of the ladies. But he did know the other lady on sight...and feel...

And every which other way, too.

His heart lifted in his chest.

Beatrix.

"Dev," Imogen said—at his back.

His feet had begun moving—toward Beatrix.

"We still have two rounds."

"Of course." He couldn't keep the indifference from his voice.

As the contest resumed, he tracked Beatrix from the edge of his eye as she mingled through the gathering, which had grown in size since he and Imogen had begun shooting. She did so easily, as this was the world to which she was accustomed.

Further, he recognized the other woman. *Lady Artemis Keating*, sister of the Duke of Rakesley. As Lady Artemis was rumored to be both intelligent and a woman who went her own way, Dev immediately saw how the women would be friends. Birds of a feather, those two.

At last, the round concluded—which happened to coincide with Beatrix and Lady Artemis venturing within speaking distance.

"You're looking lovely today," he called out.

A delighted laugh trilled from Imogen, but her smile fell when she saw she wasn't the object of the compliment.

A light blush pinked Beatrix's cheeks.

He was speaking the words of courtship one would say to a fiancée. So, there was an element of speaking for show. But these words… He meant them.

Beatrix did, indeed, look lovely in her delicate ivory muslin gown and silver-threaded navy velvet spencer that brought out that hint of violet from her eyes.

Lady Artemis cleared her throat, prompting Beatrix to say, "Lady Artemis, may I introduce Mr. Deverill to you?"

Dev bowed, and the lady dipped in a shallow curtsy. "Pleased to make your acquaintance, Mr. Deverill. It's the rare man who could sweep Beatrix off her feet. I look forward to discovering how you accomplished it." The serious glint in her eye said she would be successful, too.

Another throat cleared with a light, feminine lilt.

Imogen.

He'd rather forgotten her for a moment. She was waiting for him to perform another introduction. "Lady Bridgewater, may I introduce Lady Artemis to you?"

As Imogen held the higher rank through marriage, Lady Artemis dipped in a shallow curtsy. "Ah, Lady Bridgewater, what a delight."

Imogen nodded like a queen, as if the world had been set right with her place in it acknowledged. "Dev and I were just enjoying a shooting contest."

The air went suddenly too still.

Dev.

She'd called him Dev—publicly.

Further, she'd placed a hand on his arm.

It felt…*proprietary.*

He wanted to shake free, but resisted.

Beatrix and Lady Artemis noticed, with the latter subtly lifting an eyebrow. Beatrix glanced away.

"Do you ladies enjoy archery?" asked Imogen.

"I shoot the odd round here and there," said Lady Artemis.

Imogen's gaze narrowed on Beatrix. "And you, Lady Beatrix?"

"Can't say it's been a pursuit of mine."

"It's very simple, really." Imogen appeared to make up her mind about something on the spot. "I shall give you a lesson."

Before Dev could think through the consequences of his actions, he was stepping forward and saying, "I'll show her the basic steps."

Beatrix's gaze darted between him and Imogen, as if unsure which prospect horrified her more.

Imogen's mouth curved into a tight smile. "What a generous and thoughtful fiancé you are, Dev."

"I'll shoot with you, Lady Bridgewater." Lady Artemis signaled for a servant to bring her a bow. "Though I'm not dressed for it as you are. Could you lend me your brace and shooting glove as we go?"

"Of course," Imogen tossed over her shoulder, as she strode to the haystacks and plucked arrows from the targets.

Lady Artemis followed—which left Dev alone with Beatrix.

She met his gaze with the lift of an eyebrow. "I haven't the least interest in archery."

As he was naturally wont to do, Dev saw opportunity. "You're my fiancée, remember?"

"How can I possibly forget?"

"Then be a good fiancée for all these nice aristocrats observing us and humor me."

She was annoyed, as she had every right to be. Dev was playing dirty by alluding to their arrangement to influence her compliance. Well, hadn't she learned by now he wasn't above it?

Bow in one hand and quiver of arrows in the other, he led her to the last pair of haystacks in the row, which kept them in view of all, but not within hearing. She crossed her arms over her chest.

He held up one hand. "This is a bow." He held up the other. "These are arrows." He pointed. "That is the target."

"I'm not a complete dunderhead."

"You fit the nock of the arrow—that's this little notch—to the string." He illustrated each instruction with the corresponding action. "Then you lift the bow, pull the string on an inhalation, aim, and...release." He left out the bit about offering a quick prayer heavenward that it would hit the target.

Proving that prayer worked, the arrow—*improbably... miraculously*—buried itself into the very heart of the gold circle.

A reluctant smile curved Beatrix's mouth. "Impressive."

So he wouldn't follow the compulsion to bask in the not-quite-warm glow of her praise, he extended the bow and an arrow. "Your turn."

Her smile fell. "Dev," she began, her tone absolutely reasonable. "Must I truly—"

"You must," he cut in. "*Truly.*"

He knew why he insisted—and she would, too, in a moment.

She took the proffered implements without joy, the lift of her chin mutinous.

"Now..." He stepped closer.

Her brow creased with alarm. "What are you doing?"

"Instructing you, of course," he said, all innocence—and anything but. "Position your body perpendicular to the target. Like so..." He touched his hand to her waist and applied light pressure until she followed the movement. "Now, you'll want to fit the bowstring into the nock."

Telling, that rasp in his voice.

Not only to him.

She would know it, too.

His hands remained on her waist, even as the rest of him remained apart from her, separated by a sliver of air. How his body ached to close that distance.

"Like this?" she asked.

And there it was—the telling rasp in *her* voice.

He angled and peered over her shoulder. "Yes," he said, his voice a low rumble. He imagined a shiver purling down her spine.

She lifted the bow and began pulling the string. "Here," he said, reaching around and placing his hands over hers—purely in the interest of instruction, of course.

As they bent the bow together, he felt her tremble. It could've been down to typically unused muscles being put to work. But it wasn't. It was their bodies touching, him flush against her back, his cockstand rising. The ragged tremor of her inhalations and exhalations matched his.

How intimate and precious was the air around them.

"Now," he muttered. "*Release.*"

As one, their fingers unclenched, and the arrow let fly, hitting the haystack, but missing the target.

It mattered not.

Her head angled, her gaze lifted, black-fringed gray eyes meeting his. "Like that?"

Their mouths weren't an inch apart, so close her words whispered across his lips. It would be so easy...so natural...to shift that complicated increment and press his mouth to hers...

Then he felt it—a wet splat square on the bridge of his nose, followed by another on the tip of an ear.

She blinked, as if waking from an altered state, but remained as she was. "Rain?"

A drop landed on her nose, and he resisted the impulse to lick it off.

"Of course," he said on a wry chuckle.

Her expressive eyes rolled toward the darkening sky. "We might be the cure for drought."

And Dev felt it—an echo of the friendship they'd formed before they'd become *something more.*

"Beatrix!" Dashing straight for them was Lady Artemis, her three-legged dog keeping pace at her side. "Let's go inside!"

Dev held Beatrix's gaze for a full second longer, willing her to stay, the elements be damned. Then she inhaled a steadying breath and called out, "I'm coming!"

And she was off—and Dev was alone, watching her sprint for cover beneath the solid slate roof of the manor house. He didn't blame her, but how he wished she'd stayed.

Though both guests and servants alike scurried and scrambled this way and that—a good, hard rain ever held the power to turn humans into squirrels—Dev felt no need to rush. Instead, he assisted the servants as they collected tea service, blankets, chairs, bows, arrows, and scattered newspapers—all the equipment of a morning's archery outing.

A solid half hour had passed before he stepped into the boot room, thoroughly soaked.

Which was precisely what he'd needed after the archery lesson with Beatrix—a good, bracing cool down.

CHAPTER TWENTY-SEVEN

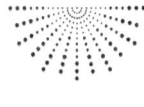

EVENING

*I*n the end, Beatrix had attended the evening meal.

But, oh, how she'd struggled with committing to the decision.

As fiancée of the host, she was the hostess by default. Her presence was expected by the guests—and the host himself.

Seated at one end of the long dining table, Dev at the other, she'd mostly conversed with Artemis to her left—as she'd fed a patient Bathsheba every other bite of her food—and to Lord Ipswich to her right, who was altogether too eager to relate in specific detail his most recent battle against a toenail fungus.

Every so often, her gaze had caught upon Dev as he continued to make the case that he had every right to breathe the rarified air of the *haut ton*. The fact was he made his case well. There likely wasn't anyone in attendance who hadn't come around to the idea.

Of course, that was all destined to change.

When he incited a divorce between the Earl and Countess of Bridgewater—for there was little doubt in her mind that he would be successful in the endeavor—the *ton* would close ranks around their own.

Not that Dev would care.

He would have what he wanted—and Dev always got what he wanted.

The thought inspired a slow shiver that made its sinuous way up her spine.

Now, she was stuck in the drawing room with the ladies while the majority of the men smoked cigars and drank brandy in the study. She lacked the patience for needlework, and the gossip being bandied about wasn't all that fresh.

Her gaze caught on the only gentleman present. *Lord Wrexford*, positioned beside the piano, turning sheets of music for the eldest Miss Shaw while she played. Both were blushing as furiously now as they had been earlier.

Beatrix knew a blossoming love match when she saw one.

As for Artemis, the instant the meal had been over, she'd stood and declared Bathsheba in need of her evening ramble, after which, her friend would be taking herself to bed. "I keep country hours now."

As Beatrix sat and smiled and nodded with distant agreeability, she found herself wishing she had a useful dog.

"Ah-ha," came a jolly voice from the doorway.

Instinctively, Beatrix winced.

"Here's where my lovely harem ran off to," continued Lydon, producing a chorus of feminine titters.

Beatrix suspected they were less provoked by Lydon's flattery than by the presence of Blaze Jagger at his side. The frisson of excitement that enlivened the air couldn't be denied.

Her brother.

Blaze Jagger was her brother.

And he was here… *Why?*

To keep a close eye on his investment?

Or perhaps to prove something?

The latter felt as if it edged closer to the truth.

"Now, I know needlework gets you lovelies all het up,"

continued Lydon. "But how about we enjoy an activity a little less exciting, like…cards?"

Of course, Lydon would suggest cards. Any form of gambling, really. He couldn't be long away from it. Beatrix could only hope there were no roosters prowling about Primrose Park. He'd have them sparring by midnight.

Along with the other gentlemen ambling into the room, Dev entered. As he caught wind of the direction the evening was taking, he quietly conferred with servants. Soon, tables and chairs were being brought in to accommodate an impromptu evening of cards.

His gaze cut over and caught hers.

He winked.

So quick it was, she could've blinked and missed it, for he'd been immediately pulled into conversation with Lord Ipswich. Beatrix hoped he was prepared to become acquainted with the anti-fungal properties of apple cider vinegar.

"He's quite a man, isn't he?" came an admiring feminine voice.

Beatrix took the split of a second to brace herself before turning to face Lady Bridgewater. "I presume you're not speaking of Lord Ipswich."

Lady Bridgewater giggled, delighted. "You're funny." A smile remained perched upon her perfect bow-shaped mouth. "Congratulations on being the one to catch him."

Beatrix didn't feel like she was being congratulated. The glint in Lady Bridgewater's eyes suggested curiosity and…challenge.

Beatrix was being tested.

"I'm not sure *catch* is the correct word," she said. "I don't recall him running away."

Neither Lady Bridgewater's smile nor the glint in her eyes faded. "A woman who fashions herself a wit." She eyed Beatrix up and down. "I wouldn't have thought Dev would fall for one of those."

Beatrix was certain she'd been insulted to her face, but had no interest in taking offense. "And what sort of woman did you think *Dev* would fall for?" She hadn't missed that use of *Dev*—and the familiarity implied.

Lady Bridgewater's smile turned feline. She didn't need to speak the answer aloud. They both knew it.

Me.

And really, that was all the answer Beatrix needed.

Lady Bridgewater yet harbored a passion for Dev.

"We grew up together, you know."

"He mentioned it."

Lady Bridgewater gave a subtle lift of her brow. "Did he? I would've thought he'd want to keep that to himself."

"Oh, Dev and I don't hold any secrets from one another."

Beatrix was definitely toying with the countess, and she should stop, truly, but she couldn't seem to.

It wasn't that she was having fun with the woman's emotions, but she thought the countess could stand to have her horizons broadened.

It would be to her benefit.

The fact was Beatrix didn't take issue with the countess.

Simply, the woman was a product of her environment—an environment that told women their only value was in their beauty and the fecundity of their wombs. A society that pitted them against one another when it grew bored, which was often. A society that discouraged women to use their minds critically.

What was clear to Beatrix was that the countess subscribed to it all—many women did.

Yet though she understood this about the countess, that didn't mean she could ever be friends with the woman.

They didn't view life from the same angle.

And now that she'd gotten to know Dev, she wouldn't have thought he did, either.

But that only illustrated how much she understood about the motivations of men.

"No secrets? How very convenient for you, Lady Beatrix," said the countess. "I'm sure that bodes well for your wedded bliss. Although—" She snorted. If a snort could've been ladylike, hers was. "If there is bliss to be found in the wedded state, I wish someone would tell me the secret."

Like that, Beatrix felt badly for every unkind thought and opinion she'd entertained of this woman. Certainly, the countess had been a title huntress, but the Earl of Bridgewater was known to have cruel proclivities of the sort both publicly acknowledged and those only whispered about. The countess had likely already paid the price for securing a title—and would continue to do so.

Until she ran off with Dev, that was.

More than ever, the possibility appeared an inevitability.

The countess shifted her gaze, her cheeks uncharacteristically high with color. Abashment hung about her, as if she'd said too much and was now embarrassed.

"Dev has nothing but wonderful things to say about his childhood," said Beatrix. Then for some unfathomable reason, she added, "And you."

Lady Bridgewater blinked, and for an instant, her mask slipped. She looked younger and fresher, her beauty so vibrant she was almost too much to behold directly.

In this instant, Beatrix saw the Imogen he knew.

"He does?" she asked, slightly breathless.

Beatrix nodded.

An unguarded smile flirted about the countess's mouth before her arch mask slipped back into place. "How very sweet of him."

And she left that as her farewell as she pivoted in a swish of silk skirts and took her place at the card table to join a game of Whist just forming.

As the room settled into card play, Beatrix understood she had a choice.

Stay and endure a long, slogging night...or slip discreetly away.

Before her mind could counter instinct, her feet were on the move and exiting the room at a swift clip that couldn't be characterized as a run—*just*.

She pointed them in the direction of the kitchens. That was where she would find Cumberbatch. He would be awake, of course. His intermittent naps throughout the day served to bank his energy for the night. She needed to see how he was faring.

His bunions might need tending.

She would stop by her bedroom for the castor oil—just in case.

* * *

DEV SETTLED into a leather armchair and idly exhaled a stream of cigar smoke, a brandy lolling in his other hand. He was aware of the picture he presented to the gentlemen presently circulating the supremely masculine domain of his study.

He was one of them.

Almost.

These exalted men had happily partaken of his hospitality these last two days, but it was clear they still didn't know what to think of him.

"So," began the lord in the adjacent armchair—an earl, "you didn't inherit the business from your father?"

The earl was only giving voice to what many in this room found incredibly difficult to reconcile—the foreign idea of a man building something from the ground, rather than having had it passed to him through inheritance, as their titles and place in the world had been handed to them.

The exception in this room was Blaze Jagger, of course. Dev had been keeping an eye on the scoundrel for a variety of reasons —reasons too many to enumerate. Suffice it to say, this house party presented myriad opportunities for Jagger to create havoc, if he so chose.

"My father is, in fact, very much alive," said Dev, "and presently touring the Lake District with my mother."

The information elicited a further gathering of more than a few eyebrows.

From the corner of his eye, Dev noted Lydon edging along the periphery of the gathered. He avoided acknowledging him. The truth was Dev didn't much like being pulled into the orbit of such a man. For all his titles, Lydon was naught more than a rotter in aristocrat's clothing.

However, Dev was left with no choice when Lydon pushed in further. "My sincerest apologies for interrupting this absolutely riveting discussion," said the marquess, inserting himself without apology, "but might I request a word with my lovely daughter's future husband?"

"Of course," said Dev, rising to his feet and leading Lydon to the set of doors that opened onto the terrace.

Outside, the rain had eased off, so they were able to step beyond the protection of the roof where they could converse with privacy. He didn't know for a fact what Lydon wanted to discuss, but he could hazard a guess.

Lydon didn't hold him in suspense for long. "Now, about what we formerly discussed."

"You'll have to refresh my memory." Dev was in no mood to make it easy for the marquess.

"The bit of pocket money." And Lydon was in no mood to be misunderstood.

"Ah, yes," said Dev, nodding sagely. "One hundred pounds, was it?"

An edge of steel glinted within the gray of Lydon's eyes. "Every week."

"Indeed."

"And you missed last week."

"Right."

The moment dragged on a beat too long. Dev wasn't the least discomfited. He wanted to see if the old scoundrel would crack.

His gaze remained steadier than Dev had ever seen it.

This was deadly serious business.

At last, Dev relented. This was Beatrix's father, after all. "I'll have the two hundred pounds delivered to you by morning."

A sudden, hale-and-hearty smile lit across Lydon's face, utterly transforming it. He slapped Dev on the back in the jocular manner of carousing mates. "Good man."

A marquess who knew when to leave before minds could change, Lydon had disappeared from sight before the next three seconds could elapse. Dev snorted and took another puff of cigar. The gentlemen had already begun moving from the study to join the ladies.

Dev entered the drawing room only to find Lydon proposing an evening of cards. It surprised him not in the least. Lydon had never met a penny he didn't want to gamble away. The two hundred pounds would already be committed to debts of honor before it even arrived in his rooms by morning.

Dev sent for the housekeeper hired temporarily for the house party while his parents were away—really, he would consult with his mother to make the woman a permanent addition to the staff —and conducted a quick consultation about transforming the drawing room into a makeshift gaming hell.

Through the evening, he'd kept half an eye on Beatrix—and now was no different. In truth, he'd expected her to bolt to her rooms after the meal. Sometimes, he could forget she was made of sterner stuff.

They needed to talk.

He would've thought they had all the time in the world for a private moment or two.

But the opposite held true.

A spare or idle minute wasn't to be found anywhere.

And they most definitely needed to talk.

The *something more* they'd been indulging in... Well, the proper thing would be to say it needed to stop.

But the problem was he wasn't sure he possessed the strength to say it.

Echoes of her feel...her touch...yet resonated through him.

He glanced toward the spot beside the mantle where he'd last seen her, and though he found her there, someone had joined her.

Imogen.

Not only that, but the two women were talking.

He couldn't say he exactly felt good about it.

In fact, a feeling of dread stirred and began crawling through him.

Somehow, he dragged his gaze away and kept to his role of benevolent host, seeing to table arrangements and pausing for small talk. But all the while Beatrix and Imogen remained at the periphery of his vision—his true focal point.

He didn't like comparing them, for they were as opposite from one another as the north pole from the south.

Yet he found himself doing so.

The physical differences between them were, of course, apparent. Imogen possessed the sort of overblown beauty that flashed and sparkled and commanded attention. While Beatrix's beauty was quieter, more delicate. It made no demands on one's attention, but once captured, one wasn't quick to look away.

She was lovely.

But these were the surfaces of the two women and, while appealing, weren't as interesting as the essences of who they *were* below.

He'd known Imogen for so long, he found it difficult to articulate who she was. Simply, he'd always known her—so he knew her.

As for Beatrix, surprisingly, he felt the same way.

As if he knew her down to the marrow of her bones.

For over a decade, he'd been sure no woman compared to Imogen. But as Beatrix stood beside her, a new possibility occurred to him.

Perhaps no one compared to *her*.

This was what unsettled the ground beneath his feet.

Since he'd been able to want anything, he'd wanted Imogen.

And the truth of it was, he felt close to making her his.

It was in the way she'd been interacting with him—the playful flash of the eye here and there—and speaking to him—*Dev*—and the fact that her marriage was clearly an unhappy one.

And yet another fact.

He knew her.

Behind that lush beauty of hers ran a streak of wildness—and willfulness, too.

In fact, it was these very qualities he'd sought to exploit in his pursuit of her.

And now she was almost *his*.

Though he could all but taste the victory, it yet failed to excite the part of him that reveled in vanquishment.

"Quite the country estate you have here," came an East End voice behind him.

Dev turned to find Blaze Jagger's mouth curled into a cocksure smile, his diamond stud winking in greeting. The rogue cut a flamboyant figure in his evening blacks and garish fuchsia silk waistcoat.

"A right inspiration to us honest working men."

Dev's brow lifted. "Is that how you think of yourself? An *honest* working man?"

Jagger's smile increased in width and arrogance. "Let's leave it at *working* and call it a compromise."

Dev didn't join in the smile. In fact, he had a few words to speak to this man. "Join me on the terrace."

Once out of earshot of the card party, which was growing

more boisterous by the second. Dev got to it. "This debt you're holding."

Jagger cocked his head, a sudden serious glint in his eye that disconcertingly mirrored his sister's. "That's between me and the marquess."

Dev gave his head a slow shake. "It affects Beatrix. If you turf Lydon out, you'll be turfing her out, too, and damaging her reputation along with it."

Jagger wagged a finger. "Now, see? That math doesn't add all the way up. The lady will be marrying a man who is rich as—or more like, richer than—the king himself, so I don't see how Lydon's troubles affect her at all."

Of course, Dev wouldn't be explaining his arrangement with Beatrix to this man, but Jagger wasn't one to accept anything at face value. He would always be on the lookout for the angle—or the lie, as it was. Dev would have to present him a new angle to consider. "Beatrix doesn't have anyone fighting her corner."

Jagger's brow lifted in utter disbelief. "Doesn't she have *you?*" A beat. "Her fiancé?"

"It's complicated."

"Seems simple to me."

Dev wasn't sure if Jagger realized he'd done it, but he'd squared up to Dev.

A startling possibility occurred to him.

Was Jagger feeling...*brotherly?*

Dev saw an opening to say what needed to be said and seized it. "I'll pay off Lydon's debt."

Jagger gave a low whistle. "That's right generous of you."

"With one caveat."

"I do revel in a good negotiation."

"You can buy as much of Lydon's debt as you like. But you don't send correspondence to Little Stanhope Street. Lydon won't see it, but Beatrix will, and she'll feel responsible for it."

"How is that?"

"She's that sort of person."

"Nah, I get that about her." Jagger sucked his teeth. "The other thing. How will she see Lydon's mail? Won't she be living in happily-ever-after bliss with her husband and opening *his* mail?"

Out of anyone currently beneath Primrose Park's sloped slate roof, Jagger would be the one to scent something out-of-the-common with his and Beatrix's relationship. "You should try getting to know your sister," he said, under no obligation to give the man a direct answer. "You might like her."

Jagger sniffed. "Lady High-and-Mighty would deign to favor a scoundrel like me with her attention?"

Dev took the response as one of insecurity, a self-protective instinct—and he didn't have time for it. "She did for me. It's who you are in *here*"—he poked a finger into the center of Jagger's chest—"that matters to Beatrix. That's not to say she'll just give you the time of day. You'll have to earn it, but it's worth it. *She* is worth it."

That last part... It was absolutely true.

How much more interesting was his life since she'd entered it?

For his part, Jagger wasn't ceding any conversational ground, but Dev knew he was collecting every word and adding them up.

He just had one more thing to say to the man. "It's best if you get back to London."

Jagger would understand it wasn't a suggestion.

Dev wasn't finished. "And take Lydon with you."

A quick smile transformed Jagger's features. "Now, that will cost you extra," he said with a nod and wink of farewell.

Relief poured through Dev. He didn't know how matters would turn out with Beatrix, but she would no longer have Jagger lurking in shadows.

He returned to the drawing room and found card play in full, lively swing. He knew even before a scan of the room confirmed it that Beatrix was gone. He felt the heat of several pairs of eyes upon him, but one in particular.

Imogen.

She'd saved a place beside her at the card table.

Even as he pretended not to notice and moved in the opposite direction, he questioned himself. He was on the verge of having everything he'd always wanted. Anticipation and excitement should've been thrumming through his veins.

Yet the only feeling he could conjure was a strange, dissatisfied emptiness. As if what he'd always wanted wasn't actually what he wanted at all.

As if he'd taken a wrong turn somewhere and kept hurtling headlong in the wrong direction.

Unsettled...rattled...shaken... These were new feelings for him.

He couldn't help but notice when these feelings had been introduced into his life.

When Beatrix had entered it.

CHAPTER TWENTY-EIGHT

NEXT DAY

*T*he rain had decided to make itself an uninvited guest and stay all through the night and into the morning, making it necessary to cancel all the day's activities, which were to have taken place out of doors.

This was how Beatrix found herself—unexpectedly and improbably—stepping inside Deverill & Shaw Company, their steam engine manufacturing factory in Camden.

When she'd awakened this morning to the admittedly dreary day, the idea hadn't yet formed. After midday tea, it was the Countess of Bridgewater who had spoken the fateful words. "Oh, I know what we can do. Let's visit Dev's—Mr. Deverill's factory."

Beatrix had kept her mouth shut and waited. Artemis had begged off and taken herself and Bathsheba to the stables. She'd needed to see for herself that the animals were being cared for properly. Most of the other ladies had been content to stay by the cozy fire, do needlework, and gossip. Many of the gentlemen were similarly engaged with billiards and cigars—and gossip, too, no doubt. Men weren't immune to the seductive whisper of tittle-tattle. Besides, it gave them an excuse to imbibe spirits before evening tea.

Still, that left many in need of something to occupy them. Which was the only way Beatrix could explain the round of ready agreement to the countess's proposal.

"It's only a factory," said Dev with an unbothered shrug. "I can't imagine you'll find anything of interest there."

Lady Bridgewater glanced around the room, undeterred. "Raise your hand if you've ever been to a steam engine factory—or any factory at all, for that matter."

Only Dev, Shaw, and Mrs. Shaw lifted their hands.

Lady Bridgewater smiled in the manner of a woman accustomed to having her way. "See? It'll be a lark."

A bolt of annoyance flashed through Beatrix. *A lark.* That factory was Dev's livelihood. It paid for this roof over their heads and the sumptuous meals they'd been enjoying, even the fire in the hearth had its beginnings with a servant paid to start and stoke it. *A lark!*

Dev's piercing aquamarine gaze cut across the room and met Beatrix's. "And you, Lady Beatrix? Will you be joining us on this lark?"

She detected a spark of the serious and urgent…

Will.

He was willing her to say *yes*.

"I wouldn't miss it," she said, and he smiled.

That smile was why she'd assented. To please him—and to please herself, it must be admitted. She was curious about his factory.

An hour later, she was entering the receiving room of Deverill & Shaw Company, which was not at all as she'd imagined. She'd thought they would step through the doorway and find themselves suddenly coated with grime and grease. But the room was tidy and clean.

Then they were passing through the threshold of another doorway and into a large, cavernous space with high windows that provided ample light, even on a rainy day. This was the factory proper, machines in various stages of assemblage filling row after row.

It was the silence Beatrix noticed next. The odd giggle or whisper peppered in by a lady here or there didn't break it, for it was the near oppressive silence of a typically loud space—as if the cacophony were only just held at bay.

Dev had explained on their twenty-minute carriage ride that as Saturday was a half-day, the workers had already left. They had Sundays off altogether. In their wake, the workers had left this quiet that would burst back into life first thing Monday morning.

Ahead, Dev began leading the group slowly along the rows, explaining this or that part or machine. Beatrix lagged at the back. Not that she had no interest in learning about this place— she was curious about *everything*, in fact—but she wanted to form her own impressions first.

For a lady of the *ton*, she'd always felt she led an interesting life. At least, one more interesting than that of her peers. True, she didn't have money or a husband or children, but she did have freedom. And even though she would readily trade that freedom for money, husband, and children, she daily took advantage of her freedom to float through society as she willed—from a resplendent ball held by a duke to the odd lowly racecourse on a Wednesday afternoon.

Yet as the reality of this factory—of Dev's real life—sank in, she saw that her *freedom* existed firmly within the structure society had laid out for her. She never truly stepped outside it.

But this factory...this life of Dev's... It existed in an altogether different realm from hers. Not only did he experience true freedom of mind and practice, he contributed to the world in a meaningful way.

Dev led an interesting, free life.

Dev led the life he wanted to live.

It was a revelation to Beatrix—and it rattled the foundations of the good, solid life she'd always thought she'd wanted no small bit. For it inspired a question: was that life nothing more than another sort of prison?

Ahead, Lady Bridgewater tossed her head back and laughed as if Dev had just said the funniest thing in the world. Lord Bridgewater had stayed back at Primrose Park, presumably to partake of billiards and the copious amounts of spirits he was so fond of. Which gave his wife leave to flash her beautiful smile about and laugh and take none of what Dev said seriously. Just as a lady would, of course. Wasn't this a lark, after all?

Beatrix experienced another flash of annoyance.

But, *oh*, how attractive Dev was at this moment. So handsome and deliciously wicked. The former a quality known to the world, and the latter known only to her.

And possibly—*probably*—to Lady Bridgewater.

Again, the flash of annoyance.

A low, persistent thrum at this point.

As he demonstrated his knowledge, skill, and talent, there stood a man who knew his business.

It rivaled both handsomeness and wickedness in attractiveness.

"It was a lucky day when I met Blake Deverill."

Beatrix turned to find Mr. Shaw smiling at her. "Was it, indeed?" She kept her tone light, even as she noted his unwavering sincerity.

"Aye," he said.

"There are likely others who feel that way about Mr. Deverill."

The words had left her mouth before she could contain them. That they were the truth mattered not.

Not every truth needed to be spoken aloud.

Mr. Shaw nodded, pensively. "I hail from a family of landed gentry who have done well for themselves over the generations."

Beatrix understood he had something specific to say to her and he would come around to it in his own time. She waited and listened.

"I was a younger son and wouldn't be inheriting. I understood that from the moment of my birth," he continued. "Because my father was a good man, he saw me educated, and upon my graduation, he gave me my inheritance all at once, rather than as an annual allowance. *'This way you'll have both the blunt and the incentive to make something of yourself in the world.'* There would be no more where that came from, was what he was saying."

"Sounds like a fair man."

A nostalgic smile crossed Mr. Shaw's features. "The best man I ever knew." He cleared his throat. "Anyway, I took the money and invested in a few factories. Textiles, for one. Then shoes. They kept me in a comfortable living and able to have a household and family. But they were nothing with vision." A dry laugh escaped through his nose. "Then came the night of Baron Whitsby's supper party."

Beatrix's head tilted slightly to the side. *Whitsby...* "Lady Bridgewater's father, correct?"

"The very same," said Mr. Shaw. "Whitsby wanted to show off the brilliant local lad he'd put through school and who would be his future estate manager. Except I saw right from the moment Deverill opened his mouth to describe his inventions that he was no future servant. He was that rare visionary with the skill to put his ideas into practice."

"You saw all that over the course of a single supper?" Beatrix wasn't surprised, in truth. Dev was a force.

"I pulled him aside and told him I had the experience to help him realize those plans of his. I proposed we immediately go into business together and never once looked back. So, in answer to your question, aye, a lucky star was shining its light on me that night."

That Beatrix felt the same was yet another realization for her.

One it was better not to think about presently.

Another of Lady Bridgewater's gales of laughter caught Mr. Shaw's attention. "They grew up together, you know."

Beatrix nodded.

"I think he thought he would marry her."

Beatrix swallowed against a suddenly tight throat. "I think you're correct."

How very straightforward was Mr. Shaw. While Beatrix appreciated his candor on one hand, she very much did *not* on the other.

"But it's for the best he didn't."

"No?" Beatrix's heart became a sudden hammer in her chest.

Mr. Shaw met her question with a smile. "He wouldn't have had the chance to marry *you*."

"Oh…right." She couldn't quite believe she was having this conversation. "Of course."

Arms crossed over his chest, Mr. Shaw rocked back and forth from heel to toe. "I've found the stars align in configurations of their own reasoning and in their own time. We mustn't question their logic."

"How very mystical of you, Mr. Shaw."

He smiled. "Only what life has shown me thus far on the journey."

Somehow, Mr. Shaw made stars aligning and shining down their good fortune sound pragmatic. But then, a person who took lofty ideas about how engines could work and translated them into functioning machines would. Daily, he and Dev made stardust tangible.

"Is he telling you how all our workers have started calling me Mr. Devil?" came a familiar voice behind her.

Dev.

She'd been so engrossed in her conversation with Mr. Shaw, she hadn't noticed him approach.

"It's a compliment," laughed Mr. Shaw. "No one can puzzle

out how you come up with your ideas. *Devilry* is the easiest explanation."

Dev shook his head. "Nothing so interesting, I can assure you. Time spent tethered to the draftsman's table into the wee hours."

Mr. Shaw winked at Beatrix. "Night is the best time to catch stardust. Now," he said, "I'll continue with our guests, shall I?"

As he went on with the factory tour, Beatrix remained at the back with Dev.

"So, what do you think?" The way he was watching her—*intently...* He wanted to know.

"It's amazing what you do here."

A chuckle rumbled from his chest. "Is that all?"

She couldn't help laughing, too. "Everyone knows this is how you made your fortune, but to see it makes it real, if that makes sense." She couldn't help adding, "I'm impressed."

His brow lifted. "I've impressed you?"

"You have." Her smile grew pensive. "Daily, more and more, it seems."

The moment stretched beyond the limits of one second to the next as their gazes held. Beatrix could neither draw nor release her breath. Into the moment, Dev said, low and gravelly, "Bea, can we talk...*please.*"

Please.

That *please* penetrated and quaked through her.

A *please* that couldn't be denied.

It wasn't in her to deny it.

Except...mustn't she?

One day—today...tomorrow...or the next day—she must deny him.

She must deny herself him.

A change of subject was necessary. "Where will this batch of steam engines be heading off to?"

Dev looked as if he wanted to press her, but he answered

smoothly, "They will be going to France. I was thinking of seeing them to Paris myself."

Beatrix felt a smile tip about her mouth. "I've always wanted to visit Paris. I hear it's lovely."

"You should come with me."

"I…"

She couldn't finish the thought aloud. She didn't need to, for he knew how it ended as well as she.

She wouldn't be going to Paris with him.

"Such intense conversation the two of you are having."

The Countess of Bridgewater was approaching, a feline smile perched on her lips, and Beatrix wondered if anyone had ever told her to shut her mouth.

"Of course," continued the countess, "Lady Beatrix could be speaking of the weather, and it would be an intense conversation."

It was meant as a put-down, a joke at Beatrix's expense.

The countess would have to do better than that if she was aiming to needle under her skin.

"Lady Beatrix observes the world in a thoughtful manner," returned Dev. He sounded…defensive. "Thus, she experiences life deeply."

Lady Bridgewater narrowed her eyes. "I suppose that's what made you fall in love with her."

All the breath left Beatrix's body, and she went entirely too hot.

Love.

What a word to be spoken aloud on a factory floor.

What a word to be spoken in relation to her and Dev.

She dared not glance his way.

"We…" she began, somehow, the croak in her voice rivaling that of a toad. "We were discussing the destination of these steam engines."

The countess observed her with an air of impatience.

"Paris," Beatrix supplied.

"Oh, Paris," said the countess. "Bridgy took me there for our honeymoon. Well, he said it was our honeymoon, but there was a horse to purchase, of course." Remnants of past annoyance yet lingered. "Anyway, Paris holds an appeal, I suppose, but, oh, the stench." Her eyes went bright with a sudden idea. "Oh, I know. You could elope to Scotland right quick, then dash off to Paris with the steam engines for your honeymoon."

It wasn't meant as a sincere idea, but rather as a joke. Or even a dare, Beatrix supposed.

Lady Bridgewater was all but explicitly daring Dev to follow through with a marriage to the too-intense Lady Beatrix St. Vincent.

"But not in August," continued the countess. "Paris is dreadful in August. Worse than London." She gave a dramatic shiver. "Now, Dev, you are needed to tell us precisely what provided the inspiration for *this* device." She'd already begun ambling ahead.

"*Later,*" said Dev, urgent and only to Beatrix. "Later, we shall talk."

And he was gone.

Except he wasn't truly.

That word yet reverberated through her—shaking her... rattling her.

Later.

She had the promise of him—*later*.

She didn't have to deny him—or herself—yet.

Which was, of course, a state of denial in itself.

That was all reprieve was...

A state of limbo.

A state of grace.

The fact was she'd like to stay here a bit longer.

To know Dev better.

To know herself better, too.

The woman she became when she was with him.

And she understood.

Later couldn't happen.

Within *later* lay the sort of fantasy Dev was so expert at weaving.

She must resist.

Not him.

But her own self-defeating desire to surrender to its lure.

CHAPTER TWENTY-NINE

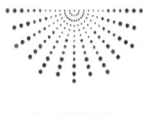

LATER

*U*ntil tonight, Dev had never appreciated Primrose Park as a house exceedingly suited to entertaining.

Literally, it had been built for the party presently taking place beneath its roof.

The older gentlemen and ladies had taken themselves to bed an hour ago, which had signaled to the younger set it was time for the real festivities to begin. The atmosphere had grown decidedly less formal with everyone floating between the ground floor common areas of drawing room, library, study, billiards room, and other rooms of whose existence Dev yet remained ignorant. All the while, piano music drifted through the air, sometimes gently, sometimes raucously, as various ladies and gentlemen took turns at the instrument. Any other night, Dev would've enjoyed the convivial atmosphere, for there was no doubt this house party was a roaring success.

But not tonight.

Tonight, he simmered and stewed.

Beatrix had been elusive all evening.

At supper, her eyes hadn't met his even once from the opposite end of the table. Then the behavior had continued into the night as she'd avoided him altogether by keeping to the opposite side of any room he entered—like now.

Book open in one hand, she stood before a bookcase in the library, pointing out a passage to a younger Shaw daughter and behaving as if she hadn't noted his presence the instant he'd set foot inside this room. However, if he were to step any closer, she would begin moving.

Really, he should try it at a run and test his theory. What would the gathered think of Lord Devil chasing Lady Beatrix St. Vincent in circles around the furniture? Weren't they supposed to be in love?

It was the last question that had him exiting the room and seeking the nearest liquor cart, which happened to be in the billiards room. He poured himself *one...two...three...*fingers.

"I'll take one of those."

He turned to find Lady Artemis approaching. He poured a generous splash and held the tumbler out to her. They lifted their glasses in a silent toast. While he knocked his back, she took a sip, her deep brown eyes watchful above the crystal rim. Lady Artemis wasn't here for the whiskey. She was here because she had something to say to him.

She cocked a hip onto the billiards table, as if settling in. Her head tipped to the side, the shadow of a smile curving her mouth. When she was good and ready, she asked, "You, Lord Devil, are an associate of my brother's wife, no?"

Heat flared through Dev. His dealings with Gemma Cassidy, now the Duchess of Rakesley, didn't exemplify his best moment. "That's ancient history."

Lady Artemis's black eyebrows gave a mild lift. "I'm not sure I would call a few months ago *ancient* history. More like last spring, methinks."

Dev was in no mood to be toyed with. "May I help you in some way, Lady Artemis?"

Her bright, sunshiny smile said she wouldn't let him minimize the past—or get away with it. "This engagement of yours to Beatrix," she said. "True love, is it?"

Well… An unexpected shift, that.

Love.

Today, everyone was exceedingly comfortable bandying the word about.

Everyone, that was, except him and Beatrix.

"Of course," he said. Really, it was the only thing to say.

Lady Artemis narrowed her eyes. "Do you know what Beatrix called it?"

Dev gave a wary shake of the head.

"Affection," she said.

"Affection?"

She nodded, as if just as mystified as he. "And do you know what I said to that, Mr. Deverill?"

"I'm sure you'll enlighten me, Lady Artemis." He didn't bother masking his exasperation.

"I said," she began, "no one shocks the world with a surprise engagement over *affection.*" She spread her hands wide, helpless to the facts. "It simply isn't done."

Lady Artemis… Through her smile composed of light and air shone a worthy adversary.

And she wasn't finished… "So, what I want to know is what are you playing at, Lord Devil."

She'd started calling him Lord Devil again.

That wasn't promising.

"Ah, be a good man, old chap," came a three-sheets-to-the-wind voice from the opposite end of the billiards table, "and pour me a tumbler of the good stuff, will you?"

The owner of the voice stepped into view. *The Earl of Stoke.* As Dev hadn't moved from his place beside the liquor cart, the earl was addressing him.

"Of course." Dev was relieved the earl had staggered into the room. Anything to pull him away from Lady Artemis's inter-rogation.

He handed a half-full tumbler to Stoke and darted a glance toward the lady. She was staring at Stoke as if she'd just seen a ghost. "Are the two of you acquainted?" he asked.

That would come as a bit of a shock, considering Stoke was a known wastrel—albeit of the harmless variety—and Lady Artemis wasn't the sort of woman to suffer such a fool lightly. Lest one forget, she was the daughter of one duke and sister of another. She was the rare lady who didn't need to make herself attractive to every earl who happened across her path.

For his part, Stoke snorted. "That would be one way of putting it."

An opacity entered Lady Artemis's eyes. "We became acquainted through a misunderstanding."

Stoke shook his head wonderingly, as if still mystified by the past to this day. "How could your mother have gotten it so upside down, anyway? Sharp as a needle, that one."

Lady Artemis's body became a straight, rigid line. "My mother?"

"The duchess."

"I know who my mother is," she returned, carefully enunci-ating each word. "*How* did she get *what* so wrong?"

Stoke shrugged, and the past was gone. "No harm done, anyway, eh?"

An extra beat of time ticked past before Lady Artemis said, "No, none."

The light in her eyes had dimmed. Dev noticed that much, though Stoke wouldn't have as he reached past Dev to top up his tumbler.

"And your family?" she asked of Stoke. "How is Lady Gwyneth?"

It was small conversation of the sort one made with an acquaintance, but the question emerged tight, as if asked through a constricted throat. For Lady Artemis, the light question held weight.

Stoke pulled a long-suffering face. "My sister thinks she should have a season."

Lady Artemis's brow gathered. "Lady Gwenyth must be approaching her nineteenth year. She hasn't had a season yet?"

Stoke waved a dismissive hand. "So she can buy a load of expensive dresses and attend a bunch of balls? And for what? To bankrupt me?"

The question hung in the air, unanswered. How was the earl *not* yet bankrupt? That was the question. His youth, Dev could only suppose. Stoke was only in his mid-thirties. Years lay ahead for him to bankrupt himself properly.

Stoke snorted, his grievance apparently not fully aired. "The chit is a knocker, no doubt about it. She's had three perfectly suitable offers of marriage from three neighboring landowners this year alone."

"Perhaps she doesn't find those gentlemen perfectly suitable to *her*."

Again, Stoke snorted. "I wouldn't wish a sister on my worst enemy."

Lady Artemis inhaled deeply and exhaled. "And Lord Branwell?"

The question was a simple one, but Dev sensed more to it—as if this were the question she'd been wanting to ask since she'd laid eyes on Stoke.

"Surely, you heard."

The tumbler she'd been bringing to her mouth froze, mid-lift. "Heard what?"

"That my brother went off to play at being a soldier in the deep, dark heart of Africa."

The earl's dismissive tone rubbed Dev the wrong way. Men didn't *play at* being soldiers. Men didn't *play at* putting their lives in the path of bayonet and cannon shot for their country.

"I'd heard round he was in the south of Africa." Lady Artemis's tone was pitched to encourage more information than Stoke's attention span appeared inclined to give.

"Returned a blasted war hero, wouldn't you know it." Stoke shook his head. "Typical of Bran."

Lady Artemis's brow crinkled. "Lord Branwell is back in England?"

A mean smile curved Stoke's mouth with as-yet undelivered bad news. "The glorious hero nearly had his leg blown off."

Lady Artemis's free hand flew to her mouth on a shocked gasp.

The cruelty within Stoke's smile remained. It was clear he bore no good will toward his brother. "End of Bran's illustrious career. Seems His Majesty doesn't have much use for a soldier with a gammy leg."

"And he's..." Her next question reached air with a struggle. "He's well?"

"Oh, he's as well as a man can be who can't even ride a bloody horse. Hasn't left the family pile in months." He held up a finger. "Actually, that's not true. He should be up in Yorkshire by now."

"*Yorkshire?*" Surprise was writ clear upon Lady Artemis's face. "I have an estate in Yorkshire."

"Yeah?" Stoke couldn't have sounded more disinterested. Again, he reached across Dev for the whiskey.

Lady Artemis, however, appeared undeterred. "What's he doing in Yorkshire?"

"Oh, his barmy old godfather sent for him."

Suspicion darkened Lady Artemis's brow. "Who is his godfather?"

Stoke cleared his throat and brought himself fully upright. He must've thought it comical. No one smiled. "Sir Abstrupus Bottomley," he said importantly. "You know him?"

Lady Artemis blinked. "His estate borders mine."

"Well, there you have it. Everyone in Yorkshire knows each other," said Stoke. "Now, if you'll excuse me—"

"Why would Sir Abstrupus send for Lord Branwell?"

Stoke ignored the question. "How old do you think the old geezer is, anyway?"

"Rumor puts him at ninety and a few years besides."

"Mayhap he's getting ready to shed his mortal coil," Stoke offered. "Settling debts and scores and whatnot."

A dry laugh escaped Lady Artemis. "I can assure you Sir Abstrupus has no intention of shedding his mortal coil anytime soon."

"Anyway, Bran has been summoned." From the crinkling of his brow, it was clear an irritating thought had occurred to him. "You don't think he's giving Bran the lot, do you?"

"I've never met a man who held onto every last farthing in his possession with more tenacity."

That seemed to settle Stoke's mind. Yet again, he reached for the whiskey decanter. Dev placed it in the earl's hand and said, "No harm in holding on to it."

Stoke nodded sagely and made to tap the side of his nose, but missed and struck air. "People say you're naught but a gamester." His words were beginning to slur together. "But in the future, I shall countenance no such aspersions to your good name, old chap."

Lady Artemis made no attempt to mask her thorough disgust as she turned to Dev. "Shall we see what entertainments are to be had elsewhere?"

Dev was only too happy to oblige.

Upon entering the drawing room, they found a game of charades underway, led by none other than Imogen.

Imogen had always loved a game of charades.

From their place at the periphery, Lady Artemis said, "My, but the countess is skilled in games of pretend."

No doubting the undercurrent to that observation. The truth

was, even though she'd been married for a couple of years, Imogen was much the same as she'd always been. Beautiful... vibrant...keen to have her way...happy that everyone was keen to let her have it.

She hadn't changed.

Yet...as he watched her, she wasn't the same to him in some other, intangible way.

The change, he saw with sudden clarity, was in *him*.

For example, how easily his gaze moved from her and scanned the room until he found...

Beatrix.

She stood well back from the proceedings, engaged in conversation with yet a different Shaw daughter. Her back was half turned to him, which put him out of her line of sight. Golden opportunity presented itself—and he seized it, nodding a swift farewell in the direction of Lady Artemis.

He'd closed the distance in fewer than five seconds. When Beatrix glanced up and started upon finding him at her side, he couldn't help the smile that curled about his mouth. He'd caught her, and she knew it. Her irritated gray eyes told him as much.

"Mr. Deverill," she said. He'd forced her hand—and she didn't like it.

Too bad.

Wasn't this how madly-in-love, affianced couples behaved? Talked and enjoyed one another's company for all the world to see?

"My sweet Bea." He reached for her hand and brought it to his mouth, kissing the back through white satin gloves.

The Shaw daughter gasped and giggled, then blushed, too, for good measure.

"Miss Shaw," he said. "I take it you're finding the evening to your satisfaction?"

"I...yes." The blush had spread to the roots of her hair.

"Do you enjoy charades?"

"Oh, indeed."

"Then why don't you…" Pointedly, he shifted his gaze toward the game at play. His suggestion was clear—that she leave.

It took only three or four seconds for her to catch his meaning. "Oh!" Eyes wide, she bobbed a quick curtsy—as if his moniker Lord Devil, in fact, made him a lord and a devil—and scurried away.

Beatrix crossed her arms over her chest, a single eyebrow winging high on her forehead. "That was only barely not rude."

Dev shrugged. He wasn't one to apologize for getting what he wanted—which was to be alone with Beatrix.

Or alone as they could be in a room full of people.

He'd decided it best to get directly to it. "We need to talk."

"We are, in fact, talking."

"*Beatrix.*"

"Lady Bridgewater is looking beautiful tonight."

Dev could've groaned

He didn't want to talk about Imogen.

Which was a problem.

After all, the arrangement with Beatrix centered around making Imogen his. Yet…he couldn't help feeling the rules of the arrangement had shifted in some ineffable way—like they'd been amended…or amended themselves, more like.

They needed to talk about that.

But he could see from the stubborn set of Beatrix's jaw that he would get no such conversation from her.

No, what he needed to do was rattle her.

"You know," he said, an idea occurring to him even as he spoke the words—an idea he could very much come to regret acting on. "You have a rare opportunity tonight."

Narrowed gray eyes met his. "I do?"

"To find that good, solid husband you've been yearning for."

Even as he spoke the words, his jaw wanted to tense with

aggravation. *A good, solid husband.* What sort of goal was that, anyway?

Her brow lifted with incredulity. *"Here?"*

"It's as good a place as any." He glanced around the room, and his gaze landed on a potential candidate. "What about Wrexford? He seems good and solid."

Beatrix nodded contemplatively. "I believe he is a good and solid prospect, but I also believe he's good and solidly besotted with the eldest Shaw daughter."

She had a point. "Not Wrexford."

Beatrix might've rolled her eyes ceilingward. "I'm very capable of sorting my own affairs."

She was now looking as exasperated as he felt. How had he and Beatrix come to this? Weren't they supposed to be friends? Now, it felt more and more like they were combatants. Dev didn't like it. He liked the closeness that came naturally to them. They shouldn't be on the outs.

He was just about to formally request a truce—she might've found it amusing—when she said, "I suppose the Earl of Stoke would be the candidate society would suggest. After all, I'm the daughter of a marquess."

A crash of thunder roared through Dev. The woman could not be serious. *Stoke?* The man was debauched...a waster...an utter sot... "If you want to marry your father, I suppose Stoke would be the ideal match."

He had no right to say it.

He couldn't *not* say it.

Her eyes flashed fire, and Dev was bracing himself for the retort he had coming when a bright, feminine voice exclaimed, "Mr. Deverill!"

A second later, Imogen was grabbing his arm. Dev had no choice but to give over. He was the host. Fun was his duty.

For her part, Beatrix stepped to the edge of the audience, arms crossed over her chest, her eyes inscrutable as she watched

Imogen pull him into the game of charades. Glittering with mischief, Imogen leaned so her mouth met his ear. Not too long ago, that single point of contact—her soft lips touching him...the whisper of her breath—would've been enough to spark a fiery conflagration of desire.

Now, like everything tonight, it annoyed him.

It was the wrong woman's lips touching him.

"Cassanova," she whispered.

Cassanova.

Before this audience breathless with excitement, he was to play Imogen's lover.

Right.

Instinctively, his gaze flashed to the spot where he'd last seen Beatrix.

She was gone.

He could've growled.

Except...wasn't he getting what he wanted?

The way Imogen was smiling up at him... He could have her —*now*. It was plain. All she needed was the slightest encouragement, and she would be his.

It was *he* who wasn't ready.

If he crooked his little finger, and Imogen came running, that was the conclusive end of him and Beatrix.

No.

They hadn't yet talked.

Urgency and frustration clamored within him. He and Beatrix were running out of time. Tomorrow was the last day of the house party.

They would talk tonight.

But first, he must play Cassanova to a woman who increasingly feeling like the wrong woman.

CHAPTER THIRTY

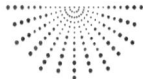

FOUR IN THE MORNING

*T*he house was silent in the way only the long deep of night could inspire.

Beatrix had lain stubbornly awake in her bed for hours, waiting for the last tendril of the evening's laughter to flutter away into the indigo ether.

She'd waited another quarter hour, just to be sure.

Only then did she slip from between the covers and make her way through the still house on quiet cat feet, a single destination in mind—the kitchens. Her infallible nose had led her straight to the desserts table. No sweet was ever entirely safe from her.

Now, she sat alone at a square, knife-scarred table, a feast of confections arrayed before her. *Profiteroles...macarons...shortbread...trifles...truffles...bon bons...eclairs...pies...cake.* She nibbled a macaron—*mmm*, strawberry—as she contemplated which sweet to sample next.

Her eye kept returning to her heart's true desire—*chocolate cake.*

She sliced a wedge twice the size she could reasonably consume in one sitting and took a slow, savoring bite, her eyes drifted shut in a moment's bliss. A good chocolate cake was a perfect symphony of complimentary textures—the moist density of the sponge...the sugary slick of icing that lit up the tongue... *Scrumptious.*

Her mouth had just closed around her third bite when a voice sounded, "Are the sweets up to your standards?"

Beatrix's gaze startled open to find Dev, his large form filling the doorway, one shoulder propped on the doorframe, arms crossed over his chest, his mouth curled into half a smile— watching her.

"What in the blazes are you doing here?"

Her righteous indignation would've commanded more authority had it not been muffled by a too-large bite of cake.

He chuckled.

The blasted man had the nerve to chuckle.

She swallowed with no small amount of struggle, before, at last, she was able to say, "If you start suggesting suitors again, I shall launch a pie at your bloody head."

Dev held his hands wide in apology, its sincerity questionable. "Peace."

The threat had been an empty one, for she had no intention of wasting a perfectly innocent pie in such a manner. In fact, she fully intended to enjoy a heaping slice of it later. But her point was made, and she was able to experience a modicum of relief. She could have her cake and her peace, too.

When Dev pushed off the doorjamb and crossed the room, her relief proved short-lived.

He pulled out a chair and sat beside her.

There was her peace gone.

"Cut me a slice, will you?"

She couldn't very well refuse the man, now could she? This was his kitchen—and his cake.

As he sank his fork into dense sponge and took a bite, she gauged his reaction. He nodded with well-considered appreciation. He even moaned. "Delicious."

She offered a smile of agreement, and they ate in silence, a measure of the tension pulsing between them dissolved into companionability. None could doubt the sure diplomatic capability of a shared sweet.

He put his fork down and met her eye. "Can we talk as we once did? Like friends?"

As we once did.

He was referring to that period of *between* time.

The specific time that ranged from *after* they'd made their arrangement to the time *before...*

The time before they'd become *something more*.

"What would you like to talk about, friend?"

That pulled a smile from him. She just had it in her to resist that same pull. "The guests seem to be enjoying the entertainments."

It was bland, as conversation went—and safe, too.

She could tolerate the former, if it meant having the latter.

"Well, they would," she replied.

His head cocked with interest. "You make it sound predetermined."

A dry laugh escaped her. "In a way, it is. This party is a confluence of everything the *ton* lives for. A beautiful house. Myriad entertainments. Delicious food. Flowing champagne and spirits. And a perfect host willing to indulge their every whim."

He nodded, slowly, as if giving the matter deep consideration. At last, he said, "You think I'm perfect?" A teasing light shone in his eyes.

She liked it.

"As a host," she teased back.

His smile turned devilish. "I must be perfect in other ways, too."

She felt her brow lift.

"One who achieves perfection in one way would surely seek to achieve it in all others."

Beatrix saw what he was so openly saying beneath his words. It was a tease, of course. But it was the truth, as well—and they both knew it.

He was perfection in other ways, too.

"You're being incorrigible."

It was what a friend would say.

A friend most definitely would *not* pick up that thread and follow it.

A friend would *not* tell him, for example, that he was, in fact, perfect at *something more.*

So perfect, in further fact, that her body hadn't stopped singing from it...hadn't stopped craving it with every cell of her being.

No, a friend wouldn't say that.

"You're not the first to make that observation," he said, as if he hadn't taken note of all she hadn't said.

She must turn the conversation in another direction.

It was four in the morning and it was only them in this kitchen and he was so very, very attractive, sitting here and eating cake and smiling wickedly with that very, very beautiful mouth of his.

His beautiful mouth... It would taste of chocolate cake.

Perfection.

"Your factory," she began, abruptly, only remembering an instant later that his factory was yet one more attractive thing about him.

His head angled with interest. "What about it?"

"It's an example of your perfection."

"I'm afraid I can't take credit for the perfection of the factory," he said. "It's all Shaw's handiwork."

Beatrix wasn't letting him off that easily. "Those machines... They're *your* vision come to life. I find that amazing."

"I amaze you?"

"You do."

"In addition to interesting you."

"Indeed."

It was the truth, but she felt strangely caught out.

As if she'd somehow become ensnared in her own truth.

"A man might like that." He lifted his brow and took another bite of cake.

Beatrix shook her head, stifling the laughter that bubbled up. Being Dev's friend… It was too easy.

It was too easy to want more.

Another question came to her—one that would prickle… "Did you enjoy the game of charades?"

"You didn't stay."

"No."

They both knew why.

She'd become superfluous to needs.

The countess was all but his.

Beatrix hadn't needed to stay to see it play out.

Dev watched her, closely, as if he saw all this behind her eyes. At last, he spoke, "Do you know what I like about charades?"

She shook her head. She was about to take another bite of cake, but found only crumbs. Another slice would be necessary—and perhaps another after that—even as she suspected there wasn't enough chocolate cake in the world to see her through the next few minutes…the next few days…the next eternity of years.

"When you play charades, you can be anyone."

That rasp in his voice…

She knew it.

But more importantly—*more urgently*—her body knew it, as it slipped beneath skin and slid through veins with every beat of her heart.

Before her no longer sat a friend—but temptation personified.

"*Anyone?*" she asked. "Like us playing at being friends?"

His head cocked. "Aren't we friends?"

"I think you know what we are."

And there it was.

The telling rasp in her own voice.

* * *

Dev detected opportunity.

An opportunity to turn this conversation into one more to his liking…

Into *something more*.

And, simply, he wasn't above it.

"We could be anyone."

Her tongue swiped across her bottom lip. "Anyone?"

"We could even be…" He let the incomplete thought tease through the air. Unconsciously, she swayed forward, as if afraid to miss a single syllable of its resolve. "We could even be two lovers who want nothing more than to ravish one another." He allowed that to sink in before he asked, "Lady Godiva Gallop, I presume?"

Her right eyebrow lifted a questioning increment. He supposed the eyebrow of the daughter of a marquess would. Yet…interest flickered within her eyes.

He managed as good a bow as one could while seated. "Lord Devil, at your service."

Surely, she saw it, too—*freedom*.

Tonight, they didn't have to be themselves, but rather these fictions of themselves.

But that was the thing about fiction.

Sometimes, it could speak the truth with more eloquence than reality.

"Your reputation precedes you, my lord." Her voice had gone low and throaty.

"Does it now? You have a slight reputation yourself, my lady."

"Is that so?"

"Oh, I've had my eye on you, you naughty, little minx, and you've been indulging in the forbidden."

She swallowed, as if her mouth had become suddenly parched.

"There's no perfect crime," he continued. "And you've left one telltale sign."

"But I've been so very discreet," she protested, slipping more fully into the role.

He angled forward, closing the distance between them, then reached up and rubbed the corner of her mouth with his thumb, taking a small, dark smudge of icing with it. He didn't shift back, but rather sucked at the sweet. Her pupils flared, she watched, transfixed.

"I'm not sure my thumb was thorough enough."

"One must be thorough," she said in a breathless whisper.

He moved further forward, easing away the inches between their lips, and swiped his tongue across the corner of her mouth —*soft...warm...sweet.*

She shifted subtly, and her mouth was pressed to his.

Like kindling lit into flame, urgency seized him as he cupped the back of her head, silky hair threading through his fingers, and deepened the kiss that was taking on a momentum of its own. He needed to touch her...*feel her...* He reached for her waist and lifted her as he stood and hoisted her onto the kitchen table. Fumbling hands were opening her nightrobe and pushing it aside, her night chemise offering a teasing view of creamy thighs. Her knees parted, and he was stepping between that sweet flesh.

A primal feeling, this.

This necessity to plant himself between her legs.

He pulled her forward so her bottom was just on the edge...so his cock could push against her soft quim, its demand clear. She groaned into his mouth and squirmed. Down her neck, his lips trailed as he reached between them and felt *her*—so slick...so hot...*so ready.*

He needed to be inside her—*now*.

Fingers shaky with need fumbled at the falls of his trousers. Her head arched back, and his name escaped those kiss-crushed lips of hers. "What is it, my naughty sweet?" he growled.

"The servants," she said in a breathless rush. "They'll be in to start their day soon."

Dev froze—and not for worry about the servants.

She'd spoken with more than a hint of Beatrix—not as the naughty Lady Godiva Gallop. She was only a few words away from becoming herself altogether.

And he couldn't have that.

He shifted back and met her eyes. "Come upstairs with me."

The longest three seconds of Dev's life ticked past. She knew what *upstairs* meant.

No turning back.

Then she nodded, and he could breathe again.

It was with great reluctance and dint of will that he shifted back so she could hop to her feet. He didn't want to be separated from her, not even for a few minutes. "This set of servants' stairs lead to the master's bedroom," he said, pulling open the correct door.

They hadn't made it halfway up the dark, narrow staircase, Beatrix a step ahead, when he reached up and took her hand, twining his fingers through hers. It was imperative that he touch some part of her.

But the next instant, it wasn't enough.

He tugged, and she glanced over her shoulder, a saucy smile curled about her mouth. On a low growl, he slipped his other hand around her waist and had her back pushed against the wall, his mouth covering hers with a near desperate need. He could kiss her all night, except…

"Do you have the faintest idea what exquisite torture it is to observe you all day and not be able to do *this*"—a hand stole around and cupped her sweet bottom—"and *this*"—his mouth trailed lower and nudged her robe aside so he could suck her taut nipple through muslin—"and most definitely *this*." He reached beneath the hem of her chemise and found the soft curls of her cunny—slick and swollen with desire...ready for him. "I could ravish you here and now," he muttered against her breast.

"Oh," she exhaled on a pleasured groan. "But..."

"*But?*"

She angled back, her mouth formed into a playful pout. "You promised me your bed, Lord Devil."

With great difficulty, he dragged himself away from her and continued up the stairs. When they entered the bedroom, he reached for her hand, but it was she who took his and led him toward the bed that was much too grandiose to be considered tasteful. Eyes glinting with mischief, she pushed him to a seat on the edge of the mattress. Clearly, Lady Godiva had a few ideas of her own. Anticipation quickened through his veins.

"You're the sort of lover who derives pleasure from giving," she said.

"I am."

No sense in denying it.

Denial only deprived one of pleasure.

"Now, it's *my* turn to give."

CHAPTER THIRTY-ONE

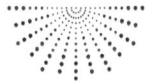

*B*eatrix placed her hands on his thighs and sank to her knees between them.

Oh, lord.

In defiance of the limits of physical possibility, Dev's cock got harder.

Sure, slender fingers unbuttoned the falls of his trousers, previous experience making light work of them, freeing his length, cool night air caressing its sensitive, velvet skin.

His cock throbbed.

Beatrix angled back and took him in.

Her mouth was inches away.

His cock ached.

She bit her bottom lip between her teeth and lifted her gaze. "Blimey, you're big."

Blimey.

It was the word a kitchen maid would use or even Lady Godiva Gallop—and it was the word Beatrix would use, too.

He liked that about her.

Fingers that held a tremble lightly brushed up and down his length before closing around him at the base. She angled forward, and he felt the warmth of her breath in the instant before she touched her tongue to him. Her gaze lifted, and he was nearly undone on the spot as she took him into her mouth and began moving both mouth and hand along his shaft, in a rhythm quickly established.

Raw pleasure struck through him, as he watched her...*felt her*...pleasuring him. A long groan scraped across his throat. Never had it been like *this*. All-encompassing pleasure because of who gave it—*Beatrix*.

Within the fiction they'd created, she was able to be entirely herself, real and present, giving herself to him, freely and without expectation.

Because she wanted him and he wanted her.

He wanted her.

And he knew.

He would never stop wanting her.

Oh, but her mouth felt so good...and her tongue had begun having ideas of its own, its skill increasing with every second. *Talented*, that nimble, velvet tongue of hers.

Too talented.

He reached out and twined his fingers through silken sable hair, resisting the primal need to urge her on until climax took him.

No.

That way lay regret.

"My sweet," he said.

Her eyes slitted open, a question within.

"You need to stop, or..." The sentence could finish itself.

Slowly, she slid her mouth off him, and a groan dragged through him. He could reach out and pull her atop him and be inside her in a matter of seconds, satisfying these base urges that demanded satiation.

But an intrusion of reality stopped him.

Tomorrow was the final day of the house party.

Tonight could be their last time.

And if tonight was the last time, he wanted it to be worth remembering.

He lifted her chemise over her head and tossed it aside. Naked, she rose and stood before him. It occurred to him that he'd never adored her properly. "You are so beautiful."

A flicker of doubt passed behind her eyes. She might have winced. She didn't see herself as he saw her.

"Beatrix," he said, reaching for her hips and bringing her close, so close he was able to press his mouth to the soft stretch of skin between navel and mons pubis. His gaze lifted. "You are beautiful."

His fingers tightened around her waist as he pulled her onto the bed. He made short work of his remaining clothing beneath her unflinching gaze.

"*You* are beautiful," she said.

He knew women saw him so.

And he knew his male beauty helped him get some of what he wanted in life—like a beautiful woman in his bed when he wanted her.

But with this beautiful woman... He had to be more than a beautiful specimen to have her.

And that she deemed him so... Well, it was a special thing.

She reached up and hooked her hand around his neck, pulling him onto the bed. Their bodies, his large and bulky... hers slender and lissome, stretched along the length of one another, opposites in every way...complementary in every way, too. His mouth met hers, and she rolled onto her back, pulling him atop her, settling him between her legs, his manhood poised and ready.

He entered her slowly...measuredly. "Oh, Dev" she sighed into his mouth as he began stroking in and out of her, her hips in rhythm with his. She was so tight around him. The experience for her had to be the push and pull of pleasure and pain, that sweet middling place achieved only by this act. Deeper, he drove into her, taking her bottom in hand, angling her hips to take him in yet more fully. Sweat pinpricked his skin, beaded down the side of his face, down the hollow of his spine.

On it went, as he maintained control and worked her body, found what pleasured her...what drove her wild...what would drive her to climax. Her gaze went interior with the pleasure received, and she began squeezing him tighter. She was reaching...striving... Climax had begun to tease at her. He steadied himself and paid attention as he thrust into her.

Her head arched back, digging into the mattress, a cry pouring from her that was equal parts pleasure and frustration. *There.* She liked her hips angled just so...his strokes just that deep...

The breath caught in her chest. Release was holding her in that specific exquisite tension just before it broke within her, leaving her crying out, her quim fluttering and pulsing around his cock, her fingernails digging into his back as he kept moving inside her, his rhythm slowed for the moment. But it wasn't long before his own release began to pull at him.

"Oh, Dev," she said, awash in satiety.

It was the feel of her that drove him wild.

But it was that look in her eyes—the look he'd put there—that pulled him over the edge into madness.

He was mad for this woman, who could slay him with a single sated glance, a curl of pleasure on her mouth. He kissed that mouth—how could he resist?—and poured unnameable emotion into this act.

All his adult life, he'd wanted to vanquish.

But now, all he wanted was to surrender—to *her.*

So, he did.

Along with release came all the pleasure promised as lightning bolted through loins and veins, but also this surrender as he floated through the ether of climax.

Here, they were one.

Here, he would have them remain—their limbs tangled and exhausted...their breath mingled...their hearts beating as one—forever.

Forever...

He'd made so much possible in his life—turned undefined visions into solid reality.

Why not forever with Beatrix, too?

* * *

An hour *or so later*

A sliver of dawn peeked through a slit in the yet-closed curtains, and Dev understood he would have to let her go.

Already, he'd kept her too long.

Already, they tempted scandal.

He almost snorted. What was the worst that could happen? That he would have to marry her?

She felt too good, curled into his side, her head snugged into his shoulder.

"Beatrix," he willed himself to say. He wouldn't expose her to the shame of scandal.

"Mmm," purred from her throat, a satiated smile curving her lips.

He couldn't resist. He pressed a light kiss to that delectable mouth.

Her eyes fluttered open. Her brow crinkled, and she blinked. Her smile fell. "I'm not dreaming, am I?"

Dev chuckled, even as he felt a vague sense of wrongness creep into the air. "I knew I was good," he said lightly. "I'll be your dream, if you like."

On a distressed squeak, she pushed upright.

He attempted to ignore the very definite wrongness in the air and slid a hand behind his head as if in idle repose. "If you're worried about the servants, they know not to enter my bedroom until I've left to break my fast. I don't have a valet."

"How very democratic of you." She gave her head a shake. "But, no, I'm not worried about the servants."

He reached for her hand. "Then what is it?"

She stared down at their twined fingers, then met his gaze. "The countess is yours for the taking now. You must know that."

Imogen?

He hadn't given her any thought in days—*weeks*, really.

Not any meaningful thought, anyway. *That* had been consumed by the woman presently pulling her hand from his and hopping off the bed. She had the chemise slipped over her head before full-on alarm began clanging through him. "What are you doing, Beatrix?"

She didn't spare him a glance. "Dressing."

He sprang off the bed and reached for his trousers, jerking them on before planting himself between her and the door. "We need to talk."

She nodded in agreement. "Indeed, we do."

Dev felt the storm gathering on his brow. She was being too readily agreeable for his peace of mind. "You first."

She shrugged her robe onto her shoulders and said, reasonably, "Well, it's obvious."

He had no liking for this conversation or the way they stood facing one another like adversaries. Only a moment ago, they'd been lovers. He wanted that moment back. "Please explain the obvious to me."

"Our arrangement has reached its inevitable conclusion. It's time to end it."

Annoyance flared through him. The woman was being too bloody reasonable. What they shared had nothing to do with reason.

"Are you so eager to be rid of me?" He tried for levity.

Her eyes had gone frustratingly opaque. "We've achieved what we set out to do."

"Refresh my memory."

Truly, he needed reminding, for whatever it was, it no longer mattered. Didn't she see that?

"The countess will be yours, and I'll... I'll be paid for my services."

"Ah, yes... So you can have that good, solid future you've always dreamed about."

If he wasn't very mistaken, fury flicked behind her eyes. "So I can pay Blaze Jagger."

"Well, that happens to be one of the things we need to talk about."

"You *are* going to pay me, correct?"

"Of course," said Dev, annoyed she would even ask. "But as for Blaze Jagger, he's been relieved of Lydon's debt."

Her eyebrows crinkled with bewilderment. "Lydon settled with Jagger?"

"He didn't."

Her brow released with revelation. "You...*you* paid the debt."

"Jagger won't be bothering you anymore."

A few moments passed while she took in and assembled these new pieces of information. "Now, I'm indebted to *you.*"

"You owe me nothing, Beatrix. Your future is yours to decide."

He started to say more—to say what was in his heart. That the future she wanted might be with him...

"Oh, yes, my good, solid future." She laughed, no humor in it. "And you'll pursue your glorious future with your Imogen, no?"

Dev couldn't articulate the exact moment he'd stopped thinking about that future, except he had. A vision of a different future—a *better* future—had replaced it.

Yet what Beatrix was saying struck something within him... something he'd been thinking for a while now and wanted to say to her… "That good, solid future you've always wanted, well, it's so ordinary, isn't it?"

She looked utterly nonplussed. "Pardon?"

"You deserve better dreams," he continued. "You could have an extraordinary life, Beatrix, if you could only risk it."

A pin could drop in the room and they would hear, so still was the silence.

"Why do you want that ordinary life?" he pressed.

"It's the life I've always wanted."

"Perhaps what we've always wanted isn't what we want now."

His lungs expressed no will to move as he watched her mind race behind her eyes. At last, she said, "You're right."

Agreement had come too easily. He couldn't trust it. "I am?"

"Perhaps that isn't the future I want."

A petal of hope peeled back inside him. "Isn't it?"

"Perhaps I don't want to marry at all."

The hopeful momentum of the moment came to a screeching halt.

How in the blazes had they arrived *here* from where they'd started?

A realization crashed down on him.

He'd missed his moment.

At some point during this evening, he should've fallen to his knees and begged her to marry him.

Or…it had already been too late then.

He should've done it the moment they'd met in Hyde Park.

"Tonight," she said, "at the dance, we'll break it off as we began."

"What does that mean?" He was having difficulty keeping up with the inner workings of her mind.

"Publicly."

As we began.

He could groan.

He could shout.

Of course, that was the inevitable end to their arrangement.

But…was that the end of *them*?

Was it, too, inevitable?

He did know this: now wasn't the time to ask. He would only make it worse.

He needed time…time to think.

Which left him with but one more thing to say… "You should leave now."

She blinked. She'd expected him to keep arguing.

Good.

He'd defied her expectations.

It was a start, anyway.

Without another word, she swept past him and out of the room.

Now, he was alone—with his racing mind.

He still had tonight.

Indeed, they would be parting ways in front of the *ton*. But that was necessary. They needed to put the paid aspect of their relationship behind them. Only then, could they start anew without artifice.

Or…it was the entirely wrong approach.

And he risked losing her altogether.

CHAPTER THIRTY-TWO

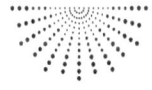

NEXT EVENING

*T*urmoil.

The only word that described how Beatrix had spent this day—in a state of turmoil.

Actually, that wasn't quite true.

She'd spent most of the day being fitted for the gown she was now wearing in Dev's magnificent ballroom.

A colorful array of ten silk ballgowns had arrived in her bedroom just as the hour struck noon—along with Madame Dubois and a few of her apprentices. From there, it was all turning this way and that and striving for perfection with every stitch.

Several hours later—and several pots of tea and all the cakes that went with it, too—they'd achieved it. The dress Beatrix now wore was, indeed, perfection—a lilac silk so pale it could be mistaken for silver.

"Lovely," said Madame Dubois in her French accent by way of London's East End. She stood back from Beatrix, head tilted, assessing her work with a critical eye. "You'll be the loveliest lady at the dance."

"Oh, no," said Beatrix. "That honor will go to Lady Bridgewater the instant she steps foot inside the ballroom." She'd regretted the words even as she spoke them—and the acid contained within.

Madame Dubois subtly narrowed her gaze. Now, she was assessing the woman within the dress. "I'll grant you that Lady Bridgewater is one of the most beautiful women in the *haut ton*. Rather like a summer rose in full bloom. Complete with the thorns, too, you can trust me on that." She cleared her throat. "But she isn't lovely like you. There's a difference, and Mr. Deverill has a discerning eye. He sees it."

Dev.

Of course, he'd sent this dress—along with the nine others and the modiste, too.

Dev.

The source of her turmoil.

Perhaps I don't want to marry at all.

When she'd spoken those words, it hadn't been a case of the dramatics and there was no *perhaps* about it.

She no longer wanted a good, solid future—not after Dev.

She would never have what she'd shared with Dev with anyone else, so it only followed she wouldn't have anyone else.

Oh, the logic was bleak.

A slick of perspiration coated her palms. The time was nearing that she would have to finish the job—*publicly*.

What had come over her to make such a suggestion?

The question was disingenuous.

She knew.

Their end didn't need to be public for the sake of the *ton*.

It needed to be public for *her*—a clear dividing line between *before* and *after*.

Before—the time when their arrangement bound them...when *something more* bound them, too.

After—the remainder of her days.

"Your future is yours to decide."

He'd paid off Jagger.

It annoyed her.

How very presumptuous and high-handed of him.

It was sweet.

And that annoyed her, too.

"You owe me nothing, Beatrix."

With those words, he'd set her free.

They should've been everything she wanted to hear…a weight lifted off her shoulders.

Except…with those words, nothing bound them any longer.

She was free—free of Lydon's debt…free of Blaze Jagger's threat…free of Dev.

Freedom never felt so bad.

"I thought I'd find you here," came a welcome voice behind her.

Beatrix turned to find Artemis approaching her quiet patch of wall. "Habit, I suppose."

"Let's speak our farewell now," said Artemis. "I'll be setting out before dawn. It's a long road back to Yorkshire." She gave Beatrix a thorough once-over before narrowing her eyes. "Exquisite dress, but you look terrible."

A miserable laugh chirruped from Beatrix.

"No, it's true," continued Artemis. "If this is how being blissfully engaged affects your looks, then you might consider breaking it off."

"That dire?"

Artemis narrowed her eyes with assessment. "It's the dark circles under your eyes. Your cheeks have lost their roses."

"Is that all?"

"What you need is—" Artemis signaled a passing footman. *"Champagne."* She plucked two sparkling coupes off the tray and handed one to Beatrix. "Now, drink that."

Beatrix took a compulsory sip.

Artemis shook her head, as if Beatrix had failed a test. "All the way in one go."

Understanding she had no choice, Beatrix began drinking. What could it hurt, anyway?

Once she'd downed every last drop—and emitted a small burp into the back of her hand—Artemis nodded and took the empty glass, replacing it with a full one. "Now, sip that one."

Strangely, Beatrix was starting to feel…not better, exactly… but *lighter*. "I'll miss you, my friend."

"You must visit me at the Grange."

"You have no plan to return to London?" Beatrix wasn't surprised, but still sorely disappointed. Her future in London was looking so very decidedly bleak.

Again, that awful word.

"I shall," said Artemis. "But the time isn't yet right. A few matters have come to my attention and must be dealt with."

She pulled Beatrix into one of her fierce embraces, then was off, Bathsheba trailing behind her. Only Artemis would bring a dog to a dance.

Beatrix remained fastened to her patch of wall and cast her gaze across the room. The affair was an informal one, as it was outside London and the number of attendees was too few to deem it a ball. Except one wouldn't know it from the opulence of the ballroom with its gleaming mahogany dancing floor and three matched, five-tiered crystal chandeliers that threw warm, sparkling light in every direction. Then there were the quality of the diamonds gracing the necks and wrists of the ladies and the exalted titles of the lords that were of equal quality and flamboyance. Any ball in London would be deemed the success of the Season with such a resplendent gathering.

Her eye caught upon two figures on the opposite end of the dancing floor—*Lord Wrexford and Miss Shaw*. They weren't dancing, but rather their heads were bent close in deep conversation. Beatrix wasn't sure whose eyes shone brighter or cheeks bloomed redder. A match was only a matter of time—he, an earl and future marquess...she, an heiress and lovely with impeccable manners and a fine mind. It would be that rare love match that was also socially appropriate.

Of a sudden, the air in the ballroom changed, as if a match had fired and sparked it to life. Beatrix knew that change in the air. Her heart a variable butterfly in her chest, she scanned the crowd until she located the source—*Dev.*

Oh, but he was handsome in his impeccable evening blacks.

Lord Devil.

That was the man the *ton* wanted him to be—to fill that role for their entertainment.

And wasn't she, too, guilty? Only last night, in his bed, she'd indulged in fantasy with Lord Devil.

Her thighs still ached from the experience.

Yet she saw more to him, and she wasn't sure if that was better or worse.

Was it *better* to see him beyond his surface? To see more beyond his handsomeness and wealth? To see his intelligence, ingenuity, and genius? His thoughtfulness... His sweetness... To see all those qualities and know he would never be hers?

Over the shoulder of a lady who had planted herself firmly in his path, his gaze lifted and met Beatrix's. Without a word, he sidestepped the lady, leaving an irritated feminine *humph* in his wake. As he erased the distance between them, one sure step at a time, he dared Beatrix to look away—as if she could. Lord Devil was coming to claim her.

Oh, the champagne was having its way with her thoughts.

Somewhere between an eternity of years and the snap of her fingers, he came to a stop before her. *Close*—too close...uncomfortably close. So close she could feel the familiar pulse of his energy and heat...pick up his scent of pine and sea and *him*... reach out and caress his stubble-shadowed cheek and tangle fingers through the hair that curled against his collar.

"May I have this dance?" he asked, the question a low, velvet rumble that quaked through her one syllable at a time.

Was music playing?

She couldn't hear it.

Her senses could take in nothing beyond what related to him.

The entire room was watching, either directly or from the corner of their eyes.

But that wasn't why she nodded and allowed her hand to be taken into his and her entire self to be led onto the dancing floor.

She wanted to dance with Dev.

To experience the enlivening, buoyant feeling dancing stirred within her—with him.

To feel herself in his arms once again.

It was the latter feeling she wanted most.

With all her being, in fact.

And the two coupes of champagne she'd consumed had blurred the reasons that stood between wanting and having.

CHAPTER THIRTY-THREE

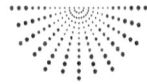

*D*ev understood the plan.

In the general sense.

He and Beatrix were to end their arrangement—*publicly*.

Really, he felt she had a stronger sense of how the plan would unfold.

But it was the *after* that he was concentrated upon.

He would take her some place where it was only him and her, then drop to one knee and proclaim his love and ask her to make another arrangement with him—*privately*.

An arrangement that had naught to do with anything other than what lay within their two hearts.

He'd strode into this ballroom with the sole intention of proceeding exactly so.

Then he'd seen her, standing against an inconspicuous stretch of wall, looking so utterly lovely. And when he walked toward her, it had naught to do with the plan.

It was need that drove every step—the need to touch her…to hold her in his arms…

"May I have this dance?"

He always found the most efficient means to achieve his ends.

An uncertain beat of the heart later, she stepped into his embrace, her chin lifted so her gaze fixed on a point over his shoulder. The hand on her ribcage slid around and lower to the small of her back. *Improper.* Even more improperly, he pulled her close—so close their bodies brushed one another as they stepped into the whirl of dancing couples and the brisk *one-two-three* of the waltz and all was right with the world.

For the few minutes of this dance, she would be his.

But there was little satisfaction in it.

It wasn't enough—and it wouldn't be enough until it was forever.

"Are you enjoying the evening?"

The sort of banal question a man would ask the lady he was attempting to woo, which he supposed made it the perfect question.

The space between Beatrix's eyebrows crinkled slightly. He'd surprised her. "I, *erm…*" she stammered. "Yes…*no.*"

"You look lovely tonight." If he was courting, then he might as well do it correctly.

She blinked.

"You're the loveliest woman in the room, in fact."

Her eyes narrowed. "I suppose Lady Bridgewater hasn't arrived yet."

"I wouldn't know."

It was the truth.

A complete shift in his thinking had occurred.

No longer did Imogen have anything to do with what bound him and Beatrix together. She never really had. The connection had charged between him and Beatrix from that very first moment in Hyde Park.

Well, that might be overstating the case. He had, after all, nearly run her down with his horse, which wasn't the best way to endear oneself to a woman's heart.

Beneath the hand on her ribs, he sensed held breath. She was evaluating his words from every angle. Soon, however, she would understand there was but the one angle from which to view them —as the truth.

"Shall we get this over with, then?"

"Define *this*."

"Our arrangement."

It was, in fact, what he wanted more than anything.

Then they could get on with the matter of the rest of their lives together.

He nodded and said, "Do you have a plan for how—"

Without warning, she planted her feet in the center of the dancing floor, bringing them to a sudden standstill and stopping the rest of the question in his mouth. Events moved so fast he had no opportunity to grasp the intent of her plan when she lifted her right hand off his shoulder and, with unaccountable fury in her eyes, delivered a decisive, walloping slap to his left cheek.

The moment and ballroom were shocked into silence, as she tore the white silk glove from her left hand, jerked the ruby engagement ring off her finger, and flung it at his chest. He only just caught it when her voice rang out, clear and indignant, "Enjoy the rest of your life without me, Lord Devil."

Then she whirled in a swish of silken skirts and fled the ballroom, a chorus of shocked gasps and titters at her back.

As plans went, it was effective.

In the newly scandalized eyes of society, Lord Devil and Lady Beatrix St. Vincent were finished.

Now, they could begin a real future—as Dev and Bea.

Yet…a feeling niggled within him.

A bad feeling.

That slap and the fury in her eyes… In combination, they felt like more than a bit of theater performed for the sake of society.

The slap… She'd really put her back into it.

The fury in her eyes… It had been real.

This plan... It had been a mistake.

He'd thought to wait a short while before following her. Allow enough time to pass where he could receive commiseration from the other males, who were already sending him condoling shakes of the head.

But, no, that would be a mistake, too.

He must catch her—*now*.

He'd taken not three steps when a hand closed around his upper arm. Annoyance shot through him as he glanced over his shoulder. *Imogen*, mouth curled into a satisfied smile.

The bad feeling curdled into a solid mass in his stomach.

He'd gotten everything wrong tonight, hadn't he?

He should've broken things off with Imogen today. Except... In reality, there was nothing to *break off*. He and Imogen weren't actually together—or in any way connected.

Not anymore.

Not in years.

How had he missed that fact for so long?

"May I help you, Lady Bridgewater?" he said, cold and indifferent—and not for the benefit of others.

"Don't you think it's time you told me something?" No missing that self-pleased light in her eyes.

He began nodding. Actually...*yes*.

He'd made a right mess of matters—there was no denying it—but a quick conversation with Imogen would be a pivot in the right direction.

He'd been too unclear—with himself...with Beatrix...with Imogen, too, apparently—which was unlike him.

He was known for clarity of mind and purpose.

For knowing what he wanted and pursuing it—and achieving it.

But somewhere along the way that clarity had become clear as mud.

Everyone, it seemed, thought they knew what he wanted—including himself.

Yet it wasn't what he wanted, not at all.

And now the time had arrived to clear the waters.

Beginning with Imogen.

He allowed her to lead him down the corridor, up a staircase, and down another corridor, at the end of which they entered a disused room. As she shut the door behind them, it became obvious she'd planned for this little *tête-a-tête*.

She arranged herself on the room's chaise longue in a seductive pose and curved her mouth into a practiced smile. Had she always been this transparent? "You've made your point, Dev."

He propped a shoulder against the closed door and crossed his arms over his chest. "What point is that?"

She trilled a light, feminine laugh that sounded rehearsed. "With Lady Beatrix, of course."

Dev went very still. He didn't like that laugh. It held an edge of malice—aimed squarely at Beatrix.

Imogen didn't notice the sudden snap of tension in the air. "As if you would marry her."

"Wouldn't I?"

Another laugh—the same malicious note ringing through. "Of course not. Why would you spend the rest of your days with her when…"

Her eyes glittered with expectancy. Impatience struck through Dev. He shouldn't be here.

Yet another mistake made.

"*When* what, Imogen?" He was in no mood for games.

"When you could spend them with *me*?"

It took the split of a second for his mind to catch up. "Are you saying you would—" The thought was too incredible to finish.

"Run away with you?"

A single wary nod was the only response he was capable of at the moment.

"Yes, I believe I shall."

Imogen was speaking the words he'd been waiting to hear for years…

And they inspired nothing in him beyond…absolute panic.

Bloody hell.

"I rather fancy being a ruined lady." Her tone was that of someone describing the weather.

"Imogen…" He scraped his mind for something—*anything*—to say to this woman he truly didn't know. "When you were sold into marriage to Bridgewater—"

"*Sold?*" Her brow creased and her head canted, as if she were conversing with the biggest dunderhead in England.

Actually…maybe he was.

"Well, weren't you?"

She flicked her wrist. "Oh, I don't care about being a countess."

See? he wanted to say to an imaginary Beatrix. Imogen didn't care about such things.

He'd been right about something, at least.

Her smile turned positively feline. "Not when I can be so much more."

Dev's brow furrowed deep trenches into his forehead. A glint had entered Imogen's eye. "*More?*" he asked and braced himself for whatever next was about to issue from her mouth.

"I can be more than a countess. I can be infamous. Bridge-water was merely a stepping stone." She shifted forward, her eyes alight with excitability. "Without him, you and I would simply be a mister and missus when we set out for our notorious future."

Was Imogen possibly…*mad*?

No, not mad.

Ambitious.

All this time, Imogen had a plan of her own.

"My beauty will achieve legend," she continued. "If we put our minds to it, I could best the Duchess of Devonshire or Lady Worsley for notoriety. Where on the Continent shall we go first?"

This future wasn't based on revenge or conquest or even love.

Her intention was to use him as the instrument of her ruination.

Use him.

Had it always been so?

From the moment they met all those years ago… Had he been doing her bidding all this time?

The answer his mind suggested…

He didn't much like it.

"Oh, first," she said, a new thought occurring to her, "there's the matter of your little business."

"My *little business*," he repeated. "Are you speaking of my factory?"

"You'll be selling it, of course."

"The first I've heard of it."

"It's served its purpose, hasn't it?"

"Which is?"

"To achieve…*me*."

Beatrix would never think or say such a thing. Strangely, though his arrangement with her involved money, she wasn't the sort of woman who could be bought.

But Imogen was.

Further, Beatrix respected his work. She understood it was a fundamental part of him and his identity. Which led him to yet another logical conclusion…

Imogen didn't know him at all.

Beatrix's words returned to him.

What she represents to you is a fantasy.

Beatrix had seen that truth from the beginning.

And just as Imogen had been a figment of fantasy for him, he'd been the same to her.

They didn't actually know each other in a meaningful way.

And as was the way with one truth, it led to another…

He and Imogen never had the spark that he and Beatrix shared.

Oh, it had been a spark, but one born of youth and infatuation…of lust and inexperience.

A fleeting spark that didn't hold the necessary heat to catch.

But what he and Beatrix shared burned brighter and hotter with every moment of each passing day…

That was love.

Of course, he could be wrong—*yet again*.

"But Lady Beatrix St. Vincent?" Imogen gave her head a disapproving, little shake. "I know she's the daughter of a marquess, but really…*truly*."

"What about her?"

"She's not exactly a diamond of the first water," she scoffed. "The woman's practically a spinster, and you're *Lord Devil*, Dev."

"Meaning?"

Imogen ignored the question. "Not to mention she rather thinks highly of herself, that Lady Beatrix."

"Why shouldn't she?"

"As if she's more intelligent than the rest of us," continued Imogen, unwittingly venturing deeper into dangerous territory. "You wouldn't be able to suffer such a woman for long."

"Oh, I don't know," said Dev, his voice betraying none of his barely contained fury. "Intelligence has its uses in a woman."

Imogen's perfect eyebrows lifted. "Oh? Like what, pray tell?"

"Like it would prevent a woman from making a fool of herself and throwing herself at a man who no longer loves her and who suspects he never did."

Her brow darkened. "Dev, what are you saying?"

"I don't love you, Imogen."

A laugh of disbelief escaped her. "Of course, you do. You've always loved me, Dev."

"Perhaps what we've always wanted isn't what we want now."

Words he'd spoken to Beatrix.

The context had been different then, but the truth contained within was the same.

"But what else could you want, if not me?"

"Imogen, I wish you well in life, but that life will not be spent with me. A little advice," he added as he swung the door open. "Be happy with your earl. You earned him."

She pushed upright on the chaise longue, her eyes ablaze. "How dare you—"

But the remainder of her words were cut off when he pulled the door firmly closed behind him.

How dare he, indeed.

Through the house, he strode, a man focused on his mission, ignoring greetings from guests and queries from servants.

They could wait.

When he reached Beatrix's bedroom, the door was cracked an inch. Warily, he pushed it open. *Empty.* He stepped inside and understood immediately.

She was gone.

Not a trace of her remained.

He'd had it all perfectly planned. Payment for services rendered was to have been delivered during the dance, putting an official end to their business dealings and making it possible to start their future from a fresh place.

What he hadn't anticipated was a pair of arresting gray eyes glaring up at him with hurt and anger.

Too late.

Two simple words, but when arranged in that configuration, they held the power to fill the rest of one's life with regret.

All his life he'd vanquished.

But there was no vanquishing in love.

Only surrender.

And he'd surrendered too late.

He'd once thought nothing would ever be enough until Imogen was his.

But that wasn't the truth of the matter.

It was the shallow thinking of a young man.

What he felt for Beatrix shafted deep into the core of him.

Simply, nothing meant anything without her.

Her absence stripped all meaning from his life.

But it wouldn't last.

Surely.

Surely, she would see that truth and understand she felt the same.

Through hurt and frustration came another emotion— *annoyance.*

He loved her.

And against her will, she had come to love him, too.

He knew it with absolute certainty.

Someone like Beatrix wouldn't give herself so entirely to another person, like she had with him, without love.

So, why had she fled?

Why hadn't she stayed and fought for him...for *them?*

He wouldn't pursue her tonight.

Or tomorrow.

Or even for the next month, if necessary.

He would give her time to sit and reflect—and stew.

He would give her time to miss him.

To see if she could live without him—to see that she couldn't.

They weren't finished.

That much, he knew.

He just needed her to realize it, too.

CHAPTER THIRTY-FOUR

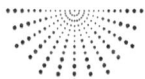

LITTLE STANHOPE STREET, TWO WEEKS LATER

*B*eatrix stood in the center of the kitchen like an extra appendage, utterly unnecessary to the preparation of tea, as the servants were more than skilled at their vocations.

The servants…

They were still here.

She couldn't seem to get rid of them.

"But I haven't been paying you," she'd said after the first week.

"Oh, we're being paid," said Cook.

Dev.

He was the only explanation.

He knew she wouldn't use her own money on servants.

He knew her that well.

Quite well, in fact.

Too well.

She shook the man from her mind.

Over the last two weeks, she'd almost become good at it.

Anyway, it was nerves that had her standing in the kitchen while servants whizzed by like a well-choreographed hive of bees.

She was to share this sumptuous tea with a visitor.

As if on cue, a firm *tap-tap-tap* echoed down the corridor that led to the front door.

The visitor had arrived.

"I'll answer it," she said, inhaling a steadying breath and willing her feet into motion. As she made her way, she found Cumberbatch seated on a high-backed chair just outside the drawing room where she and the visitor would take tea.

"Are you feeling tired today, Cumberbatch?"

Immediately, she realized her error. It was there in the contentious angle of his jaw.

Oh, dear.

"I won't be moving from this spot for the duration of your tea, milady," he said, confirming her fears. "You can rest assured."

"I do so appreciate your caution, but—"

He clenched and unclenched his right fist. "Destroyer of Worlds will be ready."

"Let us pray his services won't be necessary."

Cumberbatch gave a doubtful grunt.

The door knocker sounded again.

Nerves flittering through her, Beatrix wrapped a mildly trembly hand around the handle and pulled the door open.

"I didn't know ladies opened doors for themselves," said Blaze Jagger, cocksure smile curving his mouth, the diamond in his left ear winking hello.

She lifted her chin a notch. "Well, I do."

This was Blaze Jagger, and it wouldn't do to cede him any ground.

She stood aside and allowed him into the receiving hall. She'd arranged this tea so they could talk. After all, they were family, and she didn't really know him. Rather, she knew *about* him—which wasn't the same thing at all.

"If you'll follow me." She shut the door and swept past him into the drawing room.

Of course, they would have to pass Cumberbatch to enter.

From his perch, the aged valet glowered at Jagger, who appeared to take it in stride. "Cumberbatch," he said in greeting, "how's the day treating you so far?"

Cumberbatch grunted his reply, and Jagger nodded.

Inside the drawing room, Beatrix indicated a settee for Jagger to sit upon as she lowered herself into the one opposite. Brow lifted, he glanced around, his sharp eye undoubtedly taking in every detail. "It's a grand old room, isn't it?"

She gave a slow nod, sensing another observation to follow.

He didn't make her wait long. "Not much grand in it, though."

"You should've seen it before—" She bit off the lone remaining word of that sentence.

Jagger cocked his head. Of course, he would've caught her hesitation. "*Before?*"

She shook her head—freeing it from that word.

Dev.

"Suffice it to say," she continued, "this room has looked far worse."

And not too long ago, she left off.

Thankfully, a kitchen maid entered the room bearing tea. In the familiar timeworn sequence, the tray was placed on the table, tea poured, and cakes plated. The servant left the room.

All the while, Beatrix felt Jagger's eyes upon her. He was trying to gain a feel for her, just as she was with him.

As they settled back with their cups of tea, a tetchy silence beat out between them. Though she abhorred small chat, she had no choice but to ask, "How did you find the house party at Primrose Park?"

Oh, why had she asked that question? Couldn't she have asked about the weather?

But she knew why.

It was those mental roads of hers.

They all led back to Dev.

"It was an experience, I reckon," he said with a shrug, his

teacup and saucer held before him. He wasn't impressed, his tone and manner suggested.

For a notorious East End scoundrel, he was certainly honest.

Gray eyes eerily similar to hers bored into her. "But you didn't invite me here to discuss fancy house parties."

"I didn't." No use denying it. "Can you tell me something about yourself? Something about your life? I would like to know you better."

His head cocked with suspicion. "And why is that?"

"Because you're family."

He blinked. She'd surprised him. *Good.* He needed to be set back on his heels every so often.

Quickly, however, he recovered. "Your tale first."

Fair play, she supposed.

"My mother perished before I could form a memory of her," she began. "I've been told on more than one occasion that I'm like her in personality." She gave a bemused shake of the head. "Which tells me her marriage to Lydon couldn't have been a felicitous one."

Jagger didn't smile. Rather, he attentively took in her every word.

"I spent much of my youth at the racing courses with Lydon and his cronies."

"You don't call him your pa."

A bitter smile curled her mouth. "He's not the sort who wishes to be called Pa."

Jagger nodded, as if she'd confirmed something for him. "I didn't miss much in not knowing him."

"You didn't."

A few beats of silence ticked past before Jagger said, "I spent my childhood, such as it was, with my grandad. He runs a tavern in Wapping."

"Oh." She might've expected his story to be brushed with

tragedy. "Is your mother—" She stopped herself there. An indelicate question, to say the least.

"*Dead?*"

She nodded.

"Nah, she's still among the living." A slight hesitation. "But she's not the sort of woman who can care for a child on her own."

"Oh."

Of course, she knew the stories of such women. Women who became dependent on drink or other sorts of libations to the point they didn't care about anything else in the world. Further, it wasn't surprising to learn that Lydon would've created a child with such a woman and that child would've grown into the man sitting across from her.

"I'm sorry," was all she could say—to all of it.

Jagger's eyes narrowed, as if he were privy to the inner workings of her mind. "It's not what you're thinking."

Her brow lifted. "Oh?"

"My ma is the loveliest woman you'd ever lay eyes on, if you were to see her." His tone had gone on the defensive. "And her singing voice has been known to transfix the lowest scurvy scoundrel and reduce him to a puddle of yearning tears."

Beatrix sensed a *but* embedded within his words.

She waited.

"But…" He tapped his temple. "Her mind is mostly off with the fairies."

"Pardon?"

"My ma is simple." He spoke the words plainly. "When she was born, the midwife said she'd been in the womb too long and there would be a need to watch in the coming years that it might've affected her noggin. She'd seen it happen before." He lifted empty hands, helpless to the facts. "And time proved her right."

"*Simple?*" Beatrix repeated. It wasn't the fact of Jagger's mother's mental disability that she wasn't able to comprehend, but rather the implications it presented.

"She'll keep living with my grandad above the pub until he goes. Then she'll stay with me."

Beatrix's stomach dropped to her feet, and she was speaking those implications aloud… "Lydon took advantage."

Fury lit into flame within Jagger's eyes. "She's been singing nightly in Grandad's tavern since she was a wee one. That was how Lydon first saw her—and had to have her. She was sixteen."

Shock ripped through Beatrix. "He forced her?"

Jagger shook his head. "He didn't need to. The waster has that ability to charm, doesn't he? Anyway, she fell in love with him and began sneaking off, as happens." He shrugged. "Then she came up with child—as also happens."

"*You*," confirmed Beatrix.

"Aye, me."

"And Lydon abandoned her."

It wasn't a question.

The fury that blazed in Jagger's eyes… Beatrix experienced a responding fury within.

And through that fury came a realization.

Never again would she lift a finger to help her father.

And the man before her—*her brother*—she felt a new understanding and respect for him. "You've made it your mission to ruin Lydon as thoroughly as he ruined your mother." She saw how it drove him—that simmering fury. Which led to a question… "Are you going to keep collecting Lydon's debt?"

Jagger showed no surprise at the question. He'd been thinking about it himself. "Maybe…maybe not."

And she understood what it was she needed to say to this damaged, determined man… "You've made something of yourself, Blaze." It was time they were on a first-name basis. "At some point, that will have to be its own revenge *and* reward. My advice?" He wasn't asking, but she was giving it, anyway. "Take up a new hobby. Lydon is determined to waste his life. Don't let him waste yours along with it."

Blaze took in her words and gave no sign how they affected him. At last, he spoke. "Since we're on the subject of advice and the unprovoked giving of it..."

Tension pulled through Beatrix. He was about to turn the conversation on her—and she wasn't going to like it. "Yes?"

"From where I'm sitting, I'm seeing something, too."

"Oh?"

"You've earned some happiness in your life, Lady Bea."

"You can call me Beatrix. Or Bea, I suppose."

His mouth curved into a slow grin. "Nah, Lady Bea suits you. But what about the other part?"

"What other part?"

"The happiness part." He had the look of a man curling his adversary around his little finger. "Don't you think you deserve it?"

"I... I..." The question absolutely flummoxed her. "I've never thought about happiness."

"Well, from where I'm sitting, you're the only one standing between you and it."

"Pardon?"

"You heard me."

Of a sudden, the meaning of his words struck Beatrix... "Are you referring to my broken engagement?"

"*Indeed*, as you nobs like to say."

Beatrix drew herself squarely upright. "I believe you're laboring under a misapprehension about myself and Dev—Mr. Deverill."

It felt strangely distancing to call him *Mr. Deverill*.

But she'd managed it—and that was the important thing.

Blaze's eyebrows lifted, and it occurred to Beatrix that he might be having fun with her. "Oh?" he said, all innocence. "And what misapprehension might that be?"

"We were never truly engaged to marry."

If only it were that simple.

Blaze's brow formed a thunderous furrow. "Do I need to challenge the man to a duel?"

Beatrix resisted a sudden bent toward laughter. It might veer too close to the hysterical. "We had an arrangement."

Blaze didn't relent. "The question stands."

He meant it.

That was the thing.

Surprisingly, it warmed her.

It was a threat of the ultimate violence and could in no way be encouraged, but the gesture was...*sweet*—and perhaps brotherly.

Over the course of their conversation, a feeling had tiptoed into her mind. Now, it made itself known.

She liked Blaze.

Further, she wanted a relationship with him, even when he was being slightly annoying—like now.

He was her brother, and they just might need each other.

"Mr. Deverill and I had an arrangement," she said, quelling. "That's the extent of it. It was all mutually beneficial."

Blaze waggled his eyebrows. "It's always better when it's mutually beneficial, eh?"

A sudden blush washed over her to the roots of her hair. Still, she managed to say with all the primness of an eighty-year-old spinster, "Quite."

A loud guffaw sprang from Blaze. Beatrix was discovering younger brothers could be decidedly irritating creatures. "Well, aren't we a grand old family of adventurers."

She saw his point and, reluctantly, conceded it. Her dealings with Dev from start to finish were possibly—*definitely*—those of an adventurer.

"Except," continued Blaze, "why did you end it with him? That's what I can't figure."

"We'd each gotten what we wanted." She only realized what

she'd said when Blaze opened his mouth with what promised to be another naughty rejoinder. She lifted a staying hand. *"Don't."*

He heaved a defeated sigh, eyes glinting with mischief. "What was the arrangement?"

She didn't see any harm in telling him. "He paid me to be his pretend fiancée."

"Why?"

"There was a certain lady he wished to spur into action."

"Did it succeed?"

"I believe so, yes."

Although, it was strange that she hadn't yet heard even the faintest whisper about Dev and the Countess of Bridgewater—and she would have. Daily—and to her everlasting shame—she scoured every gossip rag in London for the news.

Still, it was only a matter of time.

Blaze wasn't finished. "What did you get out of it?"

"Ten thousand pounds." She saw no reason to hide it.

Blaze pursed his lips into a low, appreciative whistle. "You were going to use that to pay me off, eh?"

She gave a curt nod.

"You're an upright one, aren't you?" He winked. *"Mostly."*

Beatrix wished she could stop blushing.

Blaze set his teacup and saucer down, then shifted back and laced his hands behind his head. "You want to hear what I think?"

"I'm not sure."

"Wise woman," he said on a dry chuckle. "But I'm going to tell you, anyway."

Beatrix's grip on her teacup tightened. She might just snap the handle.

"It's obvious to anyone with eyes that the man is madly in love."

"That's what I was trying to tell—"

"With *you.*"

351

Frustration poured through her. "I believe that look of love was intended for another."

"That countess chit?"

A laugh escaped Beatrix. She was really coming to like her brother. "Yes, *that countess chit.*"

Blaze pursed his lips. "Nah."

"*Nah?*"

"Nah," he said, definite. "You see, your Lord Devil's eyes weren't lighting up when that countess chit entered a room."

The breath froze in Beatrix's chest.

"Now, when *you* entered a room…" He let the sentence hang in the air for dramatic effect. "That was different."

"It was?"

"When you entered a room, Lady Bea, there was no one but you."

She shook her head, firm. "It was all for show."

"Ah."

"*Ah?*"

"You can't see it, can you?"

"See what?" she asked, suspicious. This feeling—heart racing…lungs struggling for breath—it was as if panic were chasing her.

Concern shone within Blaze's eyes. "You can't see when someone loves you."

It was as if all the air had been sucked out of the room.

"My youth wasn't a perfect one." He'd angled forward and made his voice low and soothing. *Sympathetic.* That was her brother in this moment. "In fact, I was a right handful—still am. But I always knew one thing for certain. My grandad and my ma love me without conditions. But you, Lady Bea, who loved you more than they loved themselves? Who showed you that love?"

A single name wanted to push itself to the front of her mind.

Impossible.

Dev loved another.

"The man is madly in love with you."

Instinctively, she opened her mouth to refute every word.

Then she closed it, as several facts flooded in at once. First, Blaze hadn't needed to speak those words. Second, it was plain he believed them. And third, as an outside observer, he saw everything from a different angle. He didn't have her past clouding his view.

If she were to view her relationship with Dev from that angle of sight, what would she see?

A single, surprising word sprang into her mind.

Magic.

She'd conveniently convinced herself it didn't exist. That Dev and the spell he wove were fantasy—and all fantasies must end. The money...the servants...the pantry filled with food...the dresses... She'd been able to dismiss them as part of the superficialities of their arrangement and remain protected inside her cocoon of emotional safety, the barren landscape that it was.

Yet, their arrangement was over, and here those material things remained—and now she understood why. They had never been about the image they presented to the world. They demonstrated Dev's caring...his sweetness...his...

Love.

With those things, he'd given love in the only way she'd been able to receive it—through the terms and boundaries of their arrangement.

For here was the entire, unassailable truth—she'd been too afraid to trust in Dev's magic.

She'd known its loss would devastate her.

And she'd been correct.

Hadn't she been living holed up in her house these last two weeks like a devastated woman? She hadn't accepted a single society invitation or attended a single horse race. She could hardly compel herself to roll out of bed in the morning, in fact.

But love... Love was giving and receiving—*allowing* oneself to receive it. And the only way one could receive it was to open oneself and risk devastation.

Fear and shame.

Those two emotions had been guiding every step of her life since she could remember, and her one attempt to break free as a debutante had failed.

But hadn't Dev offered her a different path to tread and possibly share?

Her gaze sharpened into the present and her brother across from her. "*Magic.*"

His head cocked, and he watched her from the same distance one might observe a bedlamite. "Yeah?"

"Sometimes magic is real."

"Only because it's you saying it, Lady Bea, I'll take your word for it."

"Oh, you'll experience it for yourself someday, Blaze. You'll see." Her teacup and saucer clattered onto the tabletop as she stood in a sudden swish of muslin skirts. "I must go."

Blaze clearly felt no such urgency as he settled back into the settee. The blasted man even balanced an ankle on the opposing thigh. "Where are you off to, sister?"

"Mivart's."

"He's not there."

Her throat constricted. "Has he run off with—" The sentence refused to finish itself.

"He gave up the suite, is all."

Ah... She could breathe again. "He's in Primrose Park, then?"

"I reckon he's nearly made it to Dover by now."

"*Dover?*"

"Accompanying a shipment of steam engines to Paris, I've heard."

"How do you know all this?"

"I have sources." He sucked his teeth, nonchalant. "I keep an eye on anything related to my sister."

A tiny roar of frustration escaped Beatrix. Younger brothers were decidedly annoying. "I must hire a coach."

"You can use mine," he said. "It needs testing on the open road."

A possibility occurred to her... "Did you come here knowing I would be in need of it?"

He snorted, but didn't deny it.

She wasn't about to let him off easily. Fair play and all that. "Does anyone know how sweet you are?"

He exhaled a long-suffering sigh. "We'll keep that sort of language amongst ourselves."

She'd beaten about the bush long enough... "Do your *sources* know if the Countess of Bridgewater is with Dev?"

"Would it stop you if she were?"

And she knew... "No."

She was going to fight for Dev.

Shame...rejection... Too long they'd been her familiars, dogging her every step, influencing her every interaction with the world.

Preventing her from seeing love and seeking happiness.

With sudden efficiency, Blaze unhooked ankle from thigh and stood. "I'll speak with the coachman while you pack a few *accoutrements* for your journey."

Accoutrements?

Where had he picked up *that* word?

But now wasn't the time to sort out her brother.

Now, she must *go*.

"Blaze?" she called out.

Already halfway across the room, he tossed her a glance over his shoulder.

"Thank you, brother."

A smile curved his mouth, one lacking mischief and arrogance. A genuine smile from a brother to a sister. Their relationship was too new for them to be beloved to one another, but she sensed they would be—and it felt *right*.

Love.

One had to be brave and generous with it.

In the giving of it to others.

In the receiving of it for oneself.

There was no shortage of it, but one had to see it…nurture it.

And that was what she wanted more than anything—to nurture and grow in love with Dev.

Oh, Dev.

He'd bungled it on their last night together. He hadn't spoken what was truly in his heart.

But if he had, would she have been able to hear it?

No.

The answer was swift and uncomfortable.

She'd bungled it, too.

And now she must set it right.

Or try, at least.

CHAPTER THIRTY-FIVE

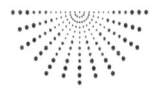

DOVER, NIGHT

*D*ev rattled the dice in his loosely closed fist, a silent chorus of held breath surrounding him as he prolonged the suspense for a few more shakes, then let fly. Dull ivory skittered and bounced across worn, knife-scarred oak, showing all combinations of numbers until they, at last, fell still.

A one and a one—*aces*.

The collective groan that followed was instantaneous.

Dev had thrown out.

The weathered sea dog to his right scooped up the dice and blew on them for luck, and the impromptu Hazard game moved on.

Relieved of his throwing duties, Dev settled back on his bench and crossed his arms over his chest. He hadn't been at all inter-ested in the play, as he wasn't a gambler, but it was a way of passing the time before the Channel crossing, which wouldn't be for another few hours, if the storm presently raging outside had its way.

It was all manner of folk presently crowded beneath the roof of The Crown—reputable sailors...disreputable smugglers... those of the middling class and gentry...a few lords and ladies...

the other sort of ladies, too. The ones of the night. Locals and foreigners, alike. Nothing like a blowing storm to bring all and sundry together beneath any roof that offered shelter and sustenance.

When everyone had first crammed into the taproom, the air had fizzed with barely contained annoyance that wanted to give way to all-out fractiousness. Then the drinking had commenced, the cards and dice revealed, and all found themselves in a jollier and more accepting frame of mind.

Everyone, except Dev.

His frame of mind had been decidedly, immutably dour these last two weeks.

Drink and gaming weren't the answer for him, either. He'd witnessed the attempt to drown one's sorrows in the bottom of a bottle on too many occasions. The endeavor never met with success. No, drink wasn't the answer—work, however, was.

He'd accomplished more work in this last pair of weeks than he had in the last pair of years. Tethered to his draftsman's table, he'd been.

It was the only way.

The only way to stay away from her.

For that was his true accomplishment these last few weeks.

He'd kept away from Beatrix.

Though it had been necessary to give up his rooms at Mivart's. One mad night, he'd drawn a detailed street map of Mayfair and had begun charting routes to her house—which hadn't been a useful exercise. The knowledge that a full-on sprint could have him at her doorstep in a matter of four minutes and fifty-three seconds hadn't been good for his peace of mind.

So, he'd decamped to Primrose Park, where he spent his nights, then his days at the Camden factory. A far better use of his time and mental faculties, which had mostly served to keep her in a back corner of his mind.

Mostly.

Shaw inquired about Lady Beatrix once a day, as did Mama and Papa. They were rather ruthless in their inquiries, in fact.

He'd thought Beatrix would've come to her senses by now.

Wasn't it as obvious to her as it was to him?

They were meant for each other.

But he'd heard not a single, solitary word from her.

Which was why he'd agreed to accompany the steam engines to France. London wasn't big enough for the both of them—and neither was England. Not if he were to keep away from her.

Not if he were to allow her to come to him.

Possibly it was a terrible plan.

No.

It wasn't.

For them to have a chance at happiness together, they needed to leave what had brought them together behind—*money...his idiotic pursuit of another...*

For them to be happy, apparently they needed to be miserable first.

The fact was he missed her—as a friend…as a lover…

It was an ache that ever strummed in the center of his chest. He woke with it in the morning and took it to bed with him at night. He'd experienced nothing like it in his life—and that was how he knew it was true.

This wasn't about winning or losing…vanquishment or defeat.

It was about something bigger.

It was about the possibility that he might not spend his life with her.

Actually… Was his plan a good one? Didn't plans need to be discarded sometimes? He understood that from his own work. Sometimes a plan contained a fundamental, catastrophic flaw and needed to be scrapped and tossed into the rubbish.

Oh, he was a fool.

Beatrix wanted to see Paris... He was going to Paris... Didn't a new plan work itself out from there?

Perhaps the storm was a sign... That he return to London, bundle Beatrix into a carriage, and haul her to Paris. Except he wasn't sure kidnapping was the most expedient way to achieve a viable future with a woman.

Yet...he couldn't put two countries and a large body of water between them without talking to her.

A new plan came to him with sudden urgency.

He would pay the ship captain an exorbitant amount of blunt to hold anchor for a few days—and return to London.

He wouldn't cross the sea without knowing his fate.

"Well, aren't you a dark and stormy one?" came a throaty voice that sounded as if it had been worn out by all manner of life.

He angled back to address the lady who had replaced the sea dog at his side. She wasn't one of the respectable ladies, but rather the other sort said the saucy smile on heavily rouged lips.

"If you will pardon me." He made to stand.

A hand clamped around his forearm, preventing his progress. "I never did mind a storm-tossed bed," she continued, as if her invitation hadn't been clear. "With the right sort of chap."

He had no time for this. He dug a crown from his pocket with his free hand and held it up in the scant space between them. "Not tonight."

Or ever.

The coin was plucked and tucked within the considerable depths of the strumpet's bosom before he could blink. "Your loss," she said with a toss of the head.

Not one to look a gift horse in the mouth, he shot to his feet and zigzagged through the taproom, a majority of whose patrons had begun belting out rollicking sea shanties, before finding himself outside beneath a shockingly clear night sky. The storm had blown itself out, leaving an almost eerie stillness in its wake. The Channel crossing would be possible inside an hour.

No matter.

His mind was made up.

He was returning to London.

Beneath a fresh indigo sky glittering with rain-washed stars, he made straight for the packet, determination in every step. On his way to seek out the captain, the first mate intercepted him on the deck. "Is that Mr. Deverill?"

"Aye." He hardly slowed. "What is it?"

"Your, erm, *friend* arrived."

Dev's eyebrows crashed together. *"Friend?"*

Even as the question emerged, his feet stumbled to a stop, and he knew.

Imogen.

She was another reason he'd left London.

She'd taken to writing him, daily—at first.

Then twice a day.

When he didn't respond to her letters—letters that were by turn angry and accusatory, then cajoling and repentant—she'd taken to arriving at his door in the middle of the night.

Imogen had never been rejected in all her life, and she wasn't taking it well.

Now, she'd tracked him to Dover—and would have to be dealt with.

"Lady Godiva Gallop," the first mate informed him.

Lady Godiva Gallop?

Belief refused to take hold inside Dev.

Could there be another *Lady Godiva Gallop*?

The first mate shook his head. "She insisted, so I put her in your cabin. I didn't know what else to do with her."

Dev tossed a hasty, "Thank you," over his shoulder, his feet already on the move.

Lady Godiva Gallop.

There couldn't be another one, yet he was too afraid to let hope in.

Not until he burst through his cabin door and beheld her with his own eyes.

Beatrix—seated primly on a three-legged stool, pencil suspended mid-air, journal flat on her lap, she scratched out one last thought, then lifted her gaze.

Oh, how he'd missed this.

The way she could look at him as if she could see straight into him.

And, tonight, he hoped she did.

Straight through to his heart.

"Lady Godiva Gallop, I presume?"

He hadn't intended those to be his first words, but as they were the only ones that came to him, he supposed they had to suffice.

Her mouth curled to one side, even as the intensity within her eyes remained, and she nodded.

Sometimes, it was easier to speak the truth as someone else.

But there was also a time to speak the truth as oneself.

That time had arrived.

"Beatrix, what took you so long?" Before she could open her mouth to reply, the reality of the moment struck him. "What are you even doing here?" And another reality... "Did you travel through the storm?"

She gave an indifferent shrug. "Blaze's coachman is quite skilled with the team of horses, although the weather did deliver a few vicious swipes here and there."

"*Blaze?*"

"He lent me his coach-and-four," she stated, utterly unflustered and matter-of-fact.

Dev's anger only amplified. "He let you travel in this weather?"

"I knew it wouldn't harm me."

The certainty with which she spoke something so wholly unreasonable had him gently asking, "Bea, did you hit your head?"

"Of course not," she said with a light laugh. "Don't you see the weather has been bringing us together from the beginning?"

He supposed her reasoning held a sort of logic.

Uncertainty flickered within her eyes. "Was I wrong to come?"

In an instant, she appeared so vulnerable and small, her composure suddenly shaky. He wanted nothing more than to take her in his arms and, in fact, took a step to do precisely that when she held up a hand. "I think it's best if we keep our distance for the moment."

She did have a point. They tended to let instinct, rather than intellect, guide them when they were close. Still, it was with great difficulty that he crossed his arms over his chest and propped a shoulder against the cramped stretch of cabin wall.

"Our arrangement," she began. "It really was a bit of foolishness, wasn't it?"

Dev's brow creased. He wasn't sure he liked the direction she was taking this conversation. Still, honesty would be the only way through. "Poorly motivated on my end," he admitted.

Imogen had been the poor motivator, to say the least. That knowledge shone in Beatrix's eyes.

"But," he continued, because he had to, "I don't regret it."

"Oh, neither do I." She had yet more to say. "But how could I when it was the best thing that ever happened to me?"

Again, he had to suppress the urge to close the distance between them. The words Beatrix was speaking, they weren't simply honest words.

They were brave words.

And he needed to let her brave them.

"You, Dev," she continued. "*You* were the best thing that ever happened to me." She set pencil and journal aside, placing them carefully on a table, every movement deliberate as she came to her feet, her hands clutched before her. "In my life, good things never just *happened* to me. Any good, I made happen. Then you came charging into my life."

"I am still very sorry about running you down with my horse."

A smile teetered about her mouth. "I'm not. The twisted ankle was worth it."

Dev groaned. He truly was going to have to spend a lifetime proving to this woman that one didn't have to suffer the bad for the good to happen.

But one step at a time.

They had to get through this conversation first.

"Then I kept finding excuses to be near you—sneaking into your hotel suite…agreeing to play the role of your fiancée. I told myself it was about the money, but really it was something else."

"It was?"

"Well, it was somewhat about the money, but it was also what I sensed in you. Contrary to the Lord Devil society christened you, you are good, Dev. I'd never had any *good* in my life, not beyond my friendship with Artemis. And I couldn't keep away from you. So, I told myself every lie, even when the truth stared me in the face. *Especially* when the truth stared me in the face."

"What truth is that, Bea?"

"You said to me that perhaps what we've always wanted isn't what we want now."

"Yes?"

"But I couldn't hear what it was you were actually saying."

He waited, his heart a solid lump in his throat.

"You don't love the Countess of Bridgewater."

"I don't."

"You…" She blinked back the tears that had begun pooling in her eyes. "You love *me*, don't you?"

"I…yes."

"Well, I love you, too."

It was likely the most unromantic declaration of love in history.

This wasn't the stuff of poets.

It was better.

Their love didn't need flowery adornment.

It was simple and true.

"You showed me love, Dev. That I can love and be loved. That love—*true* love—is a safe harbor. I can surrender to it—with you."

"Beatrix—"

She held up a hand, staying the words in his mouth. She wasn't finished. "Dev, you excite me in ways I'd never thought possible from a good, solid man."

"Now, wait a minute," he protested.

A good, solid man...

Him?

They would have to discuss that.

She went on, undeterred. "You've shown me I can have it all. I can have the good in life, and the love, and the magic, too. The fact is you've ruined me for any future that doesn't involve you."

She'd erased the distance between them, her head tipped back so she could hold his gaze.

At last, she'd come to him.

His plan hadn't been rubbish, after all.

Yet still they didn't touch.

Which had to be rectified—*immediately.*

"Can I please touch you now?" he nearly growled.

"Yes, my love," she whispered, as she hooked her arms around his neck.

He just held off from kissing her. There were words he must speak to her, too. "All my life," he began, "I've had this ability to narrow my mind to a singular focus and use it to inspire and drive me. A drive to vanquish and a craving for more beyond—to have what I wanted when I wanted. Somehow, Imogen became tangled inside that idea, and I used her—the idea of her—as fuel.

But that was all she was. I never knew the true her, you were correct on that point. I only saw a fantasy, but I was too blind with my own drives to understand that—until I met you, Bea."

A smile wobbled about her mouth. "Oh, Dev, how I do love being correct."

His own mouth gave way to a smile. "I didn't know what caring and friendship and love were before I met you," he continued. "I didn't know that love—*true love*—could be intense and fun and every emotion between. I want to please you...love you... make love to you. From the moment I met you, there was no other, only it took me too long to see it."

She gave her head a firm shake. "Not too long. We both had the blinders on."

"Now, they're off."

"At the right moment."

"You taught me there is no vanquishing in love, only surrender," he uttered into the intimate space between their mouths. "And I surrender to you, my sweet Bea—body, soul, mind, and heart."

He angled down and, at last, pressed his mouth to hers in a slow, languorous kiss that was in no rush. This kiss had all the time in the world—and he intended to use it.

He scooped her into his arms, and she muttered against his neck, "Are you taking me to Paris with you?"

"Aye," he said, his feet already on the move. "But first, I'm taking you to bed."

He'd always needed *more*—and perhaps that wouldn't change.

But with the woman in his arms, he had not simply more, but *everything*.

EPILOGUE

FRANCE, A WEEK LATER

From her perch beneath the expansive bower of a weeping beech tree, Beatrix sat with a pencil lolling in her hand and a journal in her lap and took in the view before her—Dev beyond earshot, explaining the workings of a steam engine to his client...the bright countryside outside the shade of the canopy...the lazy drift of clouds across a blue Norman sky...

She resisted the impulse to pinch herself.

For the hundredth time this week.

She would've been black and blue by now, for—*impossibly*—this was her life.

Though she'd long wanted to visit France, she hadn't been prepared for its beauty. Normandy held the specific coolness of the countryside in summer—a soft, slow quality that invited one to relax and enjoy. Further, it was less tamed than England, but then France was still picking itself up after events a little too recently experienced to have faded into the annals of history just yet.

She and Dev had gone to Paris first. But the warnings had proven correct. It was miserably hot in the city. So, they'd followed the shipment of engines to their next destination in Normandy.

Actually, their journey hadn't been quite that linear.

There had been a stop between Dover and Paris—St. Peter's Port on the Isle of Guernsey. Their time on the island had been all of three hours, but when they'd set sail again, they'd done so as husband and wife.

She held the ruby and gold ring up to the sun, the light imbuing the gem with a warm crimson glow. Dev had kept it on his person at all times during those two weeks they'd been apart.

"For when you came to your senses," he'd said.

Oh, arrogant man.

She twirled the ring. Though she'd been married for all of a week, it was already a habit of hers.

What a whirlwind... But that was life with Dev. He knew his own mind, and one couldn't help getting caught up in its controlled, fearless whir, secure in the knowledge that one would land safely on two feet.

She contemplated the blank page below her pencil. She'd been writing this last week, too—jotting little notes and observations. Dev was encouraging it. "You see the main thrust of a point and have a way of conveying it with words. And when you're good at something and enjoy doing it, that's the thing you should be doing."

The subject matter for her writing had shifted, however. Now that she didn't have to write to put bread on the table, she could write about anything and everything that interested her—the trilling music of birdsong high in the trees...the sweet deliciousness of a rather transcendent apple and caramel crêpe...the verdant hills that rolled and rolled out from where she presently sat.

In a way, it felt too free, this mode of writing. Lacking in structure...*aimless*. The fact was while she hadn't enjoyed writing gossip, she did enjoy writing about people. Though they didn't necessarily know it minute to minute, people always had an aim. She might try her hand at writing about people of the fictional variety.

But in this moment, her pencil remained silent, as it was wont to be when her gaze found itself lingering on her husband—as it was wont to do.

His forearms.

Lightly dusted with black hair and tan from hours beneath the sun, Dev's forearms held the power to transfix her when his sleeves were rolled up just so.

At this moment, his focus was on his work, which was assisting a client with setting up his steam engine correctly to get the most efficient functionality from it. Her husband was exceedingly focused on functionality and efficiency and the increasing importance of miniaturization and portability in regard to engines of all sorts, both present and future. He could really go on at length about it.

She found it both interesting and utterly, incredibly attractive.

This man she loved…

This man who loved her…

He was complex.

Over this last week, she'd come to see that his nickname—*Lord Devil*—wasn't entirely unearned.

He was ruthless in matters that affected him—in perfecting and refining his mechanical creations…in his business dealings… in his bed dealings…

He was deliciously ruthless there, too.

Here it was again—the compulsion to pinch herself.

Dev was her husband, and she was his wife. She hadn't the faintest idea what it meant to be a wife—but neither did he have experience with being a husband. Yet what she and he didn't know didn't matter. They would spend a lifetime together as friends…as lovers…as partners discovering what lay around the next bend in their joined path.

They wouldn't be tarrying long in France, for they had business to attend to in London. First, she needed to sort out Cumberbatch. She could use his assistance and opinions on the purchase of a townhouse in Mayfair. He would grouse and grumble, but he wouldn't have it any other way, for she now understood something about him that she'd been too blind to see.

He'd been protecting her for years.

Further, as it happened, Dev was in need of a valet. And since Cumberbatch wouldn't be retiring until he was six feet beneath the ground, well, the solution to both problems worked itself out from there. Though she'd informed neither man of this plan as yet, in the end they would see its neat reasonability.

The other reason for their imminent return was the Race of the Century. It was fast approaching. Next month, in fact. Dev said it no longer held any interest for him, but it did for her. In a way, horse racing had brought them together. If he hadn't won Little Wicked in a card game, their lives at this very moment would've been completely different.

Besides, the love of a good, competitive horse race yet ran hot in her blood, and the Race of the Century promised to be the best she would witness in her lifetime.

Dev had agreed, but with a single condition—that she assent to sail across the Atlantic to visit the Territory of Orleans with him. He'd heard tell of the innovations being made to the steamboats that cruised the Mississippi River and wanted to see them for himself. He very much wanted to meet the inventor Henry Miller Shreve, who he called a "visionary."

Across the distance, Dev shook the client's hand, signaling the conclusion of their business. Then as she'd known it would, her husband's gaze cut to the side and met hers.

Her breath caught in her chest, as ever.

These last couple of months—this last week, in particular—she'd learned something important about life.

Life was a mundane affair.

The daily mechanics of it, at least—wake in the morning, eat, get on with the business of the day, eat, sleep, then do it all again the next day...and the next. When done with stability and resources, that was a good, solid life.

Which was why one needed magic.

It was the magic that gave it meaning and joy.

A smile tipped at the side of Dev's mouth, and he began moving toward her.

Her heart picked up its pace—as ever, too.

This new life of hers... She could have never imagined it. It was good and solid and wild and adventurous. It contained the mundanities—and the magic.

He extended his hand and she took it, their fingers twining together as he pulled her to her feet, his warmth and strength making its way through her. Words from not so long ago came to her as she reached up and caressed his cheek, his beautiful mouth angling toward hers.

Would you like to be my something more?

She was his something more.

And he was her forever.

The End

ALSO BY SOFIE DARLING

All's Fair in Love and Racing

Odds on the Rake

The Duchess Gamble

Wager With a Siren

Devil to Pay

Win Me, My Lord

Shadows and Silk

Three Lessons in Seduction

Tempted by the Viscount

Her Midnight Sin

To Win a Wicked Lord

At the Pleasure of the Marquess

One Night His Lady

Nell and the Runaway Duke

ABOUT THE AUTHOR

Bestselling and award-winning author Sofie Darling's passion for historical romance began in middle school the moment she cracked open *Wuthering Heights* by Emily Bronte. An instant and enduring love affair was born.

Sofie spent much of her twenties raising two boys and reading every romance she could get her hands on. Once she realized she simply must write the books she loved, she finished her English degree and set pencil to paper. (Ticonderoga #2 is her quill of choice.)

When she's not writing heroes who make her swoon, Sofie enjoys a nice weekend hike, a visit to a crumbling medieval castle whenever she gets the chance, and a slightly codependent relationship with her beagle, Bosco. Visit her website.